THE WORMLING II

The Sword of the Wormling

THE WORMLING
BOOK II

The Sword of the Wormling

JERRY B. JENKINS
CHRIS FABRY

Tyndale House Publishers, Inc., Carol Stream, Illinois

Visit Tyndale's exciting Web site for kids at cool2read.com

Also see the Web site for adults at tyndale.com

TYNDALE and Tyndale's quill logo are registered trademarks of Tyndale House Publishers, Inc.

The Wormling II: The Sword of the Wormling

Designed by Ron Kaufmann

Edited by Lorie Popp

Published in association with the literary agency of Alive Communications, Inc., 7680 Goddard Street, Suite 200, Colorado Springs, CO 80920.

Library of Congress Cataloging-in-Publication Data

Jenkins, Jerry B.
  The Wormling II : the sword of the Wormling / Jerry B. Jenkins, Chris Fabry.
    p. cm.
  Summary: Having accepted his role as Wormling, Owen Reeder and his new friends from the Lowlands continue their search for the King's son while keeping safe from the evil Dragon, in a dangerous attempt to fulfill the prophesy of uniting Owen's world with the Lowlands.
  ISBN-13: 978-1-4143-0156-3 (sc)
  ISBN-10: 1-4143-0156-1 (sc)
  [1. Adventure and adventurers—Fiction. 2. Good and evil—Fiction. 3. Dragons—Fiction. 4. Fantasy.] I. Fabry, Chris, date. II. Title. III. Title: Wormling two. IV. Title: Sword of the Wormling.
  PZ7.J4138Wos 2007
  [Fic]—dc22   2006033335

Printed in the United States of America

13 12 11 10 09 08
  7   6   5   4   3   2

For Brandon and Colin, who love swords

"You can observe a lot just by watching."

Yogi Berra

✝

"Your heart is free. Have the courage to follow it."

Malcolm Wallace, *Braveheart*

1

Rivulets

Sediment and silt trickled down the sides of Mountain Lake, carried by tiny water rivulets, channels cut into the soft mud—"rain tracks," as Owen Reeder had called them when he was a child. Days of rain turned the crystal clear lake muddy. Ever since the Wormling had come, gray clouds hovered, angry at the earth.

Such surrounded the gigantic lake at the mountaintop, resulting in a cone of darkness that spread over the land. But that is not to say it rained only there. The Valley of Shoam got its share. In fact, most of the inhabitants of the valley huddled inside their humble dwellings even now as the relentless rain beat on their thatched roofs, invading their cupboards and living rooms, seeping into the walls. Small animals moved on the dense forest floor, looking for some dry place, curling up by the base of a tree or under bushes.

Two droplets fell in tandem, twin tears from a grieving sky, and descended on the valley. If you were inside these droplets—well, you would have to be very tiny—you would pass the tip of the mountain that rises beyond the lake into a sharp, rocky point, then travel down the side to the hole the Mucker had dug to allow the Wormling passage from the Highlands to the Lowlands.

You might land on a pine needle, exploding into several droplets before reaching the ground, or you might fall on a scrumhouse, the small building behind each home known as an outhouse to those in Owen's world. He had never seen one until he happened on this valley.

Call it fate or happenstance, but these two raindrops that hurtled toward the ground at a frightening rate (and didn't seem the least bit bothered by the speed) separated and remained an arm's length apart until one landed on the boy we know as Owen and the other on his new friend Watcher.

The former was a young teenager out of his element, out of his comfort zone, with piercing brown eyes and a shock of light brown hair. He was of average height and slight build—which is to say that Owen did not look like the full-armed football players back home but more like a chess-club type. He wore clothes from his world—jeans, a T-shirt, and a backpack—under a cloak the Lowlanders called a tunic, made from the skins of forest animals. He had accepted it as a gift from the woman inside the cottage behind him after her husband, Bardig, had died, a victim of an otherworldly being named Dreadwart, a being Owen could have never even imagined only a few short days before.

The latter was a smaller being, Watcher, whose face looked much like a Yorkshire terrier's. Let us be clear that Watcher would have been infuriated to know we had compared her to a dog from the Highlands, a dog that, unlike her, can't speak and walks on four legs. Her eyes were soft and delicate, and when she blinked the water away from her brown-and-blonde matted fur, it made her look sad, as if tears pooled there. But do not be fooled by her cute, gentle appearance, for, as you will see, inside Watcher beats a ferocious heart.

Watcher's ears made perfect sentinels, listening for anything out of the ordinary: the flap of a wing, the call of some strange animal, or a cry for help. She had been trained since a youngling to be alert to everything around her, and that training had paid off when she had heard the arrival of the Wormling and paved the way for him. But he was not as welcome to the rest in the valley as she wished.

Owen, the Wormling, and Watcher had been together

since the passing of Bardig. Owen had wanted to immediately search for the King's Son, who, it was said, would unite
Owen's world with the Lowlands and everyone would be
saved and happy and blah, blah, blah. But with the time of
mourning for Bardig and the heavy rains (which had coin-
cidentally come at the same time), Owen had relented and
stayed in the small dwelling, sleeping on the back porch
while Bardig's wife and a few townspeople sat inside crying
and moaning and trying their best to sing comforting songs.

"Why do they sing so softly?" Owen had said.

"Singing is forbidden," Watcher said, "along with the reading of books." She nodded at *The Book of the King*, Owen's
huge, animal-skinned tome that weighed as much as an old
dictionary. "As far as I know, you carry the only book in the
entire kingdom."

The book contained prophecies and stories, most of which
Owen did not yet understand. But those weren't the parts that
bothered him. It was the parts he *could* understand. The book
invigorated and unnerved him. It caused his heart to soar at
one moment, imbuing him with great courage and mettle,
and in the next, it frightened him. It called him higher, gave
him purpose, and with its stories made him realize he was
not alone, that the world was much bigger than his tiny slice
of it. Most chilling to Owen was that *he* had been given the
responsibility of keeping the book and delivering it safely to

the King's Son, who was out there somewhere, even now, in this rain-drenched world.

You might ask why Owen and Watcher were standing outside in the cold, pelting rain. Why would they not gravitate inside near the fire like the others? Well, that's where they had been, but at the perking of Watcher's ears they had hurried outside, peering first at the forest, then toward the mountain, then down at the valley.

"Invisibles?" Owen said through chattering teeth.

Watcher shook her head. "A stirring. From the valley."

Ever since Owen had arrived, he had not moved from this mountainside retreat. He asked about the Lowlands, its regions, what the people did to stay alive, whether they ever went on vacation (to which Watcher had responded with a blank stare), and whether there were other valleys or rivers or even oceans.

"I've lived here all my life," Watcher had said, pointing. "Up there. Waiting for you. I've heard of all the different places, of course. And, yes, we do have an ocean, and there are islands and a huge river that way. But passage is difficult and dangerous. The town council forbade us long ago from sending a runner, even when there was a death of a family member."

Owen wiped water from his forehead and turned toward the valley where Watcher looked, sniffing, ears twitching, head cocked.

"Visitors," she said.

Three hooded figures slogged up the mountain, their boots covered with mud, walking right where only days before Dreadwart had flattened a schoolhouse and trees. Owen had to look away, the fear of that day threatening to return.

"Let's leave," Owen said. "Let's take what Bardig's wife packed and find the King's Son."

"You can't, Wormling. The initiation—"

"No one here can read the scroll you showed me. I can't even read it. How are we supposed to go through some ceremony where no one knows what to say?"

"It is required."

"It's a ceremony. It means nothing compared to finding the King's Son so I can—"

"Anger," Watcher said, nodding toward the three who marched with even more determination up the muddy hillside. "There is rage among these."

"I don't care—"

"Perhaps you should."

"—if someone is mad. I don't care if people expect me to go through some ritual that proves I'm a real Wormling. It's not even in the book."

Watcher narrowed her eyes at him, and the fur beside her mouth drew itself into a knot. "Bardig gave his life to protect you, to keep you from the enemy. He was the one taught in the ways of the Wormling, the only one who still believed you would come."

"Other than you," Owen said, calming.

Watcher seemed resolute. "He was clear that when you came—not *if* but *when*—the initiation must take place. It is more than just words. It is required. Period. I would think you would be more respectful of the dead and abide by his wishes."

Owen followed Watcher up the hill to another tree ripped out by its roots. Fresh worms crawled in the moist earth as if even they were looking for a dry place. Small animals scurried, obviously sensing something.

"I can't be expected to live up to the expectations of people I don't even know," Owen said. "They didn't send me here."

Watcher turned on him. "Can't you trust in people who want you to succeed but who know there is more to your quest than simply finding someone and handing him a book?" Her ears twitched again, and her eyes widened. "The animals are telling us something. Danger is near."

"Another attack?"

"Worse. Much worse." Watcher loped up the hill as fast as any creature Owen had ever seen. She stopped and turned. "Wait here. Try to stay out of trouble."

Owen rolled his eyes. He was wet, cold, and eager to be on his way.

2

The Son

Had Owen known what was about
to occur, both with the three
who approached from below and the
onslaught that would come from above,
he would have sounded an alarm, gathered his book (and the pack of food
carefully prepared for his journey), set
off through the tangle of vines and
junglelike forest, and let Watcher find
him with her heightened senses.

But Owen did not leave, did not
gather the precious book given to him
by a strange man in the other world,
a man with weird clothes and eyes
every bit as fierce as those he had seen
in these people. Something about the
man had caused Owen to trust him

almost immediately, so when the winged beast had plunged toward them and blown its fiery breath, Owen had feared losing the man more than dying himself (though, of course, he feared that too).

Owen turned at the sound of a door slamming. Two of the hooded figures stood on Bardig's ramshackle porch, their faces shrouded.

A whoop came from inside, where the third figure had to be, and Owen quickly made his way back down. It was Bardig's wife who cried, keening—half wail, half sob, all pain.

"What's wrong?" Owen called, but the hooded figures did not turn.

Owen ran to a window in time to see the third hooded figure stand before Bardig's wife and remove his hood. He was a younger, slimmer Bardig!

"I came as soon as I heard," the man said. "Word travels slowly."

"Oh, Connor!" Bardig's wife cried, clinging to him like a vine to a rock wall. "You shouldn't have come. You know it is forbidden."

"The rules of the evil one mean nothing to me. I should never have left you." He held her tightly, and Owen was warmed by his words.

But there were also whispers in the room. Owen suddenly felt self-conscious, as if the whispers were about him. He was the reason Bardig was dead. Owen and the man's determination to protect him at all costs.

"Is he the one?" Connor said, wet hair hanging before steely eyes.

Owen moved quickly from the window. These people should grieve alone and in peace.

"You!" Connor shouted, bursting onto the porch. "Wormling! Are you such a dog that you would crawl away, afraid to face the son of the man you killed?"

Owen stopped and faced him. "Your father protected me from one who would have taken my life. For that I will be eternally grateful."

Connor jumped down, his eyes locking on Owen's. "You speak confidently for a boy who killed my father."

"The beast killed your father. You do him a disservice to say otherwise."

Connor pushed back his cloak and pulled from his scabbard a large sword. "A true Wormling is fearless, my father always said. A true Wormling would bring healing. You brought death. And this infernal rain."

"I have no power over the elements, but I am sorry for your loss."

"You are the *reason* for my loss!"

A crowd gathered behind Connor, people from inside as well as a few who had heard the commotion from the village below. Owen supposed this event was the only real entertainment these people had.

"You will stay and you will fight," Connor said. "For the honor of my father."

All the way up the mountain,
though it took her half the time it
would have taken the quickest human,
Watcher muttered about the Wormling
and his timid ways. She had hoped for
a strong leader, a wise, barrel-chested,
fire-in-the-belly type of man who would
take on their world the way Mucker
had chewed through the miles of dirt
and rock to get here. Instead, they had
been sent a shy and hesitant Wormling,
more of a schoolboy than a fighter, a
milk-fed kitten rather than a lion.

Her best friend in the world had
been Bardig, so it is no surprise that
she would speak to him, even though
she knew he was dead.

"I don't understand it," she said, looking to the heavens. "All the things you told me made me think the Wormling would be different. He seems more eager to get back to his own world than to save ours. He has to have an older brother or even a sister who is stronger. Why couldn't they have been sent?"

She scuttled up the mountain, grabbing at saplings and rocks to propel her. Strangely, the farther she got, the softer the ground became. Her small padded hooves left footprints much deeper than she was accustomed to, and she was glad to get to the stony ledge that led to the mouth of the lake. From there she could usually look out on the lush valley, green and flowering, the trees rising before her. The ground was so steep she could almost step out and walk on them. But today, with the clouds and a mist so thick it hung like sackcloth over the water, it was all she could do to even see the path that led around the lake.

"Why would such a weak, hapless human be sent to a place like this when what we need—?"

Like a whisper on the wind, a voice pricked Watcher's ears. "He is the one. Listen to him. Help him."

It was not Bardig's voice, though it could have been. He had said the same thing to Watcher moments before he had been killed by Dreadwart. Bardig had been convinced that though Owen was small in stature, he was bigger in heart than most warriors in the Lowlands.

Watcher's eyes darted. "How can I help someone I don't believe is worthy to be called Wormling?"

The voice didn't answer.

With her next step, Watcher's breath was sucked away. Her hoof sank a few inches in the trail along the crater lake. The rain had forced small gullies in the bank to sweep down the mountain. The lake had risen to within a few feet of the top of the crater, and the softness of the embankment led Watcher to believe the village didn't have much time to prepare.

"Warn them," the voice whispered. "Tell them to leave now."

It is difficult to tell where a person is going until you understand where that person has been.

Owen had read that in *The Book of the King*, but it hadn't dawned on him until now, looking at Connor's gleaming sword (yes, it gleamed even though it was cloudy and rainy, a sure sign it was sharp and well cared for). Why had Connor moved so far from his family? Why hadn't he attended his own father's funeral?

"You must be suffering over your father," Owen said haltingly. "I am too. I don't want to fight you. He was my friend—"

"Whether you *want* to fight is not

the question. The question is, *will* you fight when I raise my sword?"

"I'm unarmed," Owen said, holding out his hands.

"My father said the coming Wormling would be a strong warrior," Connor said, circling Owen. "All his life he clung to that hope. I hung on to that story until I grew old enough to realize it was a fable. And now you come, filling people's minds with talk of a book and a prophecy."

"I didn't ask to come here. I didn't want to be a Wormling."

"So you're on *our* side then and not on the side of the Dragon?"

"The Dragon came after me in the other world—"

"And you bowed to it and worshipped it, didn't you?"

"No! I would never bow to the Dragon. Only to the true King and his Son. That's why I've come, to search out the Son so that—"

"He can lead us in revolt against the Dragon and unify the two worlds—yes, I know. I heard it my whole life until I grew weary of all the talk. And then I decided to do something. We have an army." Connor threw his head back. "We have begun our own rebellion against the Dragon."

Some in the crowd gasped and stepped back. Owen saw a few old men in tears. Mothers pulled children close and covered their heads with kisses.

"If you are a true Wormling, if you are the one my father spoke of, you will have no problem joining us. Get your things. Take up your weapons and follow."

Owen stared at Connor's fiery eyes. He took a breath, unable to shake the thought of all these people listening and watching. He thought about the speech he was supposed to give in class—how frightened he had been. Compared to this, the speech was child's play, though the thought stirred something old in him.

"You cannot fight this enemy with conventional weapons," Owen said. "Even if you had all the swords and spears in the land and all the courage you could muster, this will require more."

"Why do you let this dog speak to you?" one of the hooded men spat. "If he won't fight with us, he's against us. Kill him."

"I'm not against you," Owen said. "I'm for the King and his Son. The Dragon will be defeated but not this way. Not your way." He looked toward the hill where they had buried Bardig. "Not at such a cost."

"Why can't we fight?" Connor said. "What is your battle plan?"

"The book," Owen said. "It was given to me by Mr. Page, and I used it to follow Mucker to this world."

"He's brought death to us," a woman called.

Others agreed.

Connor waved his sword, as if slicing the Dragon in two. "Let him fight with his book then. I will use my sword, and we will see which of us has the better plan."

A man ran from Bardig's house holding *The Book of the King* above his head. "I found it in his pack!"

"Connor, don't do this," his mother begged.

Connor's eyes were locked on Owen's. "Stay out of this, Mother. We will teach the Wormling a lesson he can't read in any book." He caught the book with one hand, then flipped it to Owen. "Fight!"

Connor thrust his sword straight at Owen's heart, but Owen thrust the book in front of him at the last second, absorbing the razor-sharp tip. It slid between his fingers and sank two inches, slicing through the animal-skin cover and all the way to the first few pages. Owen gasped, wondering if Mucker (who had returned to his normal size) might have been hurt. Connor yanked and yanked, with Owen holding fiercely, being pulled about the mud-splattered yard in an awkward dance. Connor finally worked the sword free, raising it over his head as Owen toppled in the mud.

"Stop!" came a scream from above.

Connor's two hooded compatriots rushed to their leader's side, brandishing their own swords.

Watcher rushed down the mountain, the hair on her face pressed back as she ran, mouth agape, tongue lolling. Owen could not imagine a more beautiful sight—not that Watcher was beautiful, though to her kind she probably was, but the sight of a friend running toward him made his heart leap.

"Run!" she yelled. "The lake is about to overflow!"

Connor scowled. "Overflow?"

"Watcher is in league with the Wormling," someone said. "Don't trust her."

"The lake has never overflowed!" someone else shouted.

"She's just trying to save her precious Wormling."

Watcher pulled to a stop, gasping, hooves caked with muck. "The trail around the lake—it's usually hard. You can find rocks to skip. Now the trail is spongy and soft. It can't hold much longer. We're in danger—and the villages below. We must ring the warning bell."

Connor stepped up and held his sword to Watcher's throat. "Swear on your life that this is true, halfling."

She glared, a fire as intense as Owen had ever seen, and pushed the sword away with a hoof. "I don't have to swear to you or anyone. A wall of water, millions of buckets full, is ready to crash through here. If you won't do anything about it, I will."

Several in the crowd ran for their homes as Watcher helped Owen up.

He cradled the book. "Get the scroll. I'll ring the bell."

High in a tree in the middle of the village, in a twist of

gnarled branches, hung a bell that had once sat atop the school building in town. After Dreadwart had destroyed the building, the men of the village hauled the bell to the strongest tree in the square. "How many times should I ring it?"

"As many as you can before the water comes," Watcher said.

Connor raised his sword to Owen. "Not so fast, Wormling. You might fool others here but not me. Now we fight."

Owen faced Connor, speaking quickly. "Your father cared for these people. Fight for them and their freedom. Protect them, and let me do what I must!"

A hooded one blocked Owen's way.

Owen glanced at the tree and the bell swinging in the cold rain and wind.

Watcher turned, ears trembling, face twisted. "Invisibles!"

5
Call to Arms

Far above the people and animals and rain-slicked countryside, through the thick clouds and into the next realm, lay the kingdom of the Dragon. Though he transcended the Highlands, the Lowlands, and the dominion invisible to human eyes, he spent much of his time watching and planning how to make people miserable.

Looking out on his regiments of warriors, repulsive creatures with demonic eyes and faces, the Dragon called his aide, RHM or Reginald Handler Mephistopheles. This being, almost as revolting as the Dragon himself, was not only grotesque on the outside with scales, horns, and a stench that made Limburger cheese smell like perfume, but inside he was also equally hideous. Hideous squared. He cared for no being but himself and obeyed the Dragon only because the evil one was more powerful. Though the Dragon had no inkling, RHM had designs on the throne, just as the Dragon coveted the throne of the King.

As for the Dragon, he was not content with subjugating his kingdom's citizens. No, he longed to rule everyone in every sphere. So great was his concupiscence (a word you would not want to get at a spelling bee that means, among other things, an unusually strong desire) for power that he had lied, stolen, murdered, and even called his underlings bad names before scorching them with the fire that constantly gurgled in his throat. One burp and you were toast.

When RHM arrived, crunching through the leftover bones of charred aides, the Dragon spoke, his back to him. "After the death of Dreadwart, we agreed the best tactic for this Wormling was to allow him access to the Lowlands."

"Yes, sire. To lull him. Give him a sense of invincibility."

"It seems to me," the Dragon rasped, "that the region deserves more punishment than Dreadwart inflicted. They must expect retaliation for the killing of one of my council. Which I anticipated."

"You knew he would die, sire?"

"I was prepared for it, yes."

"What do you desire?"

"Send a squadron of demon flyers to the area. Give the inhabitants no warning."

"Annihilation, sire? Incendiaries?"

"No, no. Not fire. Purge the Valley of Shoam with water. Breach the lake wall. Those who survive will be left with nothing but the memory of what happens to those who cross the council."

RHM bowed and stepped backward, knowing full well that one order not fully followed would mean his bones taking their place on the Dragon's floor.

"And one more thing," the Dragon said, a rattle in his chest. "Send a Stalker with the squadron to bring back news of this book the Wormling possesses."

"Would you have it stolen, sire?"

"I would have it destroyed but not at the moment. If the Wormling loses the book in the flood, we have him right where we want him. If he keeps it, we'll follow him on his search for the King's Son. Until he discovers the truth."

6

The Deluge

Watcher disappeared into Bardig's home, accompanied by the dead man's wife.

Owen rushed down the hill toward the Bell Tree, aware that Lowlanders were following but not looking back to prove it.

Suddenly horrifying cries filled the skies, cries of war and attack. The air seemed filled with beings, clouds roiling in wind-driven mania.

Owen had seen news footage of tornadoes, but he had never seen anything like this. Like low-flying missiles the invisible army swept through the valley, headed straight for the mountain.

Owen tested the steps on the tree, placed the book on a low-hanging branch, then climbed to the top, grabbing the rope and swinging the bell as fast and as hard as he could. Below him the frightened villagers dashed for their homes, the worst places they could go. Others headed west, through the thick groves of pine to another ridge that overlooked the valley. That was where Owen would run when he had the chance.

Connor stood below him now, brandishing his sword, yelling at him, but the bell drowned most of his words.

Gong! Gong!

". . . avenge my father . . ."

Gong! Gong!

". . . cut you down like . . ."

Gong! Gong!

". . . so come down from . . ."

Gong! Gong!

The last gong was interrupted by a terrific explosion. People on the hill pointed at the lake, where a single half-moon hole had been left by the tail of a flying creature. Water gushed from it. Above them, hissing and screaming, came the chilling cry "For Dreadwart!"

Then another half-moon opened in the crater and more water gushed. The wall of the lake had breached, and the villagers could only watch in horror. Seconds later, another salvo from the demon flyers hit the wall, this time farther down. Waterlogged sludge and mud and rocks and dirt spilled from the side of the mountain in slow motion, sending a deadly cascade toward the trees and houses and animals and people.

Owen had been horrified of a school bully, the Slimesees, the Dragon, and more. But he had never seen anything as intent on destruction as this barreling wall of water.

With a mighty roar, the water crashed through the trees, knocking them down like spilled toothpicks. The water gained momentum, throwing trees into boulders and moving them like toys.

Connor suddenly fell silent, sheathing his sword, gathering his men, and running for the house on the hill. They were running toward the water! Owen yelled at them to run for the ridge, but they either wouldn't listen or couldn't hear.

Watcher raced down the hill, the initiation scroll of parchment in her mouth. She made it to the tree just as the water reached the town.

"The book!" Owen yelled, pointing to the lower branch. "Hand it to me!" He looked up as the water slammed into Bardig's shack, turning it around until the walls collapsed and the cottage became part of the rushing stream.

Watcher kicked the book to Owen as another tree slammed into the Bell Tree with a terrible shudder. Watcher fell into the water. Owen reached desperately for her, but it was no use.

His friend paddled as best she could, then slipped under the muddy torrent.

Screams. Terrible screams from above as people on the ridge overlooking the valley called out to friends and family. A woman holding a baby floated by as if on an amusement park ride. A scrumhouse with all four walls intact passed Owen. The water rose so high he could have reached out and touched the building. It soon slammed into a rock and disintegrated.

Though he could not swim, Owen had survived the attack of the Slimesees before arriving in the Lowlands. Now he could think of nothing but staying in the tree and avoiding the gushing rapids, the book in his hands. Surely the lake would drain soon and the deep water would recede. But it appeared as if a giant had come through with a rake and simply wiped the hillside clean of trees and rock. Tons of debris cascaded in the bubbling brown swirl.

Foot by foot the water rose, and the Bell Tree branches swayed, the trunk shuddering and jerking with each unseen underwater bomb—a tree, a boulder, a house.

Owen slipped but regained his grasp, barely holding on to the book. He closed his eyes and begged for help. He remembered the voice that had saved him from the bully's attack and had spoken about courage. Owen had named him the arm in the night.

No help came.

The tree bent under the weight of the rushing water, snapped somewhere below him, and with a sickening creak, turned like Bardig's house. It crashed into the murky water with Owen clinging for his life.

7

The Guardian

A good emissary does the bidding
of his Sovereign without hesita-
tion—not out of fear but out of duty
and honor. But standing on the ridge
overlooking the violent water, this
strange being, unseen to those around
him, wondered at the orders tucked
tightly in his belt. He had read them
countless times in all manner of set-
tings—in the other world outside
Tattered Treasures bookstore and at
the school, above Mountain Lake as
the rains first came, even behind a
draped section of the dungeon where
he had spoken with the King.

Until the book was lost—until it
fell into the hands of the enemy of

all souls (which was the plan of the Sovereign)—this being could not intervene in the affairs of the Wormling or any whose fate now hung in the balance. Oh, be assured, he wanted to, but his orders did not permit this.

And he could not, under any circumstance, explain or expound upon why he was shadowing Owen (at some distance, as Watcher was now close to the Wormling). He could only protect the Wormling and the book until the time was right.

In fact, it could be argued that the being had already over-stepped his bounds in the school hallway when he assisted Owen in pummeling a group of testosterone-laden teenage boys. But the case could also be made that Owen's life had been in danger, so intervention was imperative. Plus, that very conflict had set Owen on a path that led to Mr. Page.

As the branch of the Bell Tree Owen clung to dipped toward the water, this invisible being moved effortlessly toward him, hovering, watching, noting the shift and pitch. Watcher had finally resurfaced, coughing and sputtering despite the initiation scroll in her teeth. She had frantically latched onto a rock outcropping with her forelegs and was try-ing desperately to hang on. But the being's charge was Owen, and if he had to he would follow the Wormling anywhere— even to the farthest reaches of the Dragon's realm.

The threat posed by Connor had almost gone unnoticed by the being, because he had been busy guiding Watcher to warn others of the impending flood. But when he saw the sword slice through the book, he nearly jumped to Owen's rescue. Fortunately the danger had been averted by the young man himself. Though Owen was yet to become even an apprentice, he was learning the ways of the heart.

From overhead came the ghastly cries of the scythe flyers, their huge, moon-shaped tails cutting like sharpened pendulums. Of all the hideous creatures under the Dragon's control, the guardian being hated this regiment most. The devastation they wrought was ruinous, obliterating every target their leader assigned: town, lake, or living creature. No one could prepare for an attack of such force and reckoning. They could only cower.

Owen's tree stuck on something and he smiled, breathing again. But just as quickly, the tree broke loose and was swept downstream toward the valley. People floating by grabbed for the branches, but most flew past, caught in the current.

Owen gripped the book with all his strength. Shivering, his head dunking under as the tree rolled, he scrambled to keep the book above water. He rode around the curve of the mountain, dropping into another channel the water had cut into the ground. The guardian cringed when he saw houses strewn about the hillside, people clinging to trees, children stripped bare, shoes and clothes and kitchen utensils and farm equipment hanging eerily in treetops.

Only a hundred yards ahead of Owen lay a precipitous waterfall. The being moved quickly and decisively.

†††

Owen hung on for dear life as the tree flew along. The rushing water picked up momentum, and the waves cut a relentless path in the ground. Then, as if something in the water had stirred (a Slimesees or a whale catching the tree and moving it against the current), the tree shifted and rode toward the bank of a raging river.

It caught on a mighty oak, and Owen nearly flew off. He clung desperately to his perch and saw Watcher—fur matted, ears wet—struggling against the tide, trying to survive. She swam with hooves outstretched, her head—and the scroll in her mouth—barely above water.

"Watcher!" Owen yelled. "Grab my hand!"

When Owen leaned toward her, she shook her head, as if to protect him. That made him only more determined to reach her, and he leaned farther, supporting himself with his other arm around the book and a sturdy limb. Owen realized he could not reach Watcher, so he wedged the book in the crook of a branch and, with one foot around the sturdy limb, leaned out with both hands.

As Watcher bobbed, Owen grabbed her, cradling her head in both hands. She hooked a foreleg around his arm as a wave crashed, knocking the book into the water. Owen shouted, not just because he had lost the very thing he was supposed to protect, but also because Watcher let go and dropped back into the murky depths.

Without thinking that he did not know how to swim or that he might sink, considering nothing but his friend and the book and the scroll (and Mucker, of course, who was inside the book), Owen plunged in. He struggled to keep his head above water, finally realizing he needed to hold his breath and go along for the ride.

Watcher went under again and resurfaced downstream, near the floating book.

Suddenly a terrible roar met Owen's ears, as if a million screaming demons lay ahead.

Watcher struggled, then turned and with a hoof lifted something heavy and dripping over her head.

The Book of the King!

Owen slapped the water and laughed, but his joy turned to horror as Watcher rose before him on a wave of unbelievable height and plunged over a cliff. In the next instant Owen was swept up in the wave. At the peak of it, just as he was about to plunge, something caught him—a hand, an arm—and warmth flooded his body as his feet skimmed the surface and he was carried to a flat rock.

Owen crumpled there, shaking his head, spitting water,

and straining to look over the precipice for any sign of his friend. The remnants of a house floated past, then plunged over. Owen watched, helpless.

He heard the voice again. "The journey is long, Owen. And a man who finds a friend finds a good thing."

He recognized the words from the book. As he leaned out, he spotted Watcher on a ledge below, clinging desperately to a tree limb *and* to the book.

"Watcher! Hold on!" Owen scrambled over the bank to where debris had washed up. He quickly fashioned a coil from tree bark, tied one end to a tree, and yelled to Watcher, "Hang on! I'll get you out."

8

The Aftermath

When Owen pulled Watcher from the water and up the falls, she didn't even look like herself. Her matted coat stuck to her body, making her appear about a third of her size, like a cat that has emerged from a pond, its fur having shrunk.

She nudged the book and the scroll toward Owen with a hoof, thanked him with her eyes, and stumbled into the forest. There she coughed up a sizable amount of water and shook herself, spreading a stream from her fur.

The book was in good shape for having been submerged, and the first thing Owen did was check on Mucker. He seemed fine, even invigorated.

The book's animal-skin covering had protected the pages, and though they were wet, the writing hadn't faded or smudged.

Owen gathered armloads of wood and started a fire. His backpack had been firmly strapped to him, and inside he found food and brought it to Watcher.

She devoured it, licking her lips and sighing. "How many are dead?"

"I'm not sure yet. Many are meeting on the ridge. Let's hope the villages heard the warning and made it to high ground." Owen stirred the fire with a stick as it slowly dried the wood and began roasting it. "Watcher, why could we see Dreadwart but not those monsters that attacked the lake?"

Watcher closed her eyes. "Dreadwart wanted us to see him. He was part of the council. He could have remained invisible, but he knew the sight of him would frighten us even more. Others from the Dragon's world have the ability to change form and appear as animals or even humans."

"I think I met one of those."

"These demon flyers are cloaked with invisibility so they can attack without warning. Others are smaller and can be seen. There are many types. They fill the people with terror."

"And kill and destroy, just like their leader."

Watcher nodded.

Owen pulled the parchment from a stick near the fire,

where he had placed it to dry. The writing was in script he could not decipher.

Watcher's ears twitched and she sat up. "Someone's coming."

Owen hid the book and the parchment and grabbed a long stick—a crude weapon but better than nothing.

The figure, shrouded in darkness, approached slowly but appeared unafraid. It was Bardig's wife.

"I hoped I would find you," she said, appearing ready to drop from fatigue. She handed them some crusts of bread and some fruit, then rubbed her hands over the flames, her eyes heavy. "Connor blames you for what happened. They're coming for both of you."

"I can't believe he survived," Owen said.

"We tried to warn them," Watcher said.

"Some listened," the old woman said. "Most are looking for someone to blame." The light of the fire danced in her eyes. "You must leave, but I need to tell you something before you go. Bardig and I enjoyed a full life together, and I do not regret one moment of it. He had two goals in life. One was to raise a son who loved the King and would follow him selflessly. And the other was to live long enough to see the Wormling. That was always on his heart. Always a part of his soul. Often on his lips."

Watcher touched her arm. "He lived to see the fulfillment of the prophecy."

"Yes. Now, Wormling, your success depends not just on yourself. An army follows a leader because a battle looms, not just for the exercise."

"I don't understand."

"You play an important role here, but so do we. It does not surprise me that a Wormling would find himself without honor in the very country he comes to help."

Owen had read a passage strikingly similar just the night before.

"My son is against you," she continued. "I hope that will change, and I will try to persuade him, so that when you return with the King's Son, he will embrace you as a brother rather than an enemy."

"I'm sure the King's Son can use a warrior like him to fight the Dragon."

"It's impossible to defeat such an enemy," Watcher said. "You saw what happened today. How do you fight an enemy you can't see?"

Bardig's wife smiled sadly. "'With the truth in your heart that was written long before the Dragon ever drew breath.' Bardig used to say that." She tilted her head back as if trying to remember. "He also often said, 'Greater is the one who creates than the one created. And if he is with us, why do we care who is against us?'"

"I miss him," Watcher said.

The old woman leaned over and kissed Watcher's forehead. "I know, child. It will not be easy without him, but what good thing is easy?"

"Where do we go?" Owen said. "Bardig was the only one familiar with the initiation rite."

"Bardig always said it was imperative that the Wormling be given the initiation *exactly* as written in the scroll. Evidently this will give you some special power or ability, or perhaps it will reveal some ability you don't even know you possess."

"But, please," Owen said, "hurry. Tell me what you know of the rite itself."

"Bardig said it was a shame he was the only one left who could perform the initiation—that the only other person who even knew the language was Mordecai."

"Mordecai?" Watcher said, sitting up straight.

"Yes. The King himself had Mordecai deliver the parchment. This, of course, was before the fire and the attack. It was almost as if he anticipated . . ."

"Who is Mordecai?" Owen said.

Watcher and the woman exchanged glances. "Mordecai was here in our village before his . . . banishment."

"Banishment," Watcher said. "You can't be serious. You say he is in exile. Guilty of high treason."

"Regardless," the woman hissed, "you need him. It is the

only way. I would never suggest you walk unprotected, let alone to the islands of Mirantha—"

"Islands?" Owen said.

"Not a nice place," the woman said.

"You've been there?" he said.

"I've heard."

"I don't see what this Mordecai can offer. I just want to find the King's Son and get back to my world."

"Be careful to do what the book tells you."

"The book says nothing about this."

"Yes, but it is part of what we know to be true. And it comes from the King himself."

"So this Mordecai delivered the parchment. If he was exiled for treason, we might be walking into a trap."

Bardig's wife closed her eyes. "Wormling, the people here do not believe. Make this journey. Fulfill in every way the mission the King has for you. Study and discover. I will consider it my mission to convince those here to support you upon your return."

From the woods behind them came whispers and footsteps.

"You must hurry," the woman said. "And may neither of us fail in our mission."

After Bardig's wife left, Owen and Watcher covered the fire with wet leaves and moist soil.

"Follow me," Watcher said. "I know a quick way down the other side of the mountain."

It is impossible to relate all that goes on in the mind of a young man sent into another world and given a task— the importance of which he cannot hope to comprehend—while feeling as alone and estranged as a human can feel. All Owen had for comfort, other than the book, was Mucker, the worm that wriggled inside the book, and the cute but cautious Watcher. Faces and places filled his memory: his father, the evil Karl, his friend Petrov at the Blackstone Tavern. Plus the people at his school and Clara. Blessed Clara. Owen couldn't help but dream that one day he would return, and Clara would be waiting for him. He fell asleep nights thinking of her, wondering what it would be like to talk with her uninterrupted by Gordan and his gang. Owen could talk with her for hours.

⚜

Equally impossible is to do justice to the mind of the being beside Owen, who had been content with living in one place her entire life, listening, sensing, devoted to the task of simply waiting for something to happen. A week. A month. A year. A lifetime. Watcher did not care, for she was committed to her craft.

Now, with the sound of footsteps behind them, other questions invaded Watcher's mind.

How long will the journey take?

Are the islands of Mirantha as scary and desolate as I've heard?

Is this Wormling really the one I have been waiting for?

And what of the Kerrol that is said to live in the waters? Should I tell the Wormling about it? And if I do, might he turn back?

These would have to be answered in due time. Meanwhile, sending a chill down her spine and making her stomach prickle were the questions of whether they would find

Mordecai on one of the islands, and if they did, whether he would perform a ceremony for a King he had disowned.

Mordecai held a mythic place in the stories of the Lowlanders, and it was difficult to separate fact from fiction. Some said he had turned into a cannibal, attacking unsuspecting travelers from the tops of palm trees or high rocks (though it was unclear who those unsuspecting travelers might have been). Others said he was strictly a vegetarian and killed travelers only for sport, separating them, then hunting them with arrows or spears (again, the storytellers did not elaborate on the identity of these travelers). Those he did not kill he tied to anthills and slathered with wild honey or dangled over shark-infested waters surrounding the islands.

He was supposed to have invented other unspeakable tortures, and Watcher was inclined to believe all of them. Part of her assumed these were just stories to keep people from the islands, but on the other hand, she knew of no one who had journeyed there and ever returned.

Watcher sensed the Wormling's fear and thought it best not to divulge too much about Mordecai. She had little doubt that if Mordecai was still alive, they would find him. Her gift was to sense things, to be aware, but she had no idea if their destination would lead to a bright discovery or a painful death.

With only the pack that had survived the flood and food Bardig's wife had brought from the ruins above her home, these two misfits set off in the pitch blackness, with just a few deep-set stars to accompany them.

Those and the 10 people pursuing them, thrashing about in the woods, carrying torches, and trying to stay quiet.

✦

Owen followed as closely as he could, at one point grabbing Watcher's fur, now dry. She moved deftly and without wasted steps, as if she'd played on this hillside as a youngster. Watcher had to know the hills and trails as well as Owen knew the stacks back home at Tattered Treasures.

Owen was quickly spent and tugged her to a stop. "Why so fast?"

She turned, eyes fully dilated, no doubt seeing things Owen couldn't and probably never would. "Connor and the others trailing us are angry. They speak of death."

"Okay," he said. "Just don't lose me."

✦

It is tempting for us to go into detail about the flora and fauna of the Lowlands, the various deciduous and nondeciduous trees, the fertile soil, and the animals scurrying about in the night. However, let us leave that to your imagination—the theater of the mind—and not bore you with information unless it affects Owen and his companion.

That said, understand that the rains and the torrent of the breached lake had changed the land. It was difficult to walk, let alone run, through the forest and over the hump of a hill where Watcher now pulled Owen like a large dog dragging its master by the leash. And when she came to the top of the not-so-well-worn path, instead of feeling the fronds of the familiar ferns that grew along it, all she felt was the mud that became thicker as she scrambled up the slippery path.

Suddenly Watcher's hooves flew from beneath her, and with Owen holding tight, she fell headfirst into the slimy mess. Both plunged down the slope like it was a flume and they were the logs. She screamed and heard him doing the same as the goo covered them.

⋔

Owen quickly shut his mouth, trying not to swallow any mud as they cascaded faster and faster. Watcher seemed to be frantically reaching for anything to grab on either side of the path, but the plants and trees had been washed away. They were speeding into the darkness when Owen felt the ground give way to nothing but air.

Like cartoon characters suspended in midair, the two wind-milled arms and legs and feet and hooves. Owen was aware that daylight might have shown exactly what it was they were falling into, and at that instant he decided it was just as well he didn't know.

They plunged into a deep body of water with a huge splash, and Owen's world became a gurgling, dark cave. With *The Book of the King* secure in his pack, he struggled against the water's icy pull and sucked in a lungful of water. The shock sent his body into spasms; then he fell limp and sank.

♦♦♦

Watcher soon surfaced and searched for Owen. "Wormling!" she cried. *I'll have to teach him to swim.*

She dived into the murky depths, feeling with her hooves for his body. She had descended nearly a hundred feet when she felt his backpack and realized it was still wrapped tightly across his chest. She pulled him to the surface and helped him to the shore, positioning him faceup, his feet still in the icy water.

Convinced the Wormling was dead, Watcher wept. She felt responsible. Now he couldn't fulfill the prophecy, and the villagers would never know true freedom.

But Watcher's ears suddenly stood at attention as her hooves, resting gently on his chest, were pressed hard in a pumping motion, as if some other being had taken charge of the rescue.

Owen began to cough and sputter, making Watcher laugh

through her tears. She laid her head on the Wormling and sighed.

Above them in the distance, along the ridge that stretched all the way to Mountain Lake, Watcher saw the torches of villagers who searched for them in vain.

"Rest easy, Wormling," Watcher whispered. "That fall assured we won't be caught tonight."

10

Questions

Reaching the islands of Mirantha would not have been easy at any time of the year, but this being the rainy season in the Lowlands made it especially difficult. Rivers were swollen and difficult to cross. Owen could hardly believe that, even this far from Mountain Lake, many villages had been destroyed by the flood, scattering families to higher ground.

His lungs now free of water, Owen was rejuvenated. He and Watcher discovered a cave where they rested, carefully venturing out occasionally to hear the voices of Connor and the others echo through the valley.

At nightfall they set out again through the muddy tangle of trees and plants. As they walked, Owen tried to explain his world, and he could tell Watcher was mystified.

She seemed most astounded that the animals there couldn't talk. "Was it a big change getting used to—me?"

Owen nodded. "But I don't think of you as an animal. You're more of a person to me. You remind me of someone from home, but I can't think who it is."

"I remind you how?"

"You know, your sense of humor, the way you talk. The things that make you *you*."

"Is it someone you like?"

"Well, I like you. How could I not like someone who saved my life?"

Watcher, leading him through the wilds, turned and walked backward, her stubby tail wagging. "There was something about that, which I didn't tell you. Something strange."

Owen stopped. "A voice?"

"No, but I heard one at the lake, earlier in the day, telling me to warn everyone of the flood. Then, when you couldn't breathe, I felt hands on mine, pressing your chest. It had to be an invisible."

Though Owen had told only his father about the voice, he now told Watcher about the arm in the night and that voice—strange yet comforting.

"Exactly," she said. "Every other invisible I've encountered has scared me. They either attack or they're stalking, planning an attack. But this one helped, as if he was on our side."

They slept in hiding during the day and continued their trek each night, speaking in hushed tones, Watcher pointing out landmarks by the moonlight.

On the third night Owen could still see the outline of Mountain Lake looming behind them. "What lies beyond what's left of the lake?" he said.

"Wilderness as far as you can imagine. And a place known as Perolys Gulch."

"Who lives there?"

"A race of cursed people. Outcasts. Diseased. If you ever speak of going there, you will go alone. I've known no one to return from there alive."

Owen pondered her fear, and they walked a little farther. He could tell Watcher was upset just talking about such a place.

"In some places in my world we have mountains you can see for miles while driving."

"Driving?"

Owen had to explain the concept of cars, which made Watcher gasp. That led to his telling her of all the differences between their worlds. When he mentioned school and every child learning to read, Watcher stopped and stared. "I can't imagine owning a book, let alone reading one."

"I can teach you," Owen said.

"It is forbidden."

"By whom? Surely not the King."

"The Dragon. The King is in hiding. We live under all kinds of rules."

"And how does he make known these rules?"

"Each village is part of a township, the townships divided into regions. Representatives from each region receive the rules from a member of the Dragon's council."

"And the citizens have no say?"

"Anyone who has ever argued or even questioned a rule has been killed. Bardig was our representative, but Connor will probably take his place."

"Is he not afraid the Dragon knows he is a rebel?"

"He fears nothing and no one. Bardig tried to persuade Connor not to mount an attack until the time was right. Until the Wormling came."

So there it was again: the responsibility that made Owen shiver. He was having a hard enough time taking care of himself. Now others depended on him for their very lives.

"Anyway, you can't teach me to read," Watcher said.

"Don't be so sure. The Dragon is not my sovereign. He has no authority over me. In fact, as far as I'm concerned, he has no right to rule this kingdom. He appointed himself. He destroys. He kills. He's done nothing but keep the land under his thumb, if he has one."

Owen grabbed a stick and wrote the first few letters of the alphabet in the sand. "We'll begin with the basics."

"And someday I'll be able to read that big book?"

Owen smiled. "Maybe one day you'll write one."

⁂

When Owen and Watcher seemed to have distanced themselves from the voices, they settled into a comfortable pace. Now they walked by day and rested at night. Every day at first light they set off, moving steadily until they couldn't see the path in the darkness. They slept under trees or in burrows or caves. Watcher was able to determine which dens were vacant merely by her keen sense of smell.

Owen had worried about what they would eat when Bardig's wife's treats and the few soggy provisions in his backpack ran out. But they found berries and other fruit along the way, and they occasionally stocked up from the vegetable gardens and fruit trees of villagers. Watcher assured him it was understood among the Lowlanders that any traveler was welcome to the bounty at the edges of each property.

Just when Owen believed he had had enough fruits and vegetables to turn him into a salad, Watcher—quick footed and able to pounce—would catch a pheasant or a turkey or a rabbit and they would roast it. Owen had never enjoyed food that . . . well . . . fresh, but he learned quickly that hunger is always the best seasoning. He also discovered he had a natural talent for cooking the meat to perfection.

As they walked and talked all day, Owen told Watcher stories from his many hours of reading. *Treasure Island* was one of his favorites, as were the Harry Potter series, the Hardy Boys, and countless fairy tales. He took her into the world of *Robinson Crusoe*, shipwrecked and alone—or so he thought— on a deserted island.

Watcher could hardly stand it when Owen stopped a story in the middle and told her he would tell the rest the next day, but he knew that would keep her interest and make her even more eager to learn to read.

Every day at sunset they found a place to spend the night, gathered wood for their fire, ate, and then Owen read from *The Book of the King*. Often he read the prophecy of the Wormling, then a story from another part of the book. There were so many to choose from. Some told the exploits of daring knights and kings, others of sojourners like him and Watcher, and still others were simple fables.

"Read the smiling story," Watcher said one night as they finished their rabbit. She looked exhausted.

"You sure it won't put you to sleep? You've heard it so many times."

She shook her head and her ears twitched.

Owen opened the book and began to read.

"Gretchen was a young girl with only one smile left in a land where no one smiled. Not even at birthday parties. People were glum. Serious. They didn't have time for childish things like fun or laughing.

"It had been Gretchen's practice in the evenings to lock the door of her room, sit in front of the mirror, and smile. It made her feel so warm and good that she couldn't wait to do it again. But something told her— and she had every reason to believe it—that she had but one smile left. She was saving it for just the right moment when she needed to feel wonderful.

"Walking home from her village one day, her last smile tucked away so she could enjoy it when she chose, she came upon a lad sitting by the roadside, tears streaking his dirty cheeks. He had somehow twisted his ankle, leaving it swollen and puffy. He wouldn't let Gretchen even touch it.

"She tried to help him up, but still he cried.

"From her basket she pulled a piece of candy, a sucker that made his tongue turn blue, but still he cried.

"Gretchen knew one thing that would make the boy feel better, one thing she could give him that could change his life. But she had only one left, and she wanted to save it for herself.

"Gretchen had to make a choice. Save her last smile or give it away.

"As she gazed upon the weeping child, she made her decision. She took the boy by the shoulders, looked deep into his eyes, and smiled.

"Of course he had never seen such a thing in the land of no smiles. And so the change in him was instantaneous and dramatic. He couldn't help but respond, and instead of taking the smile and running away with it, he gave it right back.

"So Gretchen had one more smile to enjoy for herself . . . or to give away again. She learned that you can never lose what you freely give."

Watcher sighed and brought her forelegs up under her, the firelight flickering in her eyes. "I love that story. I know it's about learning to give, but it also makes me want to smile more often. That sure makes life more enjoyable."

Owen scooted closer to the fire and curled up. He was teaching Watcher to read, but she was also teaching him. And the next day they were to learn even more.

11

The Enchantment

A hint of salt blew on the wind, and Watcher told Owen the islands of Mirantha were still at least a day away.

As they slowly picked their way through the wilderness, Watcher kept reminding Owen to be quiet.

He whispered, "Why?"

She nodded toward a barren region of rolling hills filled with tumbleweeds and upturned earth. "The Badlands," she mouthed.

It appeared to Owen as if the bad part stretched a thousand miles. The land before them had turned from forests and glens to rocky crags, desolate save for scrub oak and the occasional cactus. On either side of the path sheer rock walls created a narrow passage. It was the only way in or out, and they had to move in single file.

Dark clouds foamed and roiled as if a storm was about to explode. It made the passage look like a black tunnel of death.

"This must be Forbidden Canyon," Watcher whispered. "It is said that the Dragon lived here for a time after his fall from the King's court."

"The Dragon used to serve the King?"

Watcher lowered her voice even more. "Something terrible happened between him and the King. I know only what Bardig told me."

"How did Bardig know?"

Watcher stopped suddenly, and her ears twitched. She looked up. "Demon flyers. Come!"

She pushed Owen inside the canyon as a blast of wind swept over them and a giant wing flapped, reminding Owen of the terror of the Dragon pursuing them at the B and B. Owen ducked a jutting rock and fell into the sand. Watcher joined him as the flyer passed.

"Are they looking for us?" Owen whispered.

Watcher shook her head and closed her eyes. "Demon flyers herd and gather their prey."

Owen studied the rock walls. Something drew him, but he couldn't place it.

"You're not thinking of going up there, are you?" Watcher said.

"Perhaps the King's Son is there. If we follow those flying things back to—"

Watcher pulled him down. "Another!"

The air swirled violently, and an unearthly cry echoed off the walls, penetrating Owen's heart. It sounded like the screech of some demonic beast.

Watcher said, "Come, hurry, before it's totally dark in the canyon."

Lightning flashed and thunder rumbled in the distance as Owen squinted to try to see. Stones skittered down the walls, forcing Owen and Watcher to take cover. Floating through the chasm came an eerie, mournful lament, as if someone was rehearsing deep regrets and sorrows.

"That's an enchantment," Watcher said, raising her shoulders to cover her ears. "Hurry. Don't listen."

But Owen was already caught in the grasp of the music. He looked up as it swirled around him like smoke from a campfire. He noticed movement—eyes peering down. He quickly caught up to Watcher.

"If you get trapped in this, Wormling, I will have to leave you! There's no hope for you if you become enchanted."

The music followed them, and Owen thought he heard movement above, perhaps voices. Was this part of the enchantment? Something stirred deep within him. "How can there be music," he whispered, "when it's been outlawed for so long?"

They could see only a thin strip of the dark sky from this deep in the canyon, and Owen noticed mist descending. Thunder cracked closer, and the music became even more somber, sounding like a funeral dirge. Owen had been to only one funeral in his life, for an old man whose workshop had been next to the bookstore. The music had been played soft and slow, as if the room couldn't handle the people's silence. It was the one thing Owen remembered, other than the strange symbol on the dead man's ring.

Suddenly drums joined the music, and it grew so loud that the ground shook.

Owen glanced up to see Watcher's mouth form an O as she stared at something behind him.

Owen looked back just in time to see a wall of water every bit as tall as the breached lake bearing down on them. No way could they outrun it, but still Watcher ran, Owen hanging on to her fur and being dragged along.

"Find high ground!" Owen yelled.

When they reached a widening in the canyon, Watcher shook Owen free and jumped, climbing the wall.

He followed, scrambling to reach a ledge just as the water engulfed them. It was freezing and made Owen feel as if he were standing in the foam of a milk shake.

"Flash flood," Watcher panted.

"They can come out of nowhere, and the water is channeled through the gorge."

A steady current flowed a few feet below them, but it was slowly rising. "No wonder the walls are so smooth," Owen hollered over the din. "We need to go higher."

Watcher was easily the more adept climber, making footholds of just about any spot on the rocks. Owen did his best to stay close, but the water was rising faster than they were, and the current was so swift he had no doubt they could be swept into a wall and smashed like pumpkins at any moment.

The water had reached their knees when Owen spotted a ledge above with a deep darkness behind it. "Cave!"

"A cave won't save us from this!" Watcher shouted.

They pulled themselves up onto a ledge, just above the waterline, and Owen saw fear in Watcher's face.

"We're going to be all right," he said, trying to believe it himself. Had the music stopped? All he could hear were the rush of water and claps of thunder.

The cavern was eerie—barely light enough to see the white foam ascending toward them. The sheer walls rose hundreds of feet, but their smoothness made climbing impossible.

Lightning struck above them, and thunder immediately roared off the rocks. In that instant, Owen spied a solitary figure on the ledge above them, poised to shoot a sharp arrow directly at him.

"Stop!" Watcher shouted. "We mean you no harm."

"Go back the way you came!" The voice was raspy and high, Munchkinlike but menacing. "You're not welcome!"

"We can't go back!" Owen called. "We'll be killed!"

"Come farther and you shall surely die!" The being waved to call forth 10 more like him from the shadows, bows and arrows poised.

The water covered Owen's feet now, and he struggled for a grip on the smooth rock until his fingers ached.

"Please!" Watcher said. "We're headed to the islands of Mirantha! We won't bother you! We just need high ground!"

"What is your business on the islands?"

Successive flashes of lightning allowed Owen to study the man. A mere four feet tall at best, he had silky brown hair that hung straight to his shoulders, and his eyes were dark slits in the matted fur of his face. A black pug nose pushed his cheeks back, and in the tangle of whiskers sat a mouth more human than Watcher's, with cherry lips. His long ears hung from the top of his head. He wore a tight-fitting coat that looked like camel hair and heavy pants that came to the tops of furry boots.

"What do we do, Watcher?" Owen whispered.

Watcher raised her chin, facing the tiny leader of the band of archers. She looked and sounded unafraid. "I live high in the Valley of Shoam. Near Mountain Lake."

"We have heard it is no more," the being said.

"The demon flyers breached it and flooded our whole valley."

"Many died?"

"But more escaped."

"Then what brings you here to face our flood?"

"We didn't know the danger," Watcher said. "I am taking my friend to the islands."

"For what purpose?"

Watcher sniffed at the air. "Please, can we at least come up to the dry ledge to speak with you?"

He waved them forward, and as Owen and Watcher carefully crawled onto the ledge, all but the leader stepped backward.

"I'm taking the Wormling to meet with—"

At the word *Wormling*, the leader's eyes widened, and he dropped to one knee. The others followed, emitting a strange hum.

"—someone for an initiation ceremony."

"Forgive us," the leader said, peeking at Owen. "Why didn't you tell us you were the Wormling? News of your arrival has spread through the land. Come with us before the water covers you."

He led them to rough-hewn steps that went straight up. Bowing from the waist and motioning Watcher and Owen to go first, he said, "I am Erol. Welcome, Wormling."

They reached the next level, with Erol and his charges right behind, just as a new wave hurtled through, flooding the cave below.

"Don't worry," Erol said. "The water has never reached the top cave. You will be safe."

"How many caves do you have?" Owen said.

The group chuckled, and Erol put a hand to his chin. "We recently counted more than 300. Most are single dwellings and difficult to get to, but many, like this one, are accessible through our vast series of tunnels."

As his eyes grew accustomed to the light, Owen was stunned to find a cozy retreat with a fire in a hearth. Erol pointed Owen and Watcher to chairs before a stone table bearing a large bowl of fruit. They ate hungrily. Owen could hear the roar of the water as it coursed through the canyon, but he felt safe and warm. He awkwardly leaped to his feet when a woman delivered steaming drinks, and Erol introduced her as his wife, Kimshi.

"Meet the Wormling we've heard so much about," Erol said.

Kimshi covered her mouth and backed away, bowing. "What we have is yours."

Erol gathered in his wife and stood with his arm around her. "Excuse our surprise, but of course we've never had a Wormling in our midst. Please sit."

"If you don't mind my asking," Owen said, sitting again, "what sort of beings are you?"

The room grew quiet, and Watcher cleared her throat.

"I didn't mean to offend. It's just that I've never seen . . . I mean, just like you haven't seen a Wormling, I've never seen anything quite like you."

"We should play it for him," one of the creatures whispered.

"Quiet," another said.

"We are musicians," Erol said. "Even though it is forbidden by the Dragon, we make music."

"Are we safe from being heard?" Owen said.

Erol cocked his head. "Never completely, but we have sentries on the ridgeline. That's how we knew you were coming."

Several of the creatures left and returned with bells, tambourines, shakers, stringed instruments, and what appeared to be flutes or recorders made from some exotic shiny redwood. Three carried drums around their necks with leather belts holding them in place.

Erol took one of the stringed instruments and tuned it. A rush of discordant sound filled the room as the others tried to tune to his instrument. Finally Erol bowed slightly and said, "For your enjoyment, a song written by my wife."

Owen liked all types of music, but what he heard in the cave that night was the most original, most joyous he had ever experienced. The delight on the musicians' faces made plain that they were doing what they were created to do. And when Erol began to sing, Owen thought his heart would burst. Watcher's eyes filled.

"*Waiting, watching, wondering,*
A stirring from our King.
When will he come?
Winter? Spring?
The signs all around.

"*I hear the future.*
I feel the past.
I see light from a distant star.
It could be today or ten thousand years.
We wait for you, Wormling.
We wait for you, Wormling."

That night Owen was escorted
through a series of tunnels and
stairs to the deepest part of the caves,
where a guest room had been set aside
for royalty.

"We have entertained visitors of
importance before," Erol said, "but we
have never been this excited."

"Thank you," Owen said. "And my
friend . . . ?"

"She has a room of her own, and
Kimshi will see to her needs."

A gaggle of tiny children had followed Erol and Owen and now stood
pointing and whispering and tittering.

"Don't stare, children," Erol said.

"It's all right," Owen said. "They've never seen a Wormling, and I've never seen their kind."

He smiled and motioned them forward, and they came running to his side, giggling and gawking. Owen picked up the smallest girl, and her eyes grew big when he hoisted her almost to the ceiling.

"Are you really a Wormling?" an older boy said, sniffling and rubbing his nose.

"So I'm told."

"But did you come through the earth, following the chomper?"

Owen nodded. "What's your name?"

"Starbuck," he said, beaming.

"Well, Starbuck, would you like to see him? hold him?"

"Could I?"

The children looked at one another, mouths wide, squealing.

Owen pulled the book from his pack, and everyone gasped. "This is Mucker," he said, exposing the tiny worm to the torchlight.

Mucker seemed to roll his eyes at Owen, clearly having just awakened and not in the mood.

Starbuck carefully examined him, tickling his cheek to try to see his teeth.

Mucker looked at Owen pleadingly.

"He's a bit shy right now. Let's let him go back to sleep." As

Owen put the worm away, he described how big Mucker had become, and the children looked incredulous.

"I wish I could be a Wormling," Starbuck said.

"Maybe if things go well," Owen said, "there won't be need for another."

"We must let our guest get some rest," Erol said. "Come, children."

The kids groaned, and Owen had to shake each one's hand. Then several wanted hugs, which made the first few envious and they had to return for hugs too. Owen laughed and ate up the attention. Starbuck tried to linger, but Erol yanked his ear and told him to get to bed.

When the children were gone, Owen asked Erol if he would like to see *The Book of the King*.

"Would it be permitted? I don't want to overstep."

Owen pulled the book from his pack again.

"My thanksgiving to you, sire."

"Please call me Owen."

"I could never."

"I insist."

Erol took the book and opened it carefully, running his fingers over the ornate lettering. "We have a song about the book we'll have to sing before you leave."

"How do you remember your songs?"

"Some are passed down from our forebearers. And of course

we invent new ones too, but none of us read or write. You could say they are written on our hearts."

"Would you like to hear some of what the book has to say?"

"Oh! Could I?"

As Owen read, Erol closed his eyes and seemed to breathe in the text, its very language appearing to transport him. When Owen stopped, Erol wiped away a tear. "I could write a thousand songs just about what you have read. Imagine the songs my people could sing if we could read."

"One day you will, Erol. The Dragon will be defeated, and his curse will be lifted. All the land will read and sing and rejoice."

"Oh, how I long for that day."

Finally Owen was alone in the secluded room at the back of the cave. The bed consisted of a huge sack filled with straw that smelled like a fresh hayfield. What a luxury after having slept on the ground for days!

But even after settling into the deep softness, Owen couldn't sleep and found himself listening to the receding water. He tried recalling all the hills and valleys he and Watcher had traversed, but still sleep eluded him. Rising quietly, he climbed into the antechamber above, past the room of the snoring and snorting Erol and Kimshi, and found the ladder to a hole in the ceiling of the cave.

The clouds had retreated, and a billion stars twinkled from

the dark sky. The moon crested in the distant west, and Owen found a crag where he could sit and study the land. No way could he and Watcher climb here and walk to the shore. One wrong step and it was hundreds of feet to the bottom.

"A thousand pardons, Wormling," Erol said, padding out and sitting next to him. He yawned and stretched. "Something on your mind?"

Owen pointed. "The Badlands. Watcher sensed invisibles there."

"Demon flyers."

"She says they are herders, but herders of what?"

"Your kind," Erol said, stroking his hairy face. "Humans. Sometimes we can see them with the viewing circle." He held out his hands, shaping what it looked like, and Owen guessed it was a telescope.

"What do you see?" Owen asked.

"Smoke from campfires in the night. Lines of beings moving in the early light to underground entrances."

"Caves?"

"Mines. Because the people are evenly spaced, Kimshi believes they may be chained together. It seems a good theory."

"What would they be mining?"

"Whatever the Dragon requires," Erol said. "We have seen sparkling piles on the ground there. In the middle of the day, when the temperature becomes unbearable, vapors rise from the desert floor, and it's like looking into a furnace."

"Why would the Dragon need minerals from underground?"

"I have no idea. Perhaps it's fuel for the fires of his thousands of encampments."

"Those people must be miserable," Owen said.

"I don't see how anyone can live in such heat, let alone work in it."

"Have you ventured there? tried to help them?"

Erol sighed. "It is all we can do to stay safe here, given our size and the dangers. The young ones sometimes yearn to leave. Starbuck has been after me to let them go on a camping trip. We can't let them because they're no match for the demon flyers. But we did let them go on a picnic."

A lump swelled in Owen's throat as he thought of the humans of the Badlands. "There must be something we can do. Even if we tried to communicate that help is on the way."

"The way to help them, Wormling, is to fulfill your mission. Find the King's Son. When the two worlds are united, the Badlands will be transformed. Doesn't the book prophesy that?"

"It doesn't specifically mention the Badlands—at least, not that I've read so far. But it does say that every low place will be raised, every mountain will descend, and the rough and rugged land will stretch out like a garden and be fertile. Then the inhabitants will no longer live in fear."

"How wonderful!" Erol said. "To think that this mountain will be leveled and we won't have to live in caves or fear the invisibles or hear their shrieks. Oh, to be able to put down our weapons and take up our instruments!"

Owen and Erol chatted all night, talking of the past, the future, and where the King's Son might be. Just when Owen felt drowsy enough to sleep, the sun emerged over the peaks in the east and took away his breath. Pink and purple clouds filled the horizon, and Erol rose quickly, telling Owen to wait there a moment. As if he could have pulled himself away.

The little creature returned with a crudely fashioned telescope. "Look there—not at the sun but below it."

Owen pointed the lens, twisting it to bring the scene into focus. Water rippled as it reached the shore, and in the distance three distinct landmasses rose from the sea.

"The islands of Mirantha," Erol said.

Owen had never seen an ocean except in pictures. The beach looked inviting, and he imagined children building sand castles and teenagers playing volleyball and throwing Frisbees.

"Have you been there?" Owen said, unable to take his eyes from the shore. "Have your children seen it?"

"My children do not know it even exists," Erol said gravely.

"We never mention it in front of them. Starbuck would set out the same day."

"They would have so much fun."

"And they would die. If the demon flyers didn't get them, the Kerrol would."

"Watcher mentioned the Kerrol on our way here but didn't give details. What is it?"

"Your friend told us you survived an attack from a Slimesees. I have never seen one of those, but I have watched the Kerrol ascend from the depths of the waters and leap into the air. It is enormous with hideous teeth and scales. When we sing the song of the Kerrol, the children make us stop. It gives them nightmares. Believe me, no one dares enter those waters."

"Then how did Mordecai get onto one of the islands?" Owen said.

"I do not know this Mordecai, but we have seen the smoke from strange fires there in the night. We always believed the islands to be deserted and these fires some natural phenom- enon. We also believe the Kerrol forages on the beaches for wild hogs and monkeys."

As the sun rose, vapors lifted from the earth to the north in the Badlands, and Owen turned the scope that way. He saw the beings—slaves?—that hurried in a single line up an incline and disappeared into the mouth of a mine. Nausea attacked and spread through him.

"If you are intent on going to the islands, Wormling, I might be able to help. Some time ago a traveler happened through and stayed with us a few days. Like you he listened to our songs, laughed with us, and ate. He said that one day a Wormling might come this way."

Owen sat up. "What did he look like?"

"Older. Graying hair. Piercing eyes."

"Did he carry a book?"

Erol smiled. "He read from it just as you have. We wrote songs about it."

"What did he read?"

Erol closed his eyes and leaned back, the morning sun illuminating his face.

> "Prepare a way. Make straight paths. For the day of relief and rescue is at hand. The Day of the Wormling."

That had to have been Mr. Page, who had given Owen the book in his own world. "How can you help me?"

Erol signaled for Owen to follow, and they moved back down into the cave. The intoxicating smell of woodsmoke wafted throughout, and Owen saw Kimshi and several other women cooking meat and gigantic eggs—each large enough for a whole family. The tiny children ran through hallways and cavorted on makeshift chin bars suspended from the ceiling.

Erol led Owen down several narrow passageways, through heavy wooden doors he had to unlock with keys strapped to his waist. "No one from the outside has ever been to our innermost chamber. Few even here are allowed. But you are the Wormling."

Erol pushed open the last heavy door and lit a torch on the wall. The small room was filled with expensive-looking clothing draped over the backs of ornate furniture. Pearl necklaces hung from hooks on the walls, along with scarves and coats. In the corner a metal box bore a small lock. Erol opened it and pulled out a small vial of liquid. "Jargid musk," he said, popping the cork.

Owen nearly passed out from the smell. It was as strong as a skunk but even worse. Owen coughed. "What's a jargid?" he managed.

"I've never seen one. The man who passed through gave this to me. He said that if a Wormling ever came through headed for the islands, we were to give him this. The smell will keep the Kerrol away."

"How will Watcher and I survive the smell?"

"You'll hold your nose," Erol said, clapping Owen on the back. "Something the Kerrol apparently cannot do. The man said he left a skiff at the end of the gorge. Unless the current has destroyed it or the floods have moved it, it'll still be there."

14

To the Islands

Hungry as he was and as mouth-watering as smells from the kitchens were, Owen collapsed into bed and did not awaken until late morning. Watcher was already up and rubbing her swollen stomach after a hearty breakfast. Kimshi had saved a plate for Owen, and as soon as he had eaten, he suggested to Watcher that they get their things together. "We might make it to the shore by nightfall."

Kimshi and the other women loaded them down with foodstuffs that wouldn't spoil for months. The group gathered for a song about the book and also a farewell ditty, which made both Owen and Watcher brush away tears.

Owen could hardly believe how close he felt to these tiny creatures, having been here less than one whole day.

"You will always be part of our family," Erol said, "always part of our music. And we stand ready to join you in any battle."

Owen rushed the embraces and good-byes to try to maintain his composure, and soon he and Watcher had descended to the ravine. New striations showed on the rock walls from the recent torrent, and the ground bore a new layer of soft silt.

At the end of the narrow canyon they searched and searched for the skiff, and Owen decided it had long since been washed away.

"I'm not giving up," Watcher announced. "We can't swim to the islands, after all."

"We'd better go back and ask Erol for help building a new craft," Owen said.

"That would take days. Let me keep looking."

Owen felt like a sloth, sitting in the sun while Watcher scampered about, and he nearly dozed again. By late afternoon he was feeling miserable and impatient, but Watcher had shamed him by doing all the work. He almost hoped she *wouldn't* find the boat so he could justify having done nothing all day while she wasted time.

As the sun began to descend beyond the peaks in the west, Watcher whooped from a tiny alcove.

Owen rushed to her side as she kicked away branches to reveal a flat, broad platform anchored to the rocks. The skiff!

It consisted simply of a dozen large saplings bound together over two support beams. A crude rudder was attached to the back for steering, and Owen fashioned an oar from wood he found. The whole thing was lighter than Owen expected, and they were able to hoist it onto their shoulders.

A few hundred yards from the mouth of the ravine, they heard music and turned to see Erol and his band atop the ridge where he and Owen had talked all night. The little people played and sang them a joyous send-off.

The sun had disappeared and the sky was darkening when Owen and Watcher finally lowered the skiff and fell, exhausted, in the black sand. It was warm and seemed to envelop them as they lay near the lapping water.

Owen pulled the vial Erol had given him from his pack. "This is jargid musk. It—"

"You don't need to explain that to me," Watcher said, turning up her nose. "Jargids are the most horrid creatures in the land."

He told her of the traveler and his belief that the musk would ward off the Kerrol.

"It would sure ward *me* off," Watcher said. "How in the world was he able to milk that thing?"

They built a small fire on a black dune, propping up the skiff to shield them from the blowing sand. As darkness settled, Owen studied the three faint silhouettes on the horizon, the islands of Mirantha. "If Mordecai is there, how did he make it and how did he elude the Kerrol?"

Watcher shivered and held up the vial. "I do not want to meet that beast in the water or on land."

"We'll slather ourselves with the musk and wait for the tide," Owen said.

Watcher's ears went rigid as something moved in the water. Then came a splash as if a whale had surfaced and dived back in. A hideous call echoed toward the caves of Erol.

"We'd better wait till morning, when we can see," Watcher said.

"The oil will protect us," Owen said, as if he knew it would work. In truth he could only hope.

15

On the Waves

If you remember, at the end of the
first installment of our story,
Watcher told Owen that the picture
of his mother looked like a woman
Watcher knew from a distant village.
Now, with the water lapping at the
shore and Owen listening to Watcher's
even breathing as she slept, he dug
through his pack for a morsel Kimshi
had wrapped for him and came upon
this picture once again.

Ever since he could remember,
Owen had been told that his mother
had died giving him birth, and though
he knew better, he could never shake
the feeling that *he* was responsible for
her death.

He stared at the picture as he munched his breakfast, running a finger over her face. Could it be that the woman Watcher knew was a relative? No. From what he could tell, the only people who slipped from one world to another were Wormlings.

Except for Mr. Page.

And the Dragon.

Watcher stirred. The fur above her eyes had a way of creeping down her forehead and covering her eyes as she slept. When she awoke, she stretched and scratched at her hair until it rested comfortably above again. It was cute, Owen thought, and he knew she had no idea he was watching her.

She stood and saw the picture. "Thinking of home?"

"I'm thinking we've come a long way from everything I've known, and I've no idea how much farther we might need to go." He put the picture down and tossed her some dried fruit. "You won't want to eat after we've applied the oil."

After she ate, Watcher helped pack the skiff and drag it closer to the water, watching for any sign of the Kerrol.

"The woman I told you about," Watcher said, "she lives in a different direction from here. Maybe after the initiation—"

"It's all right," Owen said. "There's probably no connection."

"But there might be. If we could find her . . ."

"Let's just get this oil on and get going," he said, overcome with an anxiousness he couldn't explain.

"I didn't mean to upset you, Wormling."

Owen uncorked the bottle and poured a little oil into his palm, trying to hold his breath.

"Are you sure we can't dilute it with water?"

"It doesn't come with directions," he said, slathering it onto his arms and behind his neck. He couldn't imagine ever getting used to the stench. "Let me put some on you."

Watcher gave him a death stare. "I don't think I could stand going all the way to the islands smelling like that."

"You're going to smell me anyway. Or would you rather be devoured?"

"I'd rather stay here and wait for you," she said, coughing. "You must understand—my sense of smell is more acute than yours. This would go straight from my fur to my brain."

"Fine. If you don't want to go, stay. I'll find Mordecai myself." He jammed the cork into the bottle.

Watcher extended a foreleg. "Wait. I'd never forgive myself."

"You don't have to come," Owen spat.

She trotted to the other side of the dune and brought back a dollop of clay from the hillside, shoving it into her nostrils. "There. I can breathe through my mouth."

She closed her eyes as Owen applied the oil to her. He just hoped the Kerrol had her same sense of smell.

Owen could barely keep his breakfast down. "Better give

me some of that clay." It helped but not much. He had to smile at how they must look. A young boy and a furry Watcher, clay stuffed in their noses, boarding a wood skiff, smelling of jargid.

The water was cold and clear, and Owen saw small fish dart away as he helped Watcher push. When they reached a row of waves, the surf crashed over the skiff and turned it around, nearly knocking Owen off his feet.

After several tries, Owen finally climbed on and paddled hard as Watcher worked at keeping her balance. Then a wave knocked him from the skiff like a man waving a fly from a picnic basket.

Watcher leaped in, holding Owen above the water until they could recover the craft.

Climbing on again, Owen put his head down and rowed with everything in him as Watcher swam and pushed from behind. "Here it comes!" Owen yelled as another huge wave began to form.

"Keep paddling!" Watcher shouted.

The skiff rose and Owen felt 10 feet above the water. Finally he rode down the other side, sliding into the ocean toward the islands! "Yeah!" Owen hollered. "We did it! We made it!" He turned to help Watcher from the water, but she wasn't there. He yelled for her and frantically scanned the pounding surf behind them.

"Looking for something?" she said with a mischievous smile, head resting on the front of the skiff.

Owen helped her on and assigned her to the rudder. His rowing seemed to help, but he knew they were at the mercy of the tides now. A passage from *The Book of the King* came to mind: *Nothing good is ever easy.*

And a parallel saying: *We learn most from that which is most difficult.*

If that's true, Owen thought, *I'm learning a lot.*

16
The Two-leg Curse

If you are a casual reader who cruises through a book picking out snippets of the story, the Kerrol may appear to you much the same as the Slimesees who lived near the portal under Owen's home. But if you are one who pays attention to details, you will note that while the Slimesees may have been effective against one who had stumbled onto the portal, he was no match for Owen once he had breached it and had in his possession the most powerful weapon against the enemy of souls, *The Book of the King*. In the end, Owen had the King's authority, which made the Slimesees shriek.

The Kerrol, however, had a different *agenda* than his counterpart in Owen's world. And the Kerrol weighed as much as one and a half killer whales—about 21,000 pounds (though he had eaten a great white shark the day before and added a few thousand pounds). Neither did he care about dieting. He swam around the islands, often showing his great fin to scare anyone bold enough to think they could reach the islands from the shore. His greenish body blended perfectly with the rock formations around him.

Now the Kerrol floated deep below the surface, his stomach full but not satisfied. It was never satisfied, never knew when to stop eating. Schools of fish swam past, but they were too small to bother with. He didn't even bat a scaly eyelid. He shifted and floated down to the deck of one of the many ships that lined the ocean floor. The Kerrol had sunk many, devouring crews and passengers along with contents of their galleys and mess halls. One slash of his mighty tail would open a hole in most vessels. And when years would pass without a ship's captain having the courage to test the waters, the Kerrol would be forced to forage for his usual cuisine—anything in the water.

But eventually people would grow brazen again, calling the stories nonsense. They would venture out, flouting the danger until they saw the hideous head rise from the water. The ocean would engulf them, and the razor-sharp claws or the pointed teeth would tear their flesh.

The Kerrol was not above toying with his prey. Once, just for sport, he had allowed a ship to dock and waited under the rickety bridge that tied two of the islands. In the moonlight, when a couple of the two-legs went for a stroll, the Kerrol silently rose and suspended himself next to them. He plucked them both from the walkway and enjoyed them as appetizers.

Others from the boat came looking for them, and the Kerrol picked bits of cloth from between his teeth and positioned them along the beach. The others carried long sharpened knives on their hips as they called for their friends.

The Kerrol followed them at a distance, watching and waiting, picking off a lone searcher who got too close to the water, then two more who dared cross the rickety bridge. It was going well until a child screamed, alerting the others. It was most difficult to hide from a child. The others climbed back on their boat, only to cross the path of the Kerrol in deep water.

It was that very ship's bell on the deck of the mangled vessel that the Kerrol played with now as shafts of light pierced the water. And then, as if it had every right to be there, a flat object blocked the sunlight, and the Kerrol twisted to get a better look. With a mighty swish of his tail, the Kerrol rose, sucking water through his gills, sniffing for anything that might pass for food.

The Kerrol studied the square object that seemed familiar

and remembered who had piloted this vessel before—the sole two-leg who did not scream and thrash and attempt to flee but looked him in the eye and made strange sounds that pierced his heart.

The Kerrol flew faster toward the surface, his great webbed feet clawing at the water. Despite the white shark in his belly, it rumbled for more.

All the Kerrol could think about was the curse of the only two-leg who had ever eluded him. The stench. The courage. The falling back into the water with the waves pushing the vessel toward shore.

The Kerrol wanted revenge. And his hatred propelled him.

17

Troubled Waters

I can't wait to wash this smell off,"
Watcher said, her nose twitching.

The clay was breaking down, and
the odor was getting to Owen too.
Even breathing through his mouth
didn't help any longer. "You won't dare
wash at the water's edge," he said. "You
don't want the Kerrol attacking."

"Look at the vegetation. Green trees
and plants everywhere. There has to
be a freshwater source. I'll bet there's a
lagoon somewhere on the middle island,
if not on all three."

Owen began to despair. It was not
so much the fear of what lay beneath
them, though he feared it. They were

being driven by some unseen, uncaring force of nature, and even the pack on his back containing *The Book of the King* was of little comfort.

The report of fires on the island gave him hope that Mordecai was indeed there. If they could find him, Owen would offer food as a peace offering. But the Kerrol weighed on Owen's mind now as the sun peaked. Though the water was cold, the sun quickly warmed the skiff and Owen began to sweat, which made the jargid oil smell even worse, if that was possible.

The water level rose as something beneath them drew close to the surface.

He looked back at Watcher. "Do you sense danger?"

She wrinkled her nose. "I sense our stink."

"No, I mean the rise of the wa—"

Bubbles burst on the surface, and white foam swirled. The skiff ran down a wave, and Owen slid to the edge, barely managing to stay on. Suddenly a being so huge and hideous that Owen could hardly keep his eyes open appeared before them. But how could he not look? He had to know what was surely about to take both their lives.

18

The Crest of the Wave

Only once before had Owen's breath been taken from him so forcefully. It was the moment he had been saved from certain death by an arm in the night, when the step he had taken should have been his last, should have sent him falling to his death back in his hometown.

The sheer size of the talons and teeth of the creature before Owen made him want to jump in the water, if only he could swim. Of course, the thing would have been on him in a flash. The beast had a row of horns atop his head like the spikes on the crown of the Statue of Liberty. But worse was the look on his face. One of intelligence. As if he recognized either Owen or a good meal when he saw one.

The tiny skiff rose on the swell of the ocean, bubbles and foam engulfing Owen and Watcher as a great flood cascaded from the Kerrol.

Watcher moved forward, fighting the slippery tilt of the vessel to get closer to Owen. She emitted a low, guttural growl and clenched her teeth as if about to attack.

Owen turned quickly, stepping between her and the Kerrol. "Stop it!" he hissed. "You're making him even madder!"

"I want that thing to smell us!" she cried. "Come and get your jargid, you slimy beast!"

The Kerrol repositioned himself, clearly eager to enjoy these appetizers on the small plate.

The skiff's deck of saplings was as slick as ice now, and Owen's every step was precarious.

Watcher spread her legs and waited, as if prepared to take on the beast single-hoofedly.

As the Kerrol's colossal mouth opened and he surged toward them, his look suddenly changed from hunger to fear and revulsion, like a kitten catching sight of its first Great Dane. His horns pointed backward, and the scales on his back and sides rose.

Then, strangely graceful for such a massive creature, he

closed his mouth and silently allowed himself to slide back beneath the surface with barely a ripple.

Owen fell to his knees, relieved and eager to see where the beast was headed.

Watcher moved to the other side and peered into the clear water.

"He smelled us!" Owen said. "He looked terrified!"

"Shh," Watcher said, her ears perking. The hair on her back stood.

"What?" Owen said, scanning the sky. "An attack? That's all we need."

The wind died and the skiff bobbed calmly. Owen spotted the bridge that tied one island to another in the distance. Might Mordecai be watching, even now?

The sky began to darken into indigo—a reddish blue. The water seemed unusually calm as the skiff spun lazily. Owen knew he should be more worried about what might come from the sea than from the sky. He noticed Watcher's hackles go up again as an unearthly breeze kicked up behind them.

They had blown about 20 yards closer to the islands when Owen espied the huge green eyes of the Kerrol as he returned from the depths. When the outline of his body appeared, Owen set himself and held on.

Watcher growled as the water exploded behind them and

the Kerrol broke the surface, higher than before as if suspended by some unseen force.

A wave as tall as a building crashed over the skiff and drove it under. Owen held his breath and held on for dear life, seeing Watcher do the same. When the little craft surfaced, the Kerrol lunged at them but again stopped as his hideous nostrils jerked to one side, his face contorted, and he dived back under, his long fin disappearing. In his wake the skiff rose like a surfboard on the crest of a wave.

They flew across the water now, the wind hard at their backs, the skiff high atop the wave and vibrating. The pulse tickled Owen, and Watcher rolled with laughter, kicking, eyes wide, fur flying. As they neared the beach the sun shone on the sand.

Perfect, Owen thought. *We're headed for a soft landing.*

But just like that, the wave pushed them straight toward jagged rocks.

Watcher's laughter turned to shouts. "We have to jump!"

"I can't swim! I'll drown!"

"I'll catch you, Wormling! Jump!"

The island seemed to be racing toward them. Owen glanced back at Watcher and found her kneeling, fear on her face.

"I'm stuck! Go ahead and I'll catch up."

No way would Owen leave her. First, she was the best friend he had ever had. Second, he couldn't survive without her. Without another thought he lurched to her and tried to pry her hoof from the saplings. Watcher yelped. She was stuck solid.

Owen crawled to the back of the skiff and tugged an oar from its bindings.

"Hurry, Wormling!" Watcher yelled.

Owen pulled himself forward with the oar as the Kerrol surfaced again and just as quickly retreated, sending another wave over them.

Owen jammed the oar through the opening ahead of Watcher's paw and forced it down inside the hole. That separated the saplings just enough for her hoof to pop out, and she stumbled backward. Owen lunged for her, and they both slid into the churning water headed for the rocks.

19

Shoreline

Owen awoke on the beach to the taste of salt. The clouds had mostly disappeared, but he saw lightning in the distance.

He rolled over, his backpack shifting, and vomited. Wiping his mouth as the surf crashed against the rocks, Owen felt for the book and the vial of jargid oil. Still there. His food was wet and salty but edible. He sat up. No open wounds. No broken bones. He felt, however, as if he'd been through an entire washing-machine cycle.

Among the jagged rocks lay what was left of the skiff—saplings floating in the foam.

Not far away, Watcher sprawled on

the beach, her fur waterlogged, one eye open, staring. Owen rushed to her, fearing she was gone, but when he touched her shoulder, her eyes rolled back and she quickly stood.

"I can't believe you made it," she said. "You were under a long time."

"How did we miss the rocks?"

"I steered you away and tried to drag you here. That's the last I remember."

Owen sat, shaking his head. "You saved my life. Again."

"Wormling, you don't have to do everything. I think that's why I was put with you. To help."

"What if I'd left you back there?" Owen said. "You'd have drowned, and I'd have smashed against the rocks like the skiff. My arms would be over there, and my head would be in some lagoon."

"We need each other," she said simply, shaking the sand from her fur. "Night is coming. We should find shelter."

A few hundred yards into the forest they found a grove of date palm trees and plenty of other fruit. Watcher hurried off while Owen gathered wood.

She returned a few minutes later looking refreshed. "There is freshwater that way. You can wash there and get a drink."

Though exhausted, Owen felt almost giddy from having escaped the Kerrol and the rocks. He slaked his thirst and bathed, then headed back to the shore, where he gathered oysters and found flintlike rocks he knew would create a spark. Watcher brought dried grass in her teeth, and they started a fire.

As the flames grew and danced, they roasted oysters in the coals, listening to them pop and sizzle. Watcher said she had always wanted to try them. She enjoyed them, and Owen was surprised anew at how real hunger could make almost anything delicious.

When they had eaten, they stretched out by the fire, staring at the night sky. The stars were more brilliant here than Owen could remember at home.

Something streaked across the sky, and Watcher gasped. "A fire star. Bad luck."

"It's just a meteor," Owen said. "A tiny piece of some planet that died years ago."

Watcher stared at him. "How do you know this?"

"You learn all kinds of stuff like that in school. Did you know you can actually travel, using the stars to guide you?"

"You learn this from books?"

He nodded.

"Where does the meteor go?" Watcher said.

"It just burns out." Owen suddenly realized the meteor was a lot like him—on a journey, his fire quickly fading, unable to figure out where to go.

Watcher sighed. "I think I would like your world, with its books and teachers and learning."

"You'd like some of it."

They fell silent, Owen lulled by the sound of the water lapping the shore.

"What are you thinking about?" Watcher said finally.

"The people of the Badlands. And the King's Son. Maybe that's his prison."

"He could be a thousand different places," Watcher said. "You'll know more after the initiation."

"If we can find this Mordecai."

Watcher looked as if she was about to drift off.

Owen heard animals skittering between the trees, insects calling from the dense foliage, the surf pounding the rocks, and a gentle breeze moving palm fronds. Beautiful and peaceful as it seemed, could Owen be any farther from home? And could they be in any more trouble than to be on a remote island without a boat?

20

Company

Owen awoke to a thud in the sand next to his head. He sat up quickly to see a patch of loosened sand where Watcher had slept, but she was gone.

Thud!

Owen dived behind a bush. He heard laughter overhead.

"I thought you were going to sleep all morning," Watcher said.

He looked up to find her high in a swaying tree, kicking at another coconut. "Watch out! Here it comes! Hey, you should have seen the sunrise from here! Beautiful. I've never seen anything like it."

When she climbed down they broke

open the coconuts and roasted the white meat but spilled most of the milk trying to drink it.

Owen led Watcher to where he had found the oysters. Small animals ran from the area, leaving footprints of several species.

Back at the freshwater lagoon, a waterfall was surrounded by all kinds of plants. It reminded Owen of the lagoon Robert Louis Stevenson had written about in *Treasure Island*.

Watcher cocked her head and pointed. "These weren't here last night."

In the sand near the waterfall were human footprints, twice the size of Owen's.

"Is this Mordecai a giant?" he said, realizing that whether they were Mordecai's prints or not, he and Watcher were definitely not alone on the island.

"Haven't heard that," Watcher said. "Maybe he just has big feet."

A few yards away they found tattered socks. They ran back and covered their campfire and buried the oyster shells and coconuts to remove any trace of their presence. Then they found the footprints again and followed them up the hill by the waterfall to a small pond.

There they lost the trail, then picked it up again on a ridge leading around the northern side of the mountain. The path was only a foot wide in places, and though Watcher had no problem, Owen couldn't help but look down and imagine what might happen if he fell. A vivid imagination was one of Owen's strengths, and sometimes it allowed him to imagine the worst. He could just see his body—or what was left of it—on the rocky shoreline, now free of the jargid oil. There the Kerrol would find him and roast him on a spit.

"You coming?" Watcher said as he lagged.

Working their way along the well-worn path, Watcher paused to examine a footprint, but Owen knew she was just letting him catch up. When they came to a huge rock jutting out, they stepped behind it to rest. From there they could see the southern tip of the island, the makeshift bridge across the water, and the beach stretching out before them like a black stripe.

"I wish Bardig could see this," Watcher said breathlessly.

"Maybe he can." Owen smelled smoke and heard something that caused him to look up. There, in a rocky crag, lay a cave surrounded by weird-looking trees, almost like the bonsai trees in Mrs. Rothem's classroom. Hanging from one of the trees was a rope of sorts, several inches in diameter, which had been fashioned by twisting several vines into one. It looked like it could bear a thousand pounds.

"We've got to find out who's up there," Owen said.

"The only way up is the grapevine," Watcher said. "You ready?"

Owen nodded, but before he could move he heard a grunt and a carcass flew out the mouth of the cave, shot past them, and fell on the beach. All he could tell was that it was bloody and had very little meat left on its bones.

Watcher winked at Owen. "Whoever or whatever lives up there shouldn't be hungry at least."

"Comforting," Owen whispered.

Watcher climbed behind him, suggesting places for Owen to step. It was slow going, but he held tightly to the grapevine and tried not to look down. About 10 feet from the ledge leading to the cave, Owen sent a loose rock skittering down the slope. No sooner had he looked down to watch it than his head spun at how high he was. His arms ached, his hands trembled, and his legs felt like rubber bands.

"Just a little farther, Wormling," Watcher said. "You can do it."

He took a deep breath and fixed his eyes on the goal above. He had taken one more step when something big and hairy emerged from the cave. Two enormous eyes peered over the edge and then disappeared.

"Keep going!" Watcher said.

But as Owen reached hand over hand, he froze when all he could see was an arm the size of a tree trunk with a machete in its hand. It swung toward the grapevine.

21

Mordecai

N o!"
Owen's shout must have
startled the bushy being, because his
machete blow didn't hit squarely, and
he cut only half the grapevine tied to
a massive tree. Watcher and Owen
hung precariously (which is to say they
nearly wet themselves), swinging and
hearing the sickening stretching and
tearing of the vine.

They were utterly at the mercy of
Machete Man.

"We're friends!" Owen cried.

The man peered over the edge
again, this time with an ugly sneer.
"Go back down, and I'll let you live!"
His voice boomed like thunder.

Retreat after all they'd been through? Though terrified, Owen couldn't imagine it. Something had changed within him, and he found himself willing to risk death rather than turn back now.

"Are you deaf?" the man roared, drawing back the blade again.

"You can't kill us!" Watcher yelled. "He's a Wormling!"

Owen had shut his eyes, waiting for the second, fatal slash of the machete. But all he heard was silence. He glanced up to see the man leaning over the edge, angling his head so he could see past Owen to Watcher.

"What did you say?"

"A Wormling!" she said, speaking faster than Owen had ever heard her. "I'm a Watcher in the Valley of Shoam and he arrived just days ago and we've come for the initiation!"

"Shoam? You know Bardig?"

"Of course! At the head of the valley. But Bardig is no longer with us. Dreadwart killed him."

"Dreadwart," the man said, the bombast gone from his tone. It was as if he remembered something Owen could not even imagine.

"But Dreadwart was killed too," Watcher said.

"That ought to reap the Dragon's ire."

"Oh, we've suffered since then," Watcher said. "That's why we need the Wormling initiated. Bardig's widow told us only one person knows the initiation rite. We have the scroll, but no one can read it."

Owen hung there, just feet from the ledge, his body screaming for relief. His fingers were knotted around the now-flimsy vine, and his legs and feet cramped with the effort of hanging on.

The man who held their fate seemed to study them, his gaze darting back and forth between them. His face had been over-taken by his beard, mustache, and eyebrows, like a rock wall engulfed by vines, and his eyes peeked out from deep caverns. His hair was black and thick and curly, covering his head like a helmet. His great beard, which flowed like a forest from his chin to his chest, bore flecks of gray and red. Owen wasn't sure if this was his natural color or something left over from dinner. His lips and prominent nose were as red as cherries.

He wore simple sleeveless clothing made of animal skins, the tails of which hung from his back. His pants were ragged and dirty, rolled up at the cuffs. The knees were worn through.

Most striking was an ugly scar of red patches and skin growths visible even under all that hair. It seemed to begin at his cheek and run all the way across his face and down his neck to the end of his right arm.

"Please let us come up," Owen said, dizzy from fatigue.

"Who are you looking for?" the man snarled.

"Mordecai," Owen managed.

"No one here by that name. Now go."

When the man backed away from the ledge, Watcher nudged Owen. "What are you waiting for?" she whispered. "Go on up! He knew Bardig. He has to be Mordecai. Do you see anyone else on this island?"

Owen hung there as the cut in the vine creaked and stretched even wider.

"Go, Wormling! Now! Please!"

"Watcher! Hold still! You're breaking the vine!" They swung as the vine fibers began to snap. Owen should have moved when she told him, but now it was too late. It was giving way—and fast. "Grab something!"

Before Watcher could react, Owen felt the final snap and the sickening knowledge that they were free-falling into the abyss. There was nothing to grab on to, so he squeezed the vine even tighter. Weightless now, he could only pray that he would somehow lose consciousness before impact with the stone canyon floor.

Owen had plunged only a few feet when the vine grew taut again and they stopped and hung in midair. The jerk made him almost lose his grip, and he found himself slipping, his feet resting on Watcher's shoulders.

"Sorry!" he hollered, but Watcher was looking up past him.

Not only had the vine stopped, but now it was being lifted! Owen turned and saw the hairy man pulling the vine, hand over hand, as they slowly ascended. Finally, the man grabbed Owen's jacket and pulled him to safety. One more pull and Watcher scampered onto the ledge.

Owen dropped to his knees, exhausted, but noticed Watcher gazing out over the beach and the ocean. "Quite a view," she said, panting.

The hairy man sniffed. "I didn't come here for the view."

"What did you come here for?" Watcher said.

The man just headed for his cave.

Owen quickly rose and followed him, somehow no longer afraid. "We came all this way to find Mordecai. We risked being eaten by that *thing* out there and almost died on your vine. The least you could do is tell us who you are."

The man turned and stared at Owen with his pinpoint black eyes.

"Are you Mordecai?" Owen said.

The man ruminated like a cow chewing its cud. "What difference could it possibly make?"

"Tell us!"

The man paused. "I used to be called that. No longer."

"Why?"

"That is not your business, nor is it your business to be here. You'll find fresh vines behind the tree. Wedge them tightly before you go down."

Watcher drew closer, brushing Owen's elbow with her

shoulder as the man disappeared into the cave. "We have risked everything to find you," she called after him, her voice echoing. "If it were up to me, I wouldn't trouble you further. But there are lives at stake. Please look at the scroll. The Wormling has it in *The Book of the King.*"

Mordecai returned to the mouth of the cave, eyes wide. "You have the book?"

Owen nodded.

"Where did you find it?"

"I didn't find it. It found me. A man named Mr. Page visited my father's bookstore—"

Mordecai held up a hand and scanned the sky. "Come inside. Both of you. Quickly."

22

The Cave

Owen couldn't place the odor at
first, but after a few steps inside
the cave, he realized it was a hint of
jargid musk.

Mordecai had hewed a crude fireplace into the wall, and some kind of
animal was roasting over the coals.
Pelts of an animal Owen didn't recognize were stacked beside a blocky wood
table. Fruit and vegetables hung on
a vine strung at the back of the cave
near a hammock—again of skins—suspended between four huge timbers.

Mordecai plainly did not care
about venturing into the civilized

world ever again. Owen found it difficult to tear his eyes from the man, with his great fields of hair and the nearly endless scar.

"The book," Mordecai said, grabbing a torch and pointing to the only chair.

As Owen sat and placed his pack on the table, the big man settled on the floor and Watcher edged closer. Owen set the half-empty vial of jargid musk beside the pack and reached for the book.

Mordecai squinted. "Where did you get that stuff?"

Owen told him.

"Erol and his clan are a good bunch."

Owen nodded.

"Do you know why the Kerrol hates jargid musk so much?"

"No idea," Owen said.

Mordecai swirled the oil in the bottle and set it back on the table. "Nor do I. I didn't know sea creatures could smell." He rose and turned the spit, muttered something under his breath, and sat back down. "I hoped the Kerrol would end my life. It feeds on such as me. And you. But whether it was the stench or that it couldn't stand to eat something as ugly as *it* is, I don't know."

"We're not ugly," Watcher said.

Mordecai raised an eyebrow. "Come, come, the book."

Owen dug it out, and Mordecai cradled it like a long-lost baby, running his massive, scarred hand over the cover. "Describe the man you say gave you this."

"Older, longish gray hair under a large hat. A coat that reached the ground."

"Did he wear a ring?"

"I'm not sure."

Mordecai inched closer. "What about his eyes?"

"Two," Owen said.

Watcher giggled.

Mordecai was clearly not amused. "What color? Anything different about them?"

"Blue," Owen said. "And when he looked at me, it felt like—"

"He was piercing your soul?"

"Exactly. You know Mr. Page?"

Mordecai pulled the scroll from the book. "Why did he give this to you?"

Owen sensed Watcher's unease and turned to try to calm her. But before he could speak, she pursed her lips and shook her furry head. "You don't have to answer these questions. You're a Wormling. He should bow to you."

Owen turned back. "Mr. Page must have known I was a Wormling. He told me to read the book, and now I know I'm to search for the King's Son. But it was the initiation I was unaware of, and Watcher and the others say I need it."

Mordecai looked from the scroll to Owen and back as he pored over the letters. He handed it back. "I wish I could help you, but I can't. I'll prepare another vine for your descent."

"You can't or you won't?" Owen said.

Mordecai stared at him, then rose and lumbered out of the cave.

"That's it?" Watcher called after him. "We come all this way and you won't help?"

Mordecai returned, dark eyes fierce. "You don't know what you're asking. The rite calls for more than simply reciting a few words and patting him on the head. There's work involved. Training. Lots of it."

"I'm not afraid of training," Owen said. "If it will help me find the King's Son—"

"You'll never find him," Mordecai snapped. "You won't last a day out there."

"We've come this far," Watcher said. "We made it past the Kerrol. The Wormling escaped the Slimesees. And Dreadwart, the demon flyers—"

"The Dragon will never let you find him." Mordecai sighed and sat near the fire, turning the meat again. "He has too many weapons, too many eyes."

"That's why I'm here," Watcher said. "Extra eyes and ears for the Wormling."

"A Watcher cannot engage in battle. You can only warn him of danger, not prevent it."

"But if you trained me," Owen said, "I could counter anything he throws at me."

Mordecai shook his head. "No training can prepare you for that kind of evil. He devours. He destroys. He kills. He burns." He furrowed his brow. "Why would Page have gone to another world and chosen you?"

"Do you not trust this Mr. Page?" Watcher said. Mordecai looked startled, like a deer in headlights. "If Mr. Page were here and asked you to initiate the Wormling, would you do it?"

Mordecai looked away. "Of course."

"Mr. Page sent this Wormling here to find the King's Son. If you refuse to help, you'll go against Mr. Page's wishes."

Mordecai moved to the spit and tore off a chunk of meat. He broke it into three pieces, popped one in his mouth, and handed the others to Owen and Watcher.

It did not look or smell as appetizing as the hanging fruit, but when Watcher sniffed hers, bit into it with her gleaming teeth, and shrugged, Owen tentatively tasted his. Though it was gamy and salty, he was able to force it down. But even after a breakfast of only coconut, his hunger was not enough to season this meat.

Mordecai paced. "I can see you have a fire inside you. Whether that is enough to survive the slings and arrows of the evil one remains to be seen. I would hate to see you sliced by a demon flyer."

"You'll train him?" Watcher said.

Mordecai wiped his face. "Only if you're dead serious about it, Wormling." He pulled a hook from the wall and took down the fruit, revealing an inner cave. "You can sleep there, out of sight of the invisibles. They don't bother me much anymore."

"How long will the initiation take?" Owen said.

"Depends on how you take to the training. We'll know when the time has come for the initiation ceremony." He handed Owen another piece of meat.

"Is eating this part of the training?" Owen said.

"As a matter of fact, it is. Not to mention a pleasure. Jargid is my favorite."

Owen's stomach clenched.

"My clothes are made of jargid skins. I also have jargid jerky curing near your sleeping quarters. I've been eating it since I was a boy."

23

Firelight

As Owen slept on jargid skins in
the back chamber of Mordecai's
cave, he dreamed fantastic scenes. The
sky was black, the landscape shrouded
in fog, and people ran in fear. Though
he did not recognize them, somehow
he shared their dread. They looked
over their shoulders as they fled, fright
etched on their faces. Women gathered
children in their arms as men trailed
them, pushing, urging them faster.

And then, out of the gloom, they
were cut down one by one, some
killed, some injured, some burned and
screaming.

One boy ran ahead of the rest of

the villagers. He wore moccasins and loose-fitting clothes of leather. His long hair was tied in the back, like a rat tail. He ran swiftly and was one of the last survivors. In Owen's dream, he struggled to catch up to the boy, following him to the crest of a hill. Above Owen appeared the long talons of some creature, and a burst of flame turned the hill into an inferno.

As the fire pummeled the earth, the boy looked back, and it was at this point that Owen, shaking his head in his sleep and thrashing about in the jargid skins, saw his face. Just before the fire engulfed him and burned him to a crisp, Owen bolted straight up and bumped his head on the cave wall. The boy's face had been his own. Owen was the boy in the dream.

Owen smelled smoke and squinted to make out the silhouette of Mordecai stoking embers. No wonder his dream had included fire.

Watcher slept soundly just outside the opening to Owen's chamber, mouth open, tongue lolling, ears flopped back. "I'm going to catch you," she said in her sleep, then laughed as if she were playing.

Owen rearranged himself under the jargid skins, trying to stay warm. He'd assumed sleeping in a cave would guarantee warm nights, but a heavy mist had blown in with the surf, bringing with it a damp cold. The nightmare had shaken him, and now sleep was elusive. He draped the largest skin around his shoulders, padding out to the fire.

"Bad dream?" Mordecai whispered.

Owen nodded.

"It's a good night to dream," Mordecai said, "but nightmares are never pleasant."

The fire flickered on the man's face, and Owen was suddenly overcome with pity. How sad to live alone in a cave on a deserted island guarded by a sea monster.

Mordecai set down the poker and crossed his arms, sighing. "So, what was yours about?"

Owen told him every detail, and Mordecai winced.

"You don't suppose," Owen said, "it could be more than a dream, perhaps a premonition?"

"Wormlings are rarely prophets. Leave that job to those it falls to."

"So it was just a bad dream, meaning nothing?"

Mordecai drew up one of his massive feet and scratched it. "I believe our dreams often reflect our fears. Like anyone, I fear the Dragon. But my greater fear is that I have lost the will—or the courage—to get involved."

"Forgive me for saying so, sir, but Watcher and I got the feeling you *had* given up."

"Ah, I was just testing you, trying to determine whether you really had greatness in you or only a taste for adventure. Call me banished or exiled or whatever you wish, but the better part of me is just biding my time, waiting for my moment. You know what I mean?"

Owen tried not to look surprised. In truth, Mordecai had been very convincing as a bitter old man with no interest in the future. "I think you are a good man. I don't know what brought you here, but I believe you know right from wrong and will seize the opportunity when the time comes."

Mordecai cocked his head and seemed to study Owen. "I do not envy you, Wormling. You still bear the notion that one life can make a difference."

"If you don't agree, why train me?"

"For one, you and your sleeping friend there would not be dissuaded. Annoying as that is, it is also admirable. And Mr. Page carries a certain weight with me—"

"Why?"

"That is not your concern. Suffice it to say, I will honor his request, even though I fear it will be a waste of time and energy."

Owen sat with his thoughts, then said, "It is not even close to dawn, is it?"

Mordecai laughed and shook his head. "There are many hours before the sun."

"Then why are *you* up?"

Mordecai drew a long breath through his great nose and

stared at the fire. "I suppose because I believed all this was behind me, that I had come far enough that it would not follow. After all this time my hopes and dreams became simple. I hope that the storms will stay away another month. I long for a bigger supply of jargid meat, a steady source of freshwater."

"And then I showed up."

"And then you showed up."

"You weren't really exiled, were you, Mordecai? You chose to come here."

"There are different types of exiles. Yes, mine was self-imposed. I came here of my own will. And I will remain here."

"But why? What made you want to leave everyone? Don't you have a family?"

Mordecai turned away from Owen in silence and busied himself with the embers again, though the fire seemed to be doing well on its own. When he finally spoke, his voice became husky. "You should not concern yourself with my story. It is yours, Wormling, that must be told."

"But *The Book of the King* says every story is important."

"The happy ones, perhaps. The ones that end well and never disappoint."

"Some stories are sad because they are only half finished. Like reading a book only halfway through."

"Believe me, Wormling, my story is finished. It is a tragedy not fit for a young mind like yours. Nor for old minds, for that matter."

The fire had begun to warm Owen, and sleep pursued him. Yet, strangely, he realized his time reading *The Book of the King* had made some deep impression on him. He couldn't imagine arguing with an adult in his world, let alone trying to advise one, but the wisdom of the book seemed to penetrate his soul and mind. He found himself eager to share his new insights.

"But, sir, doesn't it take tragedy to appreciate triumph? What would the mountain be without the valley? There's a lesson in that for those who believe their lives are over or that they have no purpose left."

Though Mordecai appeared uncomfortable with all this, Owen believed he might be getting through.

"Tell me this, Wormling: what about a person who has failed at the only important task ever given him, someone responsible for the deaths of ones he loves and the driving of others into the darkness?"

"One failure does not ruin a life," Owen said. "We all fall short of perfection."

"Some fall shorter than others."

"But we must not be defeated by one defeat. Think of the great inventor Thomas Edison and how many failures he endured before creating the lightbulb."

"The what? Who?"

Owen flushed, remembering he was in an entirely different world. He could have used the example of writers unable to get their manuscripts accepted by publishers but who went on to become important in people's lives, but that too would be foreign to Mordecai. "At what point do you stop trying—100 failures? More?"

"Remember that question in the morning, Wormling. You *will* fail in your training, but you will also grow. I promise to make sure of that." He squeezed Owen's shoulder with his scarred hand. "Now back to bed with you. You have a long day ahead."

Why can't they be clearer with their descriptions, RHM?" the Dragon rumbled, having incinerated yet another underling on the floor of his vast meeting room.

As the poor creature's ashes smoldered, the Dragon's aide, RHM, bowed low, eyes to the floor. "Sire, because the Watcher stays so close to the Wormling, it is imperative that our people stay far enough away that they can't be detected. This is why the details are, shall we say, sketchy."

"How can details be sketchy?" the Dragon growled. "They would then cease to be details, would they not?"

RHM paused. Had you been in the

room, you would have sworn that the being was amused with the Dragon, tempted to make fun of him. But he quickly thought better of it. "What of the boy in the Highlands? Have you found him yet?"

"O great one, he continues to elude us. Without the beacon, it seems nearly impossible."

"You know how important it is that he be found," the Dragon roared.

"I do, and we are doing all we can. However, in the meantime, allow me to introduce an invisible you might find most suited to the job at hand."

He ushered in a tentacled being with snakelike eyes who seemed to bear no fear of death, despite having to step over the room-temperature remains of his predecessor.

The Dragon's brows—if that's what we may call the bony protrusions over his languid, watery eyes—seemed to rise with interest at the very brashness of this creature.

"Sire, this is Veildrom, the last of the Stalkers to have seen the target Wormling. Allow me to inform you that he—"

"Enough, RHM," the Dragon said, studying his own everlengthening fingernails. "Allow Veildrom to tell me what he will and quickly. I am so weary of vagueness."

"Your Majesty—" Veildrom bowed—"I bring you a secondhand report from the Badlands, where—"

"Secondhand?" the Dragon spat. He inhaled as if about to spit fire.

"Indulge him, sire," RHM said, and when the Dragon whirled to glare at him, RHM added, "Please?"

"We do not normally rely on demon flyers for reports, but under the circumstances—"

The Dragon sighed and waved. "Yes, yes, out with it."

"They tell me they saw two beings in the narrow gorge that borders the territory of the mines. One was a Watcher and the other a human, a young man who very well could be the Wormling."

The Dragon rolled his eyes. "Could be?"

Veildrom told him how the two had barely escaped the flash flood.

"Pity they didn't perish." He turned to RHM. "Are we doing too much with the water thing? The whole deluge from the Mountain Lake and all that? I hate to get into a rut."

"The flash flood was a natural disaster, sire."

"Yes, well, let's just not become too predictable, hmm? We do have other tactics."

"The two were spotted a day later in the sea on a flotation device," Veildrom said.

"They did not approach the Badlands?" the Dragon said.

"The Wormling appeared to gaze upon it during the wee

hours of the morning, using some kind of looking device provided by the musicians of Erol."

The Dragon shook his head. "I thought we took care of that clan."

RHM stepped forward, hands clasped. "Mostly, sire. Those left have hidden themselves and no longer constitute a concern. They are, as it were, contained, having no influence—"

"They apparently had some influence on the Wormling and this Watcher! Food, encouragement for the journey and the task ahead, no doubt. That's all we need—aid to those miserable creatures and their measly lives."

"Would you like me to—?"

The Dragon dismissed RHM's notion with a wave and turned to Veildrom. "Anything else?"

"The demon flyers watched until the two were attacked by the Kerrol just off the islands of Mirantha."

"Then our worries are over," the Dragon said. "You should have started with that."

"Not quite, Your Majesty. They have since been spotted on the islands, though their skiff is in pieces on the rocks."

The Dragon's crusty face contorted with confusion. "The Kerrol has *one* job! Is he past his prime? too old and feeble for the task? Have his teeth fallen out from poor hygiene?"

"We're as puzzled as you, sire," Veildrom said. "For only

recently the Kerrol sank a vessel north of the islands and consumed the crew and passengers."

"And yet he's bested by a tiny Watcher and a young human?"

"They've obviously been helped, sire," Veildrom said.

"Obviously. But by whom?"

"We don't know."

"I don't like that answer," the Dragon said, a rattle deep in his throat.

Veildrom approached the Dragon. "I visited the caves of Erol."

"Why not the islands of Mirantha?"

"The Watcher would have sensed me."

"Don't make me drag this from you. What did you learn in the caves?"

"There was talk of a liquid the Wormling used to repel the Kerrol. Even more interesting was where they got it."

The Dragon's eyes were slits now. "*Will* you get on with it!"

"An older gentleman visited these outcasts some time ago and left a vial of liquid the leader was to provide a Wormling with should he ever come through."

"*He* has been there," the Dragon said, his throat foaming. "But what would the Wormling be looking for on the island? Surely not what is hidden there."

"The musicians spoke of a man who could perform some

sort of ceremony for the Wormling. The Wormling and the Watcher seemed desperate to find this man."

The Dragon huffed. "RHM, tell me the only other living person who can perform the initiation is the King!"

"Unless someone close to him also knew," RHM said.

"No!" the Dragon wheezed. "*He* can't still be alive."

"Who?" Veildrom said.

"A pathetic character who swore allegiance to the King long ago. He was killed in a fire at the castle."

"Or so we thought," RHM said. "But even if he survived, how would he have made it to the islands of—?"

"Veildrom," the Dragon said, "do you know anything else?"

For the first time, Veildrom seemed shaken. "One other thing, sire. Erol's clan still sings and plays. I said nothing to stop them, of course, because I didn't want them to know who I worked for."

"They are harmless," the Dragon snapped. "Contained, as RHM said."

"But their songs have taken a triumphal turn. No more laments about the past. They sing jubilant tunes regarding the Day of the Wormling. And they have written some that . . ."

"Yes?"

"Well, that question the length of your reign, sire."

"Indeed?"

"They seem confident, derisive about your abilities to contain the uprising the Wormling is sure to mount. They sing that you will be defeated by the good that will one day rule the hearts of men."

"Fools! They shall pay dearly. You have done well, Veildrom. Haste to the island and bring me news. If you fear the Watcher, kill her if you must."

When Veildrom was gone, RHM asked the Dragon if there was anything else.

"I must figure the best way to make Erol and his lot truly suffer. Not fire but something more painful. Something that lasts. And I must slow this Wormling. If he reaches initiation before we stop him, there's no telling what havoc he might wreak."

"Allow me to suggest something, Highness," RHM whispered, leaning close, which was not easy, given the girth—and the stench—of the Dragon.

When he had finished, a hideous smile curled the Dragon's lips. "Excellent idea. I like it. Maximum effect on the maximum number, *and* we will be free of the threat of the Wormling without so much as lifting a finger."

The two laughed until the Dragon threw back his head and gave a triumphant roar, shooting fire from the castle top, illuminating his kingdom.

Watcher snorted and rolled onto
her stomach, her fur hanging in
her eyes. She stretched and tried to get
the fur smoothed in a polite manner,
but there was always a tuft sticking up
somewhere. She just hoped it gave her
a certain style.

She couldn't remember sleeping so
well since the Wormling had come
to her world. Every night in the cave
she felt more and more at home. She
yawned, her tongue snaking out and
curling, and arched her back, feeling
her spine crackle.

On the first day of Owen's training she made sure she went along—to

protect him from the behemoth if nothing else. But as the days wore on and Owen and Mordecai worked on new tests of strength, Watcher became bored and began exploring the island or watching for the Kerrol from treetops. She had even strung herself a hammock, made from leftover vines near Mordecai's cave, at one edge of the place.

Now the standard breakfast was on the table—fruit and the jargid jerky Mordecai had cured. At first it had been difficult to sleep with food hanging right over her, but she had gotten used to it. And she had actually developed a taste for the meat of an animal that made a skunk smell nice. Watcher ate the fruit quickly, then stuffed the dried meat in her mouth. She could make it last an hour or the whole day.

On the table lay a hand-drawn map of what Mordecai had planned for Owen today. Owen had also drawn a picture on a leaf with a piece of blackened wood. The picture showed a big man with a boy by a mountain stream. Several landmarks were included.

When Watcher ventured outside, the sun was glowing on the horizon, and clouds passed so close that she could almost touch them. Down on the beach the waves lapped peacefully, and a great, white-winged bird glided.

The new grapevine hung from the tree near the cave, and like someone who had become used to walking on scaffolds hundreds of feet in the air, Watcher approached the ledge like it was no big deal. She wrapped her legs around the grape-vine, the leaf tucked tightly under her chin, and hurtled over the edge until her hind legs cushioned her against the rock wall. Mordecai had tried to motivate Owen by saying, "Why can't you do it like *she* does?"

♦♦♦

After the Wormling had gotten used to climbing down the mountain, Mordecai ran him nearly to death all the way around the island. He began at sunup and ran the sandy shores barefoot until he returned to where he started. Mordecai gave him until sundown that first day, but Owen didn't make it until well after dark. He was exhausted and hungry, his feet aching, but Mordecai made him get up the next morning at the same time and do it again.

Pushing, always pushing, Mordecai taught Owen many things, not the least of which were endurance and patience. While Owen ran the entire island, Mordecai went across the middle and met him on the other side just to tell him how far behind he was and how many more times he would have to run this same course if he didn't hurry. It was tempting for Owen to take a shortcut as well, but to his credit, he didn't.

When the Wormling made it to the end as the last rays of the sun disappeared, Mordecai showed him the obstacle course he had designed. The elaborate gauntlet was filled with dangerous traps. If at any point the Wormling made a wrong move, he could badly hurt himself.

"The real Wormling will be able to do this," Mordecai said.

All Owen could think of was what a klutz he had always been at sports, even in gym class.

The Wormling hated climbing trees the most—that is, until Mordecai discovered he couldn't swim. He took Owen to the waterfall and shoved him into the deep pool beneath it until the Wormling was forced to learn to float and breathe and paddle. More than once, Mordecai had to shed his tunic and jump in to pull out the choking and coughing Wormling.

♦♦♦

Watcher made it to the rapid stream down from the pool just as the Wormling whined, "How many more of these am I going to have to do to prove I'm who I say I am?"

"As many as it takes to make me believe *you* believe you're who you say you are," Mordecai bellowed, laughing. "Now try again. And be careful of the oil on the fish's body."

The Wormling stood in a rush of white water, struggling to keep his footing on the slippery rocks. He studied the surface, then lunged as something brown and red jumped up at him. "It hurts!"

"Of course, if you don't do it right. That's why they call

them shock fish. They send a charge into the water when they sense danger. Again."

As the next fish jumped, the Wormling tried to cradle it like a baby, but the effect was even worse. He danced on his toes like a barefoot man in a briar patch, yelping as the fish charged the water again and again.

Watcher could not help laughing. The Wormling must have heard her, for he turned, red faced, and rushed her. In midstream he tripped and fell on his face, which made Mordecai laugh. The Wormling arose, soaked and with red marks on his arms.

Mordecai's laughter filled the woods. Watcher had never before heard genuine laughter from him. His guffaws echoed off the rocks.

"You think it's so easy, Mordecai. You try it," the Wormling said.

Mordecai knelt, leaning over the water, waiting. When the fish jumped, he shot out a massive arm and grabbed it around its middle, tossing it onto the shore. "Can't be easier than that."

"Not fair," the Wormling said. "You have so many scars; you can't feel the sting."

Mordecai eyed the Wormling with a sour look. "My scars are none of your business." He rose and stalked away.

"I didn't mean to insult you," the Wormling called after him, but Mordecai kept going.

Watcher shook her head. "One moment he was laughing like a child, the next he was quiet . . ."

". . . as a child," the Wormling said.

"Let me try," Watcher said, kneeling on the bank as another fish jumped. She missed the first but was able to lean down far enough to kick the second to the ground beside her. She laughed as the fish flopped and gasped. On the end of its mouth sat a shiny gray patch that glistened in the sunlight. It was this that sent the shock.

"If you got out of the water," Watcher said, "they wouldn't be able to sting you."

"Grounding," the Wormling whispered. "That's it. When I'm in the water, I'm part of their world, but on dry ground . . ." He took his place on the bank just like Mordecai and Watcher, lunged at the first fish, and fell into the spray.

It was all Watcher could do not to fall over laughing. She helped him up, and he grabbed the next fish without getting stung, but it slipped from his hands back into the white water. He was successful with the next, tossing it onto the pile with the others.

††††

By noon, Owen had finished catching all the shock fish they could carry, so he tore from a plant a thick frond, as big as an elephant's ear, and stuffed all the fish inside. Watcher held

one end, and they carried the heavy load to the beach near
the grapevine.

Mordecai had started a fire and stuck a thin, sharp knife in
a stump. "Clean the fish there."

"I don't know how."

Mordecai grabbed a fish by the tail and with one slice
opened the belly and spilled the insides onto the stump.
That didn't seem to bother Watcher, who had caught and
eaten lots of fish, but to someone who had grown up over a
bookstore and had never fished in his life, it was disgusting.

Mordecai had laid out several vegetables called brawn,
which looked like cucumbers with the edible part surrounded
by a shuck, like an ear of corn (without the silk). Mordecai
pulled out the vegetable and placed a fish inside, then
wrapped it tightly. He sent Owen to look for skolers, a potato-
like vegetable that grew in the moss-covered regions of the
inner forest. Mordecai wrapped these in the skin of the brawn
and put them in the fire next to the wrapped fish.

They rested in the shade while the meal cooked, Mordecai
evidently content to let Owen have an afternoon off. Owen
already felt the difference in his body, a strength that started
in his feet and ran through his legs, all the way up to his neck.
His arms had become stronger too from doing chin-ups in the
trees.

If he went back to school in his own world now, Owen

wondered whether he would be able to handle Gordan and his crowd without help from the invisible force.

The slow-cooking fish and vegetables smelled delicious, but as Mordecai and Watcher dozed, Owen felt restless. He wandered toward the waterfall, where a huge jargid crossed his path, waddling toward the water, apparently unaware of Owen. Usually the animals sensed humans and fled, but Owen stalked the animal as Mordecai had taught him. He grabbed its tail, making the animal shriek and run. Mordecai would have wanted Owen to kill and skin it, but he couldn't bring himself to kill more than they needed.

Hungry as he was, Owen knew if he just waited for the meal he would be crazy with anticipation. He waded into the shallow pool where the stream flattened out and watched the cascading water. He couldn't have conceived of a place so beautiful, so full of life, so wild, so dangerous, and he wished he could share it with someone, someone like Clara Secrest back home. They had talked only a couple of times, but there seemed to be a sharing of their souls, a connection Owen couldn't get over.

The sun was slowly making its way down the other side of afternoon when Owen noticed something in the waterfall he hadn't seen before—a break in the white water, a blackness behind it. He moved closer and reached into the falls to feel the powerful surge. The sound and the coldness combined with the force of the splash on the rocks made him feel like he was visiting some place from his past, some echo he had never heard.

Owen moved onto the rocky path behind the waterfall between the rushing water and the face of the wall. Looking out through the sheet of water into the sun-drenched stillness of the island reminded Owen he was in a whole new world. The island took on an even more surreal tone, as if it existed only in some artist's mind.

He inched along, his back to the wall, careful of snakes or anything else that might slither along these slippery rocks. Suddenly, as if the wall behind him had moved, he backed into an opening, turned around, and found himself enveloped by a dense blackness. As his eyes adjusted to the darkness, Owen saw he had entered another cave.

Curious, he moved along a narrow corridor, the rocks so close together that he thought he had come to the end. But just beyond the narrow passage, the cave opened into a wide expanse. He had the same feeling as when he had discovered his father's secret underground hideout, but here there were no torches on the wall nor any stone staircases.

The floor was damp and trickles of water dripped, echo-ing. A pinpoint of light came from above or Owen would not have been able to see a thing. He cautiously stepped deeper into the cave until he came to a long stone table. On it sat a long padlocked chest and what looked like finely woven robes of velvet.

Owen was scanning the area for a key when he felt a hand on his shoulder. He jumped and turned, holding his breath, unable to speak, facing the dim outline of a face.

"So you really are the Wormling then."

26

The Sword

The voice was Mordecai's. He rested a hand on each of Owen's shoulders as if to calm him, then moved toward the table. "You found the secret stash. I figured it would take you a lot longer. This was to be your final test—finding this place."

"What is all this?"

"Remnants of the attack on the King's castle. Garments stolen. Some of the looted treasure."

Owen stepped back. This was why Mordecai had been exiled? He had stolen from the King? "You brought this?"

Mordecai shook his head. "I found it here, along with the key." He ran a hand along the padlock. "Perhaps hidden by whoever attacked the castle. Perhaps by someone else."

"What's in the chest?"

"Coins. Parchments. Records of the King's family—those who survived the fire. And one other item that should interest you."

"I'm listening."

"The Sword of the Wormling."

"I get a sword?"

"Since you do not battle only against flesh and blood, your weapons are often of the mind and the heart. *The Book of the King* tells you all you need for battling evil. But there will come times when you need to wield a physical sword." Mordecai unlocked the padlock and removed it. From within the chest he pulled a long sword.

Owen could tell from the glow of it under just the pinprick of light that it would gleam like the noonday sun outside, but we will not add anything to this story that would not make sense to a rational reader like yourself. Suffice it to say that it looked magical.

The handle sported the head of a lion in full roar, the rest wrapped in thick leather up to the blade, where all the design and pomp ended. It was simply two sharpened edges that ran to a pointed tip. Even in Mordecai's massive hands and strong arms, Owen could tell it was heavy.

"Take it and learn quickly," Mordecai said. "Your time is nearly at hand."

Owen grasped the sword, feeling as if something missing from his life had suddenly returned. All fears, all questions faded with the great weapon in his hands. It was too heavy to maneuver now, but he was already stronger than when he had arrived, and he would grow stronger still.

He couldn't wait to show it to Watcher.

27

Dinner and Treasure

Mordecai removed the coin boxes and other heavy items, then carried the chest back to the fire, where Watcher was tending a fresh roasting of skolers and fish. Owen followed with the huge sword, which seemed to render Watcher speechless. She just stared at it and at Owen.

Owen left the sword with her when he moved to the water to wash up. When he returned, Watcher was looking at herself in the reflection of the blade. She seemed fascinated with her face, opening her mouth, looking at her teeth, and pulling a tuft of fur from over her left eye.

"You need a mirror, not a sword," Owen said.

"What's a mirror?" Watcher said, sticking out her tongue and moving it from side to side.

Now famished, Owen finally sat with his mouth watering. He had eaten only breakfast and lunch each day on the island, snacking on pineapple or coconut milk to keep his strength up. That had made him stronger and leaner. He had more stamina and grew faster and more agile every day.

Mordecai skewered the fish and skolers and removed them from the fire. He pulled a green fruit from his pocket, sliced it with his knife, and squeezed the juice onto the fish. He poured coconut milk onto the skolers and let it soak in until the milk bubbled, then put all the food back on the fire. He rubbed his hands on his tunic and opened the chest. "I need to show you something."

Owen sniffed at the chest. It still smelled of the smoke that had permeated the scorched papers and jewelry.

Watcher picked up a gold necklace and gasped, "It's beautiful."

"It belonged to the Queen," Mordecai said. He took if from her with his scarred hand. The necklace matched the color of Watcher's fur, but its beauty made Mordecai's red scars look even more hideous.

Owen took it and held it up to the sunlight. It had become darkened by soot, but Owen was still impressed to actually be holding a piece of jewelry owned by a queen. "How do you know it was hers?"

"I just know."

Owen put the necklace back in the chest and took out a watch.

Again, Watcher was agog. "What is that?"

"A timepiece," Mordecai said. "It tells you how far the sun tracks across the sky each day and then the moon at night."

Owen thought that was an interesting way to explain a watch. "I have the same thing on my arm. Only it doesn't have hands, just numbers."

Watcher examined the black digital watch on his arm, which had become dirtier the more he trained. It was one of the few connections with his world, other than his clothes and his backpack. And the book. Always the book.

Owen pulled from the chest promissory notes, papers that said a certain person owed the King money. There were also forgiven debts, people for whom the King had canceled the money they owed.

"Seems like a pretty nice guy," Owen said. "He sure helped a lot of people."

"He was the best," Mordecai muttered.

"So who do you think hid this in the cave?"

"I don't know," Mordecai said. "Perhaps someone trying to put all the pieces of the King's life back together. His plan. He was a man of ideas, always sifting information, anticipating events."

Owen wondered how Mordecai knew so much about the King, but he wasn't ready to ask. "It wasn't just a thief then, stashing the loot?"

"Oh no. Think, Wormling. A thief would have long since sold the coins. And the sword and the jewelry would claim quite a price too, from the right buyer. No, whoever stashed all this was probably looking for something. Or someone. A clue to the whereabouts of the King, perhaps. Or maybe something about the King's Son."

"Maybe they wanted to lure someone here," Watcher said. Owen and Mordecai looked up at her, and she stepped back. "You know, as bait. Maybe they thought the Wormling would come here at some point, and they could do him harm or worse. Why are you looking at me like that?"

Mordecai coughed. "Pardon me, but I hadn't thought of that. It shows you're . . . thinking quickly and with a good head."

"Well, you needn't appear so amazed. Excuse me if I'm feeling less than appreciated." She strutted off in a huff.

"Watcher, come back," Owen said. "It's almost time to eat and you'll like this. Please."

But she had already disappeared into the jungle.

Owen rose to go after her, but Mordecai put a hand on

his arm. "We've offended her somehow. Give her time." He retrieved a fish from the fire and examined it. "You should be glad she's accompanying you. She really does have a good mind—and not just for watching."

Owen nodded and helped Mordecai remove the food. They let it cool while Owen examined a few more pages from the chest. One was burned and almost unrecognizable, but at the bottom of the page was a footprint, the kind you see on birth certificates.

Owen showed Mordecai and the man recoiled. "That is the royal certificate for the King's Son."

Beneath it was another, not quite as charred. "And this?"

"His sister. Gwenolyn."

Owen flinched. "No one told me he had a sister! Perhaps she knows where her brother is."

Mordecai sighed. "There is much to learn, Wormling. Not just about the sword and how to work with Watcher. I fear for your future."

Owen's shoulders slumped. "Why does this have to be so complicated? I really believed I could simply find the King's Son, he would unite the worlds, and I could go back home."

"You will need to go back. That's certain."

"Why?"

Mordecai shook his head. "There is much to tell. Let me show you something. Wait here." He climbed the vine to his cave with surprising agility and quickness for such a large man.

The sun was setting now, the smell of the food overwhelming. Owen couldn't resist opening the frond and picking off a white piece of fish. The taste exploded in Owen's mouth. He couldn't wait to dive in.

Soon Mordecai returned, the vine creaking under his weight. He held a parchment similar to the one containing the initiation ceremony, but Owen could tell it was much different.

"Your presence here means something is happening in the invisible world," Mordecai said, "and in your world as well."

"That's what Bardig said."

Mordecai handed Owen the fish and skolers, along with a crude fork. "He was correct." Mordecai ate with his fingers and downed the fish in three bites.

"I can't read this," Owen said.

"These are orders intercepted from the Dragon. Special orders for his elite troops. It talks of the truce between the King and the invisible kingdom. It confirms rumors of talks between the Dragon and the King. Whether it was face-to-face I don't know."

"Can there be a truce with a being such as the Dragon? He doesn't seem like the kind who would keep his word."

Mordecai nodded. "I wouldn't trust the Dragon to live up

to any agreement that called for his doing less than controlling both worlds as well as the invisible realm."

Mordecai took a bite of skoler and closed his eyes as if the taste had transported him. He licked his fingers and spoke with his mouth full. "The Dragon, it says, was prepared to sign the treaty of peace between the two worlds, but the agreement calls for his delivering the two 'packages' wrapped and intact. This can mean only one thing."

"The Dragon had the King's children kidnapped."

"Exactly."

"But why? Couldn't the Dragon have just killed the children?"

"Yes, quite possible. Probable even. But it strikes me that the Dragon wanted these two alive for his own purposes. They give him leverage to make a different deal with the King, perhaps."

Owen studied the scroll. "Where did you get this? It wasn't in the chest, was it?"

Mordecai popped the rest of a skoler in his mouth and stared at Owen. "What does it matter where I got it? I have it today."

"Where would the Dragon have taken the children, Mordecai?"

"No one knows, of course. This may be why the King disappeared. He conducted a search of the kingdom himself, checking every hamlet."

"But *The Book of the King* says the Son is in prison, so we know that much."

"Read it to me."

Owen dug the book from his pack, and as he began reading, Mordecai closed his eyes and a smile crossed his lips. The words seemed to bring him life, like a man dying of thirst given a goblet of the best drink in the land.

When Owen read that the Son would one day save both worlds and unite them, Mordecai finally opened his eyes. "Now I can see why you were so determined to be initiated. I have heard those words before, but they were only whispers on the wind, hope and freedom in the darkness."

"Do you remember when there were books?" Owen said. "Do you remember what the land was like?"

Mordecai nodded. "Knowledge was esteemed. People hungered for it. They would sit and listen to stories of old as their hearts turned to fire, and they wondered if there could ever be anything as good and as nourishing as apt words. And then came the fire, the burning and looting of wisdom. It began with the books and continued with the minds of my countrymen. We no longer hunger for knowledge."

"*Your* countrymen?" Owen said. "You count yourself among them, and yet you live here?"

"Are you a Wormling or a meddler?"

Owen smiled. "Maybe both."

28

Watcher's Quandary

A sensitive being, Watcher knew there were scarier things than just invisibles. At least she could tell when one of those was coming. With the humans, she could never tell when one would anger or betray her. She'd had her doubts about the Wormling at first, thinking he was just out for himself. The death of her trusted friend Bardig had been no small thing. But gradually she had come to trust the Wormling and believe he truly wanted to help his own world and hers achieve wholeness, as the book said.

But as soon as the Wormling had begun his training, Watcher sensed a change. Owen was becoming more aware of himself, more sure, more capable. He learned to swim. When she saw him with his sword, her stomach turned. She was losing him to a world of battle and crusades that could take him in any direction.

It was during these lonely times that Watcher sought solace in her hammock at the end of the island. Mordecai seemed so wrapped up in the initiation training that it seemed he, too, wanted her to fade into the background, seen but not heard.

And so she did fade, for a time, becoming a mere specta-tor actually taking delight in some of the exercises. One of her favorites had been at the hissing stones near the bridge that had been torn apart. In a shallow pool at the end of a lagoon lay a mist-enshrouded spot where water bubbled with heat from under the earth. Watcher did not believe this water could really be hot when the ocean was so cool, but one leg into the pond convinced her.

The Wormling's task had been to make it from one side of the pond to the other without falling in. Mordecai instructed the Wormling to study the water and traverse it barefooted when ready. The Wormling took his time—too careful for Watcher's taste—planning each step.

Watcher became so frustrated with the Wormling that she stepped in front of him and bounced over the rocks with ease, sure-footed and confident. Mordecai had laughed, but the Wormling had not. Especially when he nearly fell.

Enamored with Mordecai's attention, Watcher made a return trip, but at the next-to-last rock, something hot shot up her back and she screamed, falling.

Mordecai howled, and Watcher did not appreciate the laughter at her expense. The Wormling tried to help her up, but she would have nothing to do with him. She watched from a distance as he went back and forth over the rocks, even anticipating the gusts of steam.

"Good," Mordecai had said. "Excellent. Now we will try it again, only this time blindfolded."

To Watcher's surprise, the Wormling almost made the trip successfully. Almost. Near the edge, the steam zapped him from behind and he fell into the hot water. She had laughed hysterically, but that seemed to make him all the more determined.

Now, as she lay in the hammock watching the stars begin to appear, her stomach growled at the thought of the fish and skolers and brawn. She was the one missing out on the feast, not them. They probably didn't even miss her.

Watcher thought of her family, the meals her mother used to cook, the way her father relished each morsel and complimented the woman. Watcher closed her eyes and remembered the laughter, the love, and a pain struck deep in her heart—pain of loneliness and fear at the loss of both parents. She would never see them again, at least not in this life.

In that hammock, swinging gently with the wind, Watcher decided to return home. She would make a skiff of her own, and she had enough jargid skins and oil left that she could slather herself and keep safe from the Kerrol.

The Wormling did not need her any longer. He wouldn't even miss her. He could go on his one-man crusade, find the King's Son, and be the hero of both worlds without her help. She was sure of it.

Her mind filled with these thoughts until her ears twitched and her body went rigid. Something was coming. Something terrible.

O wen removed his heavy pack and
set it down as he ate by the fire.
"Why would I have to go back to my
world to fulfill my mission?"

"The prophecy," Mordecai said.
"Are not the four portals included?"

"Yes, it says that when they have
been breached—"

"And who can breach the portals
but a Wormling? Who has the power?"

Owen let another bite of fish lie
on his tongue, enjoying the taste. He
couldn't remember enjoying a meal
as much. "There is so much to do. So
much to remember. What if I make a
mistake? What if I fail?"

Mordecai grinned. "You are not

alone, Wormling. There is more to your journey than simply your efforts and the efforts of those who travel with you." He leaned back in the sand and put his hands behind his head. "I am hardly one to speak about such things, but there is purpose even in the mistakes."

"Sir?"

"Do you think it was a mistake that Bardig's life was taken?"

"It was a tragedy."

"Of course, but was it a mistake? Were the consequences of his death—the confrontation with his son and the flood in the Valley of Shoam—all blunders?"

Owen thought a moment. "I believe I was brought here for a purpose, and that purpose included meeting Bardig. But it also included Dreadwart and the terrible . . ." He shivered. "I don't even like to think about it."

"Oh, but you must. For your quest has as much to do with what's up here"—Mordecai pointed to his head—"as it does here"—he pointed to his heart—"and here." He spread his hands to encompass the island. "Do you *really* believe there was a clear purpose for your presence here? Until you believe it with everything in you—your mind, your heart, and the hands that will hold the sword—you cannot truly embrace what you must do."

"I have to believe the death of Bardig was part of the plan? How could something so awful result in any kind of good?"

"It brought you here, didn't it?" Mordecai said.

"And through dangerous waters and past the Badlands . . ." Owen looked at the sky, a thousand thoughts filling him. "Erol. His clan. I would never have met them if it hadn't been for Bardig's death."

"Yes, yes. And no doubt things happened to you in the other world that were equally distasteful, that you wished you could change, but they happened for some purpose. Perhaps the Lowlands will benefit from one of those."

"If I hadn't run from Gordan, I wouldn't have felt the arm in the night."

"Excuse me?"

Owen told him what had happened; then his mind turned, as minds are wont to do, and he directed Mordecai's words back to the man himself. "If what you say is true, there is a purpose in everything that happens, good or bad."

"We see good and bad from only our own perspectives, Wormling. There is a higher perspective."

"I see," Owen said, as if grasping one of the shock fish and tossing it Mordecai's way. "Then whatever brought *you* here, whatever gave you those scars and made you want to be eaten by the Kerrol, all that was part of the plan as well. All of that had purpose."

Mordecai's mouth dropped. "You are a meddler, aren't you?"

"I'm trying to understand. If your words are true, they are true for both of us."

"You don't know what I did."

"You yourself said there is purpose even in the mistakes."

"And I live with them every day."

"But do you embrace them, Mordecai? Do you see that they sent you here, brought us together, and allowed you to find the stolen chest and the birth documents and the Queen's jewelry?"

Owen had not seen Mordecai look so disgruntled since their first meeting when he nearly cut the vine. "What do you know?" Mordecai snapped. "If it hadn't been for me, none of what happened to you would ever have taken place. Why, I—"

Owen was sitting forward, eager to hear the secrets, the awful things that had made Mordecai an exile, when a powerful wind every bit as devastating as the waves in the ocean swept over him. It nearly sucked him off the ground and was accompanied by the violent rustling of leaves in the bushes near the beach trail.

"Visibles!" Watcher shouted. "Scythe flyers!"

"To the cave!" Mordecai yelled, closing the chest and putting it under his arm.

Owen grabbed the sword and followed Mordecai to the vine.

"There's no time!" Watcher screamed. "They're on top of us!"

Mordecai was already 20 feet off the ground, his big hands taking in yards of vine as he scaled the wall like a stepladder.

Owen leaped to the vine just as the huge tail of a scythe flyer appeared above the trees. The massive wings eclipsed the moon, and the horrifying screams of the animal made Owen cringe.

Owen was only a few feet up the wall when another flyer slashed his tail across the vine above Mordecai, cutting it like a hot knife through a ripe brawn. Owen looked up in time to see Mordecai grab in vain at smooth rocks and tumble backward, the giant man's backside blotting out the sky as it hurtled toward him.

"No!" Watcher yelled, darting from the bushes, her momentum carrying her into Owen and knocking him to the ground just as Mordecai landed with a terrific thud in the sand. The chest landed next to his head.

The man sat up, gasping, leaving a huge indentation in the sand. Gaining a little air, he struggled to his feet and retrieved the chest.

"So, what was the purpose of that?" Owen asked Mordecai.

"Sometimes . . . the only purpose we can see . . . is to run . . . and survive. Now let's do it."

The three ran into the jungle just as another scythe flyer skimmed the trees. Owen thrust up his sword, but the tail clanged on it and knocked him to the ground.

"Don't worry, Wormling!" Mordecai said. "There will be time to fight these beasts!"

"I thought you said these were invisibles," Owen yelled at Watcher.

"No, I clearly said visibles!"

Something smacked Owen from behind and sent him sprawling, the sword plopping into a stream. The sword began to smoke, and at first Owen feared it was disintegrating. Instead, it was producing a covering for them.

"Pick it up!" Mordecai yelled. "Head for the waterfall!"

30

Dominoes

I'm sorry I wasn't here to warn you," Watcher said, catching her breath inside the cave behind the falls.

"Yes, where were you?" Owen said.

Watcher looked away.

"Can they get in here, Mordecai?" Owen said.

"They hate the water, and the smallness of the opening will deter them," Mordecai said. "I've never had them attack like that." He put a hand in the small of his back and stretched, grimacing. "Probably smelled our dinner. Can't blame them."

"Your pack, Wormling!" Watcher said.

"Oh no! The book! I left it out there!"

In a flash, Watcher was out of the cave, shooting through the waterfall and the lagoon, Owen not far behind. He held his sword high, and steam poured from it as he ran through the shallows and the forests, trying to keep up.

Owen's training kicked in, and he felt strength in his legs and upper body from running and climbing the vine so many times. Still the sword felt heavy, but he was determined to use it if forced to.

Owen pushed through the fronds and bushes near the beach and finally stopped beside Watcher.

Someone or some*thing* was hunched over Owen's backpack. Its back looked like a giant praying mantis with large, striated wings tucked firmly in place. It was dark, like cola, the same as a cockroach, with gnarly, elongated fingernails that resembled the claws of some wild bird. When it turned, Owen saw that the face was humanlike, with a beak nose but with aspects of an insect or a reptile. At the ends of its long, sticklike arms were sharp pincers. Its eyes were huge and round with thousands of hexagonal segments. It tilted its head at Owen and Watcher, as if studying them. Owen swore he heard a zoom lens and a click.

Most frightening, it held *The Book of the King* in one of its talons. Owen slowly raised his sword and pointed it at the being.

It simply stared, cocking its head the other way. Finally it spoke in a high-pitched, nasally tone that sounded like scratches and screeches. "So, it is true. The Wormling exists."

"Give me the book," Owen said with an authority that surprised even him.

The being chuckled, which sounded more like a whistling snort. It swung the book around behind its body, and two fangs protruding from the roof of its mouth dripped green liquid onto its lips. "You have something His Majesty requires. I have come to retrieve it."

"The King?" Owen said.

"The Dragon," Mordecai said, emerging from the foliage. "This is one of his minions. His RHM."

"Ah, Mordecai," the being said, hissing. "You should treat me with more respect."

"Respect for one who would kill, steal, and destroy? You are in league with the chief murderer and thief."

The eyes of the monster turned red as he moved away from the fire.

Owen held the sword at arm's length, shaking as he pointed it.

"Be careful of the venom," Mordecai whispered. "He can shoot it a great distance. One drop will kill a grown man."

"Do I detect jealousy?" the monster said as Mordecai,

Owen, and Watcher slowly separated. "That I am now chief handler of the most powerful being above or below is no reason to slander me or His Highness."

"I do not envy one destined to lose," Mordecai said, still moving. "And how does one slander a being with no character and no backbone?"

RHM laughed anew. "For being so spineless, someone seems to have left an indelible mark on your mind as well as your body." The monster twitched his nose, and Watcher screamed as the venom shot.

Mordecai barely lunged out of the way. "Don't attack, Wormling! His venom is too potent."

Owen's arms were becoming leaden. "What about the book?" he said, focused on the monster.

"We can retrieve the other copy," Mordecai said. "Let him be."

"There is no other copy, and you know it," RHM said.

"What does the Dragon want with it?" Owen said.

"Maybe he wants it for the same reason you do," the being said, now holding it in front of him. "Does the little Wormling want his precious book back? Come and get it!"

"Wormling, no!" Mordecai snapped.

"Don't waste your energy on this beast," Watcher snarled.

"Come, Wormling. His Majesty would be delighted to make your acquaintance. I can take you there now, and you can read the book on the way. Perhaps you can convince him to make some kind of treaty with—"

"There can be no treaty with a prince of lies!" Mordecai shouted.

"Silence! You must not talk about His Majesty that way!" The being again shot his venom, and the plants and trees it hit immediately shriveled and died.

The air was suddenly disturbed, and RHM looked up with a start, giving Owen his chance. The Wormling charged with his sword, knowing he had thoroughly surprised the monster. But just as he heaved the weapon back to strike, Watcher screamed and a scythe flyer split the air. The flyer blocked Owen's swing, sending the sword whirling through the air like a windmill.

RHM hovered over the ground, his massive wings spread like a tent behind him. Teeth dripping again, the monster said, "Now, Wormling, you will see who loses the battle—"

Mordecai roared, "You know the prophecy! You know what will happen if you so much as touch a hair of the Wormling's head."

The being seethed as venom dripped from his horrid fangs. "There are ways to get to the Wormling, Mordecai. And we will succeed. Just as we succeeded with the one you know so well."

Mordecai gritted his teeth.

The being rose wildly, thrusting his wings in the air, holding tight to the book.

"What prophecy, Mordecai?" Owen said. "Why can't he kill me?"

"Neither the Dragon nor his right-hand man may touch the Wormling."

"Or what?"

"No one knows. It was a secret agreement between the beast and the King."

As RHM soared away, Mordecai spliced new vines to the one hanging along the rocks. Once they were safely inside the cave, Owen collapsed on his jargid skins, as dejected and low as he had been since he had come to the Lowlands.

"Do not despair, Wormling," Mordecai said.

"Mr. Page charged me to protect that book with my life! And Mucker is inside that book. When the Dragon discovers him . . ." Owen's eyes brimmed with tears. "Without the book, what do we have?"

Mordecai sat at the foot of Owen's makeshift bed. "The book itself is not as important as how much of the book is in you."

"I haven't even read all of it yet, let alone allowed it to penetrate me. He'll destroy it, and I'll never find the King's Son."

"Remember, nothing happens that cannot be used for

good. The power of the book remains, even when it is not present."

"Can that be?"

Mordecai smiled. "Our final phase of training begins tomorrow. Rest, Wormling."

"How can I when Mucker is on his way to the Dragon's lair?"

Mordecai slipped a hand into the pocket of his tunic. "Oh, I thought you might like to see what I found on the ground out there."

In Mordecai's palm sat a small white worm whose teeth were growing back.

Mucker looked as thrilled to see Owen as Owen was to see him. He tucked Mucker in beside him and fell asleep. And even unconscious, Owen found *The Book of the King* was still with him.

As it has always been, so shall it ever be. The King is on his throne and is in control.

31

Swordplay

Owen wrote as much of *The Book of the King* as he could remember during his spare time over the next few days, jotting thoughts and phrases and stories. Watcher helped jog his memory, staying close. It seemed she had a new resolve to stick with him, no matter what the cost.

Spare time was hard to find, however, as Mordecai kept to his word about the final phase of training: really learning the sword.

"Will the Dragon destroy the book, Mordecai?"

"How can he destroy something

held so deep in the heart that even a sword would not be able to separate its thoughts and intents?"

Mordecai took Owen into the inner recesses of the cave, through a small passage that led down an entire level to a circular room with just enough space for Mordecai to use a stick to parry with Owen.

"Mordecai, what is this indentation at the top of the blade?"

"The bloodline." He drove his dagger into a melon and tossed it to Owen. "Pull it out," Mordecai said.

Owen pulled, but he had to put the melon on the floor between his feet to get the dagger out.

"You want to be able to pull your sword out of your enemy and continue, not have to put your foot on him like a melon." Mordecai took the sword from Owen and had him toss the melon into the air. "The bloodline enables you to plunge the blade in," he said, catching the melon on the end of the sword. "Then you simply dip the blade, like this, and pull it out, resuming the battle."

Mordecai tossed the sword to Owen, who easily caught it by the hilt. Mordecai swung his long stick at his young friend. "Fight."

When Owen first began swordplay, he had flailed and jerked, trying to avoid Mordecai's stick. His battle was defensive, sometimes even running around the room. But the more he practiced and imitated Mordecai, the more he found that by simply turning his wrist or moving one foot, he could gain the upper hand.

Mordecai also threw things at him, including scalding water, and Owen learned to deflect or elude it. Within two weeks he was able to swing the sword as quickly as Mordecai swung his much-lighter stick.

When Owen finally knocked the stick from Mordecai's hand and brought the tip of the sword inches from the man's neck, he believed he was ready.

"Well done, Wormling. But you have more to learn about your weapon. Besides its ability to create a mist covering when it touches water, it can, with a word of encouragement, fly to your hand from quite a distance. Imagine the advantage of this in a crisis."

Owen tried calling the sword but missed when it flew near him. Once it knocked him down. Another time he missed the hilt and nearly grabbed the blade.

"The sword also has healing qualities," Mordecai said. "The ultimate goal of a weapon is peace. Good triumphing over evil. Destruction is not your main goal but health and wholeness. Those who fight you oppose those ideals." Mordecai wielded his stick again. "Fight."

Owen warded off numerous jousts, and when he saw an opening, he drove the sword down at an angle. Instead of blocking it, Mordecai stepped into the blade and it sliced through his sleeve to his arm.

"I'm sorry!" Owen said.

"No, it's all right," the man said, wincing, blood flowing. "Now put the side of the blade here."

Owen did, and when he took the sword away, not so much as a scratch or a drop of blood remained on Mordecai's arm.

"What? How?" Owen said.

"Ask the one who forged it," Mordecai said.

32

Initiation

Mordecai led Owen and Watcher
to a clearing he had prepared
at the end of the island. He simmered
several jargid over a fire, along with
shock fish and skolers.

As twilight approached, and with
waves crashing along the shoreline,
Owen knelt in the sand by a swaying
palmetto, where Mordecai touched
both his shoulders with the sword,
conferring on him the full rights and
responsibilities of a Wormling in the
Lowlands.

"And, Watcher, I charge you to act
and speak in a manner worthy of a

Wormling's aide. The trust he has put in you is sacred. May you live up to his calling."

Mordecai stood on a rock and lifted his voice above the night sounds. He read the scroll in lilting tones in its original language, which sounded as if it had come from heaven itself.

After each sentence, he translated. "The Wormling is called as protector and warrior on behalf of the King. It is his sacred duty to follow the King's wishes and do as he bids. This trust is bestowed upon you not because you have been deemed worthy, but because you have been chosen."

The word *chosen* rang through Owen's body like a low note on some magical instrument. All his life he had felt like an outcast, a person on the fringe, rarely included in games, anything but part of the "in" crowd. But here, in a quiet spot on an island in another world, he not only felt part of the plan but was also welcomed. Chosen. Important. Years of reading and soaking up the stories of great writers had helped prepare him for this moment.

"Look not to the left or right from the narrow path prepared for you. Study the words of the King to show yourself approved, a Wormling ready to battle, to heal, to find, to rescue. May your efforts cause the King's enemies to stumble and fall, while his friends become your friends."

As Mordecai read, his voice broke. "And remember that wherever your journey leads, there will be one who never takes his eye from you, never leaves you alone, and will always be with you."

Mordecai bade Owen to rise, and when he did he felt different. He had wondered why the initiation had to take place at all, but now, after the training and the commission, he knew.

Mordecai instructed him to say whatever came to his mind, and something wonderful happened. In class after class Owen had despaired of even answering a question from the teacher, let alone addressing the class. His hands shook, his face burned, and his back was soaked with perspiration.

But now Owen placed the sword in its scabbard, a new dark brown tunic wrapped around his shoulders, sporting a hood. Gazing at the golden horizon and his two friends, he said, "There is no place in this world or the other I would rather be than right here, right now. And there is no destination I'd want to reach than where my King—though I have never met him—sends me.

"You have taught me much, Mordecai. You have been faithful and true, and I can only hope that what you have taught has freed you from much of your past.

"And to you, Watcher, my friend and companion, I pray that one day you and I will be greeted by the King himself and that our friendship will never wane—that together we will find the Son, the prophecy will be fulfilled, and we will see the day of deliverance for both worlds.

"Where two or three follow the King, there the spirit of the King dwells richly."

"Long live the King," Mordecai said.

"Long may he reign," Owen said, reaching for the bearded man's hand.

Watcher lifted her hoof atop the two hands and seemed to search for something to say. She finally settled on, "Let's eat."

The three ate their fill, with their bare feet (and hooves) buried in the sand as the moon rose. Watcher soon fell asleep, but Owen was so excited he wondered if he would ever sleep again.

"Where will we go first?" Owen said. "You must have an idea."

Mordecai looked sad. "I will not be accompanying you, Wormling."

Owen sat up so quickly that he made Watcher stir. "We're much stronger together, Mordecai. You must come."

"Walk with me."

They moved up the beach, just out of reach of the tides. "Can't I command you to come? Now that I'm a fully commissioned Wormling?"

"You could, but you won't. You were chosen because this Mr. Page you speak of saw in you a heart of compassion. You won't force me."

"But we have the same goal, the same mind, the same heart."

"I have scars, Wormling."

"I no longer see them. I don't even think about them. You are my friend and my mentor."

"But the scars remain and not just the physical ones."

Owen put a hand on Mordecai's shoulder. "If you won't join us, at least tell me what happened. I need to understand."

Mordecai threw a stone into the surf. "I suppose I owe you that."

They walked on until Mordecai finally turned and faced the water, which reflected the night sky. "My parents were killed by the Dragon, leaving me a halfling passed from family to family in the village until one day the King and his wife rode through in a carriage. I had been left alone that day and sat watching the procession. The King inquired whose child I was, and someone told him the story. The King and his wife had compassion on me and agreed to take me in—to work at the castle. I worked in the stables, but the good lady insisted I be taught to read and write."

"The Queen herself?"

Mordecai nodded. "I learned from the best teachers in the land, and as I grew, the King took me under his wing as one of his own. I still remember walking the fields in the early morning dew, hunting fowl or rabbits, and coming across a den of jargid. He knew how much I loved the meat and would let me eat as much as I wanted from his table.

"When I was old enough, he sent me away to train as a warrior. And then an officer. And finally, he trained me himself, showing me some of what I have shown you. I was named captain of the guard, highest officer in the castle, and given the task—" Mordecai picked up another stone and flung it farther in the water. He paced in the sand, running a rough hand through his unruly hair.

"What task?" Owen said.

"Of protecting his wife and children first. I was to protect him too, though he did not need my help; he was so capable a warrior. But he would go on trips—to attend councils or to make treaties. It was while he was away on one of those trips that the castle was attacked. I wish we had had your Watcher. Quickly and without mercy, a fire erupted in the royal chamber.

"I did not hear the cries of the Queen and her children, because I had fallen asleep from too much wine. When I finally awoke and staggered into the room, flames had engulfed the netting over the crib and the boy was crying. I threw myself into the fire, grabbing the boy. But no sooner had I done this than I was hit from behind by a blast of fire. I threw up this hand to protect me, while cradling the Son. I awoke in the infirmary, bandaged. The Queen had survived the attack, but both the boy and the girl were gone. Stolen."

"Was the Son burned like you?"

Mordecai shook his head. "I don't know. All I remember is his face. Cherubic, like an angel's. Soft eyes that bored a hole through you, just like his father's."

"You did all you could, Mordecai."

"I should have been alert enough to prevent the attack. If I hadn't let them down, the King would be with his children, and the Queen would still be in her castle."

"What happened to her?"

Mordecai bowed his head. "I left in the night as soon as I could walk. As I wandered, I heard rumors that the King and Queen had searched for their children. Eventually the castle was restored, and the King sent out spies to continue looking for them."

"Did you ever return?"

"I could never show my face to him again. He had put his trust in me, giving me full access to all he had—his lands, his hunting grounds, a home for my family . . ."

"You have a family?"

"Had," Mordecai said, raising a hand, and Owen knew this was not a safe topic. "All he asked was that I protect his family." He paused. "I would love to see what the boy looks like now."

"One day you will, if we can be sure the Son is still alive."

Mordecai sighed. "I feel it to the very marrow of my bones that he is. If he is not, what hope have we?"

"I also feel something deep inside, Mordecai." Owen unsheathed his sword and Mordecai stood back. "I feel that if the King were here right now, he would forgive you. He would tell you that he loves you." Owen laid the blade against Mordecai's heart. "He would bid you to come back and fight with him. Search with him. To let him heal the wounds you have suffered so long."

Mordecai looked at the ground. "The sword's power to heal does not extend to wounds of the heart."

"Come *with* us, Mordecai. Fight *with* us."

Mordecai hung his head and walked down the beach.

Owen waited until the moon reached its zenith, and Watcher joined him, wiping the sleep from her eyes.

With Mucker tucked safely inside the initiation scroll, Watcher and Owen prepared for their journey off the island. One of Owen's training exercises had been to cut down a huge tree with a small ax. That came in handy, and Owen quickly fashioned a canoe from the fallen tree.

After a long, tight, tearful embrace of Mordecai, Owen and Watcher rubbed on jargid oil and put skins of the putrid animal in their new craft to ward off the Kerrol, then launched on the early morning tides from the south side of the island. Twice the beast slithered to the surface through the mists, and Owen wished it would get close enough for him to test his sword. But as if he had long since learned his lesson, both times the Kerrol plunged back into the depths with a kerthunk.

As Owen rowed he thought of Mordecai, and the more he thought, the sadder he became. *The Book of the King* contained many passages on forgiveness and restoration and said it was the glory of a King to overlook a mistake. Owen was sure the King still loved Mordecai and didn't hold his offense against him. Clearly Mordecai had never forgiven himself. Owen guessed it would take a visit from the King himself to free the man from his regrettable past.

Owen was soon glad to be back on the mainland, not surrounded by water, the canoe hidden in sea grass. His sense of mission—to find the King's Son so he could unite the two worlds and free the people—drove him.

His destination was the Son's prison, wherever he was held. Mordecai had offered several guesses as to where he might be, leaving Owen to dream restlessly every night, often awakening sweating and out of breath. Always it was the same: A young man in tattered, royal robes sat in the dungeon of some isolated stone prison, his hair and fingernails growing to enormous lengths. Watchmen on the walls bore hideous, scaly, horned faces. Torches lit every entrance. In his dream Owen got as far as the barred window that allowed him to see the Son just before he was discovered.

He raced from the fortress, pursued on foot, on horseback, and in the air.

Owen was now in search of the prison—or one similar to it—of his dreams. As he and Watcher reached rocky soil, several musicians of Erol leaped from trees and high rocks, alighting all around them.

Owen grinned. "Friends!"

But it quickly became apparent that the musicians were not smiling. Was it possible they didn't recognize him? thought he was a trespasser? They surrounded and subdued Owen and Watcher before he even thought of defending himself. Two lugged his heavy sword to a cliff and pitched it down a ravine, where he heard it clanging on its way.

Soon Erol himself emerged.

"Why do you look at me that way, old friend?" Owen said.

The man's eyes were not filled with hatred but with tears. He pulled a dagger from his tunic, his fist clenched around it so tight that his knuckles were white. "I'm sorry, Wormling," he said, clearly unable to meet Owen's gaze, "but I must kill you."

"May the
King Grant It"

Erol leaned close and whispered, "I
must cut out your heart and give it
to the Dragon. He has invaded. I have
one chance to restore what I have
known and loved all these years."

"What happened?" Owen said.

"The demon flyers attacked our
young ones picnicking in the glen.
They took a dozen and carried them
toward the Badlands. They have
announced that your heart is the
ransom."

"But I can help you get them back.
Killing me will only mean you lose
them forever."

Erol shook his head. "Their leader, a

most hideous creature, said our children would die unless we did as he commanded. We are to kill the Wormling and present his heart to the Dragon. He held out *The Book of the King* and said it was written that you would die by our hands—"

"He lied!" Watcher screamed, her voice echoing through the valley.

Owen nodded. "The truth is not in him," he said quietly. "The enemy seeks to make us fight those we love rather than our true enemies. If he divides us—"

"I cannot risk losing my children!" Erol said, moaning as he raised the dagger. "We must place your heart high upon the rock where he can see it."

Owen closed his eyes, took a deep breath, and raised his voice. "Sword!"

From the ravine came a clang and a whirring.

Owen spread his legs and shook off the musicians, grabbing the sword from the air. "The fate of your children and the kingdom depends on me."

Erol looked taken aback by both Owen's strength and his voice. The little man quickly held the dagger to Watcher's throat. "Consent or your friend dies."

Watcher's eyes darted and Owen heard her whimper.

"I promise on my life I will get your children back," Owen said. "But you must listen to me, not this being from the Dragon. He means only to devour you and your kind."

"Our women weep," Erol said. His voice was pitiful and weak.

"I will turn their mourning to dancing and their cries to shouts of joy. But you must—"

Before Owen could finish, Watcher tried to escape and Erol's blade sliced her foreleg, blood pouring on the ground. "Wormling," she gasped.

Owen stepped forward with the sword.

"Wait!" Erol said. "Do not end her life! This wound is not fatal."

"Stand back!" Owen commanded.

Watcher wobbled, clearly weakening.

Owen pressed the sword to her wound, and immediately the cut closed, completely healed.

Erol and the others fell back.

"My power is not my own," Owen said. "It comes from the King."

"Our fate is in your hands, Wormling," Erol said. "But how will you save the children? The Badlands are forbidden territory."

"*The Book of the King* says, 'Whatever you put your hand to do, do it well and do it with all your heart.' The King will prepare the way. And he will show us the way to his Son as well."

"We dare not doubt you, Wormling," Erol said. "Forgive me!"

"You are forgiven. I understand."

"Now, how can we help? Shall you take our most trained?"

Owen looked at the sky. *He* had been chosen, though weak and afraid. *He* had been entrusted with *The Book of the King*, though just a boy. "Was your son taken?"

"No," Erol said. "Why?"

"I am here," Starbuck called, bounding out from behind a rock.

Owen caught Erol's eyes with his, eyebrows raised.

"Him?" Erol said.

Owen put an arm around the boy. "There is power and strength in the humble. Great armies are no match for the lowly, honest heart. The rulers of the darkness look on the outward appearance. The King looks at the heart. I perceive your son has the heart of a warrior."

"I don't know," Erol said. "His mother would never—"

"But, Father! You must trust one such as the Wormling, who speaks with authority, though he is not much older than I!"

"While his mother and I consider it," Erol said, "you must tell the others of your time on the islands."

"Yes!" someone said. "Was the scarred one there?"

"With the face of a lion and the skin of a lizard?" another said.

"Who has married the Kerrol?"

"And has spawned children who roam the land?"

Owen held up a hand. "Enough! Yes, he is scarred, but all the rest is false! The King never had a truer friend."

Erol and his wife, Kimshi, eventually emerged. She wept and sang Starbuck songs from his childhood. The boy kept telling her in hushed tones to stop, but her son would accompany a Wormling into the most dangerous region of the land, and so she carried on. Owen had never experienced the tears of a mother. He watched, fascinated, as she held Starbuck like a baby, kissing him and repeating the songs again and again.

The fathers whose children had been taken prepared to accompany the three, sharpening weapons, preparing nets for the demon flyers, and gathering supplies.

But when darkness fell, Owen stood before them. "We will take no weapons, save my sword." He held up a hand to quiet murmurs of protest. "There will come a time when you all will be asked to join in the battle. And anyone who fights with the King will be rewarded. But this mission is a rescue, not a battle."

"Promise our children will be returned to us," a woman said.

"I can promise only what has been revealed. The prophecies say there will be singing and jubilation in this world and in the other when the Dragon is overthrown."

The elders gathered around Owen, Watcher, and Starbuck and began a tune so soft and low that Owen couldn't make out the words. The musicians sang in a glorious blend, without instruments. The notes seemed to spring from their very souls, echoing through the canyon.

When they finished, the elders placed their hands on the three.

Erol said, "Go with the urgency of the hawk. Run swiftly through the barren land. Train your eyes so that no attack from above or below will go unnoticed. And may our children be returned to us."

"May the King grant it," Owen said.

And the clan of Erol repeated after him.

35

The Badlands

Watcher was plainly peeved at
Owen for bringing Starbuck,
probably because he had not consulted
her. She strode ahead of him so there
was no way he could miss her feelings.

But Owen was resolute. As he had
addressed the clan, a voice, still and
small, told him, "Take the boy with
you."

At first Owen had resisted. How
would they control such a youngling?
But Owen himself had been chosen
as a Wormling. Nothing qualified him
to be given the charge of saving these
worlds. Someone must know something about the heart of this lad.

Starbuck looked like his father,

minus the rotund belly, with a long snout and a confident walk. The tender eyes were his mother's. Owen envied the boy's stories of the things his family did each night, saying good night and singing to each other.

Starbuck skipped and climbed along rocks. As they neared the border of the Badlands, he sidled up to Owen. "I've been out here before. You knew that, didn't you?"

Owen knew nothing of the sort. "How far?"

He pointed. "Past the Valley of Zior and halfway to the camp."

"How did you do this?" Watcher said. "Why?"

"I used my legs. I wanted to see what was there. My parents thought I was on a picnic with friends. I begged them for weeks to let me go. I simply had to see what was so bad about the place. Our village is terrified of it."

"You deceived your parents," Owen said. "You must not do it again."

"What did you see?" Watcher said.

"Snakes as big around as me and twice as long as you, Wormling. Maybe three times. And the lizards of Zior protect the camp at the edge of the mines. I saw them through—"

"Lizards?" Owen said.

"Hundreds. Thousands. They hop with long tails and catch insects and fight with each other. I suppose they're guarding the encampment for the demon flyers."

Watcher looked worried. "You knew about the lizards, but still you came."

Starbuck nodded. "The Wormling will keep me safe. I wouldn't miss this."

Three times Watcher's hair went up, and she pushed Owen and Starbuck behind rocks or covered them in the sandy soil. All three times demon flyers screeched overhead, flying toward the mines. Watcher shook each time, but Starbuck seemed excited.

"Those things took two of my best friends," Starbuck said. "How many are we going to kill?"

Watcher looked at Owen. "You brought him; you answer him."

"You heard what I said at the camp. I don't intend to kill anyone or anything."

Starbuck frowned. "I thought that's what you'd say. But what if they attack? We have to defend ourselves!"

Owen shook his head. "I'm hoping they never see us."

In the Valley of Zior the three scrambled inside an abandoned cave before the sun rose to the edge of the horizon. As the orb climbed, a sizzling sound made Owen realize the sun was literally baking the valley floor. Tiny shoots that had budded in the night withered and collapsed. The dew on rocks bubbled, hissed, and evaporated.

"Why is it so hot here?" Owen said, curling up to nap.

"They say the Dragon set up an unseen desert boundary," Starbuck said. "Those who travel into the valley are said to have abandoned all hope, because death is sure."

They slept through the day until the sun seemed to lose intensity in the long shadows. As they made their way out of the cave and into the dry and cooler air, animals were beginning to peek out of their holes, skittering among the sparse bushes and tumbleweeds.

Watcher stopped Owen just before he would have stepped on a huge snake slithering through a gully. Its head was as large as Starbuck's.

The valley was filled with the bones of animals. The moon finally appeared, softly glowing, and Owen was glad they didn't need a torch.

They came over a rise, and Starbuck stopped. "Yipping. The lizards must know we're coming. They can sense us."

"Is there any other way to the mines?" Owen said.

"They surround the camp all the way to the entrance," Starbuck said. "I saw it through the viewing circle."

"When the sun rises, they must go underground," Owen said.

"Yes, to live," Starbuck said. "You're not thinking of walking across there in daylight, are you?"

"Wormling," Watcher said, "no one can withstand the searing sun here."

"Unless we go underground," Owen said. "Or simply walk straight through the enemy horde."

"I'd like to see you do that without killing any of them," Starbuck said.

Owen felt the hilt of his sword. He whispered, "Follow me."

The eyes of the lizards gleamed green in the moonlight as Owen peeked over the crest of rock, 50 yards from the swarming creatures. He had told Watcher and Starbuck to stay behind, wanting to see what they were up against. The reptiles' snouts were long and thin with razor-sharp teeth, and that would have been enough to turn most people back, but it was the eyes that penetrated Owen's heart. They reminded him of the Slimesees'.

The lizards looked prehistoric, antsy and chattering in their own language. Tails as long as baseball bats twitched and patted the ground like unruly snakes. They stood on their back legs most of the time, unless they wanted to go faster. Then they dropped to all fours and skittered quicker than Owen's eyes could follow.

If only he had *The Book of the King* and could simply wave it before them, these creatures would crawl back in their holes and he and Watcher and Starbuck could pass. They could wait until the blistering daylight when, hopefully, the lizards would be forced underground, or figure some way to get past them before the sun rose.

At first the pack looked like nothing but chaos, but the more Owen watched, the more he became certain there was a method to the creatures' running and jumping. They hopped and squeaked and caught glowing insects and bit each other and squeaked some more. With their tough skin, they looked like an armored cavalry.

Owen waved Watcher and Starbuck forward and got out his water bottle, which was about a third full. He had another full bottle in his backpack, and though it was a risk to use water for anything but drinking here, he had an idea.

Watcher thought it a waste of water, but Owen pulled out his sword and told Starbuck what to do. The youngling listened; then a strange look came over him. Owen heard skittering and chattering lizardspeak and turned in time to see two green eyes bouncing over the sandy ridge ahead.

"A scout," Starbuck whispered. "He'll report us."

The creature's head bobbed, slithering over the ridge and back down.

Owen sensed danger even greater than the flood from Mountain Lake. He remained still, not even breathing as the scout scanned left and right. Summoning the skills learned in his quickness drills, Owen grasped the sword by the hilt.

The scout immediately stopped to look at the hulk hiding behind the dip in the sand. He looked surprised, and before he could call out to his friends, Owen swiftly brought his sword forward.

Any ordinary person faced with the prospect of being overrun by a horde of lizards might have squished this lizard like a bug or sliced him like a block of cheese. But it should be no surprise to you (though it obviously was to Watcher and Starbuck) that Owen did not cut his head off or splatter his insides against a rock. Rather, he simply brought the flat blade down on the lizard's head sharp enough to knock him senseless.

The lizard swooned, head lolling, tongue sticking out, and he collapsed in the sand, lips curled around sharp teeth, a strange look on his face.

"He'll be up soon," Owen said. "Take your places."

Owen crouched and moved resolutely toward the lizards. He imagined them attacking, life draining from him and making him just a stain on the desert floor. By morning he would be nothing but bones, another sad statistic in the life-and-death cycle that was this valley.

But no. When he was within a few yards of them, he stood tall and held his sword straight in front of him. Deafening screeches and chattering nearly unnerved him enough to jam his hands over his ears, but he simply took in the sight. The lizards began hopping atop each other, biting and clawing as they advanced toward him. The lizards that had been at the perimeter joined the others in the middle, and Owen flashed Watcher and Starbuck a signal.

37
Skirting Lizards

When the lizards were almost upon him, Owen spat a stream of water onto his sword. The blade glowed and emitted a burst of white mist that enveloped him and mesmerized the swarming horde. They shrank back, then gathered around the sword and followed like children at a carnival.

As the right flank of the lizards moved toward Owen, Watcher and Starbuck slipped past Owen and up the rocks toward the camp. Owen kept moving toward a narrow crevasse, still surrounded by lizards chattering and clucking, gazing intently at the sword.

He moved more quickly now, and

the lizards parted in front of him. At the crevasse, he poured
more water on the sword, stuck it upright in the sand, and
hurried into the narrow opening that led to the camp. At the
top, he met Watcher and Starbuck, panting, watching the
horde circle the sword.

The three moved silently uphill toward flickering campfires. The soft clink of chains and the muffled cries of children
mixed with snores from the edges of the camp.

In the moonlight, Owen spotted a guard, spear in hand,
wearing a helmet and a breastplate. Huge nostrils emitted
a ghastly sound that turned Owen's stomach. This was no
human, and it certainly didn't look like any animal he had
seen. It was sort of a rhinoceros-ape mix with a hairy body
and a head that didn't seem to want to end.

The camp was dotted with structures made of animal skins
stitched together and stretched over wooden stakes. Limp bodies scrunched up for warmth lay under animal skins. Each had a
chain attached to a wide silver buckle fastened around the ankle
and hooked to another person or to a metal stake in the ground.

The encampment covered the plateau to the edges. Every
30 yards or so a fire burned, making it easy for the guards to
see their prisoners.

Starbuck motioned Owen and Watcher toward holding
pens and pointed at the sleeping forms. Owen recognized
several from Erol's clan, younglings too large to crawl through

the openings in the pen and too small to break through the lid fastened at the top.

Watcher started to speak, but Owen put a hand over her lips and gestured above them to a narrow path before the mouth of a cave where a guard was slumped sleeping. They moved to the ledge, where they could talk. Below, Owen's sword still shone with lizards hopping and jumping around it.

"Psst."

Owen spotted an old man with gray hair sitting up under his tent. He scooted quietly across the sandy ground and ducked under the tent flap just as a guard stretched and belched.

The old man grabbed Owen's tunic and pulled him close. His breath was sour and his eyes dim. "Have you come for us?"

"I've come for the children," Owen whispered.

"How did you get past the lizards?"

"Never mind. Where do they take you when the sun comes up?"

"Into the bowels of the cave." The old man stared at Owen's face. "Who are you?"

"I have come to free the captives. And when my mission is complete, I will come back for you."

"Did the King send you? How else could you have gotten through the lizards?" He leaned closer. "His wife is here, you know. Yes, the Queen is in this wretched place." He pointed and said, "Over there. Extra guards day and night.

We expected a rescue mission someday, but . . . you are such a young one."

"What happens here?"

The man scowled. "The Dragon works us to death in his mines and throws us away when we're used up." He nodded south of the camp, where bodies lay stretched in piles, birds picking at the seared flesh in the moonlight. Owen had to look away.

"We have heard rumors of rumblings in the kingdom. A great tremor was heard not long ago, and the Queen has said something about a Wormling."

"She is wise," Owen said.

The man perked up. "It is true?"

Words from *The Book of the King* came to Owen. "'The King knows the burdens of the weary and hears the cries of the oppressed. His army is coming. His deliverance is near. He will lead his captives from the depths and bear their burdens.'"

The man trembled and his eyes widened. "Have you seen the Wormling? Do you know if he is here?"

"I know this," Owen said. "The rumbling you heard *was* the Wormling. The King's forces are moving. When the Son is found—"

"The Son! The Queen was overheard talking of the Dragon's council held just days ago!"

38

The Queen

The threatening pink of daylight caused a stir. Chains clinked as people sat up and the guards made the rounds to release their leg-irons. The prisoners trudged through the chow line, eagerly receiving a bowl of pasty mush they ate with their fingers. Heads down, shuffling, they plodded up the dusty path single file to the cave.

The old man with the long silver hair, however, smiled at the guards, chuckled as he shoved the food into his mouth, then quickly handed the bowl back. As he began the steep incline, he craned his neck and looked to the holding pen of the Queen. "Good mornin', my lady," he cackled. "Nice day for the Son to come, isn't it?"

The guards had to assume he was saying "sun."

The Queen, dark haired and with olive skin, did not even turn her head. She merely stared at the ground.

"Keep moving, you old buzzard," a guard said, poking him in the ribs.

The old man just smiled.

♦♦♦

Owen, Watcher, and Starbuck sat on a ledge high above the room where precious metals were separated from the mined rocks, watching people shuffle by and the guards treat them cruelly.

Owen's heart broke at the sight of a mother weeping for her child, separated at the previous tunnel. The guards had snatched him from her arms and thrown him into the eleva-tor operated by pulleys. All the way down the shaft the child screamed and cried, and Owen had to close his eyes and breathe slowly, so great was his anger.

Finally a woman with black hair, an olive complexion, and less-tattered clothes strode regally into the hall below. Owen could hardly keep his eyes off her. People bowed until she sat.

Owen waited until the line dwindled to a trickle and the guards took their positions. One of the biggest stood outside, carefully watching those who brought in wooden boxes filled with rocks. A blast of hot air hit Owen, and a bright light shone through the cave. The guard below him moved down the tunnel, yelling orders to block the entrance and the searing heat of the sun.

Seeing his chance, Owen motioned for Watcher and Starbuck to stay where they were and dropped to the ground, rolling into the separating room.

The dozen people around the table recoiled. A man stood, lips pursed. "Bow before royalty."

Owen put a finger to his lips and spoke to the Queen. "I mean you no harm, Your Highness."

The Queen stood. "Guard! Guard! Return here immediately!"

"I tried to send you a message this morning. The old man who spoke to you—"

Another woman stood and glowered at Owen, holding a black rock above her head.

"Wait!" the Queen said. "What message?"

Owen told her what he had told the old man to say.

A guard was coming, huffing and puffing.

"Please, Your Highness," Owen whispered, "just hear me out."

Something in her eyes let Owen know she would. As the guard arrived, Owen ducked under the table.

The Queen waved. "Just a misunderstanding." She looked at the woman across the table. "Go back to work."

"See to it," the guard said, shoving the Queen into her chair. The others gasped, and the guard sneered as he left.

The Queen leaned down. "You have one minute before I report you."

"I'm here to help. I'm the Wormling."

The table went deathly silent; then 11 other chairs pushed back.

"He's too small," a woman said.

"The Wormling is supposed to be a giant, isn't he?"

"Certainly not as puny as—"

The Queen snapped her fingers. "Keep working." Then she leaned closer to Owen and whispered, "Speak."

"I've been sent to find your Son. I've just come from the island where Mordecai has been hiding—"

"Mordecai?" she hissed. "He betrayed us."

"He was the only one left who knew the initiation and training."

"Bardig knew—"

"Bardig is dead. Killed by Dreadwart."

"Who sent you?"

"A man with a book; he called himself Mr. Page."

"What happened to him?"

"He left the book with me and fled. The Dragon was chasing us."

"In the Highlands?"

"Yes. And now I'm looking for your Son. He's the one—"

"Who can bring both worlds together, yes, I know. I would trade all the unity-of-the-worlds talk for the return of my child and husband."

"I will get you out of here," Owen said, "as soon as I find your Son. There was talk of a conference, that you and the Dragon spoke."

Her face turned ashen. "He said my Son was being held at the Castle of the Pines."

"Your home?" Owen said.

She nodded. "It's been years since I let myself believe he was even still alive. Perhaps this is a cruel trick by the Dragon to raise my hopes. Well, it worked. I pray he was a born liar telling the truth, but even if he was, what difference does it make? You'll never get out of here. And if you do, you'll never make it across the desert to the castle."

"I made it here, didn't I?" he said.

The Queen was silent.

"He has a point," a man said.

"I'm here to rescue the children of Erol," Owen said, "but I promise I'll come back. And when I do, I'll bring your Son with me."

"Do that and I will make you the richest man in the kingdom."

"I don't want to be rich, Your Highness. I simply want to

finish my mission and go home. I feel someone is waiting for me there, that there is a purpose in going back."

The Queen bent and looked into Owen's eyes. "Find my Son. Tell him where I am." She drew a map to the castle with a piece of coal. "Forget the unity of the worlds, the talk of peace and love and tranquility. Just bring my Son to me."

39

Escape

Owen pulled a huge cloak one of the prisoners provided over his tunic, and with Watcher and Starbuck also hiding beneath it, he carried a box of rocks down the tunnel. They were stopped only once—by a guard who would awaken an hour later with a terrific headache. He would tell his friends that the youngster under the cloak was much stronger than he looked, that the way he drove the smooth rock into his temple, just under his helmet, was military in its precision. The others would laugh, saying a child had gotten the better of him.

The three climbed down where they saw light flickering and water dripping from the sides of the cave—an oasis in the midst of a desert. They drank until they heard the screams of children.

"That's Dalan!" Starbuck said. "My friend!"

"Easy," Owen said, grabbing his shoulders. "We have to keep our wits."

The air was thick, filled with black dust.

"Get up there into the hole!" a guard bellowed, lashing Dalan with a leather whip.

The other guard laughed.

"I saw a snake!" Dalan said, chest heaving. "Its head was as big as mine."

"Then make your choice—the snake or my lash!"

Before Dalan made that choice, Owen slipped up behind the second guard and hit him in the back of the head with the smooth rock. The beast slumped as the other guard turned. He raised his whip, but he had no idea that the boy before him had spent the past few weeks knocking coconuts from their branches with only small rocks. Owen had become so good that he could throw with just enough force to knock the coconut down, creating a small hole through which milk gurgled. Mordecai had trained him to catch the coconut before it hit the ground.

Owen let the second guard slump with a thud while the children screamed with glee at the sight of Starbuck. They swarmed him, and Starbuck laughed and hugged them back.

Watcher looked at Owen as if all the trouble they had experienced had been worth it, if only to experience this moment.

Owen reached inside his tunic and pulled out something small from an inner pocket. He whispered into his palm as he moved toward the rough wall of black rock, and the children could not have understood the significance of the chomping sound.

The children stilled as Mucker began eating away at the rock. His teeth had become dull and broken on his trip from the Highlands to the Lowlands, and the last time he had used them was in the fight against Dreadwart. Since then, sleeping and becoming restored, Mucker had grown stronger and his teeth now seemed even more powerful than before. Mucker began to grow as he took bigger and bigger bites from the wall.

"Stay close to me, children," Owen said. "The rock will fall in on itself behind us."

The group huddled close to Owen as Mucker wrapped his tail around them, pulling them with him as Owen recited words from *The Book of the King* that brought life to his soul and propelled Mucker.

"Whatever you choose to do, employ your whole heart in the task. You are not working for yourself or for others, but you are working for the very King himself and his purposes. You serve at the pleasure of the King, and if you please him, he will prosper the work of your hands."

♦♦♦

Commotion grew in the mines when the injured guards were discovered. They spoke of a strong-armed giant who overpowered them. The children were missing, and the pile of rubble sent rumors flying. People came running to the elevator, pushing past the guards to rescue the children.

In the separation room, the Queen fielded questions from the workers at the table.

"Do you think he was really the *one*?"

"Could this be the beginning of the war?"

"Are the children safe?"

The Queen sat stone-faced. "I do not know what the future holds, but I do know who holds the future. And if I am right, there is more at work here than simply an intruder into the Badlands. We must be vigilant now. Do not lose heart, for when the time comes, we will be asked to join the fight."

40

The Good Heart

As Owen and the children followed
Mucker out, rocks falling and
dust settling, the children stepped
into the fresh air. The mountain cast a
long shadow, since the sun was on the
other side. The group sat and sipped
water from flasks Owen, Watcher, and
Starbuck carried. The children wanted
to know how Starbuck had been
chosen and how they had crossed the
desert. Owen let Starbuck spin his tale
while he met with Watcher.

Watcher believed the children
should head across the desert by themselves with Starbuck. "We need to get

to the Castle of the Pines as quickly as we can and not traipse back across the desert."

"*Traipse?*" Owen said. "Where did you learn that word?"

"From you."

"Watcher, we can't let them cross the desert themselves. If the lizards or the snakes don't get them, the demon flyers will."

"Then I'll go with them. I can alert them of the flyers. You can see us through the lizards and then turn around."

Owen shook his head. "I know you're trying to help, but—"

"These children are not your mission," Watcher whispered urgently. "You are to find the King's Son. Anything that side-tracks you only prolongs the agony of the people. Now you must go."

Owen knew she was right, but when he looked at the children of Erol, he glanced back at her through teary eyes. "My mission is to follow the one who sent me. To listen to his voice. Mine is not simply a task to be accomplished. It involves friends. Like you. Like them. I am to find the Son *for them*. For us. For the kingdom. What good is it if both worlds are united, but we lose our friends?"

"You should not detour."

Owen turned Watcher around and nodded toward the children, who sang and giggled and played in the sand. "How could *they* be a detour? Don't get so caught up in the goal that you miss the good right here in front of you. The King loves even the smallest, even the most insignificant. And he will see that all who are broken are made whole, no matter their station."

Her whiskers trembled as she looked at him. "Where did you learn this?"

"It comes from the book and seeps into the bones," he said. "I still have much to learn and much to accomplish, but I must see these children back to their families before we go to the castle."

"You and I both?"

"Watcher, I could no more leave you to those ravenous lizards than I could lay down the Sword of the Wormling."

She raised her eyebrows.

"Right," Owen said. He raised his voice, as Mordecai taught him, and gave a mighty yell. "Sword!" The laughing and singing stopped as Owen held out a hand. A sharp whistling pierced the air, and a gleaming object hurtled toward them. The children covered their heads and hunkered down, but Owen stood tall and grabbed the sword.

Just as quickly he dropped it, shaking his hand and hopping. The children laughed as Owen blew on his hand. The sun had baked the sword, but water from his flask cooled the metal and one touch from it healed his blistered palm.

They set out at dusk, and Owen took them as far north as

he dared. He stopped short of the bogs of Milosa before heading through the desert. He told them to keep quiet and listen for the yips and chattering of the lizards Starbuck had warned them of.

Traveling with the children was hard, because they were thirsty and quickly drained the water supply. Their stomachs ached because they hadn't been fed properly. Desperate for food in a barren place that offered none, Owen led the little band to the cave he had found on the first morning of his journey, and the children slept. He walked through the heat to find any plant with moisture. When a jargid popped its head out of a hole and rooted for food, Owen used the sword and took the animal back to roast.

The children awoke to the cooking meat and seemed to happily eat their meager portions. Soon they set out again, and the moon was still high as they came within sight of the rock walls and caves of their village. The children began to run, and who could blame them, having gone through the most horrific time of their lives?

Watcher's ears pricked, and she stopped beside Owen. "In the sky. Not far. Coming closer."

Owen yelled, trying to stop the children, but it was too late. They had seen home and couldn't wait to get there.

More than two dozen scythe flyers descended and quickly targeted the children.

Owen let out a war cry, holding the Sword of the
Wormling as high as he could.

The children heard him and stopped, unaware of the
danger.

He motioned for them to get down, and just as the first
wave of flyers reached out to grab them with their sharpened
nails, the children buried their faces in the dirt. Watcher and
Starbuck also dropped to the ground, but when the first flyer
looked back to see why it flew empty-taloned, Owen rushed
him, sword back and ready. He lopped off both feet of the
lead flyer and they plopped near one of the children, making
her scream. But her cries were drowned by the shriek of the
scythe flyer, which lost its balance, darted wildly, and spun
out of control, hitting a large rock with a bloody splat.

But here came the second wave's leader bearing down on the
children. Owen sidestepped, and the flyer flew straight toward
him. Owen struck the wing of the beast, sending it spiraling.
The third wave's leader got the sword in the heart—thrown
expertly—and fell like a stone, dust and rocks kicking up.

Owen called, and the sword slid from the bone and gristle
of the flyer and shot into Owen's hand just as another flyer
swung its massive tail at his head. The tail fell harmlessly in
the dirt as another flyer was downed.

Owen killed six of the creatures before the rest retreated.
The children gathered around him and followed closely as

they were met by Erol and his clan at the border. Mothers and fathers gathered their children with long hugs and kisses, then passed them around, everyone taking turns in the celebration.

Owen stood back with his arm around Watcher, laughing.

Finally Erol made his way to Owen and took Owen's hands in his. "How can we thank you?"

"No need," Owen said.

Erol choked up. "And to think I believed the creature the Dragon sent. I almost killed you."

"Never believe the Dragon or his agents," Owen said. "Trust in the King."

Owen cut the hearts from the six dead flyers and instructed Erol to place them on the rock where RHM had said his should be placed.

You must remember that Owen Reeder was still a teenager, with teenage concerns, though admittedly not of the usual sort.

Owen's main concern was whether he could measure up to the task ahead. Did he have what it took to find and rescue the Son? He'd been through rigorous training, sure, and he felt the muscle and brawn in his arms and chest every time he wielded the sword, but had he really become extraordinary?

As he and Watcher moved along a trail that skirted an enormous lake, Owen reminded himself that he was the doofus who had lost *The Book of the King.* He had been given the responsibility of guarding it and protecting it and preserving it, and he had failed. Some hero.

"What's wrong?" Watcher said.

"Wrong?" he said.

She pointed behind him to a long line in the sand. "Your sword is dragging."

Owen cleared his throat. "Just tired, I guess."

"We will grow much wearier long before we reach the castle. Keep walking."

By evening they had walked as far as a feeder stream, and clouds rolled in. They camped under a covering of trees, and when it began to rain, Owen fashioned a tarp of jargid skins over the branches to shelter them.

Lightning made Watcher shiver, and rivulets of water formed a new stream around them. Owen recalled how much he had loved watching a storm from his room above the bookstore back home. He would look past the alley to the mountain beyond town, wondering if there was a place for him in the world. He would wonder where he might wind up, what job he might land, and imagine himself in any of a hundred professions.

Actually sitting out in the storm, however, Owen didn't care as much for the lightning and thunder. And somehow he could no longer imagine himself in some mundane job in the other world. He did, though, conjure an image of his friend who worked at the diner. He couldn't shake the feeling that he and Clara had connected and might have had some sort of future . . . not that he would trade it for this adventure.

♦♦♦

Owen awoke the next morning wet and cold. Watcher had just returned with two fish she had caught at the water's edge. Owen tried to make a fire, but the wood was too wet. Watcher simply ate her fish without cooking it, devouring scales and all. Owen gave her his and found berries to calm his grumbling stomach.

Low, dark clouds still hung over the lake, making Owen long for just a moment of sunshine. But not even a sliver of blue appeared in the sky during the next two full days of hard walking. He trudged along, head down, heels scuffing, sword dragging, until he ran into Watcher, who had stopped. "Sorry," he mumbled.

When she didn't move, he looked up. She seemed to be watching him for a reaction. Owen glanced past her to the horizon, where a huge dark tower rose against the sky. Speechless, he passed Watcher and moved toward it, more and more of the massive structure coming into view. It appeared to have been built on a section of land someone had dug around in order to make an island.

When Owen spotted guards positioned on the parapets, he pulled Watcher into the trees and peered through the viewing circle Erol had given him. Hideous, heavy-skinned creatures in military garb paced with huge weapons over their shoulders. "They're defending the place like it's Fort Knox."

"Fort Knox?" Watcher said.

"A place with lots of gold and money."

"Money?"

Owen focused on the castle. "If the King's Son is there, he's probably being held belowground; don't you think?"

Watcher shook her head. "I'd sooner think one of the towers. It would be much harder to get there than some cellar dungeon."

"Good thinking," Owen said, still staring through the glass.

Watcher nudged him. "If the Son is such a threat to the Dragon—truly the only one keeping the Dragon from ruling the kingdoms—why doesn't the Dragon just kill him?"

"I don't know," Owen said. Cryptic statements in *The Book of the King* told of someone *giving his last full measure of life for his friends*, and Owen wondered if that meant the Son would somehow unite the worlds through his death. But if so, how could he free the captives in the mines, Mordecai, the Erol clan, and those in Bardig's village? And what of Connor and his desire to join the fight, though the fight seemed more against Owen than anyone?

236

42

Between the Stones

Owen waited until deep into the starless night, then led Watcher toward the water that surrounded the castle. This was more than a moat, much too broad to be covered by a lowered drawbridge. How did people get in and out? At the edge, still short of the light from the guards' torches, Owen stuck a hand in the water. Icy. While he had learned to swim—and well—there would be no splashing about in this body of water. Watcher might have been able to ford it with her fur as insulation, but he would cramp up and drown before reaching halfway.

"They must have a system to ferry over and back," he said. "Let's look around."

As they tiptoed about, Owen was grateful for a heavy mist that blocked even the torches from reflecting off the water. He could hear the guards laughing and talking as he and Watcher searched. Finally, behind an outcropping of rocks near the narrowest stretch of water—about 40 yards from land to castle—Watcher stumbled across an ancient craft, no bigger than a rowboat.

"If this is here, that means that someone is out of the castle," Watcher said. "Otherwise, wouldn't they leave it inside?"

"Just lucky for us," Owen said.

"But they'll be back."

"We'll cross that bridge when we come to it."

"Wormling! If there was a bridge, we wouldn't need this boat!"

"I mean we'll worry about that if and when the time comes."

They quietly set the boat in the water and clambered aboard. Within minutes Owen had rowed to the rocky shore, pausing and holding his breath between oar strokes to listen for any hint that the guards heard them.

They beached the boat, and Owen said, "Wait here. If I have trouble, I'll give the signal."

"I haven't come all this way to wait outside," Watcher said.

Owen faced her. "Watcher, please. Stay here until I need you."

She rolled her eyes.

Using the climbing methods Mordecai taught, Owen slipped his hands between stones and pulled himself 200 feet up the wall of the castle. As he ascended—reminding himself not to look down—he occupied himself wondering how many times this old fortress had been under siege. How many times had the King had to flee? And how many royal families had lived here over the centuries?

As Owen neared the first terrace, he stopped and peered through the mist at where two guards were illuminated by a torch. Another torch was lit to his left, but the spot in the ramparts was unattended.

"He's coming tonight," one guard said, and Owen froze. "Preparations have already been made."

The King? The Wormling? Who?

"He'll burn half the villages on the way; don't you think?" the other said.

The Dragon! Whoever had used the boat was likely out scouting, ready to sound an alarm if the Dragon was spotted.

"We can only hope. The citizens have caused him no end of trouble. Just wait till he catches that Wormling. His forces already have the book."

"The Dragon has it?"

"No! It's here! Delivered days ago. It's magical, you know."

"I've heard. Good thing *we* have it. It would be dangerous in the hands of the Wormling."

"Wormling schmermling. They say he's just a kid."

"Then why can't the Dragon destroy him? I hear he curses the Wormling every night."

"Well, Dreadwart was wiped out. And the Wormling attacked the scythe flyers—20 or 30 chopped up with that giant sword of his."

Somehow all this exaggeration gave Owen confidence. And to know the book was here made his heart leap. He had to get inside, maybe through the unguarded rampart. But as he scurried to his left, a loose piece of the wall tumbled into the darkness. With all his weight on his feet, a foothold broke loose as well, and there he dangled, 20 stories above the ground. Only his strength training allowed him to hang on.

"Did you hear that?" a guard said. "Something just dropped in the water."

"Probably a fish. Or one of the gators. I saw one get a jargid the other night. Thing didn't even have time to squeak."

Watcher was down there at the water's edge! No doubt she was watching Owen, not paying attention to the water. If a gator devoured her, Owen would never forgive himself for making her stay. He would feel just like Mordecai.

"I'd better get back," one guard said. He moved past where Owen hung not five feet below the ledge.

Owen held his breath and flattened himself against the wall, praying the guard wouldn't look over. When the guard had passed, Owen pulled himself up and hopped over the wall, landing catlike, without a sound. He scampered across the walkway into the shadows, out of reach of the torchlight.

Owen had to do something about Watcher. He could imagine the gator floating quietly behind her. He closed his eyes, sucked in air so his belly stuck out, and pretended he was one of the thick-skinned guards with the helmet like a crown. With lips pursed and chin puckered, he strutted to the edge and leaned out, forcing himself to bellow, "The gators will make a good meal of anyone near the water tonight!"

"Aye!" other guards called out in unison.

Owen moved back into the darkness and resumed his climb. When he reached the final parapet, he climbed over and quickly entered a window into an enormous dim room. The worn and tattered drapery hung blackened by fire, and the walls were charred. Candle wax pooled on the cool stone floor. Owen tried to imagine it before the fire, a bedroom with a canopied bed and walls covered with festoonery only a princess could love. Owen opened a massive wood door with a great creak and found fine linen robes bearing intricate designs. He shook the soot off one and wrapped it around his shoulders.

Suddenly, as if a breeze had blown into a vacant room in his mind, Owen believed he had been in this room in his dreams. The drawer of a nightstand by the bed held the remnants of a child's drawing. Stick figures with round heads. Two large ones in the background, a smaller one in front, and a tiny one in the arms of the figure with long brown hair.

On the wall a frame contained a map that included the lake, the castle, the mountains, and the Valley of Shoam. Owen traced a finger over the Badlands.

Could this be the room of the Queen? Had he stumbled onto the King's bedchamber? If so, then the pile of rubble in the corner . . .

Owen knelt and picked up what was left of a post with rounded edges. The fine wood was inlaid with exquisite detail, just like the robe he wore, and a few inches of material remained—the colors of a rainbow. A child's coverlet. A wooden rattle lay underneath, along with a toy bear with tiny ears and buttons for eyes.

Was this the crib of the Son now grown, who would unite the kingdoms and bring peace and freedom and joy to both worlds? Could a baby grow up to become a liberator of people so much older and so far away? Owen trusted *The Book of the King*, so it must be true.

He slipped the bear into his pocket before a blast of air swept in and the tattered draperies fanned. Owen heard the faint call of Watcher from far below as a fiery, red-orange glow filled the window.

43

Incoming

Owen's voice from high atop the castle wall had alerted Watcher, and she pulled the boat between her and the water. Twice she saw the eyes of a gator and tossed rocks at it, sending it under. She growled at the beast as it circled.

But her growl turned to a whimper as enormous wings appeared out of a black cloud above. Her ears fell back, she dipped her head, and her fur fell close to her body—except on her back, where it stood straight. The gator had distracted her from sensing such a clear and present danger, but now that it drew near the castle, every nerve in her body was on high alert.

"Wormling," she whispered. Her job was to sense and watch and warn, but she couldn't yell or the beast would swoop down and consume her with one belch of fire.

Some in her village had criticized her for her slowness in warning—the very same ones who said her position was useless, who said they no longer needed a Watcher, that the tales of the Wormling were simply superstition and the power once vested in Watchers had left long ago.

Watcher's teeth chattered and she shook. What if the Dragon killed the Wormling? Should *she* continue the search for the King's Son? She cowered by the castle wall as the great beast circled, a phalanx of escorts flying before and after him. These flyers, though smaller, looked much like demon flyers but could maneuver more deftly. Their eyes were a luminous red, and they scanned the castle.

Far above her, the guards leaned over the wall, bowing their helmeted heads to their leader. Perhaps they feared a blast of fire.

Watcher had no idea what to do.

The Wormling can take care of himself.

Could he know the Dragon is coming?

He's the one sent for the King's Son, not me.

He'll die a fiery death.

I must keep my head and not insert myself into this fight. But I have to warn him! It's my job!

And yet he was the one who left me here, telling me to wait for his signal. I must protect myself.

The battle raged inside until the sick, pungent aroma of death that surrounded the Dragon—rancid meat mixed with smoke, a repulsive mixture of rotten garbage and burning flesh—reached her. She could only imagine how he smelled indoors.

The Dragon's wings flapped as he descended to the very windowsill the Wormling had entered, and Watcher knew she could no longer keep silent. She closed her eyes and let out a feral cry she hoped would reach her friend.

Suddenly stillness fell over the whole castle. When Watcher opened her eyes, the Dragon's flying minions had rallied and were barreling down at her, but she feared the Dragon himself even more than these.

His eyes had locked onto hers, and with a roar that made his own flying forces pull up and away, the Dragon let go of his perch and dropped in a free fall, tucking his wings for greatest aerodynamic effect. Watcher could only stare as the black mass that was the Dragon grew closer, his tongue slithering in and out, as if anticipating a tasty meal.

Indecision would kill her, she knew. Had she lingered a second longer, Owen would have found her charred remains. Instead she propelled herself with a mighty leap over the boat and into the water. She seemed to move in slow motion, trying to hurry herself as the Dragon swooped like a hawk over a field mouse.

Watcher heard the blast of the Dragon's breath—a thunderous, molten exhale—as he spread his wings to keep from crashing into the rocks. She felt heat sear her back just as she plunged into the green murky water, and it instantly turned bright orange. The icy impact took what little breath she had, but she dared not surface as the bubbling, boiling water pushed her farther down.

She was not alone. Fish and turtles were also diving for the bottom. She kicked, trying to keep from rising as the flames dissolved. But Watcher broke the surface in the midst of smoke and steam, gasping and coughing. She heard a gurgle and looked up into two red eyes. The Dragon sent another blast of flame toward her. She had just enough time to gulp and go under, swimming for the middle of the lake.

She had eluded the monster above—at least temporarily. But awaiting her was the gator she had driven away with rocks only moments before.

Owen sank into a dark corner of
the chamber as the roar of fire
and the Dragon's curses filled the air.
After the noise seemed to recede, he
moved to the window, only to see
steam and bubbling water in the lake.

When the wing flaps came again,
Owen rushed to the wall opposite the
robe closet and pressed himself against
it, trying to disappear. A stone under
his hand gave way, and the wall moved
ever so slightly. He turned and pushed
with all his strength, and the stones
crunched together as the wall slid
open.

Owen ducked inside and closed the
wall as far as he could, but before he

could lean into it with his shoulder and push it the rest of the way, dust and ash flew through the small opening and a presence as evil and dark as Owen had ever felt filled the bed-chamber. He didn't dare move, breathe, or even blink.

"Human!" the Dragon said. "I smell a human!"

"Sire, welcome!" Owen recognized the voice of the being who had taken *The Book of the King*. "A feast has been pre-pared, and we have made every accommodation for you—"

"Who allowed a human in here?" the Dragon roared.

"There are several, sire. As I said, a feast has been planned, and we shall serve some for dinner."

The Dragon sniffed. "No, I mean in this room."

"Oh, surely not, Highness. The guards have reported no—"

"Then how do you explain the Watcher I just drowned below?"

Oh no! Not Watcher!

"Begging your pardon, Master, but a Watcher is not human."

"But you yourself reported a Watcher with the Wormling on Mirantha!"

"Oh yes, you're right. I should have dispatched the disgust-ing thing when I had the chance."

"My point is that it is unlikely she was here alone. The Wormling could be close. He'll be looking for the book, from whence his power comes."

"Perhaps we could lure him into the open if we capture the Watcher," RHM said. "Are you sure she has drowned?"

"That should be easy enough to determine. Regardless, we can tell the Wormling we have her."

"Good, sire! And if she *is* alive, we can do things to her species that will create great pain and make her—"

"I know!" the Dragon said, fire sparking. "Do not lecture me."

"Apologies, sire."

"The prisoner is enough to lure the Wormling. But see if you can find the Watcher anyway, and bring her to the counsel room."

Owen heard them leave and was about to return to the room when he stepped back and nearly fell down a spiral stairway. No matter what happened, he could not take his focus off his quest. He could do nothing about Watcher after having left her vulnerable; that was sure. He only hoped she had somehow survived. Mordecai said everything happened for a purpose, even the bad things.

Owen had to find out where the stairway led. He pushed the stone entrance closed and gingerly made his way into the darkness.

45
Life-and-Death Struggle

The water grew frigid again, and
Watcher's muscles immediately
tightened. She surfaced farther out
in the lake and knew she had to keep
moving. The shore before her was
as near as the castle behind her. She
opted for the shore, as far from the
castle as she could get.

Halfway to her destination she
heard a snort and turned around,
searching the darkness as she floated.
"Is someone there?"

When she turned back around,
two reptilian eyes glowed before her.
She thought about diving underneath
whatever this was, but she was certain

it would be quicker than she was. "Who are you?" she said as confidently as she could.

"Call me Hunger. I'll call you Food."

The gator!

"I could make a quick end of you," he said. "You won't feel much pain."

"Is your stomach all you think about?"

"What else is there?"

"Freedom. Life. If you eat me, you may also seal your fate."

The eyes blinked and dipped out of sight. Watcher was startled when they appeared again to her right.

"What is this fate you speak of, groundling?"

"Death—the fate of all who serve the Dragon. But do what you must."

The gator seemed to study her. "Those who seek your life are nearby," he said quietly. "Why did the Dragon want to kill you?"

Watcher's teeth chattered. "Because I oppose him. I do not acknowledge him as ruler."

"If the Dragon is not our ruler, who is?"

"The King alone deserves our honor and obedience. Not this impostor who lies and kills. But you are dedicated to him, and you'll either deliver me to him or—"

The eyes disappeared in the blackness, and Watcher found herself in the gaping mouth of the gator. She tried to push on the roof of his mouth, but her ears popped from the pressure and her oxygen ran out as the animal dived for the bottom.

Finally, from the back of the throat came the same voice. "I'm sorry to frighten you, groundling, but I had to be sure you were on the side of truth. I neither chewed nor swallowed, though you seem tasty. I am protecting you from those above. Hold your breath just a little longer, and I will show you something you will never forget."

46
Into the Labyrinth

The musty secret passageway snaked down through the entire castle and ended in a dank underground with soggy floors and only enough light to see things scurrying in the shadows. This proved to be an expansive area with catacombs and winding hallways, providing a wide base for the towering castle.

Owen immediately heard voices echoing off the walls. He stayed out of the scant light of the sparse torches that dotted the walls as two guards in full armor passed, leaving tracks in the moist earth.

"The master will find her," one

said. "They're scouring the lake and the countryside for the Watcher."

"I'd like to sink my teeth into that overgrown vermin," the other said. "How could any self-respecting animal hold its head high and not serve the master? Makes no sense."

"Just like the Wormling. He'll wind up serving the Dragon one way or another—either delivering his food or *being* his food."

When Owen moved out into the corridor again, he passed an old curtain fastened to the wall. *Strange. Why would a curtain hang here with no window or bedchamber or bathroom to shield?*

Wood crates were stacked here and there, some filling whole rooms. Despite ornate sconces for torches and embroidered tapestries near 20-foot ceilings—evidencing the past beauty and glory of the place—it seemed to have become a dumping ground for old containers of food. Alas, what had once been the domain of a king had become home to the Dragon's forces. The guards used corners of the hallways as their bathrooms, and bones and moldy bread lay strewed about.

But why did guards patrol this lowest level of the castle? No windows or doors led outside. One could get here only from long stairways above. Why not simply guard those entrances and exits?

Great stone pillars rose from the mud to the ceiling, and between them stood timbers lashed together like a makeshift raft. In the center of the wooden edifice was a door with a tiny window. On the other side, a double door, larger with no window.

At the sound of the guards talking again, Owen scampered back into the shadows behind a stack of crates.

When the guards passed, Owen hurried toward the first wooden door, hoping for a peek inside. Around the corner sat a guard's station, a simple table and a couple of chairs. Beyond that lay a room with another long table, this one with leather straps at the head and foot. Along the walls hung chains and knives Owen recognized from a book he had read on instruments of torture.

He stole toward the tiny window and saw two cells divided by bars. Hay was bunched in the corners of both, a bucket in each for a bathroom, and in one an empty wooden plate looked like it had been thrown against the bars. Owen grabbed a torch from the wall and was able to make out a lump in the corner of one cell that looked like some barn animal curled in the hay.

At the sound of footsteps behind him, Owen scrambled to throw the torch back into its holder and jumped out of sight.

"I'll bet she didn't even make an entire meal," a guard said. "There is no end to his appetite."

"Perhaps he had the Wormling too, for dessert."

They sat at the table. "How did you hear this—about the Watcher?"

"A guard on the parapet says he saw a gator pounce and take her under. Good riddance." He rose and thumped the double door with a foot, and a growl shook the earth. "I say the Wormling will be next."

Watcher's lungs felt like they would burst. There was no light here in the jaws of the gator, just the creature's awful breath.

They descended as far as Watcher thought they could possibly go, and then they plunged farther. Her ears popped, and she felt like she was moving up toward the surface. *Oh, let it be so! I must breathe!*

Suddenly the gator's mouth opened, and they were on dry land. Gasping, Watcher stepped off his spongy tongue and into an underground cavern, where the water reflected a dim light above.

"What is this place?" Watcher said, but the gator was gone, submerged.

Watcher moved toward a tunnel but turned around at the sound of flapping wings. A creature eyed her with a tilted head, and suddenly Watcher feared this had been some unholy scheme—the gator had brought her here to be torn limb from limb and eaten. Well, she wouldn't go quietly, not after all she had been through. She rose on her hind legs and looked menacingly at the being, ready to kick and thrash with all she had.

The bug-eyed creature shrieked with laughter. "My dear, you have nothing to fear from me or my friends."

"Friends?"

"Rotag will return with another."

"Rotag is the gator?"

"Harmless, isn't he?" He wiped his nose. "Well, he certainly wouldn't have left you down here to eat. We've heard about you. It was a long time ago, but my memory is sharp." He sat on a rock and put his paws on his knees.

"How could you have heard of me?"

"Oh, you have friends in high places." He laughed again. "I remember like it was yesterday."

"What is this place?"

"Why, this is our hall of meeting, where the waterlings and undergroundlings get together to discuss important matters. And I daresay the matter before us today is exciting."

"You're an undergroundling?"

The animal's mouth dropped. "I apologize. They'll kick me

off the assembly if they find out I've been so rude. Tusin is the name. Assemblyman of the undergroundlings." He bowed to her. "Welcome, Watcher."

"Thank you. I think. So, what will happen—?"

Just then the water cascaded from below, and Rotag slid to a stop. A beady-eyed flyer with the wingspan of an eagle swooped into the cave and alighted on the rock above Tusin.

"Allow me to introduce Batwing, and you already know Rotag." Tusin stood. "Meeting of the assembly convenes on this day of the King, all members present, the honorable Rotag presiding."

Rotag rolled his eyes good-naturedly. "I have summoned this groundling to our meeting because she says a Wormling is in our midst."

Batwing flapped and Tusin clapped. Watcher felt such energy in the room that she believed the very rocks would have cried out if they hadn't responded. The noise echoed, and other voices picked up on the word *Wormling.*

"I can see your bewilderment," Rotag said. "The King, before he set out on the search for his Son, allowed certain of us to know his plan. He left us with responsibilities—"

"Which we have taken seriously," Tusin said.

Rotag continued. "The King said that one day the Wormling and a helper would come to the Lowlands in search of his Son. And here you are."

Everyone seems to know more about us than we know about ourselves.

"The King read to me from a book—"

"*The Book of the King?*" Watcher said.

"Exactly! How did you know?"

"It was given to the Wormling in his world, but it has been stolen. We think it might be in the castle."

"How would you know that?"

"I sense things. It's my job."

Rotag squinted. "Batwing? Could you . . . ?"

"At once," Batwing screeched, flying off.

"I'm curious," Watcher said. "Why did the King choose you? How did you become part of this assembly?"

Tusin said, "I could say it was because of our intellects or that we are the best specimens of our species. . . ."

"But he would be lying," Rotag said.

"The truth is," Tusin continued, "we were available. He called us to his service, and we responded gladly. How could we not?"

"How did he call you?"

"Like this." Tusin waved. "'Come here; I have something for you to do.' As simple as that. He talked of the deep things in his heart: How he grieved over what had become of the kingdom. How he longed for it to be restored, and how it would be when his Son returned. Our hearts burned with his every word. They were like red-hot pokers, stoking a fire we didn't even know existed."

Rotag said, "He made us feel as important as his own Son. He said each of us has a story, and the smaller stories fit into the larger one. It was all very mysterious at the time, but now I can see how he was right. He gave us this job—to find the Wormling, to protect him, and to help him find the King's Son."

"Is the Son here, in the castle?" Watcher said.

"Someone is being held there. I have heard the crying and moaning."

"The Wormling is in the castle now," Watcher said. "He believes the book and the Son are both inside."

Rotag and Tusin looked away.

"What is it?" Watcher said. "What's wrong?"

Before either could answer, Batwing returned, short of breath, fangs jutting. He grabbed hold of a growth on the ceiling, hung upside down, and addressed the group. "I saw *The Book of the King* in the Dragon's highest chamber. It is guarded by four demon vipers—the Golden Guard from the east, west, north, and south. It will be impossible to get past them."

"Not for the Wormling," Watcher said. "I saw him battle the beasts in—"

"Yes, yes, and lop off the feet of some scythe flyers. We have heard. Well, these are quite different. They shoot venom at their enemies. Your Wormling wouldn't be able to even get his sword close to them before he would be cut down."

"You don't know the Wormling," Watcher said.

"I know these vipers, and they will not let the book out of their sight."

"Then we must find a way to make them. Or kill the Dragon."

Batwing closed his eyes and swung back and forth from his perch. Tusin stared at the stone floor.

Rotag spoke. "If this Wormling has read the book, he knows that *only* the Son can bring the worlds together."

"He has become fearless and cunning," Watcher said. "I believe he will find the Son and return with the book."

"He will need help," Tusin said.

"The King said *we* are to help," Batwing squeaked.

Rotag sighed and gazed at Watcher. "New friend, we will do all we can."

Owen sat stunned at the news of
Watcher's death. Deep in the
night, fears are the worst and grief
can envelop even the strongest heart.
Owen could only imagine Watcher's
fear and desperation as she was
devoured. And it was his fault. She
had wanted to come with him, but he
had made her stay.

Owen had gotten off to a bad start
with her when first he arrived in the
Lowlands, but he and Watcher had
become friends, bonding in their
love for the King. And there had
been something else between them,
something more than just friendship.
Certainly not romance, for they were

not even the same species, but somehow they cared deeply for each other no matter how wrong either could be. Owen regretted the times he had had the chance to encourage or compliment Watcher but had let the opportunity slip.

Now how could he press on with the demon flyers of the enemy arrayed against him, without the one being in this world who knew the most about him and cared the most for him? Bardig had *given* his life; Watcher had hers taken due to carelessness—Owen's own.

"Psst."

Owen peeked out from behind the crates to see a face at the tiny window of the cell.

"Are you here to help?"

"That depends on who you are," Owen said.

"The guards are away! Get the key from the wall behind the desk."

Owen retrieved it but hesitated before the door.

"Hurry!" the man said, his voice making Owen guess he was in his twenties at most.

Owen fumbled with the key, ears pricked for any sound of guards and wondering if he might be freeing someone who deserved to be imprisoned.

Just as the lock clicked, footsteps approached. The prisoner opened the door and pulled Owen inside, the lock latching.

"Thanks a lot," Owen said. "Now we're both—"

"Shh!" The man pulled some hay back. "Lie down and I'll cover you."

"What's all the racket?" a guard roared.

"I'm hungry!" the prisoner said.

"Shut up or you won't eat for a week!"

The guard sat at the table and put his feet up, mumbling, "Kudzik wandered off with the key again. Idiot." Soon he was dozing.

Owen crawled out from under the smelly hay, brushing it from his hair and clothes.

"Who are you?" the prisoner whispered.

Owen looked into the man's face. Could this be the King's Son? He had imagined the Son tall, dark, strong as an ox, with a face chiseled from stone and yet with eyes that could look right through you. He assumed the Son would act in a regal manner like his mother, the Queen, the perfect blend of strength and compassion, of love and power. But the young man in front of him seemed less than regal. He had longish hair cut square around his face. His eyes stuck out so he looked more like an owl than royalty. He was tall and thin, not as strong as Owen had thought, but still Owen's heart beat wildly. Could this be the one?

"Does it matter?" Owen said. "Maybe I'm a Wormling. What would you say to that?"

The prisoner rolled his eyes and sat. "My father used to

tell of a Wormling. A dream. A fantasy. He uses the power of some book to bore through rock. Ever hear that story?"

Owen studied the man. "Maybe. Your father. Is he the King?"

"What if he is? If you can be a Wormling, I can be a prince."

Owen smiled and pumped his fist. "You're him! The one I've been searching for! You don't know how long I've been looking or how far I've come. Now the prophecies can be ful—"

"Quiet," the prisoner said. "I'd rather stay alive than fulfill some prophecies you made up."

"I didn't make them up. I read them in the book." Owen looked around. A stone wall at the back. Dirt floor. Three walls made of timbers. He pulled Mucker from his tunic and noticed the worm's teeth were shattered from chomping in the mine. "Now we have to get out of here and find the book."

The prisoner stood. "You are obviously committed to this little quest. Fine, be my guest. But I'm getting as far away from here as possible. You can stay and face whatever it was that flew in an hour ago."

"That was the Dragon," Owen said. "He wants to destroy everything your father created."

"He can have it. Destroy away. I'll be on the other side of the kingdom. I'm not risking my life for fairy tales."

"They're not just stories. *The Book of the King* is a manual to live by, encouragement to live for others and to help you when—"

"I'm not interested in whatever you're selling! I just want out of here."

"I'm sorry. I've never heard your name. What do I call you?"

"I'm Qwamay, but they'll have both our heads if you don't be quiet."

"Prince Qwamay," Owen whispered. "You will unite the two worlds."

Qwamay glanced at the guard's station, then paced. He stopped and knelt. "Do you have help? Are you working with anyone?"

Owen's face fell. "There was one with me but no longer."

"So you're it? my rescue party?"

"Yes, but I have reason to believe *The Book of the King* is here, and with it—"

The prisoner cursed. "Stop talking about that book! Just get me out of here."

"The book says each of us is in a prison, each needs rescue, and we can't do it on our own. We need someone from the outside—"

"Yes, a Wormling, is that it? Do you see yourself as a savior? You're just a boy. And deluded."

"Listen, Prince Qwamay, your father had the book written. It was delivered to me along with the Mucker." Owen showed him the worm.

Qwamay scowled. "Terrific. That toothless bug is going to get us out of here?"

Owen unsheathed the Sword of the Wormling. "And this."

Qwamay took it and studied the intricate carving in the handle. "Who gave you this?"

"A man who used to work here. You would have been too young to remember him. Mordecai?"

Qwamay sliced his finger on the edge of the blade and quickly stuck it in his mouth, handing the sword back. "You're right. Never heard of him."

Watcher followed Tusin through the cave, over slick rocks and jagged ledges. Her keen eyesight helped when they neared the surface, but most of the climbing had been in pitch darkness, relying on her sense of touch. It was tough, slow going, but anything was better than holding her breath in the jaws of a gator, no matter how good his intentions.

Rotag had taken the underwater route, and they met him and Batwing on the shore behind a grove of acacia trees. They were an unlikely quartet planning to storm the castle, but

Watcher remembered a story the Wormling had read to her from *The Book of the King.*

"Three spies were sent into an enemy encampment by the captain of the guard," she began. "The vicious and deadly force slept soundly, too drunk on the spoils of war to notice the intruders. Once inside, they moved steadily through the camp, counting the fighters and all their weapons. They counted 7,000 soldiers. Their own force was less than half that.

"They hurried back to report to their captain. He chose 15 men (the three spies included) and had them stand above the camp on a hillside. The other troops protested, but the captain of the guard said the King wanted to teach them that it is not by might nor power nor weapons of warfare that an army is victorious but by the strength of the one who sends them."

Batwing, Tusin, and Rotag seemed to hang on every word.

"What happened?" Tusin said, his voice cracking.

"The 15 encircled the camp of 7,000 in the dead of night. At a signal from their captain, they blew a note on their rams' horns. The enemies awoke in confusion. Their horses bolted from their pens, and the warriors, believing they were under attack, grabbed their swords and spears and lunged at anything and everything around them. All 7,000 were slain by their own hands.

"So the smaller army learned that victory came not from

strength in numbers but in trusting the word of the captain and following his orders."

"I take that as a word from the King himself," Batwing said. "That sounded like a story he would have told."

A single glowing light shone from a room at the top of the castle. It beckoned Watcher like a beacon, perhaps showing the way to *The Book of the King*. But where was the Wormling?

"I can't blow a ram's horn," Rotag said.

"I can screech," Batwing said.

Watcher laughed. "Let's remain quiet and search for the Wormling. Remember, the one who has sent us is greater than the one inside."

"But the one inside breathes fire," Batwing said. "And has demon vipers."

The two heavily armed guards at the front of the castle had skin thick enough to withstand an arrow. They were clumsy, oafish beings, but they looked like stone sentries now, slumbering at their posts with flies hovering.

Watcher and Tusin rode on the back of the smooth and silently gliding Rotag across the water toward the castle. When they reached land, Rotag pitched his riders off and advanced on the guards.

At that very moment, Batwing swooped out of the sky, diving for the guards, and sped past their noses. The two guards jumped, their spears clattering to the ground. That's when they noticed the gator.

"Look at the size of that monster," the first said, grabbing his spear and hurling it. It glanced off Rotag's scaly back and rattled along the rocks into the water. The other guard bent to pick up his spear, but the gator lunged at him with mouth wide.

The black-winged creature flitted about their heads, making them flail. Of course, this whole operation was designed to move the guards just far enough from the entrance so Watcher and Tusin could enter unseen. As they slipped in and disappeared around a corner, scythe flyers converged on the scene, sending Batwing racing into the night as Rotag plunged into the water.

"Waterlings have never come that close before, have they?" one guard said.

"Maybe he was hungry," said the other.

"Or maybe he smelled Wormling. But the master will have all of him."

Owen recited passages from *The
Book of the King*, challenging
Prince Qwamay to help defeat the
Dragon and unite the kingdoms, but
Qwamay would not listen. He said it
would be impossible to escape after the
sun rose, so Owen reached through
the window and all the way to the
lock. He silently inserted the key, but
when he turned it far enough to release
the lock, it clicked like a bomb. The
guard's chair slipped from under him,
and he crashed to the floor.

Owen shot out of the cell like a
cannonball and brought the butt of

his sword down onto the guard's head before he even had a chance to get a whistle to his lips.

"Finish him," Qwamay said. "We have to make sure he doesn't wake up."

When Owen hesitated, Qwamay reached for his sword.

Owen yanked it away. "I never take a life when I don't have to."

"You read too much. Well, it's your own funeral. I'll be long gone by the time he squeals."

They ran past crates and cages, coming to a musty room full of rotting food. Prince Qwamay paused, shoving a handful of turnips into his mouth. How strange to see the Son of the King of all the land resorting to eating trash.

"I'll find food fit for you," Owen said. "Just follow me."

"Never mind. I'll find my own way out."

As footsteps caromed off the walls, Owen pulled Qwamay into a corner behind the black curtain. They stood deathly still while someone passed, snarling, headed for the cell.

"Through here," Owen said, pushing the panel that led to the secret stairwell.

"Only if it leads outside," Qwamay said.

"There is no way out from down here. Come on. At least you'll be safe."

Qwamay shook his head. "Give me your sword, and I'll fight my way out."

"Don't be foolish! They'll cut you down as soon as they see you. Follow me and I'll get you to safety."

Qwamay snorted. "You really believe you're the Wormling, don't you? some kind of hero with a sword and a chomping Mucker?"

"How could I not believe? It's been proven over and over. Some who have seen do not believe, though the evidence is right before them. Listen, I promised your mother I would bring you to her, and that's what I'm going to do, whether you like it or not."

"My mother?" Qwamay said. "Where did you see her?"

Owen told him.

"And she bought your story about being this special worm child?"

"She trusts me to bring you to her and release the captives."

"She trusts too much."

"That is no place for a Queen. But if you and I band together—"

"If you're such a savior, why didn't you rescue her yourself?"

"My mission was to find *you*! But you have to step up and lead."

"Lead who?"

"There are many in the land loyal to your father; they just have to be given a vision. They perish for lack of knowledge."

Qwamay patted Owen's shoulder. "Well, good luck spreading the vision."

A shout came from the cell area and a whistle blew.

"Now you have no choice, Prince," Owen said, pulling him through the panel.

51

Caught

Watcher's ears perked up as shouts rang through the castle. She and Tusin and Batwing had found each other and hidden in an isolated room on the main floor. They were about to head out again when Watcher pulled them back. "Strong vibrations," she whispered, her eyes shut tightly. "Invisibles coming this way. Huge. Bigger than I've ever felt . . ."

These invisibles, though she did not want to tell her new friends, were different from the ones Watcher had sensed before. These seemed more evil and also had abilities other invisibles did not. They communicated in squeaks and blips and carried weapons, cloaked by their bodies.

A sudden gust whipped the decaying velvet draperies about them, and a presence moved into the room.

Watcher's eyes flew open. "Run!"

Watcher heard the squeaks and blips of the invisibles and an echoed response from upstairs. Batwing was the first out, darting and flitting like a moth on fire. A horrible burst from a weapon exploded behind Watcher, and the *thwong* enveloped Batwing. He crashed to the floor.

Tusin had turned the other way and beckoned Watcher through a sitting room that had been reduced to ashen rubble. The two raced through in search of a hiding place. Another weapon burst met Watcher's ears, and together she and Tusin lunged and landed in a heap as the blast crashed into the wall. Dust and ash fell as Watcher scrambled to her feet and pulled Tusin along. The invisible above her was joined by another, and Watcher's head filled with pain. The burst came again just as she and Tusin ducked behind a wall, and a stone fell, barely missing them.

⧓

In the chilly water outside the castle, Rotag floated and watched, somehow not associating all the commotion with his friends until Batwing flew toward a window and spiraled to the floor. Rotag moved toward the shore to get a better look and was right under the window when Tusin appeared, running headlong for the opening, followed by Watcher.

Tusin jumped just as a shock-wave burst immobilized him, and he somersaulted to the water with a slap, sending spray over Rotag. In a flash, the gator gathered Tusin in his huge mouth as a scythe flyer passed overhead.

52

Decisions

Going up the winding stairs proved a different undertaking than coming down. Though in the best shape of his life, Owen felt his muscles tense with each step and his whole body ached. Halfway up, Prince Qwamay collapsed and rolled onto his back.

"How long have you been in that cell?" Owen said.

Qwamay shook his head, gasping. "I don't even know. Tell me, how did you know of this passage?"

"I stumbled upon it."

"Really? No special worm-child guidance you received?"

Mordecai had taught Owen that

nothing happened by chance and that not even the smallest inconvenience was wasted in the economy of the King. Of course, he could not explain that to Qwamay just then. The young man certainly didn't seem ready for the truth that he, of royal lineage, was in line to reign with his father and defeat the enemy.

A terrific blast shook the stone around them. Another piercing burst and Owen was up, taking the stairs two at a time. "Sounds like an attack!"

"Who would be stupid enough to attack the Dragon?"

"I told you! There are many loyal to your father!"

"Then I should be able to easily slip away with all this commotion."

Owen's charge from Mr. Page had been to guard the book and find the Son. He had failed at the first; he didn't want to fail at the second. If he could find *The Book of the King* quickly, perhaps the King's writings would convince the Son to get involved with the mission. One look at those compelling words would make him see the wisdom of following such a wise and loving ruler. Whatever stood between Qwamay and his father, Owen was sure it could be overcome.

Gasping, Owen finally reached the top and listened at the secret entrance. He pushed the panel that opened into the bedchamber. Wings flapped outside, so he crouched low to the floor. "Qwamay?" he whispered.

But the young man had not followed.

As Owen neared the canopied bed, the voice that had protected him so long ago spoke again, this time with an unusual urgency. "Prepare your sword and shield."

Shield? Had he missed something during the initiation? He pulled the weighty sword, and merely holding it brought back the words from *The Book of the King.*

> The King is good and worthy of honor. He is a shield to all who wield his truth. Enemies shall be cut down because of him.

Owen noticed a strange glow from the hallway. Cautiously he stepped out. In spite of his fear, he knew from some instinctual place that this was why he had been called to the job of the Wormling. This confrontation was what he had prepared for on the islands of Mirantha.

In Owen's former life, he had done everything he could to remain safe. But in this world he was in constant danger. Enemies were all around, and he had to be prepared at every moment.

In the hallway he found another stone stairwell. He passed a roomful of more charred furniture. A hiss emanated from the next room, where the glow was as bright as daylight.

He reached his sword into the yellowish green light, and in the reflection saw the ugliest beasts ever. Four had planted their talons on the four sides of an immense table. They looked somewhat like demon flyers but smaller and more ghastly. Their glowing eyes made the room so bright. Their beaks were like the mouths of snakes, tongues darting as they hissed, and instead of tail feathers, these bore small casings full of tiny beads that clattered when they shook—and all four shook now.

Owen stepped into the doorway and locked eyes with a demon viper. (He did not know the creature's name at that moment, but that is what it was.) The other three arched their backs and strained, as if they wanted to fly but couldn't. When Owen moved into the room he saw *The Book of the King* on the table.

The head of the viper before him elongated like a snake's, and the other four followed suit, their rattles joining in a percussive hymn to their master. When their heads were two feet longer than when Owen first saw them, he smiled. This would be easy. One swing of the Sword of the Wormling and these creatures' heads would fly off like toy rockets.

Owen poised to strike, but he was soon mesmerized by the glowing green eyes, the fangs, and the trickle of sticky saliva from the roof of its mouth. When the sides of the viper's neck fanned out like an umbrella and its eyes turned bright red, Owen was entranced.

Liquid shot from the beast's mouth, straight at Owen's head.

The creature had struck with lightning speed and accuracy, a drop of
its venom potent enough to kill a man
by merely touching his skin.

Without thinking, Owen threw up
his sword to block the poison, inches
from his face, deflecting it into the
wall, where it immediately ate away
the stone. Owen shot from his crouching mode into a full-bore run, diving
under the table.

The other three vipers went wild
with their rattling and clacking and
shrieking. Owen rolled onto his back
to face the four sets of vipers' eerie eyes,
changing from green to red. Without
waiting for their venom shots, he drove

his feet up and kicked the table, sending the beasts flying into the wall and the sacred book sliding across the floor.

A viper screeched, and Owen saw smoke coming from its back, where one of its compatriots had apparently misfired its venom. Within seconds its screeching turned to a hiss as its body shriveled into a quivering mass.

Owen was on his feet now, sword ready, three vipers stunned by his quick action. The surviving vipers took flight, circling and eyeing him. Perhaps no one had ever countered them before; clearly they were as angry as hornets. Owen lunged at the nearest, but it darted and Owen's sword caught only the end of its tail, rattle beads clattering to the floor. Owen turned just in time to use his blade to divert yet another stream of venom, this time into the face of the third viper. It fell to its death, hissing and sizzling.

The only two left were at opposite ends of the room now, but they screeched at each other and flew straight for him.

Owen dived for the table and turned it as both beasts unleashed their poison. The table split as the vipers swooped past, coming around for another pass.

Owen reached for the book as a viper plunged at him, shooting. He blocked the spray with the book, and the venom ricocheted back at the viper, striking it in the chest and killing it. Unlike the heavy wood table, the book had suffered no damage.

The last viper dive-bombed from the ceiling, eyes afire, fangs exposed, venom dripping. Owen dropped the book and reached for his sword as another flying being entered, not as fast and looking woozy. It screeched and flew directly toward the viper, causing the enemy to change course. It was a bat! And it had protected Owen.

The delay had given Owen just enough time to raise his sword above his head, and the viper flew right into it, chopping itself in half.

The bat cocked his head. "Careful of the venom, Wormling."

"Thank you, friend," Owen said, reaching up to shake before remembering bats didn't have hands. He patted its head instead. "You know me?"

"Your friend told me about you."

"My friend?" Owen said, carefully wiping the sword on a charred drapery.

"Calls herself Watcher. Brown hair, about this high . . ."

Owen's mouth dropped. "That's her. Is she alive?"

"She was when they dragged her from the room."

"Who?"

"Invisibles with a powerful weapon. They hit Tusin and he fell—"

"Tusin?"

The bat—who said his name was Batwing—explained

everything, and suddenly Owen was hopeful again. But Batwing said the invisibles had taken Watcher to the highest part of the castle, where Owen hadn't even been.

He had retrieved the book, but the King's Son had disappeared. He had to find the Son again. But his heart refused to leave Watcher in the hands of the Dragon.

Watcher moaned and groaned, struggling to open her eyes, but the ringing and pounding in her head would not stop.

She couldn't move her legs. When she finally was able to see, she realized she was strapped to a wooden chair secured to the floor. She also sensed a presence so evil that the hair on her back rose straight up.

"Well, well, we meet the Watcher," a deep and rattly voice boomed behind her. "Did you have a nice rest, my dear? You know, few survive a blast from the concussers."

Watcher could tell by the putrid, sulfurous breath and the sound of the long heavy tail slithering about that this was the enemy of the King, the enemy of the Son, the enemy of the Wormling, and the enemy of all the citizens of her world. Just outside the door stood the being who had stolen *The Book of the King*, but when she looked at him, he quickly moved out of sight.

"Come, come, Watcher," the Dragon said. "There are so many things we could discuss. How about you answer a question from me, and then I'll tell you anything you want to know."

"You never speak the truth," Watcher said.

"Oh, please," the Dragon whined. "Of course I do. Why wouldn't I? You haven't bought into propaganda of my opposers, have you? It must have been an ordeal, traveling with someone spouting passages from that dreadful book. Tell me, is the Wormling self-absorbed, obsessively focused? That must be terribly draining for you."

"I will tell you nothing about the Wormling."

"But you have been traveling with him, hmm? Haven't you? Come, come, you can tell me. . . . Well, you are to be commended for your long-suffering. Now, as a gesture of goodwill, despite that you refused to answer, please feel free to ask me something. Go ahead. I'm dying to know what's on your mind." The Dragon finally came into view, his face lit with anticipation.

"The King's Son," she said. "Do you know where he is?"

"Hmm," the Dragon groaned. "And I promised to answer."

"I knew you would not tell me the truth."

"No, no, it's not that. It's just that at the moment I don't know. I *did* know where he was, but now . . . it seems I've misplaced him."

"What do you mean?"

"Ah, ah—that's two questions. If I answer, you must promise to answer my next one."

Watcher could not lie or her powers would leave her. Silence was an option, but she felt compelled to help the Wormling. "All right, I promise."

"Good! So, you seek the whereabouts of the King's Son. To be truthful, we had him in a dark place, very safe and hidden. Now it seems he's escaped. So, no, I don't know where he is. But as soon as he is found, believe me, you will be the first to know."

The Dragon inched closer, his ugly body squeaking as Watcher felt the heat of his breath on her neck. "My turn. And you promised. Where is the Wormling?"

Watcher gritted her teeth. "He told me to wait outside. That's the last I saw of him."

"Going in the castle?"

"Ah, ah. That's two questions."

The Dragon backed away and straightened. "No, it's one. The question is where is he?"

"The last I saw him, he was entering the castle, yes. But,

like you, I really don't know. If he found the King's Son, they could be miles from here."

"Without you? Not a chance." The Dragon snorted, and a finger of fire leaked from his snout. Clearly he wasn't happy. "Well, regardless, he'll be back for you, won't he?" He leaned close again. "Want to know something about your Wormling? He's been hiding something from you, keeping something to himself, despite your loyalty."

Watcher pretended otherwise, but he had her full attention. "I'd be surprised."

"Have you any idea who this Wormling *really* is?"

"He's told me of his life before, in the other world."

"Ah, but has he kept from you the most important information all this time? Tsk, tsk, tsk. And you, such a faithful friend. It's a shame, isn't it?"

Watcher tensed against the ropes.

"Let me guess," the Dragon continued. "There is more than loyalty in your heart for this Wormling; am I right?"

Watcher pursed her lips and shook her head.

The Dragon chuckled. "Getting too close to the heart of the matter, am I?" He leaned close to Watcher's ear and whispered in his sweetest, most cunning voice, "Your Wormling is in *love*. It's true. His heart belongs to someone in the other world, and he doesn't want you to know."

"Why would I care? He's not even of my species."

"Some things cannot be explained by science. Admit that there is some feeling deep inside that Watcher's heart of yours. I can sense it, just as you can sense invisibles."

"You don't even know him. You've never met him. How could you know—?"

The Dragon's aide stepped in, head bowed.

"I told you I did not want to be disturbed!" the Dragon roared.

"I beg your pardon, sire, but I have urgent news. The vipers. They've been killed."

"How many?"

"All, sire."

The Dragon's throat rattled and his skin flushed. "And what of the book?"

At this the being sank, his head nearly touching the ground. "I'm sorry, sire."

The Dragon shook and let loose a blast of fire from his throat that barely missed the bearer of the news. He whirled on Watcher, eyes flaming, breath like molten lava. "You'd better hope that Wormling of yours has not yet left the castle."

The Dragon strode from the room, the being letting him pass, then following.

Watcher struggled at the ropes until her ankles bled, but she could not free herself. She began to weep, not knowing the fate of the Wormling but knowing what the Dragon had said was true. The Wormling was her friend. He had shown her great kindness, and she felt as loyal to him now as she had felt for her old friend Bardig.

At her lowest, when she could not stop crying, the voice that had spoken to her long ago came back.

"Courage, Watcher," the voice said softly. "Be brave and believe."

Owen skulked through the castle
with Batwing, carefully avoiding guards and scythe flyers. He knew
demon flyers had to be around too and
wished Watcher were here to warn
him. When the Dragon bellowed from
the floor above, they moved to the
stairwell, only to hear the clambering
footsteps of his minions approaching.

Batwing raced to the ceiling and
hung there unnoticed, and Owen used
the handrail to climb to a windowsill.
The creatures were in such a hurry and
apparently in such a blinding rage that
they didn't notice him. The Dragon
lumbered down the staircase Owen
had just left.

As soon as the Dragon and his assemblage were out of sight, Owen jumped down and followed Batwing upstairs. Owen frantically searched three rooms for Watcher before Batwing circled back and waved him on. "Found her," he said.

Owen rushed to her, but before he could say a word she blurted, "Invisibles all around! Alerting the Dragon now!"

"Hold still," Owen said, and he used his sword to slice her bindings.

"Did you really kill the demon vipers?" Watcher said as they ran from the room.

Owen flashed the book from under his tunic. "And not a scratch on it."

"Where now?" Watcher said.

Owen turned to Batwing. "Can you cause a diversion that would allow us to reach the next level?"

"I can try," Batwing said.

"And alert Rotag," Watcher said. "We'll meet at the landing by the castle wall."

Batwing flew over the staircase into the huge hall, screeching and chirping.

Watcher and Owen raced down the steps, but when they were only halfway to the next floor, Owen noticed the hair on her back standing straight.

"They see us!" Watcher said.

"Faster!" Owen said, leading her to the King's former bedchamber.

Watcher kicked the door shut and eyed the room slowly. "So much pain. This is where *he* and the Queen slept. And the Son in the crib."

"We don't have time for this," Owen said. He grabbed Watcher's fur and could tell something had shot through her mind.

The door rattled and something pounded against it.

"Invisibles," she whispered.

Screeches, unearthly and piercing.

Owen dragged Watcher to the secret wall entrance, slipped behind it, and closed it just as a blast of fire shot into the room. There was a commotion followed by footsteps, but Owen and Watcher were flying downstairs, holding the walls as they took two and three steps at a time.

An eerie light flashed behind them, and Watcher slowed. "They've found the passage!"

"Go!" Owen yelled.

The air swirled and smelled of fire. What had taken Owen and Prince Qwamay so long to climb now took only minutes to descend. At the bottom Owen pulled his sword, but no sooner had they entered the dungeon and turned the corner than they were met by a horde of guards with weapons drawn. Leading the group, sword in hand, stood Qwamay.

Owen's heart sank. "You're with them?"

"Betrayal is the hallmark of battle, my friend."

Watcher pushed Owen into the corner where the black curtain hung against the wall.

The passageway door flew open, and flames shot from the Dragon's mouth. He nodded to Qwamay. "Good work." He turned to Watcher. "We never got to finish our chat. You disappoint me. On the other hand, you led me to this fine young Wormling. Rather puny, but I suppose the King has to settle for what he can get these days."

Owen brandished his sword, making the Dragon bare his dreadful teeth and rumble, "Surely you don't expect *that* to protect you. Give me the book, and I promise to make your end painless."

"You know the prophecy. You can't harm me."

"*I* didn't write the prophecy! That's just someone else's wishful thinking! Now give me the book!"

"But the agreement between you and the King—"

"Do I look like a ruler bound by signed documents? Now, this is the last time I ask politely for the book."

Owen shoved Watcher behind him. "You'll have to take it. I'll never surrender it."

The Dragon raised an eyebrow and cocked his head. Reaching with his tail, he wrapped it around Qwamay and pulled him close.

"What are you doing?" Qwamay yelled.

The Dragon narrowed his eyes at Owen. "Give me the book and I won't harm your friend."

"You said I would have kingdoms of my own!" Qwamay whined.

The Dragon clamped his scaly talons over Qwamay's mouth. "Turn it over, Wormling, and I'll not make you pay for the four vipers lying dead in my holding room. And I'll let the Son live."

Owen could not give up the book—it was life to him, and the secrets to the survival of the two worlds lay within. But neither could he allow the King's Son to die at the hands of the Dragon—even if the Prince had betrayed him.

What good was the book if the King's Son was dead? And what good was finding the King's Son if they had no book?

"Don't believe him," Watcher said. "He'll never let any of us out of here alive."

"The book, Wormling," the Dragon said. "Or I roast this Prince."

Owen pulled the book from his tunic. "I'll trade it for his life."

The Dragon wore a smarmy smile as he pushed Qwamay and he fell in a heap at Owen's feet. His face was bruised and his mouth bloody.

"Are you all right?" Owen said.

"I'm sorry."

Owen knew from *The Book of the King* that a Wormling could never go back on his word. A deal was a deal, no matter how much it hurt his cause or made his heart sick and regardless of whether the enemy felt bound by his own word. But as Owen was about to hand over the book, a voice whispered to his soul that he should open to a certain page, one he had not yet reached in his reading. As the Dragon, black saliva pooling at the corners of his mouth, drew near and reached for the book, Owen dutifully opened it and began to read:

> "Hear the words of the King. The words of this book shall not depart from your mouth or your heart all your days. Think about it day and night and be careful to do everything written in it. Those who do will be prosperous and successful."

The Dragon huffed angrily, but the guards and other beings behind him listened intently.

> "But those who oppose the King shall be cut off from the land of the living. These words will be found true of the evil one among you. He will injure the heel, but the Son will crush his head."

Owen laid the book gently on the floor.

The Dragon roared, and his eyes glowed crimson. He opened

his mouth and gurgled, making those behind him cover their eyes and ears and turn away. How many times had they seen citizens in the Lowlands consumed by his fire?

Owen held up his sword, keeping both Watcher and Qwamay behind him, but the Dragon ordered everyone else from the room. His troops raced out the door, pushing each other as the Dragon's death rattle continued.

Owen carefully backed to the corner, herding Qwamay and Watcher near the curtain to shield them from the Dragon's incinerating breath. But when the last of his forces were gone, the Dragon shot a blast of fire into the hallway, consuming everything in its path. The smell of burning wood and charred earth nearly choked Owen.

Next the Dragon raised a broad-taloned foot and slammed the door so hard it broke from its hinges and shook the walls. As the behemoth advanced, Owen noticed that a huge stone near the base of the castle's foundation jostled with each step. Might it actually be removable?

"Pull the curtain around yourselves," Owen whispered, "and see if you can remove that stone. Get out of here at all costs."

"We'll not leave without you," Watcher said.

"I'll catch up with you," Owen said. "Now you must!"

The Dragon towered over Owen as Watcher and Qwamay worked behind the curtain. The monster grinned a sickly smile. "Congratulations, Wormling. You have reached the end of your journey. I will serve you for dinner tonight and enjoy the first and largest portion myself."

The Dragon snatched up *The Book of the King* and tossed it behind him. His great tail thumped with excitement, making the floor shake and dust and mortar fall.

Owen gripped his sword and moved away from the curtain in the corner.

Nothing in all of Owen's nightmares, in all his imaginings of the most horrid, foul, and frightening creatures, prepared him for the close-up version of the animal before him. His teeth were jagged like a jack-o'-lantern's and as sharp as ice picks. His scales bore prickly spines all over his body, like quills that dripped green fluid. The Dragon appeared to be through talking. His dark eyes told Owen everything he needed to know.

Behind him, Owen heard the sliding of a stone, just enough to give him hope. He sidestepped to his left, hoping to distract the Dragon from the curtain. "Fear of the King," Owen said, "is the beginning of wisdom."

The Dragon gnashed his teeth, lunging at Owen.

Owen felt the wind from the sweeping talons on his cheek. He stepped over charred boxes, trying to maneuver to a position of strength, but he tripped on a grate in the floor and fell, his sword clanging. The Dragon pounced, and Owen rolled right, narrowly escaping the broad stomping foot.

"Sword!" Owen called, and immediately it flew to his

hand. Before he could thrust with it, a sweep of the Dragon's great tail sent it flying into the wall. The monster was on Owen now, close enough to overpower him with his smell, worse than a thousand hog pens.

Owen dived to the floor and slid between the Dragon's legs. The animal nearly toppled, turning to try to follow.

"Sword!" Owen called again. This time he grabbed it and slashed the Dragon's leg, blood flowing over the scales and quills.

Owen raced into the hall, hoping to lure the Dragon away from his friends. The Dragon thundered after him, past the bones of some animal piled in a corner. Owen pressed himself against the wall in the shadows, and the Dragon scanned the area. Standing perfectly still, Owen heard the stone clunk from its position in the wall.

Yes! They're getting away!

Owen felt on the floor and found a pebble. As the Dragon continued to search for him, Owen tossed it onto the bone pile, sending the bones tumbling. The Dragon surged toward the noise and Owen ducked past him, shooting down the corridor like lightning. He flew back into the room and skidded to a stop at the curtain. As the Dragon came stomping back, Owen whipped the curtain back and felt a cool breeze, hearing the sweet sound of water lapping against the shore. Watcher and Qwamay were already through.

Owen tried to back into the hole, but as he was pulling his shoulders through, he smelled the Dragon and felt his hot breath on his face. He tried to raise his sword, but the Dragon stood on the blade, blood dripping from his wounded leg. With an unearthly roar, the beast lunged and Owen covered his face with his hands. The Dragon's talons slashed his arm to the bone, but Owen felt hands around his ankles, and with a huge pull, he shot through the hole and found himself outside.

Qwamay and Watcher stood over him as blood poured from his arm.

"Call for your sword, Wormling," Watcher said.

Owen was nearly unconscious, but he managed to cry out, "Sword!"

The blade poked out the hole in the castle wall, but the Dragon had a death grip on its handle. The monster howled as his massive forearms were dragged through the tiny opening, the stone around it cracking. His broad shoulders were lodged tight, his nose peeking out. He tried to open his mouth but didn't have room, so his snort of fire came from only his nostrils. Choking on his own smoke, he finally let the sword loose and it flew to Owen's hands.

"Into the water!" Watcher shouted, pressing the sword blade onto Owen's wounded arm as Qwamay dragged him over the rocks. Rotag floated nearby, waiting to help.

The Dragon struggled fiercely behind them, the stones beginning to give way as a section of the castle wall bulged. The creature's ugly head disappeared as he backed up for another surge at the opening.

A line of archers appeared along the parapets, and their tiny arrows began piercing the water.

Rotag shouted, "Jump on and hold your breath!"

The three grabbed the gator as arrows rained down.

Then the Dragon burst through the opening, roaring, charging as the castle walls fell.

And Rotag the gator dived deep under the water with his three passengers aboard.

The Truth

Owen had nearly passed out from lack of oxygen by the time they made it to their subterranean hideout. Tusin helped pull them ashore, though clearly weak from his own injuries. The sword had healed Owen's wounded arm, but his energy was gone.

"What of the book?" Watcher said.

"It is enough that we have gained the King's Son," Owen said. "We can go back for the book later."

Batwing flew down the shaft and collapsed near them. "The Dragon has the book. He has ordered all his minions to pursue and destroy you."

"He knows that with my knowledge of the book and our having the King's

Son, we have all we need to overthrow him," Owen said. "It's only a matter of time."

Watcher shrieked when she rolled Qwamay over and discovered blood. Owen pushed her out of the way and ripped open the man's tunic. One of the archers' tiny arrows had pierced him through the back, the tip coming out his chest.

Qwamay grabbed Owen's hand. "My breath is slipping. You must go."

"Where?" Owen said. He held the sword to the wound, but the arrow prevented healing.

"My father had a small cabin in the woods where he would think and dream," Qwamay said. He shoved a bloody map into Owen's hand. "Retreat there and rest. Plan your next move."

"You can't die," Owen said. "You're the key to everything we've searched for. Without you, we're nothing."

Qwamay pulled him close. "I am not who you think I am. Your search is not over."

Owen lifted Qwamay. "What do you mean?"

"My father is not the King."

"Who is he?"

"Mordecai. The captain of the guard." Qwamay's eyes rolled back, and his body fell limp.

Owen and Watcher found a patch of soft ground in which to bury Qwamay. Watcher seemed aloof, as if there was something she understood that he didn't, but she wouldn't explain.

Owen longed for his home and the simple life over the bookstore, where he could get lost in a story and not have to worry about the outcome. If he didn't like the way a book ended, he could pick up another.

Still, with the words of *The Book of the King* echoing in his soul, he knew he had a long way to go in this new world before he could even dream of going home.

⋕

Two days later, under cover of darkness and aided by their new friends, Owen and Watcher reached the cabin of Qwamay's father. As Owen leafed through a crude desk he found envelopes bearing the King's official seal. They included commendations for Mordecai, and another contained a letter to the Scribe. So, *The Book of the King* had been written under the direction of the King but not by the King himself. Perhaps this Scribe would have information about the King's Son.

They stayed three days in the cabin by the lake, then set off at night. Owen still had Mucker in his tunic, certain that one day he would need his little friend's help again.

In the counsel of the unholy, the
Dragon opened the book and
laughed. The Wormling had escaped,
yes, along with his Watcher, but a mortal blow had been dealt the one they
mistook for the King's Son.

All around the table, they drank
and toasted their leader. They had
endured the power of the Wormling
and lived to tell about it. But the
Wormling had delivered a death blow
to four of the most menacing creatures
the Dragon had ever devised and had
lived to fight another day.

When the Dragon retreated to his
room that night, he took the book

with him, leafing through it, scoffing, coming up with twists on the truth and turns on the holy writ. As he looked out at his kingdom, he renewed his pledge to someday rule the Highlands, the Lowlands, and his invisible kingdom.

But the verse the Wormling had read kept coming back to him, sending a shiver up his spine.

He will injure the heel, but the Son will crush his head.

ABOUT THE AUTHORS

Jerry B. Jenkins (jerryjenkins.com) is the writer of the Left Behind series. He owns the Jerry B. Jenkins Christian Writers Guild, an organization dedicated to mentoring aspiring authors. Former vice president for publishing for the Moody Bible Institute of Chicago, he also served many years as editor of *Moody* magazine and is now Moody's writer-at-large.

His writing has appeared in publications as varied as *Reader's Digest*, *Parade*, *Guideposts*, in-flight magazines, and dozens of other periodicals. Jenkins's biographies include books with Billy Graham, Hank Aaron, Bill Gaither, Luis Palau, Walter Payton, Orel Hershiser, and Nolan Ryan, among many others. His books appear regularly on the *New York Times*, *USA Today*, *Wall Street Journal*, and *Publishers Weekly* best-seller lists.

Jerry is also the writer of the nationally syndicated sports-story comic strip *Gil Thorp*, distributed to newspapers across the United States by Tribune Media Services.

Jerry and his wife, Dianna, live in Colorado and have three grown sons and four grandchildren.

††††

Chris Fabry is a writer and broadcaster who lives in Colorado. He has written more than 50 books, including collaboration on the Left Behind: The Kids and Red Rock Mysteries series.

You may have heard his voice on Focus on the Family, Moody Broadcasting, or Love Worth Finding. He has also written for *Adventures in Odyssey* and *Radio Theatre*.

Chris is a graduate of the W. Page Pitt School of Journalism at Marshall University in Huntington, West Virginia. He and his wife, Andrea, have nine children, two dogs, and a large car insurance bill.

RED ROCK MYSTERIES

BRYCE AND ASHLEY TIMBERLINE are normal 13-year-old twins, except for one thing—they discover action-packed mystery wherever they go. Wanting to get to the bottom of any mystery, these twins find themselves on a nonstop search for truth.

CP0140

The Future Is Clear

Check out the exciting Left Behind: The Kids series

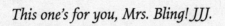

This one's for you, Mrs. Bling! JJJ.

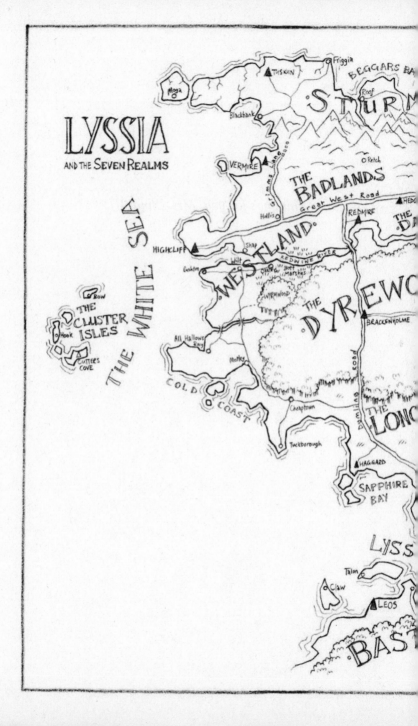

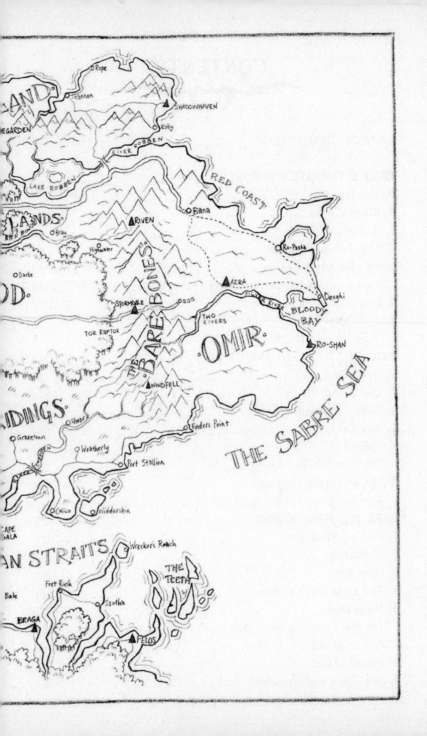

CONTENTS

CAST OF CHARACTERS

THE WOLF AND HIS ALLIES
Drew Ferran, last of the Gray Wolves, rightful king of Westland.

Werelords of the High Seas
Count Vega, Prince of Cluster Isles, sea marshal for the Wolf, former captain of the *Maelstrom*, member of the Wolf's Council. Sharklord.

Baron Bosa, the Whale of Moga, captain of the *Beluga*, former pirate. Whalelord.

Figgis, first mate of the *Maelstrom*.

Florimo, navigator. Ternlord.

Casper, former cabin boy of the Maelstrom. The son of Vega and Shah. Hawklord.

Phibians of the Bott Marshes
Kholka, a phibian Marshman.

Shilmin, his wife.

Khilik, their child.

Shoma, another phibian Marshman.

Werelords of Azra
King Faisal of Azra, true king of Omir. Jackal-lord.

Vizier Barjin of Azra, Faisal's closest adviser. Jackal-lord.

Lady Hayfa the Hyena, ruler of Ro-Shann and besieger of Azra. Werehyena.

Aldo, Hayfa's right-hand man.

Lord Canan of Omir, ruler of Pasha, rebel king engaged in civil war against King Faisal. Doglord.

Kara, Faisal's young daughter. Jackal-lady.

Bastian Allies of the Wolf

Lady Opal, the Beauty of Bast, sister of Onyx. Pantherlady.

Lord Chollo of the Teeth. Cheetahlord.

High Lord Tigara, Elder of Tigers, grandfather of Taboo. Tigerlord.

Taboo, granddaughter of Lord Tigara, gladiator in Scoria. Tigerlady.

Hawklords

Lady Shah, healer, heir to Windfell. Hawklady.

Count Carsten, leader of the Hawklords, brother of Baron Baum.

Baron Baum, leader of the Hawklords, brother of Count Carsten.

Bearlords of Brackenholme

Lady Whitley, daughter of Bergan, Greencloak scout.

Duke Bergan of Brackenholme, member of the Wolf's Council.

Duchess Rainier, wife of Bergan. Foxlady.

Lord Broghan, son of Bergan, Greencloak commander, now deceased.

Baron Redfearn, Bergan's brother.

White Bears of Icegarden

Duke Henrik, Lord of Icegarden, cousin of Duke Bergan.

Lady Greta, magister, sister of Henrik, under siege by Baron Hector.

Wildcats of Robben

Bethwyn, lady-in-waiting to Lady Greta.

Baron Mervin, ruler of Robben, Bethwyn's father.

Staglords of Stormdale

Duke Manfred, member of the Wolf's Council.

Lord Reinhardt, son of Manfred, acting leader of Stormdale.

Lord Milo, son of Manfred, younger brother of Reinhardt.

Magister Wilhelm, healer, Hector's uncle. Boarlord.

White Wolves of Shadowhaven

Miloqi, a seer.

Mikotaj, Miloqi's brother, known as the White Death.

Other Living Werelords

Lady Gretchen of Hedgemoor, former fiancée of Lucas, Drew's friend. Werefox.

Lord Conrad of Cape Gala. Horselord.

Lord Eben of Haggard, young Ramlord.

Krieg, gladiator, survivor of the Furnace. Rhinolord.

The Behemoth, gladiator, survivor of the Furnace. Mammoth-lord.

Duke Brand of Calico. Bull-lord.

Deceased Werelords

Wergar the Wolf, former king of Westland, Drew's father, deposed and killed by King Leopold.

Queen Amelie, White Wolf, dowager queen of Westland, widow of Wergar and Leopold, mother of Drew and Lucas. Killed by Hector.

Earl Mikkel, brother to Duke Manfred, slain by Doglords before the Battle of Highcliff. Staglord.

Baron Ewan of Haggard, father of Lord Eben, magister, slain by Count Kesslar. Ramlord.

Lord Dorn, son of Duke Brand, slain by Count Kesslar in Haggard. Bull-lord.

Red Rufus, killed in the Battle of Brackenholme. Hawklord.

Human Allies

Trent Ferran, Drew's adoptive brother, former member of the Redcloaks, the Wolf Knight.

Djogo, former captain of Count Kesslar's mercenaries and slaver, now Drew's friend.

Captain Eric Ransome, former pirate captain of the *Maelstrom*.

Baba Soba, a wisewoman of the Romari.

Yuzhnik, Romari fire-eater and strongman.

General Harker, commander of the Watch in Brackenholme.

General Reuben Fry, archer from Sturmland.

Bo Carver, Lord of Thieves.

Pick, young girl thief.

Lars Steinhammer, Sturmish blacksmith.

Ibal, former member of Hector's Boarguard, now allied with Bergan.

Mack Ferran, Drew's adoptive father, father of Trent, killed by the Lionguard.

Tilly Ferran, Drew's adoptive mother, mother of Trent, killed by Vanmorten.

THE CATLORDS AND THEIR ALLIES

The Lions of Leos

High Lord Leon, Elder of Lions, father of Leopold, grandfather of Lucas.

Leopold the Lion, late deposed king of Westland, father of Lucas. Slain by Lucas.

King Lucas, self-crowned king of Westland, son of Leopold and Queen Amelie, Drew's half-brother.

Lord Luc, nephew of Leon, elite Lionguard.

Lord Lex, nephew of Leon, elite Lionguard, Luc's brother.

Their Werelord Allies
Lord Ulik of World's End, the Naked Ape. Apelord.
General Clavell, brother to General Skean. Cranelord.

The Panthers of Braga
High Lord Oba, Elder of Panthers, father of Lord Onyx and
    Lady Opal.
Lord Onyx, the Beast of Bast.

Their Werelord Allies
Lieutenant Ithacus, High Lord Oba's messenger. Vulturelord.
Count Costa, member of Onyx's war council. Vulturelord.
General Skean, member of Onyx's war council. Cranelord.
General Gorgo, member of Onyx's war council. Hippolord.
Baron Overmeir of the Blasted Plains, member of Onyx's war
    council. Buffalo-lord.
Lady Giza, member of Onyx's war council. Weregazelle.

Their Human Allies
Sheriff Muller, Bandit-lord of the Badlands. Member of Onyx's
    war council.
Major Krupha, Redcloak commander. Member of Onyx's war
    council.

The Tigers of Felos
Field Marshal Tiaz, leader of the Furies of Felos. Tigerlord.

Their Werelord Allies

General Primus, cousin to Onyx. Pantherlord.

Lord Urok, the Red Ape of World's End. Apelord.

The Cheetahs of the Teeth

Lord Chang, son of Lord Chollo. Deceased.

The Rat King

Vanmorten, Lord Chancellor of Westland, most powerful member of the Rat King family.

Vankaskan, dark magister, Hector's former master. Killed by Drew.

Vorjavik, war marshal, killed by Lord Reinhardt at the Battle of Stormdale.

Vorhaas, twin of Vorjavik, commander of the Lion's army in the Dalelands. Killed by Trent Ferran.

Wyldermen and Their Goddess

Vala, evil wereserpent goddess worshipped by the Wyldermen. Killed by Drew.

Darkheart, leader of the Wyld Wolves.

Werelords of Scoria

Lord Ignus of Scoria, owner of the Furnace. Lizardlord.

Count Kesslar of Haggard, slaver. Goatlord. Killed by the Behemoth.

On the High Seas

Sea Marshal Scorpio, former commander of the Bastian Fleet
and captain of the *Bastian Empress*. Fishlord.

THE BOARLORD AND HIS ALLIES

Baron Hector, dark magister known as Blackhand, ruler of
Redmire, former member of the Wolf's Council, ruler of
Ugri. Boarlord.

Vincent-vile, the phantom of Hector's dead twin brother.

Crowlords

Lord Flint, son of Count Croke, leader of the Crows of Riven.
Killed by Hector.

Human Allies

Ringlin, captain of the Boarguard. Killed by Hector.

Two Axes, Ugri warrior.

PART I

THE WOLF RETURNS

I

THE BULL PEN

THE YOUNG WOMAN stopped in her tracks on the dockside, taking a moment to look back over the harbor while the steady stream of men-at-arms strode past. The fortress city of the Werebull Duke Brand had been liberated, the enemy fleet of Bastian warships decimated by the Wolf's navy. Calico Bay was a fractured reef of blackened masts and half-sunk dreadnoughts, their twisted timbers reaching out of the waves like the fingers of drowning men. The occasional trawler weaved between the wrecks, hopeful fishermen slowly taking back their sea from the fallen invaders as they made for the deeper waters beyond. She watched as one small vessel bobbed past the *Nemesis,* a man-of-war that blotted the sun from the sky above. The fishermen saluted the men aboard the *Nemesis,*

a mongrel crew from Bast and Lyssia who had sailed with the young woman in the name of the Wolf. The men waved and cheered back, hollering encouragement as the plucky boat headed for open water.

She admired the trawlermen's optimism, the never-say-die attitude of a people who had been prisoners within their own city for so long, already reclaiming their livelihoods just days after the tyrant Sea Marshal Scorpio had been routed. She felt hope, a strange feeling to her, and one to which she would have to become reaccustomed.

"Are you ready, my lady?"

Whitley turned to Captain Ransome and saw the elderly pirate captain straightening his gray whiskers. He waited for her on the crowded drawbridge that linked the fortress city to the docks beyond its walls. More of the ships under her command remained anchored farther out to sea, their human cargo having alighted in the harbor. There was no sign of Baron Bosa's fleet out there: Whitley had expected to find the victorious Werewhale of Moga waiting for them, but alas he had been drawn back out to sea, hunting down their enemies. She brought her attention back to the procession of exotic soldiers as they strode by. Whitley had witnessed the Goldhelms of the Werepanthers and the Redcloaks who served the Lion marching across Lyssian soil, but here was a different kind of Bastian: the Furies, twin-sword-wielding warriors of the Tigerlords. They numbered fewer than their cousins, but their

reputation was equally frightful. As they traversed the giant timber drawbridge into the city, the men of Calico looked warily down from their walls at the leather-clad Furies crossing the threshold.

"You think they're happy to see more Bastians come ashore, Ransome?" she asked, falling in beside him as they vanished into the shadows of the mighty gatehouse, the sandstone walls towering overhead.

"If they feared us they wouldn't open their gates, my lady," said the old sea captain. "There may be Bastians among our number, but the men of Calico have witnessed our friend Baron Bosa annihilate Sea Marshal Scorpio's fleet. They're right to be cautious after what they've endured, but I'd still consider this a warm welcome. I doubt Duke Brand greeted the Werefish with such open arms."

"I was expecting a king and they send me a girl?"

Whitley marched through the hall known to all in Calico as the Bull Pen, as the assembled great and good parted excitedly to let her by. Captain Ransome remained at her shoulder, back straight and jaw jutting out sharp as a cliff, as they approached the duke's table. Though old enough to be her grandfather, the former pirate had proved his worth time and again to the girl from Brackenholme, and had helped save her pelt from the jaws of the terrible Sharklord Deadeye. There was

only one other soul she would rather have by her side, and he was now far away.

"Girl I may be, but I speak on behalf of the Wolf and my father, the Lord of Brackenholme."

Her voice rose over the noise in the Bull Pen as all eyes turned back to the giant fellow who had spoken from behind the long table. He lifted his bald head and snorted at the young lady as she came to a halt before him. His neck was lost in a knot of enormous muscles piled across his shoulders. He wore a long black cloak held in place by a straining gold chain about his throat, and its ermine-lined edge trailed onto the ground at his feet. It was clear by the way his court looked to him that he commanded their utter obedience. Whether this was born out of respect or fear, Whitley had yet to decide.

"Bergan's child?" said Duke Brand.

"Lady Whitley, Your Grace," replied the girl with a respectful bow. "Thank you for opening the gates of Calico to our men. Your hospitality is most welcome."

"Good thing you sent word ahead," said Brand gruffly. "Chances are, had you turned up unannounced, we'd have blown you out of the bay with that Bastian blasting powder."

"The blasting powder that my friend Baron Bosa seized from Scorpio's fleet, you mean?"

The Bull prickled at this comment, but Whitley continued. "You have nothing to fear from my force, Your Grace."

"Who said I was afraid, little Bear?"

"The warriors you no doubt saw in my company are allied to the Wolf, sworn into his service in the name of High Lord Tigara, the Weretiger of Felos."

"Strange that those you once considered enemies are now called friends, Lady Whitley," said the duke.

"In the winds of war, alliances can shift like the grasses of your Longridings, Your Grace; often unpredictable, and occasionally fortuitous. The Catlord Forum of Elders is broken, the continent of Bast in turmoil. The Lions and Panthers fight with one another, while the Tigers of Felos are now loyal to Lord Drew. They are our allies, Your Grace."

Whitley wasn't about to be intimidated by the old Werebull. She had done a lot of growing up since the war had begun, her days as a wide-eyed apprentice scout now a dim and distant memory. What she had experienced would have broken a lesser spirit. She saw nothing to fear in Brand.

"Baron Bosa has moved on already, I hear?" she continued.

"Indeed," replied the duke. "He said there were bigger fish to fry along the Cold Coast. There's talk of even more Bastians making for our shores. I'm grateful to the Werewhale and his fleet for their timely incursion in Calico Bay. Had they not come to our assistance when they did, Brenn knows what fate would have awaited my people."

"You mention Bosa's fleet, Your Grace, but those were actually the Wolf's ships. The baron is one of Drew's men, having sworn fealty to the rightful king of Westland."

"And why does this Wolf king not show his face to us? Do I not merit an appearance from the fabled son of Wergar, the lycanthrope at the heart of this sorry war?"

"Lord Drew is otherwise engaged," said Whitley, her own annoyance just about in check. She had not wanted to leave Drew's side, but circumstances had dictated that their paths had to diverge. "He has sailed on to the desert realm of Omir, while I headed straight for Calico and the newly liberated Lords of the Longridings. My path takes me north, Your Grace, to Sturmland where our enemies await."

"Your enemies are your own business, my lady," said the Bull. "I've had as much of this war as I can stomach. You may go north with my blessing."

Whitley stood agape. "I didn't come here to seek your blessing, Your Grace," she snapped. "I came here seeking soldiers."

"You've brought soldiers of your own, I see. No need for you to take any of mine."

"There is *every* need for the men and women of the Longridings to join us on the march north. As you yourself observed, my soldiers are Bastian warriors who now fight as brothers-in-arms against our common enemy."

"More Bastians coming to fight in Lyssia?" scoffed Brand. "Well, isn't that just what we need? I hardly see how the Tigerlord's warriors are an answer to our worries. The Lion king

Lucas's Redcloak army and the Goldhelms of Lord Onyx still swamp the Seven Realms."

"The Furies are but a small fraction of the solution to our problems," said Whitley, fists curled earnestly as she took another step forward to lean against the table.

Brand waved a mighty hand dismissively. "March north, my lady, with your southern friends by your side. The Longridings never asked to be part of the Wolf's war but somehow managed to get dragged into it."

"This war was inevitable, with or without Drew's emergence in Westland. King Leopold was only the beginning of the Bastian invasion."

"And that invasion is in ruins now! You said it yourself, the Catlords are divided, their army in pieces! Let the Lion keep Westland—"

"Do you really think Lucas will be content with just a small portion of our continent? He wants the lot, Brand, as does Onyx. Our enemy may be divided, but they remain intent upon taking Lyssia for their own. They want everything."

"Mind your manners, child," rumbled the duke. "I doubt your father raised you to speak to your betters in such a charmless fashion."

"Presently, Your Grace," she said, scouring the assembled court in the Bull Pen, "I've yet to spy any betters."

Brand punched the table, enraged.

"Insolent little wretch," he snorted. "Come to my hall and disrespect me, will you?" His brow split, horns sliding out of his temples like two monstrous spears. The audience of assembled nobles gasped, stepping backward, and even Ransome quickly staggered clear, as the Werebull shifted shape before them. Only Whitley remained motionless, feet locked firmly in place, her eyes fixed fiercely upon the duke while her heart quaked. *Perhaps I should* fear the Bull after all?

Brand grabbed the table and pulled it to one side, his temper exploding in the face of the contemptuous girl from Brackenholme. His powerful legs had transformed, great cloven hooves striking the flagged floor like steel against stone.

"You seem to forget, Your Grace," she shouted, "that you have Lord Drew to thank for your freedom! It was the Wolf's fleet that sailed to your aid, scuttling Scorpio's fleet. Tell me, how close to starvation were the people of Calico before Bosa sailed into the bay and liberated you from Scorpio's siege? Before the Wolf was victorious on your behalf?"

Whitley moved now as the Werebull snatched at her, ducking under his grasp and moving around him. Light on her feet, she kept him turning, making a mockery of his frustration before his cowed and trembling courtiers. Some of the noblemen and ladies cried out, panicked. Whitley was vaguely aware of shouting and a fresh commotion at the entrance to the Bull Pen, but her attention was focused solely on the duke and his terrible horns.

"Is that how you win a war, Duke Brand?" she called out. "Hiding behind your giant walls while other men—better men—give their lives?" She turned to the cowering crowd. "What of the other Lords of the Longridings? The Bull of Calico grants you shelter, and you leave your backbones at the door? Will none of you help us?"

"Shut up, you wretched child," roared the Werebull, stamping the floor as he lowered his head, blinded by rage. "Silence or so help me . . ."

"What?" she growled back, rust-brown fur emerging from her skin. "You'll attack me? I suppose you can take me, Brand, since I'm just a girl. Perhaps you feel I'm not worthy opposition for the once powerful Lord of the Longridings? Well, I promise you this," she said, claws and teeth growing as she prepared for his charge, "I'll leave you with something to remember me by."

As the Werebull lunged at her, Whitley leapt high, seizing Brand's monstrous head. The two wrestled across the chamber, the half-transformed Bearlady gripping the duke with all her might, while the onlookers watched on in wonder. She had Brand in a headlock, twisting and turning the duke as he tried to wrestle free. The duke's cloven feet struck the ground, their clatter rattling off the Bull Pen's walls as the two struggled for dominion. Finally tearing himself loose, the Bull collapsed through a darkened alcove, crashing into the wall, plasterwork crumbling with the impact. He struggled to his feet, bellowing at his guards.

"Pass me an ax!" he snorted. "Now!"

Before any soldier could comply, a blond-maned Horselord pushed through the throng, making his way toward the two combatants. He was partially transformed and more than prepared for a fight, his eyes fixed upon the Bull.

"Have you taken leave of your senses, Duke Brand?" asked Whitley's champion, his nostrils flaring as his long face flushed with anger. "I return to court to find you trying to kill our guest?"

"She's no guest of mine," snorted Brand, glaring at the Werestallion, who positioned himself between the duke and the girl. "Stand aside, Conrad."

"Why?" said the Horselord. "So you may harm her?"

"So I may turn her out of my city!" shouted the Bull.

"Then you turn my brethren and me out, too," replied Conrad, gradually shifting back to human form as his temper subsided. "Whitley is a friend to the people of the Longridings. She is an ally of ours."

"Of yours, young Horselord."

"Of ours," repeated Conrad, pointing at the girl as her fur receded. "The Bears of Brackenholme have suffered more than anyone in this war, yet still they fight on. I witnessed her brother slain at the hands of King Lucas and saw many of her people butchered on the street in Cape Gala. We owe them our freedom, Your Grace. Don't treat her this way. The Wolf is our ally."

"Yours, perhaps," said the Bull, shifting slowly back to human form, as more plaster crumbled free from the bricks at his back. "But not mine. You remember my son, girl?"

Whitley shook her head, unable to recall if she had ever met him. "I cannot say I do."

"He was a ward to Baron Ewan, the Ramlord of Haggard. Just a lad, my dear, sweet Dorn. And then he met your friend the Wolf. Death followed swiftly, Bearlady. He took up arms alongside Drew Ferran and died for his troubles. I can never forgive the Wolf for what happened to my son."

Whitley cast her mind back, the memories now returning, but cloudy and distorted. The grim events of Lord Dorn's death had been lost among the hundreds of others she had witnessed in the intervening time. But Brand spoke the truth. The young Bull had aided Drew in freeing the prisoners of the Goatlord Kesslar in Haggard. Dorn was murdered for his troubles, little more than a boy, the same age as Drew.

"Go with her if you must, Horselord," muttered Brand miserably, remaining in the alcove's shadows. "Take your brother Stallions with you. But count me out. I owe the Wolf nothing."

2

KILLER CHARM

DREW FERRAN STARED at the tarnished mirror fixed to the wall, the swinging lanterns and jangling ephemera providing a grating chorus around him as the ship gently rocked. Oddities from every corner of the Seven Realms had been collected down the years by the *Maelstrom*'s skipper, finding their way onto the ceiling of the captain's cabin. Discolored and clouded though the mirror's surface was, there was no mistaking the young man who glowered back. His thick mop of black hair had grown down to his shoulders, in desperate need of a good cut, while his jaw was peppered with the dark stubble of a beard. His skin was tanned dark, thanks to months on the road and at sea, crossing oceans and continents, exposed to the elements.

Had it really been almost two years since his journey had begun? Drew closed his eyes, thinking back to the farmhouse where he had grown up, the night of the storm and the beast that had followed. He shook his head and grimaced, the memory of his murdered foster mother flashing through his mind, her throat torn by the Ratlord Vanmorten. Drew had changed so much, and he was not alone. What had become of his old friend Hector, the Boarlord of Redmire? He had left his bookish friend behind in Highcliff, thinking he would be safe. Nothing could have been further from the truth. Hector's path had been a dark one as he dabbled in necromancy, ultimately taking him north to Icegarden. Was he still there? Could he truly have become the monster people said he was?

When Drew opened his eyes he was no longer alone. The grinning visage of Count Vega had appeared in the mirror at his back.

"By Sosha, we could be related!" the Sharklord declared, laughing and tousling his friend's hair. He wasn't wrong, Drew had to agree: they shared the same dark looks.

"My father?" Drew teased.

"I was thinking of a more charming, handsome, slightly older brother." He clapped the youth's back. "Come. They're waiting for you on deck."

The heat was instant and punishing as they went up top, the *Maelstrom's* decks bleached of moisture and color. There were few places to shelter from the sun's fierce rays, and Drew

instantly wrapped his kash around his face. Few aboard the pirate ship had gone without the Omiri headgear since they had sailed into the Sabre Sea, the kashes providing protection against the terrible heat, especially during the midday sun. But there was another reason why the young Wolflord wore the kash: the *Maelstrom* was anchored in the deeper waters of Denghi harbor, in view of the neighboring ships within the Bloody Bay. To be spotted by anyone sympathetic to the Lion could mean the end of the impending battle before it had begun.

Drew was not the only one disguised. The *Maelstrom* had received a makeover: her pristine sails were replaced by tattered, patchwork affairs, her decks and hull cluttered with nets and lobster pots. The gun decks had been hidden away, her many shuttered windows dressed with planks and tarpaulins. For all intents and purposes she no longer looked like the dread vessel of the Pirate Prince of the Cluster Isles; she was a battered, oceangoing fishing ship, unremarkable in every way. Three more ships remained anchored around the headland, each wearing a similar nautical mask. Fully two hundred warriors from the Bastian port of Felos had been distributed among the vessels, the cuirass-wearing Furies hidden belowdecks, waiting patiently for their moment. Waiting for the bloodshed.

A rowboat was being winched aboard, the seawater painting the deck wet as the boards thirstily soaked it up. Opal, the Pantherlady of Bast, stood with her back to the quarter mast, her dark form shrouded in robes and harsh shadow. Her bright

eyes shone from within the slit of her kash, fixed upon Denghi, narrow and appraising, as she studied the Omiri port. She and Figgis, the *Maelstrom*'s first mate, were returning from a brief visit to the harbor's bars and drinking dens. As Figgis spoke animatedly to Opal and jabbed a bony finger in the city's direction, Florimo stood nearby, watching. The old navigator looked quite at home in the colorful Omiri attire, his now customary enormous pink feather drooping from his bandanna, befitting a Ternlord. The ship's youngest crewmember, Casper, crouched at his bare feet, studying coastal maps under Florimo's watchful eye. The cabin boy had only recently discovered he was a Werehawk, the son of Vega and a Hawklady, though the boy did not know the full story of his conception or who his mother was. The elderly Ternlord provided invaluable guidance for the boy as he slowly came to terms with his fearful avian abilities—guidance Casper's father, the Sharklord, was ill-equipped to offer.

"What did you discover in Denghi?" asked Drew as he joined Opal in the shade. "Is it as bad as it looks?"

"Worse," she said, her voice rich as honey. "Denghi is no longer neutral. Hayfa, the Hyena of Ro-Shan, claims the city as her own."

"The road to Azra is hers, my lord," added Figgis. "Doglords are welcome enough, but I doubt you'll encounter a Jackal in Denghi."

The fabled city of Azra was home to King Faisal, the Were-

jackal of Omir. The true prize of the Desert Realm, this was the jewel Lady Hayfa had long desired. Not content with the coastal city of Ro-Shan, the Werehyena would stop at nothing until she had seized Azra. With Hayfa's ally Lord Canan and his terrible Doglords controlling the lands as far north as the Bana Gap, Faisal's hold on his homeland was looking increasingly fragile. If the road to Azra was controlled by the Hyena, her stranglehold on the city was almost complete.

"Seems Hayfa and Lord Canan are carving Omir up between them," continued Figgis, "looking to oust the Jackals from Azra and all their lands."

"The only blessing is there's no sign of my Bastian brethren," said Opal. "Field Marshal Tiaz must be keeping his men occupied farther north, routing the Jackals at the Bana Gap."

At the northernmost edge of Omir, where the Barebones rose from the sand, a narrow avenue wound its way through the mountains. Many years ago, the land here had been claimed by Faisal's forefathers, the last refuge for travelers on their way into the Desert Realm. As time went by, the city of Bana had grown from this settlement, carved into the rock face and overlooking the gap below. As the Doglords had joined forces with the Catlords of Bast, the first city to suffer had been Bana. The Tigerlord, Field Marshal Tiaz, had been dispatched to claim the Gap for Lord Onyx, while Lord Canan wanted every Jackal within the city put to the sword. It had been besieged since the beginning of the war.

"Nothing's ever easy," Drew sighed, scratching his bristly jaw. "What news did you gather regarding the city of Azra itself? When I left it on the eve of winter, the Hawklords had flown to the Jackals' aid. I thought they could handle whatever the Catlords threw at them."

"It appears not," said Opal, a hint of pride evident in the Panther's voice. "Azra is besieged by Hayfa's forces, while Tiaz and Canan have drawn your Hawklords away from Faisal's side. It appears the Jackal believed the walls of Azra to be impenetrable. Confident of his own safety, he wasted no time charging your avianthrope allies with rescuing his brethren in the north. The Hawklords flew to the Bana Gap, carrying many of the Omiri king's greatest warriors in their talons. Maybe they suspected they would free the trapped Jackals easily. Perhaps they thought they were flying to victory, to quell a few rowdy Doglords who pawed at Bana's gates. What they encountered was Field Marshal Tiaz and the full might of his Bastian army."

"I have to believe that my friends who flew north yet live," said Drew. "I made a promise to them all that I would return."

"I saw the weapons Tiaz had at his disposal when he departed Sturmland along the Great West Road. Your allies were winging their way to their deaths."

"What weapons?" snapped Vega, tired as always of the Panther's penchant for drama.

"The Gypsian Vultures for one," replied Opal haughtily.

Drew watched the two of them speak, no love lost between

them. The Sharklord had blackmailed Opal while she was prisoner aboard his ship. True to his word, he had gone straight to her homeland of Braga while the Pantherlady escorted Drew to Leos, the Catlord seat of power. Drew's task was to sow division among the Forum of Elders, while Vega abducted the infant children of Opal, guaranteeing her cooperation. Both missions were successful: the Bastians were now at war with one another and Opal's children were under the watchful eye of the Tigers in Felos. Safe though her children were, thanks to the Sharklord's actions, there was no disguising the hate she felt for her unlikely ally.

"Gypsian Vultures?" said Drew, trying to take the sting out of their dialog.

"From the Gypsian Plateau at the heart of Bast," said Opal. "It towers over the jungle, fully a thousand leagues across. Barren, inhospitable, and miserable. The Vulturelords call it home."

"And these Vultures are a match for the Hawklords?"

"More than a match, when one considers their superior numbers. If you thought having the Hawks of the Barebones fighting your quarter in the sky would win you this war, I'm afraid you're in for a rude awakening, Wolflord."

"It's Drew, Opal," he replied with a stiff smile. "Wolflord sounds so impersonal."

"I'll stick with 'Wolflord' until our work is concluded."

Vega's laugh was as dry as the air around them. "You make it sound like a business deal."

"This is business," she said to Vega with a snarl. "I would never have sided with Lyssians out of choice. You forced my hand when you threatened my children. But what's done is done. We fight together against the Lions and my own family, the Panthers. Until the dust has settled and the blood has dried, we are allies. When that concludes . . ."

She left the comment hanging menacingly. Drew gulped, his throat parched.

"Get off your high horse, Opal," said Vega. "You wrote the rule book on how war is waged in Bast. The Catlords have spent the past sixty years kidnapping children from across the jungle continent, forcing the therian lords into submission. I'd imagine it's an unpleasant sensation, having the tables turned upon you. Count yourself fortunate that your children are alive and well."

Opal snarled as Vega turned to Figgis.

"Any other news, mate?"

"More whispers, Captain, about Bastian fleets sailing to Lyssia. I don't doubt our own ships are part of the cause of these rumors, but you have to consider they're referring to High Lord Oba and High Lord Leon as well: the Panther and Lion have each set sail for Lyssia, as well we know."

"They've probably headed straight to Highcliff," said Drew.

"Both of them?" said Vega. "Unlikely. The Panthers and Lions are at war with one another now. If they haven't stopped to fight with one another in the White Sea, then they'll have

found different ports to sail into. Highcliff isn't big enough for the armies of two warring Catlords. With no sign of my old friend Baron Bosa in these waters, one has to hope he's making a nuisance of himself with Oba and Leon. Which brings us to our own quandary: where do we go ashore?"

He turned to the Ternlord.

"My dear Florimo, did you discover anything of interest? A likely place, beyond Ro-Pasha, where we may strike land for the Gap?"

The navigator wasn't long returned from his own scouting mission, having scoured the shore for safe passage into Omir. For two nights he had been absent, moving under starlight, out of sight of the people of the Desert Realm and anyone who sailed the Sabre Sea.

"I'm afraid you won't find a welcome north of Ro-Pasha, Count Vega. The survivors of Sea Marshal Scorpio's fleet have made the Red Coast their home. His remaining ships are dotted throughout the shallows, housing those still loyal to Bast."

"Bosa really worked Scorpio over in Calico Bay," said Drew. "He's no doubt still licking his wounds after the beating the Whale dished out."

"So there's no safe place to find land?" said Vega.

"Not in Omir, my lord," replied Florimo. "Discounting Scorpio's remaining ships, there's simply too much enemy activity, with Doglord encampments all along the coastal road from Ro-Pasha to Bana."

"There must be a way in," said Drew. "Some point unguarded by the Doglords and Bastians."

"If there is, then I missed it," said Florimo with a smile and a sigh. That spoke volumes. There wasn't a keener eye in Lyssia than that of the navigator.

"We must keep looking," said Drew regardless. "I'd wager one of those Bastian captains could help us. Perhaps if we lure one of these wounded vessels out into deeper water, we'll get all the answers we need."

"You'd propose an attack on one of Scorpio's ships?" said Vega.

"It may not come down to a fight," said Florimo.

"A shame if it didn't," interrupted Vega mischievously as the Tern continued.

"They're spread out, a broken fleet. We'd outnumber a single ship by four to one."

"Two to one," Drew corrected him.

"Mathematics was never my strong suit," said Vega, "but I think you'll find we number four ships."

"There'll be only two of us taking the Red Coast," said Drew. "The other two ships will head to Azra. War awaits us on two fronts."

"Didn't I already mention that Denghi's under the control of Lady Hayfa?" said Opal. "We'd never get out of the city once we entered. The Jackals are a lost cause. The Hyena controls the road and every inch of land around Azra."

"Every inch of land, perhaps, but every inch of water?"

"Explain yourself, Wolflord," said Opal, her voice humorless.

Drew gestured beyond the port, pointing westward. "I've been here before, last year when I first encountered King Faisal. You follow the Silver River inland. It should take you to the small port of Kaza, a short distance from the Jackal city. That would be your best hope of finding somewhere to find land."

"And then what?" scoffed Opal. "We throw ourselves onto the spears of the Dogs and Hyenas? I've already told you, Azra is lost. You'd be better off pooling your resources to the north, making a concerted assault upon the Bana Gap. For what it's worth," she added pessimistically.

"And I'm telling you, I won't desert my friends. I made a promise to Faisal and the people of Omir, just as I made a promise to all the free people of the Seven Realms. I will see the tyranny of the Cats and their allies broken."

He stepped up to her, loosening his kash so she could see his face, his voice measured and meant for her ears alone.

"You swore to serve me during these dark days, did you not? The time of the Catlords is over, their union forever broken. Your own brother and father have conspired against their fellow felinthropes down the years. You've even aided them yourself. You're with High Lord Tigara now, and the Tiger is with me. I won't beg you, Opal, and I'm not going to command

you. I ask you to show the honor that your brethren from Braga have been incapable of. Fight for me, Opal. Aid the Jackals of Azra and break their enemies' stranglehold. I'll be waiting for you in Bana. I'll need you in the north when you're done."

The fire in her eyes gradually subsided as Drew's passionate words sank in. She nodded slowly.

"I'll take two of the ships up the Silver River. This will be good for the warriors who hide within their bellies: the Furies are itching to wet their blades. Lord Chollo can accompany me."

Chollo, the Cheetahlord of the Teeth who awaited Opal on another ship, was inextricably tied up with the political uprising in Bast. It was a terrible web of betrayals. Chollo had been a longtime staunch ally of Tigara, Cheetahs and Tigers as close as brothers. When Opal revealed to the High Lords of Bast that Chollo's son had been murdered by her brother, Lord Onyx the Panther, many years ago, it had caused an uproar. Onyx had killed Chollo's son out of jealousy, then framed Taboo, the Tigerlord Tigara's granddaughter. Lord Chollo now ached for revenge. Only a teenager at the time, Taboo had been banished by the Forum of Elders and sent to the volcanic isle of Scoria to fight in the gladiatorial arena known as the Furnace. This was where Drew had first met the Weretiger, and an unlikely friendship was formed. Taboo and the other survivors of the Furnace now languished somewhere in Omir—perhaps Azra or Bana—and it was up to Drew and his allies to set them free.

"That sounds like a fine plan," said Drew, chancing a smile, hopeful for one in return. He was disappointed.

"It's a plan, anyway," she grumbled. "Sharklord, take your ship around the headland. I would be reunited with Lord Chollo at the soonest. My journey must be under way."

"You see, Opal," said Vega, nodding to Figgis, who headed for the wheel, "unlike my dear young friend there, I take no offense to being referred to as 'Sharklord.' I've a sneaking suspicion you're actually rather fond of me. Can't say I blame you. As big fish go, I'm quite the catch."

Drew watched as the crew of the *Maelstrom* set about hauling anchor, the tattered sails catching the meager winds as the boat came about. Florimo joined Figgis at the ship's wheel, passing on what knowledge he had garnered from his scouting mission. Meanwhile, Vega continued his charm offensive on Opal, the Werepanther leaning on the prow rail, her back turned to the pirate prince. Drew shook his head as he watched the Sharklord.

"They say he can charm a pearl out of an oyster," said Casper, appearing at Drew's side.

His chest was puffed out and proud, his admiration for Vega growing by the day. Drew couldn't help but think of his foster father, Mack Ferran, the man who had raised him as his own, sadly gone from this world just like his mother; and of King Wergar, killed long before Drew would discover he was the deposed ruler's long-lost son. Casper was lucky to still have

a father, regardless of Vega's outspoken, sometimes outrageous, ways.

Casper chirped away. "He's a way with the ladies, my old man, doesn't he?"

Drew tousled the boy's hair with his one hand. "That way might get him killed if he isn't careful."

3

A WAVE OF STEEL

HE HAD EXPECTED MORE.

Seated in a white leather saddle upon a pitch-black charger, High Lord Oba turned about, hand resting upon the pommel of the silver sickle at his hip. He glanced back down the road, watching the sea of black-plumed golden helmets as they rose and fell at his back, marching east along the Great West Road.

When they had arrived in Westland's capital of Highcliff two days before, the Pantherlord Oba and his personal guard had found a panicked, nervous Lionguard and a city gripped by curfew. Lucas's soldiers, unaware that the union of Catlords was broken, had bowed humbly before Oba. No dignitaries awaited them; the young Lion king was absent from his throne, having taken to the battlefield, and Oba's son, Onyx, the fabled

Beast of Bast, remained camped in the Badlands with his army, waging war upon the remnants of Sturmish resistance. Highcliff had been left essentially unguarded, with the Pantherlord focused solely upon those foes who yet lingered on the frozen slopes of the Whitepeaks. The Redcloaks remained bowed as the Goldhelms disarmed them, escorting them to Traitors' House, Highcliff's old prison. As coups went, they didn't come any easier for Oba; the Pantherguard now controlled Westland's capital.

So Oba and his soldiers had taken to the Great West Road in search of his son. Personal guard was too simple a description for the force of Goldhelms who had landed in Westland with the High Lord of Braga. Here was Oba's own private army, fresh from Bast, held back from the war in Lyssia for far too long. These golden-helmeted warriors would help Oba elevate his son to the position he so richly deserved: King of all Lyssia. The Lions had had their moment and blown it. Leopold had been unfit to rule, unable to control the Seven Realms. When the Panthers had coaxed Lucas into murdering his own father, they had hoped this would herald a new beginning. How wrong they had been, replacing one madman with another. Now was the time for the Panthers. The world was theirs for the taking.

The road was a rutted affair, wide enough to accommodate six men walking abreast. The land was rolling and pleasant just as he had heard tell, with occasional gray crags breaking up the green canvas, a world away from the steaming jungles of Bast.

A lush patch of woodland flanked the road uphill to his right. Fine for hunting in, Oba suspected. He missed hunting, and was looking forward to tasting what Lyssia had to offer in that quarter. A handful of his more capable allies rode around him, therian lords loyal to Braga who had accompanied him on his epic journey. Bastian Werelords of all shapes and sizes had deserted the Cats, from Mammoths and Monkeys to Cobras and Crocodiles. Each had turned on those who had once been their masters as the Forum of Elders was sundered. All thanks to this Wolf boy, Drew Ferran, and Oba's wretched daughter, Opal. Was there any wound that hurt more than the cut inflicted by one's own blood? The girl was dead to him, and if he ever saw her again he would ensure she was dead to the world.

Oba faced forward once more, glancing up at the weak, anemic sun. These Lyssians called this their summertime. The Panther laughed, then shook his head, his thoughts returning to their eerily muted arrival in the Seven Realms. He had sent a messenger ahead, the swift-of-wing Vulturelord Ithacus. Could the avianthrope have gotten lost in this alien country? Was Onyx's army truly that hard to find? He had expected a fanfare from his son. He had expected pomp and an honor guard to escort his troops into the Badlands.

He had expected more.

"Let them have it," whispered Lord Reinhardt, and the silent signal was given.

A volley of arrows erupted from the trees, spraying the middle section of the Bastian entourage as it passed. Bushes and undergrowth were torn apart as horses leapt from the dark shadows of the woodland, out onto the lush slopes, thundering down into the broken ranks of Goldhelms. A hundred Knights of Stormdale rolled down the hillside in a wave of shining steel that broke into the invaders' flank. Famed and feared though the Bastians were as warriors, they were caught utterly by surprise, and struggled to retain a semblance of order as the plate-armored riders cut through their midst.

To the left of the panicked force, more horsebacked Lyssians emerged, charging from a gully previously obscured by the crags. They crashed into the rear of the Goldhelms, who cried out as sword and hoof pounded down upon them. With the knights now clear of the woodland, the archers advanced, choosing their targets carefully as the Bastians broke for cover. The din was sudden and deafening: horses snorting, shields breaking, soldiers screaming, limbs snapping.

Reinhardt was at the melee's heart. His great antlers stood proud on his head, dipping and goring his enemies on one side as his greatsword scythed down on the other. Other young bucks had shapeshifted in the battle, staying close by the Lord of Stormdale, their own tines tearing into the men from the south. But the Lyssian Staglords weren't the only therian-

thropes who fought. A huge red-fleshed Bastian Werebuffalo, its bearded mane rattling with beaded braids, swung an ax in a deadly arc, skittling horse and rider as they closed on it. A younger Werepanther, half the size of the Beast of Bast, lashed out, its claws and sword slashing at the knights as it surrendered to the frenzy.

Reinhardt urged his horse toward the Buffalo, attempting to draw the monster's attention, raising his greatsword to try to deflect the bone-shattering progress of the ax. The mighty blade succeeded in diverting the weapon, sparks flying as the ax bounced up toward Reinhardt's face. He turned away, feeling the impact as he tumbled from his steed onto the pitted road. He shook his head, trying to clear his vision, spying one of his own severed tines lying in the earth a few feet away.

Reinhardt dodged as the Buffalo's weapon came down, carving fresh ruts into the road. He raised the greatsword to parry the next blow, his entire right arm shuddering as the Bastian's blade struck home, hefted by two mighty, muscled arms. The sword was slipping in the Staglord's grasp now, stunned as he was by the sheer might of his enemy's attack. Blood trickled into the corner of his eye, threatening to blind him. The sun was blotted out by the raised ax as the Buffalo attempted a deadly swing.

The next sound was the Buffalo's gurgling cry as the weapon tumbled through the air, his severed forearms following it to the earth. As the Bastian Werelord staggered into the throng

of combatants, its limbs left behind, another Staglord appeared in its place. Baron Hoffman thrust his hand toward Reinhardt while flicking blood from his broadsword. Reinhardt seized his great-uncle's open palm and struggled back to his feet.

"Bit early to be lying down on the job, nephew," said Hoffman, glowering at the battle around them.

"You have my thanks, uncle!" shouted Reinhardt, his eyes searching the throng. "My brother—have you seen him?"

"Milo?" Hoffman was suddenly alarmed. "I thought the boy was to stick close to you?"

"He was," snorted Reinhardt ruefully. "He was."

Over the heads of the battling knights and warriors, toward the front of the broken column, the very boy in question had somehow found himself mere yards from the Bastian high command. Milo was on foot, having lost his mount in the initial charge. He was supposed to shadow his older brother, with Reinhardt's most trusted knights keeping their eye on the lad. But misfortune had struck the young Stag, his horse finding a rabbit hole and snapping a leg before joining the fray. Milo had been catapulted from his maimed mount, landing with a crunch within spitting distance of a gaggle of Goldhelms. Small as he was and shrouded in his soot-gray cloak, the boy looked an insignificant target to the southern warriors, the Bastians instead turning their attention to the ferocious knights.

Along the line Milo had crept and dashed, looking for an opportunity to prove his worth. So often dismissed on account of his youth, he yearned to do something momentous, strike a blow against a mighty opponent, perform an act worthy of the storybooks. His older brother, Reinhardt, was his most vocal naysayer, urging Milo to steer clear of all danger. Thankfully, his great-uncle, Baron Hoffman, was more trusting, accepting the thirteen-year-old's desire to impress. Every knight had to prove himself at some point, his uncle had said. Now he dodged through the mass of fighting men toward the leader of the Bastian battalion.

Unmistakably the most powerful fellow in the company, the Goldhelm commander sat astride an enormous dark warhorse that reared and lashed out with its hooves. The clatter of iron shoe on helm caused Milo to shudder as one after another, the knights fell beneath the warhorse's feet. The rider's black skin gleamed, flashing purple and blue in the bright sunlight, gleaming with sweat as he hacked away at the men of Stormdale with a shining silver sickle. An arrow was buried in the small of his back, and another in his thigh, but he paid them no heed, baring sharp feline teeth as he set to work. Almost seven feet tall, the rider was as large as any man Milo had ever seen, and twice as frightful.

The boy pulled back his hood, shifting his cloak away from his sword arm. The stubby antlers had already appeared upon his brow, but the discomfort of the change had been pushed

from his mind. He was a lord of Stormdale: the Stag was his birthright, his heritage, his gift. The gray cloak fluttered free, revealing a breastplate beneath, a leaping buck fashioned upon the polished steel. In his hand he held a shortsword. The blade felt heavy in his grasp, the boy suddenly weighed down with dread and doubt as the rider caught sight of the young therian.

What in Brenn's name are you doing, Milo?

In an awful moment of realization, it occurred to the lad that he had made a terrible mistake. The man snarled, his face cracking and shifting as the Catlord emerged further. Thick black whiskers emerged from the face, sharp as needles as they broke the flesh. The Panther's eyes shone green as its canines descended from its gums like guillotine blades. It lifted its sickle, spurring the boy into action. Milo darted forward, swiping down with his blade at the Panther's bare thigh, hoping to open it up. Instead the horse reared once more, its hooves looking to strike out. Before it could connect, Milo's shortsword had found another target, cutting the leather straps that held the saddle in place. Seat and rider came away from their mount, crashing to the ground as the breathless young Stag remained standing.

His moment of victory was short-lived, as the Panther's claws flew out and caught him by the breastplate. Horror seized Milo as the giant pawed hand found purchase on the edge of his chest, gripping the armor's edge beneath his armpit. He felt buckles snap and steel crumple as the Pantherlord's

hand made a fist, proud knuckles threatening to break his ribs. Milo gasped for air as the Bastian commander rose onto one knee, pulling himself steadily upright. The boy made to strike the arm that held him, his shortsword coming down only to be deflected by the Panther's great sickle. The weapon flew from his grasp, lost in the boiling melee around them as the Bastian lifted Milo toward his jaws.

"You're only a wee one, little Staglord," said High Lord Oba, "but your antlers will still make a fine trophy! My first therian kill in Lyssia. The first of many—"

The Bastian's self-aggrandizing speech was cut short. The knight came out of nowhere, his sword smashing Oba's forearm like hammer upon anvil. Instantly Oba's hold on Milo was released as bones and muscle crunched with the impact. Only the Panther's hide-like flesh stopped the sword from cutting clean through, a deep enough gash causing blood to erupt from its broken limb.

Oba caught a brief glimpse of the knight. He wore the same armor as the other riders, but his was tarnished and dirty, streaked with blood and mud. His helmet was markedly different from those of his comrades, fashioned into the style of a snarling wolf, his face hidden within the depths of those open, steel jaws. Then came the second blow, which caught Oba square in the face with the flat of the blade. A Wolfshead blade, the runes down its length shining with silver.

"Up, Milo," shouted Trent Ferran as the giant Panther stumbled backward. "To safety! Now!"

His opponent had already righted himself, coming back at Trent with a roar. The Catlord might have been much older than the agile boy from the Cold Coast, but it was a great deal more experienced in battle. Holding the Wolfshead blade in both hands, Trent parried the Panther's first strike, the sickle forced to one side of him. Oba's knee came up, catching the youth in the exposed ribs and sending the air from his lungs. He fell to his knees, sword loose in his off-hand. Trent swung behind him, looking to punch the brute again, this time in the groin—human or therian, that was a weak spot for any fellow. The beast caught Trent's fist in the hand of its broken arm, the splintered bones grating as it squeezed tight, blood pouring from the wound as the boy's knuckles began to give.

Oba looked down with surprise as the lad's scream came out wild and guttural, almost a howl of pain, ringing out loud from the snarling wolf helm. Then the young Staglord was on the Panther's back, punching away ineffectually at its broad muscled neck. Oba twisted, trying to dislodge the brat. That brief moment allowed the Wolf Knight to act. He sprang to his feet with an uppercut, his open hand tearing up the High Lord of Braga's face. The Catlord's skin came away in ribbons, the knight's fingers leaving furrows in the flesh.

The Panther threw its head back in a bellow of pain and

rage, and the boy instantly released his hold on its shoulders and tumbled to the ground. The monster brought its hands—one good, one broken—to its face as its cheek flapped, wet and ragged.

Trent grabbed Milo by the wrist, hauling the boy back as he saw more of the Bastians beginning to arrive at their liege's side, coming to his aid. To his relief, he found the Knights of Stormdale at his back, helping him and the young Staglord back into their ranks. The Goldhelms were withdrawing, those who had disengaged from the battle at the head of the column breaking away, the warriors on horseback providing their brethren cover. Trent caught sight of the Werepanther, apoplectic with fury as the Catlord's men tried to encourage Oba back onto the charger. The High Lord of Braga raged at them, swiping at them, mopping at its bloody face as it looked past them toward Trent. The youth from the Cold Coast, brother to the Wolf king, stared back.

"I'll see you again, Wolf Knight!" screamed Oba, clambering bareback onto the mount, the horse neighing fitfully as the surviving Goldhelms scarpered down the Great West Road. There had been losses on both sides, but it was clear that victory belonged to the Staglords this day.

"I look forward to it, old man!" Trent shouted back, yanking off his helmet. His blond hair was plastered to his face, slick with sweat and grime. Golden stubble covered his jaw and throat, his eyes red-ringed and weary as if diseased.

"If you're struggling to find me, the name's Trent Ferran, brother to the Wolf of Westland. Just ask about, they'll point you my way."

Oba was already wheeling on the horse, the Panther's companions urging it to make haste before the knights attacked again. The beast continued to stare back over its shoulder as they rode away, its eyes fixed upon the youth who had wounded it so.

"Made yourself a fine enemy there, Trent," said Milo at his side.

"Seems enemies are all I've got left," muttered the tired youth.

"You've got friends here," said Milo. "Always. No matter what."

Trent managed a smile as he mopped his brow. He caught sight of his hand, the one that had raked the Panther's face. Clumps of torn skin remained caught beneath the fingertips, the ends more closely resembling claws than nails. His skin burned with fever, the blood coursing through his body hot and unnatural, granting him inhuman power. Bitten by one of Lucas's Wyld Wolves, he was now gripped by the same dark enchantment that had transformed the wild men. Day by day he was changing, turning into the beasts he despised. Trent dreaded to imagine what fate would befall him upon the next full moon. He clenched his fist and withdrew it into the folds of his gray cloak.

"He's safe!" gasped Reinhardt, appearing through the exhausted soldiers behind them, limping on one stiff leg. "Thank Brenn," he said, hugging Milo.

"Thank Ferran," said one of the knights, clapping Trent on the back. "Lord Milo would've been a goner if not for the Wolf Knight's quick thinking."

Trent turned and sheepishly smiled at his companions. Reinhardt extended a hand, looking for Trent to shake it. The knight was about to accept the offer when he thought better of it, his clawed fingers twitching within the shadows of his cloak. He chose to bow instead.

"It was nothing, my lord," said Trent. "His lordship was in peril and I stepped in."

"You're making a habit of stepping in, Trent," said Reinhardt, smiling warmly.

"You're not wrong," added Hoffman, arriving on his horse. "I'm losing count of the number of scrapes you've swung in our favor, lad. I'm glad you're on our side and not theirs."

The knights cheered, clattering their gauntlets together and calling out Trent's name. The color in the youth's cheeks deepened; he kept his eyes fixed on the broken Bastian force as it disappeared down the road.

"I've never seen such a ferocious human in battle," said Reinhardt in admiration. "If I didn't know better, Master Ferran, I'd swear there was a bit of Wolf in you after all!"

His guts in knots and his skin still crawling, Trent clenched his fists, claws digging into his palms and threatening to draw blood. He smiled at his brothers-in-arms, mindful to keep his lips closed as he did so. His slightly enlarged canines were the last thing the Staglords needed to see.

4

The Patient Prisoner

SWINGING HER LEGS out from the cot, Gretchen placed her feet gingerly on the earthen floor. Righting her body she took a moment to gather her senses, a woozy wave washing over her. She clutched the edge of the bed with her hands, fingers grasping the wooden frame as she took a breath. Lights played before her, slowly dispersing as her vision returned to normal. The Werefox's gaze went to her right leg as she turned it, hitching up the brown cloth skirt to reveal the skin beneath. The scar down her calf was pronounced and ugly, stitched together crudely but successfully. She reached down, her hand fluttering over the amateur handiwork. Her fingertips rose and fell over the raised bumps where the flesh had been synched. It wasn't the work of a magister, and she

would forever walk with a limp, but the leg had been saved.

What she wouldn't give to have Hector looking after her now with his medicine bag. Only it wouldn't be Hector, would it? Her old friend was gone, if the rumors were to be believed, replaced by a necromancer who went by the name of Blackhand. They had known one another since childhood, Hector always so kind and caring. Could the Boarlord truly have turned his back on healing in favor of death? Gretchen shivered. She thought back to the night when her wound had been received, the bile instantly rising in her throat. Lucas and his Wyld Wolves had sacked the town of Bray, butchering all they encountered, including dear Trent Ferran. She would have gladly died that night, tumbling into the Redwine rather than falling into Lucas's awful claws.

How long have I been here?

Pushing the sickening sensation aside, she reached forward and grabbed the crutch that had been left for her. Fashioned from a twisted tree root, a roll of cloth swaddled around its head, it rested against the dry mud wall. Gretchen placed it under her armpit, tentatively leaning upon it as she let the crutch take her weight. She shivered as the pains shot up her lame leg, almost sending her toppling over. Clutching the stick in her pale knuckles, she leaned against the wall. She felt the cool packed earth against her face, calming and reassuring her as she composed herself. Her body was malnourished, weakened, the Foxlady having spent an indeterminate amount of

time convalescing in her cot. Herbs had been administered, poultices applied and incense burned, but for the life of her she couldn't picture her physician's face. She had a vague recollection of a shadowy figure standing over her on occasion, waking her momentarily from her fitful dreams.

The sound of laughter caught her attention. Steeling herself, Gretchen set off toward the tattered sheet that hung over the hut's entrance, the warm summer sun illuminating the weather-worn canvas. She winced and grunted as she shuffled closer, pausing to snatch at the cloth and tug it back. The light was instant and blinding, almost bringing about a blackout. The glare gradually subsided as her eyes became accustomed to the world beyond the threshold.

Reeds and tall grasses surrounded the building, swaying gently in the breeze, the bulrushes rising as high as eight feet in places. Small birds flitted between the fronds, chasing one another and trilling as they went. The steady croaking of frogs provided a constant backdrop, the little creatures out of sight in the depths of the marshland. But it was the sound of a child's laughter that had drawn the girl from Hedgemoor from the cool confines of the hut and out into the sunlight. The mother crouched beside a burned out fire pit, tickling the baby boy's belly as he rolled in the damp earth, naked as the day he had been born.

"How old is he?"

The woman looked up suddenly, eyes wide with alarm. She

snatched the child up into her arms, holding him to her chest as she backed away from the hut. Gretchen raised her free hand peaceably, the other still clutching the crutch.

"Please, don't be afraid," she said, mortified by the stranger's reaction.

Gretchen noticed the woman's unusual build, like nothing she had ever seen before. She was short and squat, her wide head sunken into her broad shoulders. Her arms seemed more distended than those of most humans, her fingers long and splayed as they clutched the baby to her bosom. The clothes she wore were unlike those one might find in the Dales or Westland, an animal hide cloak draped over a leather smock. She had the look of the wilds about her, causing Gretchen's own fear to rise. Now she recognized the telltale signs: the flint-headed spear lying on the floor by the fire, a hunting horn close by, the bone necklace around the mother's throat. *Was this a Wylderman woman? Had she been taken to a camp of the wild men?*

Her eyes flitting around the edges of the camp, searching for movement in the reeds, Gretchen took a hobbling step toward the mother and child. She could use the crutch as a weapon if any of the savages returned, but her best chance was to transform into the Fox. She was malnourished and haggard, and the metamorphosis would no doubt exhaust whatever energy she still had, but at least she would go down fighting. Her feet slipped as she advanced on the woman. Despite the heat of the summer sun, the ground around the hut and clearing

remained moist and muddy, a fine mist steaming around them.

"I don't mean to harm you," said Gretchen, managing to smile and keep the beast in check—at least for the time being, anyway. She did not want to harm the woman, but if it meant the difference between further misfortune at the hands of the wild men and living to fight another day, she wouldn't think twice. She had witnessed their vile acts, their cannibalism, their worship of the wicked Wyrm goddess, Vala. Long ago she had been kidnapped by the Wyldermen and would have been sacrificed to the Wereserpent, except for her friend Drew Ferran, who had to come to her rescue. Her torment at the hands of the wild men had not ended there, as they had hunted her and Drew's brother, Trent, through the sinister Dyrewood, almost to the point of death. No, she was done fleeing the foul men of the forest: she would fight back, or die trying.

Gretchen caught the woman's glance toward the fire pit, her big eyes clearly catching sight of the spear that lay in the mud.

"Don't do it," said Gretchen, shaking her head and waggling her finger, hoping that the woman understood the common tongue. If she did, she was paying the girl from Hedgemoor no heed. The mother edged nearer the weapon, shifting the baby against her chest and freeing a hand, ready to snatch up the shaft. Gretchen crouched, her open hand now flexing menacingly as russet-red hair appeared over its back. Claws tore from her fingertips while her teeth sharpened to needle-fine points.

"Think of your baby, I beg you," she growled, but the woman was already moving.

Gretchen pounced.

Girl and Wylderwoman arrived beside the fire pit at the same time, the mother reaching. Gretchen lashed out with her hand, grabbing the spear and launching it back through the air. The weapon came to a juddering halt, embedded into the mud hut wall. Feeling a moment of triumph with her small victory, the weary Werefox turned back to the woman. She had read it wrong, very wrong. The mother had gone for the hunting horn instead.

The sharp blast of the horn echoed across the marshes, small birds from the nearby reed beds taking to the air in flocks. Gretchen's heart sank with the knowledge that the woman's companions would be upon her in no time. Could she really stay and fight? Or should she now turn and flee into the swamps that surrounded her? She had absolutely no clue as to her whereabouts, and to be lost in the swamp-riddled marshes was to be a few stumbling steps away from certain, sinking, drowning death.

The horn's peal ceased, and the woman removed it from her lips and tossed it to the floor, clutching her child in both hands once more. The baby had the same unusual features as its parent—the stubby neck and long fingers, wide eyes fixed upon the partially transformed vulpinthrope.

In that moment, Gretchen was overwhelmed by a feeling

of great pity for the mother and child, born into a life of brutality and barbarism. She wasn't their enemy, not truly; she just wanted to be away from this place, back on the road, searching for her friends once again. Perhaps Trent had survived the attack on the town of Bray? She had seen the young man brought down by the monstrous Werewolves that had attacked under the command of the Werelion King Lucas. Could he still live? A fire had burned briefly in her heart, hopeful that she would be reunited one day with him. Instead, that one blast of the horn had sealed her doom.

She stared at the two of them pitifully as they cowered from her, backing toward the undulating wall of reeds. She clenched her fists, wondering if she was capable of ending their lives. Was it Gretchen's place to decide who should live and die? Could she truly do it? Was it worth it? Her hands were both open now, the crutch discarded on the ground. The mother's tearful face paled as she saw the look in the Werefox's gleaming green eyes.

The net came out of nowhere, landing over Gretchen with pinpoint precision. A collection of weights that lined its edge ensured she was instantly cocooned within its constricting cords. She wriggled a hand through the mesh, her clawed fingers managing to sever a few of the bonds, but she was already toppling, crashing to the damp earth. She landed on her side, the wind knocked from her chest as she kicked and struggled, helpless as a floundering fish. The woman and child darted for

cover, keeping their distance as they retreated to the mud hut. Gretchen could hear the wet footsteps approaching through the mud, coming to a halt behind her. She twisted, trying to get a look at the wild man who had launched the net at her, but she was trussed tighter than a pig for the slaughterhouse. The noises continued at her back, squelches in the wet earth suggesting that her enemy was now crouching, his shadow passing over her. She could hear his breath, feel it as it blew through her hair and across her cheek, smell its foul, fetid stench.

"If you're going to kill and eat me, get it over with, you rotten Wylderman scum," she said, spitting through the net wrapped tight about her face. "I hope you choke on me!"

She felt his hands now, cold and clammy, as they landed on her exposed forearm. She shrieked at his touch, causing the mother and child to jump where they watched on. The hand, its fingertips rough and calloused, gripped her now, rolling her over onto her back. The man looked down from where he knelt beside her, the sun shining behind his head like a halo and plunging his face into darkness.

"Kholka no Wylderman," said the stranger, his deep voice clicking unnaturally as it caught in his throat. "Kholka be phibian."

His long fingers remained clutching her biceps on either side, holding Gretchen in her place as he looked her up and down. The Fox was still there upon the surface, a thin coat of fur covering her skin, teeth and claws still on show, but she

had no more fight in her. She was helpless. His grip was firm, head bobbing to one side and the other as he studied her. Suddenly he loomed in close, causing her to flinch with fright. She could better see his face now, his pasty complexion mottled and discolored. He shared the woman's features, large eyes unblinking as he assessed the bound girl. His wide lips were thin and stretched, downturned at their edge, granting him a sad, perplexed expression. He shook his sad face gently from side to side.

"Kholka phibian," he said again. "Hate Wylderman. You behave good, so?"

Gretchen assumed it was a question, judging by the rising intonation of his pidgin common tongue. She nodded frantically. The man raised a long finger and stroked the loose skin below his chin in theatrical fashion. He truly was the oddest-looking fellow she'd ever seen, and she felt a fool for mistaking him and his companions for wild men.

"Kholka take net. Make girl free. Girl behave?"

Again she nodded eagerly. Hesitantly his fingers set to work, slackening the ropes and weighted shots where they had enveloped and entangled her. As he worried the cords apart, Gretchen allowed the Fox to recede. She could feel the bonds loosening now, falling free as the man shook the net from her. Gretchen struggled with the last of it, ripping it loose before scrambling clumsily away from where the man crouched. He bundled up the net and placed it gingerly onto the ground before him.

"Girl leg," said Kholka. "Happy?"

She looked down at her calf, the mud caking the scarred flesh.

"You did this? It was you who took care of my wounds?"

The strange man didn't answer but instead blinked, the movement of his eyelids slow and ponderous. Gretchen glanced toward the woman and baby who hid in the doorway of the hut.

"Your wife and child?"

Once more he blinked.

"Thank you . . . Kholka," she said, managing to smile, the Fox now all but gone as she turned to the woman. "And you, my lady. I'm sorry for startling you."

"Girl no bother," said the man. "Kholka wife no speak. Girl speak to tree. Tree speak more."

Gretchen struggled to rise, slipping and wincing as her injured leg caught the brunt of her weight. Kholka hopped forward, wide feet slapping in the mud as he snatched her arm and steadied her. Like his wife he wore skins, his legs naked from the thighs down. She could see the powerful muscles there now, bulging beneath his mottled skin. They truly were the most peculiar people she had ever seen.

"Where am I?" she asked, greeted instantly by a confused cocked head from Kholka. She pointed at the ground then twirled her finger in the air. "Here? Where?"

Kholka scooped her into his arms suddenly and stepped

up to the hut. Bracing himself, he jumped fully eight feet from a standing start, landing onto the broad, sloping roof. He dropped to one knee, keeping her perched on his leg like an infant, the girl staring at him with surprise. He pointed out over the reeds, his long finger extending as it made a sweeping arc across the marshes. In the distance she could see the faint, blue-tinged outline of the Dyrewood, instantly recognizable by its vast size. It filled the horizon.

"You live here alone?" she said. "Kholka family alone?"

The man shook his head, pointing out other spots beyond the bulrushes where the rickety roofs of other huts could be seen. They were all around them. Her eyes came back to the reeds, and now she saw more of the strange faces, camouflaged by the long grasses, watching on suspiciously from the edge of Kholka's clearing. When they had arrived, Gretchen couldn't say. Perhaps they had come when Kholka had first returned, snaring her in his net. He was not alone by any means. The blast of the horn had alerted the attention of Kholka's neighbors.

She glanced skyward, trying to get her bearings. The sun was directly overhead. That put the forest to the south.

"We're in the Bott Marshes?" she asked.

"Bott Marsh over river," said Kholka. "Over river."

"We're north of the Redwine, then?"

He blinked.

"Then you can get me to my friends," she said excitedly. "Take me to the edge of your lands and I can be on my way, Kholka."

He frowned now, looking at her leg once more before shifting back to Gretchen's face.

"I need to leave," she said slowly, spelling out the words loud and clear as if that might miraculously help him understand better. "I must go," she said, pointing north.

Kholka shook his flat head, the wattle of flesh around his jaw wobbling. "Not safe. Girl sleep. Girl eat. Girl stronger."

"Girl go," she said, raising her voice in annoyance, irritated by the strange man's stubborn demeanor. She moved toward the hut's edge, readying to lower herself to the wet floor below. He snatched her wrist.

"No," he said again. "Not safe. Girl stay."

"I can't stay," she said, tugging her wrist but unable to free herself from his steely hold. "I know it isn't safe, but I'm needed out there. A war is being waged, Kholka."

"No war here," he said, shaking his sad face slowly. "Marsh folk no fight. Phibian peace."

"Here as well, Kholka," she insisted. "You can't ignore what's happening to your neighbors in Westland and the Dales."

"Phibian peace," he repeated.

She yanked hard, tearing her hand from his grasp at last, rubbing her wrist with her other hand. She dipped her head

miserably. Kholka was right—she was weak and needed rest and recuperation. With the summer sun now high in the sky, who knew how long she had lain wasting away in that cot below. But right though he was, he was also very wrong.

"You know peace now, Kholka," she said. "But I warn you, it won't stay that way. There's a world beyond your marshes, and that world's far from peaceful."

"Phibian peace." Again that expression, as if it might hold the tide of violence at bay, keep the blood from spilling.

"Like it or not, war is coming," she sighed. "I fear your 'phibian peace' will count for naught when the Catlords march through."

5.

THE BAITED HOOK

TO DREW'S EYES, the *Maelstrom* had more outfits and costume changes than a dancing girl. Gone was the fishing vessel disguise that she had worn in Denghi harbor, to be replaced by something more salubrious. Only the tattered sails remained; the lobster pots and nets flung overboard when they had abandoned the city port as a place to land. Now, colorful Omiri sashes trailed from the masts, fluttering in the breeze. The long red cloths and flags marked her as a Spyr Oil trader, hinting at the great value of the goods within her hold. The *Maelstrom's* belly was full of the Furies, feared warriors of Felos, not pots of the sought-after elixir, but the *Bastian Empress* wasn't to know this fact. Famously captained by Sea Marshal Scorpio, the gargantuan warship cut up the ocean as she roared toward

the *Maelstrom,* churning the waves white in her path. In luring the Bastian flagship onto their wake, Vega had struck gold.

"How do you know Scorpio's taken the bait?" whispered Drew. "He's the commander of the entire Catlord fleet. Surely he won't bother himself with a merchant vessel?"

"How do you think one rises to power in the navy, Drew?" asked Vega from where he crouched beside him, eyes never leaving the warship. "Scorpio didn't earn his reputation through diplomacy and good-hearted deeds. Show me a naval officer who's not a pirate and I'll show you a fraud. It's in Scorpio's blood, as sure as it's in mine."

The Sharklord's hungry smile made Drew shiver. It was dusk, and the sun was setting, painting the sky red behind the *Bastian Empress.* Vega was always at his most aggressive at dusk, something the young Wolflord had become accustomed to. The mention of piracy had clearly stirred something in him, sending him back to his grim and glorious past in a moment of reverie. After all, the war aside, Vega was the buccaneer Pirate Prince of the Cluster Isles. His reputation demanded blood.

"Perhaps he's just coming to question us? Ask us our business?"

Vega shook his head. "Look at her course, lad. That's a fighting line: the *Maelstrom*'s easy pickings in her eyes. We can only hope she's looking to intercept us. The worst that could happen would be she charges our open port side. Best, she comes across our bow to slow us down. Keep her steady, Mister Figgis!" he

called back toward the wheel where his mate held the ship's course.

"And if she rams us?" said Drew anxiously.

"We get wet." Vega grinned at him. "On an entirely unrelated topic, how are you at swimming?"

Scorpio stood on the prow of the *Bastian Empress*, smiling. It was the first time he had smiled in weeks, since the debacle at Calico Bay. His siege of the Bull's city had been going so well, Duke Brand and his allies at the point of starvation, when it had all gone wrong. Where that bag of blubber Bosa had gotten the flag codes that gave the Whale passage into the heart of Scorpio's fleet, the commander would never know. Once there, the Whalelord and his allies had struck, using surprise and lashings of blasting powder to decimate the blockade. His navy in ruins, Scorpio and a handful of vessels had limped away, heading through the Lyssian Straits and following the coast to Omir. Thankfully, Bosa had not followed, remaining in Calico; if he had pursued them, the remnants of Scorpio's fleet would have been sent to the seabed.

The Spyr trader was a lean-looking ship, built for speed. He had to laugh at the idiot Omiri, flying their red silk flags and advertising their precious cargo. Did they think the blessing of their merchant guilds would protect them from plunder? Perhaps from Omiri pirates, but the ocean was an

awfully big place, and not everyone played by the same rules.

Scorpio glanced back across the decks. His men were buzzing, close to a kill. Many of his sailors had perished in the Whale's attack, and only a skeleton crew now operated the *Bastian Empress,* but that was all he needed for such easy prey. They were a worthless crew he was lumbered with, and he never wasted any opportunity to remind them of that. He relished dishing out discipline, taking the whip to their backs himself, especially after their disgraceful showing in Calico.

The sooner this sorry campaign in Lyssia was over with, the sooner he could get back to Bast and his real work, out of the Catlords' service. Scorpio was a slaver, a dealer in blood, flesh, and bone, and he had lost out on a number of opportunities since masterminding the landing of Onyx's army on this northern continent. No doubt his friend Count Kesslar was spinning gold out of Lyssia's misfortunes. Scorpio made a mental note to catch up with the old Goat once this war was done.

Poor though the fading light was, Scorpio was able to get a better look at the trader as the *Bastian Empress* lurched closer. She was a handsome vessel, with the sleek lines and swagger of a racing galleon. Perhaps she had once served in some military capacity before being decommissioned. Waste of a good fighting ship if that were the case, reasoned Scorpio. The patchwork, multicolored sails were a nice touch, suggesting that the captain was a flamboyant fellow who was happy to improvise with repairs when needed. He could hear the red flags clapping

now, proudly proclaiming the Omiri's business. Fools. Oddly, the masts and yards were in fine shape, showing no wear and tear whatsoever. Strange that a captain might keep his timber in such fine condition, yet scrimp on sails.

She was sitting low in the water, lower than one might expect for a Spyr Oil trader. That nagged at the sea marshal's mind. He noticed the hoardings that were fixed to the trader's hull, running the ship's entire length. They rattled and clattered in their fixtures, right over the lower decks where one might expect portholes. Or gun ports.

By the time he screamed his warning, it was too late. The hoardings had fallen away, the cannons had fired, and the belly of the *Bastian Empress* was riddled with holes.

Drew and Vega were already in the water before the *Maelstrom* had unleashed her surprise attack. Both were transformed, the Shark's powerful body propelling the Wolf through the waves, heading straight for the predatory dreadnought. The murky twilight and turbulent sea gave the two Werelords plenty of cover as they approached the flagship. Drew gripped the Were-shark's mighty dorsal fin, his clawed fingers digging into the tough, gray flesh for dear life. His sword, Moonbrand, trailed in his wake, safely ensconced in its scabbard, the enchanted blade's weightlessness providing no hindrance to their passage. Vega was swimming at a rate unlike anything Drew had

imagined. The Werewolf gasped for air as they powered on, snatching lungfuls before being once again submerged. Suddenly, they were alongside the barnacle-encrusted hull of the floating fortress.

Deafened though Drew was by the waves and the warship's thundering progress, the unmistakable booms from the *Maelstrom*'s cannons filled his ears. The curving wall of timber exploded beside them, the dreadnought's vast flank ripped open by the smaller ship's surprise salvo. The crew's screams instantly filled the air as timber and iron tumbled inward and out, the Bastian ship's innards exposed to the elements. An awful groaning sounded from within as the *Bastian Empress* suddenly lurched to starboard, the sea instantly finding a way into her gaping belly.

As the waves rushed in, the mighty Sharklord turned toward a yawning hole in the vessel's hull, already half-submerged, the tilting deck within alive with the frantic activity of panicked sailors. A mariner was barking orders at the men, trying to turn them back as they rushed for the top decks, but the crew were having none of it. He was quickly barged from his perch, tumbling into the inrushing waves with a splash, just as Wolf and Shark clambered out of the foaming, surging water.

None of the mariners were in a fighting mood. Some wailed at the sight of the dripping wet therian lords as they made for the staircase, while others leapt to one side to allow them to

pass. Moonbrand was in Drew's hand, but the sailors parted before the Wolf and Shark like wheat before the scythe.

On the pitching topside of the dreadnought, the chaos only intensified. The *Maelstrom* rode the waves beside her now, the count's crew cheering as their captain emerged onto the enemy ship's decks. The Bastians were working the ropes in teams, launching lifeboats over the rails. Drew spied two officers nearby fighting over the command of a gang of men, one set upon abandoning the stricken vessel, the other keen to see them remain at their posts. He saw the flash of a dagger and the stubborn mate went down onto his knees before the deserter, clutching his bloodied stomach as the men continued to release the rowboat from its mooring.

"What do we do?" growled Drew.

"We do what we came for," snapped Vega. "We get the answers we need."

"So we snatch one of these officers," said Drew, his yellow eyes narrowing as he set his gaze upon the one with the bloody knife.

"We're not fishing for sprats, Drew," said Vega, pointing a sharp gray finger toward the forecastle where a hulking figure was busy tossing sailors down the steps in their direction. "That's who I'm angling for: Sea Marshal Scorpio, high commander of the Bastian navy."

Vega strode across the decks, Drew close behind. The Shark's rapier was out of its scabbard as they passed the gang of

seamen who were swinging the lifeboat over the side. Without breaking his step, Vega whipped his blade to the side, striking the traitorous officer who had just murdered his shipmate. Drew followed the captain of the *Maelstrom*, shocked to see the growing patch of blood where the rapier had darted in and out of the mate's exposed back. A few yards farther and Drew heard the heavy thump as the man joined his former friend's body on the pitching deck.

"Sea Marshal Scorpio, as I live and breathe!" exclaimed Vega, projecting his voice over the din. "I had hoped we'd first meet under more clement circumstances. After all, it's not often the commanders of rival fleets get the opportunity for a personal chin-wag, is it?"

Drew got a good look at the captain of the *Bastian Empress* as Scorpio tossed another couple of men down the forecastle decks to block their path. He was a remarkably ugly man with a great, jutting underbite, his throat wobbling and ballooning as he bellowed commands. Scorpio's face was pockmarked and puckered with boils. Already a series of spines and quills had emerged from his head and back, rattling with irritation as he thundered about the bridge. Taking hold of another of his companions, Scorpio screamed into his ear before hurling him down to the main deck, "Get into them, you dogs!"

"Not quite the welcome I expected," snapped the Shark-lord, his monstrous mouth contorting into a terrible, jagged

grin. "Bastian hospitality's not what it was. The least I expected was you'd crack open a vintage bottle of wine!"

"Cease your prattling, Sharklord," snapped Scorpio, alone on his forecastle now as the dozen men still loyal to him fanned out below, weapons raised in defense.

"You know you don't need to die here today," growled the Werewolf, coming to a halt beside Vega as the wooden floor juddered beneath their feet. A mighty *crack* sounded below, another huge timber buckling as the wounded ship continued to take on water.

"You'll spare my life?" shouted Scorpio.

"He was talking to your men, my dear Sea Marshal," replied Vega.

"Take the lifeboats, by all means," continued Drew, stepping past Vega and swinging his huge head from side to side, gaze leveled upon the fearful sailors. "Swim for shore, or surrender yourselves to us, but don't die in the name of Scorpio."

"You underestimate the loyalty of my crew," sneered the Bastian commander as more quills emerged from his body with a flourish. "These are brave men of Bast! Any one of these is worth a dozen of your Lyssian mongrels, Wolf!"

"I don't question where they're from, Scorpio, only where they'd like to die."

The Werewolf took another step and peeled his lips back. The Bastians got a good look at his enormous canines as they

gnashed against one another, surrounded by daggerlike incisors that could rip flesh from the bone in a heartbeat. Moonbrand shimmered in his hand, its pale white glow casting a ghostly aura over the lycanthrope.

"What's it to be, boys?" growled the Wolf. "You want to die tonight? Or would you rather die in your wife's arms, having lived to a ripe old age?"

The crew of the *Bastian Empress* tossed their weapons onto the slanting deck, blades and spears clattering as they slid along the shaking timbers and vanished overboard. "You cowards!" screamed Scorpio, his eyes bulging as his throat and chest ballooned, the puckered flesh shimmering yellow. The skin of his face flashed violet and purple as spittle flew from his spluttering lips. "You filthy, rotten cowards! You'll all die for this!"

The deadly quills of the Scorpionfish stood proud over his entire torso now, rising around his head like a poisonous crown of thorns. He set off aftward, making good his escape. Vega and Drew moved quickly, each bounding up the steps after him, but the Werefish had a step on them, and would be into the sea in moments.

Jumping up onto the prow rail of the *Bastian Empress,* Scorpio glanced back, unable to resist bellowing one last bold threat of revenge.

"I'll kill you all!"

He turned, preparing to dive, just in time to feel the flat of a shortsword strike him hard and clean across the face. Scorpio

toppled backward, crashing onto the foredeck of his own sinking ship, quills embedded in the twisted timber boards, pinning him in place. He blinked, stunned, his face smeared with his own blood as he tried to focus on the figure that hung in the air off the bow of the *Bastian Empress*.

"Good work, Casper," said Drew, winking to the young Hawk as he hovered there, sword in hand.

Vega poked the floundering Werefish in the belly with his foot before crouching over the sea marshal.

"The good-bye speech?" He balled his gray, clawed hand and weighed it in the air as Scorpio blinked blearily at him. "A bad idea in hindsight, eh?"

The Sharklord's fist descended, sending the Scorpionfish into a deeper, far more troubled sleep than he had ever known.

6

BOWED BEFORE THE GATES OF AZRA

FOR LADY HAYFA, the Mistress of Ro-Shan, it had been a day of glorious executions.

The city of Azra, once proudly proclaimed the Jewel of Omir, was now a monument to death. The local saying went that so long as Azra's walls stood, the city belonged to the Jackals. That adage had proved true to a fault. Initially the Azrans had shown resilience and fortitude in the face of their enemy, with the assistance of the Hawklords of the Barebones. But all was not well in the north. With the help of the Cat-lords of Bast, Bana had been attacked by Lady Hayfa's allies, the Doglords, demanding the immediate attention of King Faisal. Directing the majority of the avian lords north along with his greatest Jackal warriors to reclaim the Gap, he re-

mained on his throne with only a handful of Omiri noblemen
for company.

The Jackal's city had survived the bleak, frozen months,
but on the final day of winter, the Dog's and Hyena's forces
had encircled the city like a hangman's noose. Lady Hayfa had
directed the bulk of her army against Azra's southern walls,
while Lord Canan's warriors besieged the northern defenses.
Cut off from the outside world, unable to contact their comrades in Bana, the people of Azra were worn down by the brutal force beyond their walls. Come summer, Bastian cannons
had rolled into the dunes beyond the city, unleashing a stun-
ning barrage of blasting powder against Azra's walls and into
her weary heart. The body count had been horrendous, and
King Faisal was at last convinced to surrender for the sake of
his people. A deal was struck: no more blood was to be spilled
within Azra. Hayfa accepted the terms. The fabled walls had
fallen, and the city now belonged to the Hyena.

Hayfa was true to her word. No more blood was spilled
within Azra. But beyond the walls, Hayfa celebrated her triumph in high style. There were no scaffolds, no executioners'
blocks, no grand speeches for the enemies of the Hyena. One
after another, the soldiers and commanders of Faisal's army and
those nobles who had remained in the city had been marched
by Hayfa's soldiers through the streets to the Silver Gate
that faced south to the river. The defeated people of Azra had
watched miserably as the brave souls who had tried to protect

them were led to their deaths. Once beyond the threshold they were driven through the sand to where the dunes met the city's broken walls. Piles of severed heads lay stacked against the polished stone, grisly cairns that marked out Hayfa's victory.

Now that the lesser nobles and courtiers of Azra had been slaughtered, Hayfa had arrived in person to witness the main event. She had kept her distance throughout the battles, consumed by a morbid fear of assassination. It had taken the Jackal's surrender to bring her to the Silver Gate. She had ordered that the executions be carried out away from the prying eyes of the people of Azra. They were the Hyena's people now, and the last thing she needed was for them to be weeping over their slain masters and turning them into martyrs. A dozen or so Azran nobles remained, the most powerful and influential of Faisal's court and closed council. Their deaths had been put on hold until the Mistress of Ro-Shan had arrived. The new Queen of Azra wanted to savor the moment.

Surrounded by her own courtiers who traveled on foot from Ro-Shan, Hayfa rode a chair high upon the shoulders of Omiri slaves, the sedan's shimmering silk curtains fluttering in the warm breeze. The Hyena's military command accompanied them. The gathered prisoners looked up as the procession came to a graceful halt before them. At their backs the walls loomed, scorched black by the blasting powder in places, crumbling from its explosive impact in others.

From where he knelt in the sand, wrists bounds at his

back, Djogo stared up at the ruined defenses miserably. The world was a changed place. Gone was the time when the most a Lyssian might fear from a siege was the ballista or trebuchet. The Bastian black powder had transformed the face of war. Cannons had replaced catapults, and sieges were concluded in a much swifter fashion. Now, at the end of it all, Djogo found himself wondering whether he had backed the right horse. In a life not so long ago he had been a slaver in the employ of Count Kesslar, the Goatlord, a villain in every sense of the word. But when he had encountered Drew Ferran, the young Wolf of Westland had had a profound impact on him—and not just because he'd lost an eye in a fight with the lycanthrope. He had gained so much more once they became allies: pride, self-worth, and a true friend. But joining Drew on his quest against the Catlords had led him to Azra, defending a city of strangers against the Dogs and Hyenas.

Djogo glanced across at the king beside him. The Were-jackal's head was held high, chin jutting out straight while those around him, beaten and broken, kept their heads bowed. Ropes bound the humans, and silver threaded cords shackled the Werelords. Djogo had been in his element in Azra, put to use by Faisal along the walls. The former slaver was an able commander and fearless warrior, and the Jackal had come to trust Djogo as he proved himself to the king time after time. The odds had seemed fair at first, even after the Hawklords had flown to Bana with the best warriors Faisal could muster.

The towering defenses and sharp-eyed archers had been able to repel everything Hayfa and her allies could throw at them. But the arrival of the cannons had sounded the death knell of the Jackal's resistance.

Djogo saw Faisal's eyes narrow in contempt as the curtains of the sedan were drawn back and the Hyena stepped out into the fierce noon sun. With elegant strides, the Mistress of Ro-Shan approached the rows of captured therian lords and human commanders, hulking guards and slaves on either side of her, one beating a fan while another carried an enormous parasol.

When Djogo caught sight of Hayfa, it took his breath away. She was as beautiful as he recalled, their paths having crossed long ago. Her face was painted white, with dark hair piled atop her head, wrapped around and within a shining crown. A multitude of gems jingled and jangled from the crown, of all colors, shapes, and sizes, casting rainbows across her flowing white dress. Her court gathered at her back as she stood before Faisal, her executioner shifting nervously behind the kneeling Jackal, scimitar in hand.

"His crown, Your Majesty," said one of the courtiers, stepping up to offer her the twined golden rope that a day ago had rested upon Faisal's brow. Her look was dismissive, as if the Jackal's crown were some beggar's bauble.

"I'm flattered that my impending death has drawn you out of your hole, Hayfa," said Faisal, his rich, honey-toned voice

commanding her attention. His toga was torn, his once-perfect face bloodied where the warriors of Ro-Shan had worked him over.

"I'm a perfectionist, Faisal."

"You're a coward."

"I want to be sure you're dead."

"Seeing my head on a longspear won't be proof enough for you?"

"In a transitional time such as this for Azra, the last thing we need is your severed head for the people to rally behind. Your skull will be thrown into an unmarked pit in some sorry corner of Omir, along with your other body parts."

Djogo saw Faisal gulp. The Hyena turned to the former slaver and smiled.

"Ah, and here he is," she said, stepping in front of him. "Kesslar's puppet who fights for the Jackal. You've made quite an impression upon my army."

"I'm no longer Kesslar's puppet," replied Djogo, spitting into the sand at her feet. The Goatlord had dealt with the Hyena in the past. "I'm a free man, Hayfa."

She laughed, the sound musical and trilling as her courtiers joined her.

"Of course you are." She looked over his shoulder to the ropes that bound his hands together. "Freedom rather suits you."

"Save your breath, Djogo," said another prisoner nearby.

Vizier Barjin was Faisal's closest adviser, a distant cousin to the king and much loved by all in Azra.

Hayfa arched an eyebrow at him. "Vizier Barjin, isn't it?" she asked, smiling as her executioner paced behind the row of prisoners.

The old man sneered at her. "If you're here to kill us, be done with it, and stop your infernal—"

His words were cut short as the executioner's scimitar descended, the vizier's head tumbling into the sand at his knees. Gasps went up from the other prisoners, turning away from the horrific sight.

"All in good time, Vizier Barjin," she said to the wide-eyed head in the sand. "All in good time."

"Your Majesty!"

Both Hayfa and Faisal turned toward the greeting. A man in a bright green turban was waddling toward them, blue and emerald robes draped over fat arms as he waved and waggled his ring-laden fingers their way. Behind him a procession of armored men followed with a Denghi Longspear escort of Hayfa's warriors flanking them on either side. They wore leather cuirasses that covered chest and upper thighs, an outfit Djogo recognized immediately.

"Queen Hayfa, Light of Omir and Mother of the Sand!"

Hayfa smiled smugly at Faisal as the colorful courtier approached, kicking up the sand and puffing his fat cheeks in his haste. Djogo heard the footsteps of the executioner behind him,

saw the blood spatter the sand between himself and the king as the man flicked it from the blade. *Am I next?*

"What is it, Aldo?" said Hayfa, as the crowd approached under the watchful eye of her Longspears. "You would interrupt my business on this glorious day?"

The man was groveling before he'd reached her, dropping to his knees as he shuffled through the sand the remaining distance.

"I plead for your forgiveness, Your Majesty, but the lady made it clear this was of the utmost importance."

"What lady?" snipped Hayfa, as her commanders closed in around her.

Two figures walked at the head of the escorted crowd, each wearing an Omiri kash that hid their faces. Djogo had to assume these were Bastians, just like the warriors who accompanied them: the fabled Furies from Felos, home of the Tigerlords. Of the kash-shrouded pair, one was clearly a woman, her movements smooth and sinuous, almost prowling as she approached the royal party. Djogo caught a flash of her skin beneath the desert cloak and robes, so dark that it seemed almost purple beneath the sunlight's glare. His heart caught in his throat: a Werepanther?

"That's far enough," said Hayfa, her voice tinged with anxiety at the arrival of these unexpected guests. "What possesses you that you should bring strangers before me, Aldo? May I assume that none carry weapons?"

"Correct, Your Majesty," replied the squat man, humbly. "I took the precaution of removing their swords when they arrived in Kaza port. They've been most accommodating."

She gave him a withering look. "Never trust anyone who's happy to hand over their blade." Eyeing the strangers, her personal guards leveled their weapons at the two kash-wrapped figures. "Well? Introduce yourselves, and be quick about it. And show the Queen of Azra some respect while you're at it."

The two reached up and unhitched their kashes, unraveling the lengths of cloth until they hung around their necks like scarves. While the woman remained standing, staring at Hayfa defiantly, the man dropped to his knee beside her, his head bowed. The fellow was well into his eighth decade, the hair atop his scalp graying, olive skin stretched thin across his fragile face. He looked weak, but the former slaver knew well enough that appearances could be deceptive. As for the other, Djogo had never met the woman—why in the Seven Realms would he have?—but he recognized the Beauty of Bast instantly, as did Hayfa.

"You brought Lady Opal here?" gasped Hayfa, her composure lost as her men began to close in around the Bastian Werelady.

"Opal will do just fine," replied the Pantherlady, raising her hands peaceably.

"As far as I know, all Bastians are our allies, Your Maj-

esty," said Aldo apologetically. "The lady said she had urgent news for you!"

"The lady is no ally of ours," snapped Hayfa, her white paint cracking as her face contorted. "She has turned upon her own. Isn't that right?"

"Your man was correct about one thing," said Opal as her guards held their blades to her and her companion. Behind her the Furies remained surrounded, encircled by the Longspears, the tension heightened suddenly by the turn of events. Djogo glanced up, the executioner shifting awkwardly between him and Faisal as the drama played out.

"And what is that?" said Hayfa.

"My news is urgent, Hayfa of Ro-Shan."

"It's *Queen* Hayfa of—"

"You will hand over King Faisal to my safekeeping, you will take your forces—abandoning your cannons—and depart back to your own lands immediately."

Hayfa barked and snarled, wide-eyed and apoplectic with outrage, her face quickly shifting, paint crumbling away. Dark hairs tore from her skin as the dark snouted muzzle of the Hyena burst forth.

"You think you can order me around, betrayer of your own brother, enemy of your own people? Word reached me well enough! You stalked into the Forum of Elders in Leos with the Wolf by your side, using duplicity to get close to the High

Lords before committing your treasonous acts. You thought you could do the same with me? I see you haven't brought the Wolf this time, though."

The Werehyena glowered at the slender old man who knelt beside Opal, his head bowed, blades lowered to him.

"Will you agree to my terms?" said Opal, her voice a low growl.

"Terms?" laughed the Hyena. "You have no terms! You've nothing to bargain with!"

"That's a no then?"

"Of course it is!"

"So be it," hissed Opal. "Chollo."

Djogo had fought foes that were faster than he was in the past, men who seemed to be one step ahead of him, moving before he had had time to think. The young Wolf was one such opponent, gifted with a preternatural speed—even for a Werelord—that Djogo had never before witnessed. But even Drew Ferran's lightning reflexes paled in comparison to those of the old man. One moment he was kneeling beside Opal; the next, he was hurdling the surrounding blades in one blindingly fast bound. The Hyenalady sprawled in the sand beneath Chollo as the fully transformed Cheetahlord encircled her throat with his claws.

"Is that still a no?" asked Opal. Hayfa's guards now looked panicked, unsure of whether to keep their weapons trained on

the Pantherlady or to turn them upon the aged Werecheetah who pinned their mistress to the ground. Opal was shifting now, too, the black fur of the Panther bristling through her skin, her teeth shining as she grinned hungrily at the terrified Hyena. The Beauty of Bast tossed her traveling clothes aside, unencumbered by the robes as powerful feline muscles rippled across her body.

"The king!" shouted Djogo as the executioner moved, making his own mind up with the stalemate.

The executioner's scimitar went high as he lunged across to Faisal. Opal was already there, having sent the surrounding guards sprawling as she leapt to the king's aid. Her clawed hand flashed, and a sickly tearing sound erupted from the executioner's throat. The man faltered as he dropped his weapon into the sand. His jaw went slack, throat yawning open as his head joined those in the dust at his back. Opal stood behind Djogo and Faisal now, ducking down swiftly to slash at their bonds, rope and silver-threaded cord tumbling loose as she freed the prisoners.

"I owe you my life," whispered Djogo, looking up at the Pantherlady in awe, but she wasn't listening. She was focused upon the Hyena, who still lay helpless in the sand, the Cheetah at her throat. The Furies were already busy disarming the Longspears who had escorted them to the Silver Gate, reclaiming their own weapons and turning them on their enemies.

"You leave your cannons, your weapons, and your dignity behind in the sands," said Opal, panting with the excitement of the kill but holding her own bloodlust in check. "Return to Ro-Shan and be grateful you still have your life, Hyena. Azra belongs once more to the Jackals."

7

THE WOLF KNIGHT

TRENT DREW THE whetstone across his sword, the droning sound of tool against steel familiar and comforting. He closed his eyes, letting the stone find its own rhythm, the Wolfshead blade whistling beneath its touch. He was back in the farmhouse on the Cold Coast, the wind singing beyond the bedroom window, rain pattering the glass, Drew snoring in the bunk above him. These were the sounds of home, the sounds of family. Yet there was something else new to the daydream. A scratching, grating sound, like fingers against slate. The noise was unwelcome, didn't belong, and it came from the window. He glanced up from his bunk and caught sight of the beast outside, clawed fingers scraping down the pane of glass. The

monster's fist struck out, shattering the window. Blood, rain, and flying shards showered the young man as the Wolf lunged for Trent in his bed.

He shouted as he stirred from his fantasy, causing those nearby who were gathered around their fires to start. A couple of knights called over to the young Westlander, showing concern for his startled cry. Trent smiled sheepishly, dismissing them with a grin before turning back to the sword and stone. The palm of his right hand had been opened, the whetstone slipping from its course as he had drawn flesh across steel. He clenched his hand, cursing his foolishness. His fingertips were dark and discolored, nails replaced by claws. *What manner of monster am I becoming?* Letting go of the sword, he looked to his left hand, the two smallest fingers missing. He had lost them in a fight with Wyldermen, as he and Gretchen had fought for their lives in the Dyrewood. Gretchen was gone now, dead no doubt, Lucas and the wild men of the forest responsible for all Trent's pains and ills.

The night of the attack on Bray, while the town blazed at his back, was burned into his mind's eye for eternity. The bite he had received from the monstrous Wyld Wolves of King Lucas had altered him forever. Wyldermen were bad enough, but these twisted souls had been transformed by dark magicks. He could feel it, day by day, his body shifting, a gradual metamorphosis from human into . . . what? Trent didn't like to think

of it, couldn't bring himself to say it. He knew enough about therianthropy to understand that it was a natural, inherited gift for the Werelords alone. For a human to change? That was a curse that would eventually kill a man, if not drive the poor fool insane. The last full moon had almost been the death of him, the fever laying him low. Reinhardt and Magister Wilhelm had watched over him, fearful for his fate. When he had come through the other side of the sickness, the Knights of Stormdale had rejoiced, praising Brenn for his favor. But Trent knew better. He had broken the back of the fever: it had its claws into him now. The next full moon, a matter of weeks away, would be quite different. *That which doesn't kill you makes you stronger:* one of Pa Ferran's old sayings.

Trent stared up at the dark night sky. She was up there, her sickly glow obscured by the clouds. He craved a glimpse of her, half-formed like a lidded eye. The moon had a strange effect on him: entrancing, empowering, nausea inducing. His skin itched and burned, reacting to her light, the hairs pricking across his flesh, thickening, darkening. *Is this what Drew experiences?* He looked down at the Wolf helm beside the fire, the orange glow dancing over the polished steel's grotesque, snarling features. He shivered.

"You cut yourself?"

Trent jumped, looking up to find the boy, Milo, standing beside him. The lad had a way of creeping up on you when you

least expected it. If he didn't make the cut as a nobleman perhaps a future in the Thieves Guild awaited.

"It's just a nick," said Trent, trying to hide his bloodied hand from sight. "What are you doing creeping about? Shouldn't you be bedding down?"

"Shouldn't you?" Milo countered. "It's an early start in the morning. My brother says we ride for Grimm's Lane—the Vermirian Guard believe the road to be theirs. Let's see if we can put some doubt in their minds, eh?"

Trent had to admire the boy's bloody-minded optimism. Surrounded by grown men, Milo played the part, a knight like the rest of them only a foot or so shorter. Trent's father had another saying: *If you're good enough, you're old enough.* He had never been sure of what that meant, but, looking at Milo in the leaping stag breastplate, shortsword on hip, it was becoming clear. Regardless, though, Trent couldn't abide seeing the boy in peril again.

"Try to keep away from the sharp end of the ruckus this time, my lord," said Trent.

The lad looked hurt. "I'm not here as a passenger. I'm here to fight."

"For your own sake, stay out of the vanguard. Please, avoid putting yourself in harm's way again."

"That's the whole point of being a knight, Trent," said Milo moodily. "Danger comes with the territory."

Trent could feel his irritation growing, the boy's persis-

tence getting under his skin as the moon emerged overhead. "Listen to me, Milo. The next time you get yourself in a hole, I might not be there to haul you out of it. I can't be nursemaiding you—"

"Nobody asked you to!" shouted the young Stag, drawing the attention of the other knights nearby, some rising to approach.

"Yet that's what happened!" snarled Trent, his head beginning to throb. His teeth felt too large for his gums, grating against one another, blood welling in his mouth. Why was the boy angering him so? He was usually patient with Milo, but not this night, not under the moon's glare.

"You don't get to tell me what to do, Ferran," said the boy petulantly, color rising in his cheeks as others approached, drawn in by the commotion. "I'm a Staglord of Stormdale. I'm your superior!"

"You're just a child," growled Trent, slapping his bloody hand against his face now as he pressed his forehead into his palm, trying to drive away the headache. His mind was fogging now, the boy's voice vexing, annoying him, a flea on a hound's hindquarters. *Just shut up, little lord . . . Shut UP . . .*

"You're not that much older than me," said Milo defiantly, emboldened by the audience now as Trent turned away.

The boy wouldn't stop, just kept on whining, needing to have the last word. *Dear Brenn, leave me be.* Trent's heart rate was rising, his hot breath coming out in short, ragged gasps.

Silence the boy. His world was turning, the moon on top of him, stifling, suffocating, his own shadow pooling out around him like an oil slick.

"Face me, Ferran," said Milo, reaching out to clap the shaking young man across the shoulder.

No sooner had the boy's slap connected than Trent was turning, his three-fingered hand seizing the adolescent Staglord by the breastplate. The gathered knights went for their weapons, but they were all too slow for the youth from the Cold Coast. His body twisted as he rose, lifting Milo off the floor, his other arm extending, brought back ready to strike. His fingers were outstretched, claws straining, his hand an open paw poised to deliver a deathblow. A tiny part of his being was aware that it was just a boy in his grasp, a foolish, stubborn but ultimately brave young boy, but it was drowned out by the rage within. A beast was roaring in his heart, wanting to rend and shred anything and everything that stepped in his path.

"Trent, no!"

The voice boomed across the camp, causing Trent to cease his assault. The circle of knights who warily encircled him separated to allow Lord Reinhardt to approach. He was flanked by Magister Wilhelm and Baron Hoffman, the elderly Staglord transformed, antlers towering above his majestic head. Reinhardt remained in human form, his face a mask of bewilderment at the turn of events. The red mist lifted and Trent blinked, as if seeing the scenario for the first time. How had he come to be

holding Milo by the breastplate, his savage hand set to strike?

"What are you doing?" whispered Reinhardt in disbelief.

"Release him," said Hoffman with a snort, his antlers groaning as they extended to their full length. "Release him this moment or, Brenn help me, I'll open you up, lad!"

Trent looked back to the young Werelord who dangled from his clenched fist, Milo's eyes never leaving his own. *Why am I still* holding *him?* He dropped him at last, the boy scrambling backward until he came to a halt at Reinhardt's feet.

"I . . . I'm sorry," Trent said, staring at his disfigured hands in horror. "I don't know what came over me."

"I know exactly what came over you," grumbled Hoffman. "That madness grips you every time we battle. I had no problem when you were channeling it against the Catlords. But turning on your own? Upon my kinfolk?"

The old Stag's broad throat rumbled.

"I swear, my lord," said Trent, glancing up at the moon before back to the enraged Werelord. "I lost my mind momentarily, but I've regained my senses. Please believe me, Baron Hoffman, I would never harm Lord Milo deliberately. I'd never harm any of you."

He turned to the assembled knights, his brothers-in-arms, and they each shrank back, sharing the same look of suspicion. He looked to Milo on the floor, the boy's stricken face staring right back.

"Please, my lord," said Trent tearfully, holding his torn and

trembling palm out to the recoiling boy. "Don't fear me. We're friends, remember?"

"Is it any wonder he shies away from you," said Hoffman, snatching a finely polished shield from one of the knights, "when you look like that?"

The Staglord rammed the curved steel sheet into the ground directly before Trent. The Wolf Knight caught his reflection. It was his turn to be horrified. An unrecognizable face stared back, patches of hair sprouting around his throat from the top of his breastplate, his jaw distended and jutting. Worst of all were the eyes. The striking blue was long gone, replaced by a boiling amber that caught the flames from the fire.

"No wonder you've been wearing that helmet day and night," snorted Hoffman.

"What *happened* to you?" asked Reinhardt, ignoring his uncle's disgusted grumbling.

Trent's shoulders sagged, his chin hitting his chest. It was time to come clean.

"When you found me in Bray after Lucas had torched the town, I should've been dead." The crowd fell silent as the young man spoke. "He had Wyldermen fighting for him, but these were no ordinary wild men of the forest. Monstrous and misshapen, these brutes had surrendered any humanity they'd had. They were men no more; these were beasts, wolves."

"Wolves?" said one of the knights, causing a chorus of murmurs that were silenced by Reinhardt's raised hand.

"Not like Drew," continued Trent, unbuckling his breast-plate and allowing it to fall to the earth. "Ghastly monsters, a mockery of my brother's nobility, they slaughtered all in their path. I was bitten and mauled but somehow survived. When I awoke the next day on the riverbank, I saw this—"

He pulled his shirt open, exposing the skin beneath. The raised white scar of a bite wound was visible upon the dirty flesh of his shoulder.

"It had already healed. I was already . . . infected."

The knights took a hesitant step away from the weary warrior, only the therians remaining near him.

"Infected?" asked Magister Wilhelm, the old man's brow creased with concern.

"Indeed," sighed Trent. "I fear my blood's poisoned by the same Wyld Magicks that coursed through the Wyldermen's vile veins. That fever that broke after the full moon—you remember it?"

"Well enough," replied the healer. "I nursed you through it."

"And I thought it would kill me, but I came out the other side. But the next time . . ."

"The next full moon?" said Reinhardt.

Trent nodded, his voice a whisper. "I fear what I'll become. Each night I can feel my body changing beneath the moon's light. Before long, I'll be a beast just like Lucas's Wyldermen."

"Then you must leave at once," said Hoffman abruptly.

"And where should he go?" retorted Reinhardt, turning upon his uncle. "Do we turn out one of our own at the first sign of illness?"

"He isn't one of our own though, is he?"

"He was while he was winning battle after battle in our name, fighting alongside us."

"You're not listening, nephew. The lad's changing. The time will come when he'll be a danger to all around him."

"We can't abandon him," said Reinhardt, shaking his head. "He's Drew's brother, for Brenn's sake. Surely there's some cure to whatever ails him?"

"Silver?" suggested Hoffman gruffly, receiving a withering look from Reinhardt. "By now, we've all heard about Lucas's Wyldermen—the Wyld Wolves, he calls them. They're a mockery of lycanthropes. If Master Ferran here is stricken, then surely a quick and humane death by silver blade is the only kindness we could show him?"

"There may be some who can aid you, Trent," said Magister Wilhelm, raising a bony finger to interrupt. "The Daughters of Icegarden are the greatest healing magisters of the Seven Realms. Perhaps they know a way to reverse the effects of whatever Magicks are at work within you."

"The baron's right," said Trent, causing them all to turn to him. "That you don't trust me is neither here nor there. *I* don't trust me, and for that reason alone, I must be on my way."

"It would be a kindness to put you out of your misery," said Hoffman. "You're dangerous, Ferran."

Trent glowered at the baron. "Care to try, my lord?"

"Enough bickering," said Reinhardt. "What *will* you do if you lose control, Trent? Who will stop you if—or when—the beast begins to take over?"

"Don't worry," said the youth grimly. "I won't allow it to come to that."

Reinhardt shivered, understanding the inference. Trent stepped over to his kit bag, yanking out his old brown breastplate as he kicked the metal greaves from his legs. He beat the dust from the leather and swiftly began fastening it about his chest.

Reinhardt stepped up to him, seizing him by the forearm, his grip firm. His face was writ with sorrow as his eyes lingered upon his friend's twisted features. Trent looked away, ashamed of the transformation that was at work within him.

"I am so sorry, Trent."

"Don't apologize, my lord," the youth replied, peeling off the Staglord's fingers. He lifted his saddle and carried it to his horse where it was tethered to a nearby tree.

"I'm going to break camp tonight. I want to be on the road as soon as possible."

"You do right, Trent Ferran," said Wilhelm sagely. "Head north, young man, and you may seek out the Daughters of Ice-

garden. Duchess Freya is the most senior among them and an old friend of mine. If she has lived through the horrors Onyx and the dark magister, Blackhand, have heaped upon Sturmland, you may yet find hope there."

Trent smiled as he fastened his kit bag to the back of his saddle and unhitched the horse.

"You've misunderstood me, my lord magister," he said, jumping up onto the horse's back and pulling the hood of his gray cloak around his face.

"How so?" asked Wilhelm, confused.

"I don't seek the Daughters of Icegarden," the mounted youth replied, his sharp canine smile visible in the shadow of his cloak. "There's only one cure I seek."

"And what is that?" asked Reinhardt, as Trent turned his horse and began to pick his way through the assembled Knights of Stormdale.

"Vengeance, my lord," replied Trent, giving his mount's flanks a stiff kick and spurring it into life. He called back as the horse soon found its gallop.

"Vengeance!"

8

THE ONLY WAY

THE GRASSES HISSED as the wind whistled through them, shadows racing over the savannah as clouds dashed by overhead. The Longridings were an open, exposed realm, with few places to shelter, let alone hide from a foe. Crawling on her belly, the young woman edged closer to the top of the ridge, her two anxious companions crouched farther down the incline behind her. Her head at last crested the slope's summit and she gently parted the grasses.

Whitley gasped as she surveyed the land ahead. The Dymling Road was no longer recognizable; the Bastian war party covered it, a sprawling mass of slow-moving soldiers and dying fires. She spied where the Talstaff Road branched off from the Dymling, bearing west beneath the Dyrewood, the route

swamped by the Lion's army. The main body of High Lord Leon's force had already headed for Westland, having landed the previous week in Haggard. So this was the Lion's rearguard, a motley collection of the supporting players that were invaluable for any army: carpenters, cooks, and clergymen, with a fair number of soldiers providing them protection. The Redcloaks of High Lord Leon were already some way north along the Talstaff, skirting the Dyrewood and avoiding the Dymling where it continued into the Dyrewood, fearful of the woodland realm's haunted reputation.

She cursed as she looked at the forest. The old road cut straight through the heart of the Dyrewood, but its entrance was invisible, the way choked by the Lionguard's advancing rearguard as they turned off onto the Talstaff. There would be no way of entering the forest without the Redcloaks spotting them, at least not via the Dymling Road. Whitley couldn't entertain the notion of leading her companions into the wilds of the woodland realm. Besides the fact that much of the forest was impassable, there were many denizens of the Dyrewood that could bring about a swift death, including those that hunted on two legs, not just four. The battle with the Wyldermen who had seized Brackenholme was still fresh in Whitley's mind. The wild men might have been beaten, but they were still out there no doubt, licking their wounds. No, there was only one way into the forest for Whitley's party, and it was via the road. She looked back down the slope, her two friends star-

ing back hopefully. Her grim visage told them all they needed to know.

"What is it?" whispered Lord Conrad as Whitley scrambled back through the grass toward them.

"Bastians," said Whitley, "and lots of them."

"But which Bastians?" asked Eben, the young Ramlord, his slightly skewed eyes wide with concern as he fingered his little beard. "Is it the Lion or the Panther?"

"Redcloaks," replied Whitley as the three of them now set off back on foot toward their small encampment. "We need to place a scout up there on the ridge, keep an eye on them while we decide what to do. The last thing we need is some of the Lion's men wandering this way and finding our hiding place."

"We're right under their noses," said the Ramlord anxiously. "You said there were lots of them, Whitley. How many is lots?"

"Best not dwell on the details, Eben," she said with a wry smile. "Suffice it to say we're outnumbered."

Baron Eben was a nervous soul, not used to the outdoor life, especially during a time of crisis. He had served as a magister to the court of Duke Brand in Calico as his father, Baron Ewan, had before him. A caring, kind young fellow, he had shown much courage when he had volunteered to join Whitley and the Horselords on the ride north to war. Judging by his sickly pallor, she suspected he was now regretting that decision.

Arriving back at their camp, Lord Conrad hastily directed a couple of his best men back onto the ridge to monitor the Lionguard's movement. Ransome was waiting for Whitley. The old sea captain had left his ship behind in the Bull's bay to remain by the Bearlady's side, and she had grown fond of the white-whiskered pirate. Ransome gladly accepted the role of surrogate father to Whitley in the absence of Duke Bergan. As she did many times each day, the girl from Brackenholme wondered where the Bearlord was now. Knowing that he had been spotted alive in the Whitepeaks had filled her heart with joy, but she had kept it in check. She couldn't afford to believe her father lived until she was back in his arms.

"What news, m'lady?" asked the pirate captain, frowning when he saw her glum face.

Whitley described the Dymling Road's blockage. "It could be days before the Lion army moves on and we can enter the Dyrewood."

"Days we don't have, m'lady," said Ransome. "Not if we're to gather your army and reach Sturmland in a fortnight."

"The captain's correct," said Conrad. "If we're delayed, Lord Drew will be arriving in the north to face the Lions and Panthers alone."

"If he even gets that far," added Eben pessimistically.

"Gentlemen," said Whitley. "We number a hundred. We have High Lord Tigara's Furies under my command, and we

have your Horselords, Conrad. We move tonight, under cover of darkness."

"Move where exactly?" asked Baron Eben.

Ransome nodded, agreeing with Whitley's reasoning. "We strike out for the neck of the Dymling Road, cut our way through the Redcloaks until we reach the Dyrewood."

Eben's face, already drained of color, looked almost translucent. "There has to be another way? Surely?"

Whitley clapped a reassuring hand onto his shoulder. "It's the only way."

Reaching the Dyrewood's border had been the easy part. Traveling at night through the long grasses, Whitley's band found the dense walls of tangled brambles that marked the edge of the Woodland Realm. The thorny vegetation and leechlike vines wound about one another, connecting tree to ground and bush to branch, creating an impenetrable barrier that ran for mile after mile. As the riders followed the border, clinging to the shadow of the forest's overhanging canopy, Whitley couldn't help but feel the twin pangs of loss and joy: loss that she was apart from her loved ones, but joy that she could reach out and touch the forest, her home.

Eben and Ransome rode on either side of her, with Conrad at the front of the column. They rode slowly, quietly, no more

than three abreast. Should the Redcloaks discover them, they would need to move fast and stay close together. But their aim was to move unnoticed, charging at the last moment when they broke for the neck. The devil was in the details; their hopes hinged upon the timing.

"I've never seen such a thing," whispered Ransome.

"What's that?" asked Baron Eben, across Whitley's saddle.

"I'm a man of the sea, my lord. This forest . . . so large a place, so vast. My mind aches at the notion of it."

"As does mine when I think of your oceans," said Eben with a shiver, staring nervously at the woodland. "I fear the Dyrewood places both of us firmly out of our comfort zones."

"The forest is the last thing to fear presently," said Whitley, gripping her reins tight as the clamor of fighting suddenly filled the air.

All around her, the sound of heels hitting horses' flanks sounded, Horselords hollering and Furies whooping as they spurred their mounts on toward battle and beyond. The column was riding hard, having emerged out of the shadows along the Dyrewood's edge and now charging beside the Dymling Road. Whitley glanced across as she saw Redcloaks moving, snatching up weapons, the makeshift camp stirring into life as the slumbering army was rudely awoken. Their destination, where the ancient road disappeared into the forest, was only a mile or so due north, but that was a mile through the Lionguard encampment.

Hooves thundered, tearing up the dry earth and flattening bedrolls and tents. Crossbows twanged as bolts were loosed, men tumbling from horses and crashing to the ground. Screams cut the night air as Redcloaks were trampled underfoot. Swords slashed, cutting riders from their mounts. Spears flew, skewering others in their saddles. Conrad led the way, the Werestallion partly transformed, his greatsword held in one hand, shattering the Lionguard in his path. Other Horselords had followed suit, swords swinging, manes billowing, spittle frothing from their gnashing teeth. The Furies fought like men possessed, shortsword in either hand, expertly controlling their rides with their thighs.

Whitley was lost among them, Eben just about at her side, Ransome gone from view. Their progress was slowing as more soldiers now surged from their tents, putting themselves in the way of the horsemen. The occasional Catlord or therian from Bast could be seen in their midst, bounding through them, unseating riders from beasts. She could hear Conrad at the head of the charge, roaring out orders, calling for his friends to follow, but the way was becoming crowded, the momentum slowing. A Lionguard reached up, snatching hold of her green cloak and pulling hard, nearly dragging her from her mount. The horse turned, Whitley gripping the reins in one hand as its neck twisted, nostrils flaring. The soldier laughed with triumph, having brought the girl's progress to a stuttering halt. His cheer turned to a scream as her claws slashed down, leav-

ing his face in ribbons and causing him to unhand her.

Whitley's horse circled as the girl struggled to find her bearings, the flow of riders all but halted as they now found themselves engaged by the Lionguard. She cried out Conrad's name in vain; hers was just another voice over the din of battle. They had underestimated the enemy, having assumed that these soldiers would be the Redcloaks they were used to, the miscreants and mercenaries that Lucas had hired. Far from it: these were warriors from Bast, and at the first sign of a fight they were up and running into the fray. Whitley twisted about in her saddle, seeing a pair of Horselords race past a few yards away, having found a gap through the melee. She spurred her mount after them, making for the opening.

The third horse came out of nowhere, crashing into Whitley's in a crescendo of snorts, whinnies, and crumpling muscle. Both creatures went down, their riders tumbling from their saddles and hitting the dust. Whitley tried to crawl clear, wincing as she felt her leg held fast beneath the felled mount. The horse wasn't moving, steam rising from its open mouth as its glassy eyes stared up at the stars. She tugged frantically, gripping her thigh and trying to worry it loose. *Come on, Whitley.* She could hear no more horses, the last of her comrades having already passed by, at least those who hadn't already been killed. She looked up, sighting a pair of Redcloaks stepping over the dead and dying horses and riders as they approached her.

One held a sword, while the other snatched up a dropped spear from the ground, shifting its point in Whitley's direction.

There was only one way she was getting out from under the slain stallion. Whitley growled and began to shift, her ursine muscles straining beneath the dead horse, making it rise inch after inch from the floor. The men saw this as they drew in, speeding up now as they caught sight of the muzzle and canines as the beast emerged. They shouted as they came, alerting their distant comrades to her presence. Whitley roared as the Werebear took control, her thick pelt of fur shuddering as she began shaking the horse loose. She snarled as she sat upright, her thick, clawed hands pushing the corpse, lifting it, almost rolling it clear. The spear came flying, aimed straight and true for the Bearlady. Up came the slain horse's saddle at the last moment, Whitley holding it between her paws as it punched clean through the leather. With a final heave she rolled the dead mount away and bounded to her feet.

Tearing the spear out of the saddle, Whitley launched it back at the fast approaching Redcloaks. The soldier who had moments earlier thrown it at her juddered to a halt in mid-stride, feet flying forward and up into the air as the missile ripped through his torso. The second managed to close the distance, sword raised high, the silver-blessed steel destined to connect with the ursanthrope. It was the wrong move; a lunging, stabbing assault would have pinned her back, while

the high slash left him exposed from below. Whitley seized her opportunity.

In the blink of an eye she crouched before springing forward and into the Lionguard, her jaws snapping and connecting with flesh and bone. The sword now descended, still in the grip of the Redcloak's severed hand as he collapsed beneath the Werebear's great bulk and bloody attack. Whitley looked up as the man burbled and bled beneath her, spying more of the Lionguard making their way toward her. She was alone, and surrounded by Redcloaks. There were a dozen of them, many pointing directly at her and calling to each other as they saw their chance for glory. Whitley could already imagine what kind of trophy her head would make when presented to High Lord Leon.

Horses charged around her suddenly, coming from behind and racing past her flanks. Warriors wielding axes and spears leaned down from their saddles, meeting the onrushing Lionguard with weapons and war cries. Their white cloaks marked them as Longriders of Calico, the bull's head boldly emblazoned upon their shields. Transformed though she was, she could feel the beast now receding, her adrenaline having been exhausted by the battle. Yet more of the Longriders charged by as she returned to human form. She soon lost count of their number, the Redcloaks crushed beneath their hooves and blades as the Dymling Road opened up before them once again.

Whitley heard a snort at her back, turning quickly to find

a great warhorse standing over her, breathing down her neck. It was larger than any stallion she had ever seen, and it needed to be, considering the giant who sat astride it. Duke Brand, his pride bruised but eyes firing with refound purpose, extended a huge shovel-like hand down toward her. Whitley smiled as he spoke.

"Do you still have room for a foolish old Bull among your number, my lady?"

PART II

THE LINES ARE DRAWN

I

DRIED OUT

"GIRL TIRED. REST."

Gretchen sucked her teeth and wiped her brow. For a change, it wasn't Kholka suggesting she take a breather. He had given up trying to persuade the girl to ease up, the glares and growls she had thrown his way being warning enough. Not so long ago, Gretchen would have seized the opportunity to stop and recover, possibly even send for a pitcher of chilled water, but that woman might as well be dead. The Werefox of Hedgemoor was a reformed character, and there were few tasks or challenges she would shirk these days.

"Worry about yourself, Shoma," she replied haughtily, bracing herself before leaping over the stream to the opposite bank.

She landed with a wet thump in the loose mud, snatching the bulrushes to steady herself and keep from tumbling back. The Marshman called Shoma glowered at her before turning and continuing on through the reeds. He stalked past Kholka, who stood leaning on his spear, a broad smile spread across his thin lips. It seemed the entire hunting party, made up of men, was put out by the idea of a woman joining them. All except Kholka. Her friend had been quite insistent at the village meeting that she should come. That had meant a lot to Gretchen. She nodded as she caught up with him.

"Thank you," she said under her breath, the two falling in step beside one another.

"Is good," said Kholka. "Shoma tired like old woman. Him needs rest."

Gretchen laughed out loud, causing those Marshmen who were walking ahead of them to look back angrily. She clapped a hand over her mouth.

"Sorry," she whispered, feeling every inch the admonished child. "They're very serious, aren't they?"

"Hunting," replied Kholka quietly. "Serious work."

The previous weeks had seen Gretchen first accepted into the Marshman's family and then gradually introduced to his wider community. Kholka's wife, Shilmin, though unable to speak the common tongue, had taken Gretchen to her heart since the girl from the Dalelands made herself useful. Whether she was peeling vegetables for the pot or playing with little

Khilik, Gretchen provided an extra pair of hands to Shilmin. She'd proved particularly popular with Khilik, the child giggling whenever he saw her and constantly trying to snatch handfuls of her fascinating red hair. Kholka had hesitantly introduced her to the rest of the village and, though wary of the stranger, the Marshmen had reluctantly accepted her presence.

Like Kholka, Shoma was one of the village elders, and appeared to be the leader of the hunting party. The Marshmen, or *phibians* as Kholka referred to them, shared the same long-legged gait as Gretchen's friend, as well as the squat necks and broad shoulders. Gretchen's beautiful boots were viewed with suspicion, barefoot being the preferred option when it came to footwear. Indeed, all the Foxlady's clothes had been treated as outlandish by the river people, leading her to don the skins they wore in order to blend in as best she could. Her boots were her only indulgence, and she made no apologies. You could take the girl out of Hedgemoor and make her survive in the wilds, but at the end of the day she remained a princess.

There were seven in the hunting party, including the Foxlady, two of the men carrying nets over their shoulders that held their catch. Those eels and fish that still lived wriggled and writhed inside the mesh, rolling over one another as they gasped hopelessly in the air. Shoma led the way, glancing back occasionally to cast his sneering gaze over Gretchen.

"He doesn't like me, does he?" said Gretchen.

"Shoma not like drylanders."

"Not all drylanders are bad, Kholka."

"All drylanders Shoma meet bad," said the fellow with a shrug. "Drylanders not like phibians."

He wasn't wrong. Gretchen had dismissed the Marshmen as myth throughout her childhood, bogeymen of the Redwine that were used to keep children away from the water. Those who said they actually existed had sworn that they were monsters, not to be trusted. Some claimed to have killed them upon encountering them, believing the Marshmen were flesh-eating villains like the Wyldermen of the Dyrewood. Gretchen now realized nothing was further from the truth.

"Drylanders fear anything that doesn't fit in our world," sighed Gretchen. "Your people look peculiar compared to the folk of the Dalelands and Westland."

"Drylanders look pee-cool-yar to phibians," said Kholka, struggling to get his mouth around the word.

"We're scared of that which we don't understand. Marshmen would fit into that category. We tend to attack that which we fear."

"Kholka scare girl?"

Gretchen paused for a moment, afraid that she might offend him. "The first time I saw you outside your home, I'll admit I was scared. You did throw a net over me, though."

"Kholka careful. Girl was crazy."

"The girl was scared," corrected Gretchen. "Being scared can make people do crazy things."

Kholka shrugged again. "Not first time girl see Kholka."

Gretchen still struggled to understand half the things her friend said, his pidgin-common tricky to follow.

"Outside your hut, Kholka," she said again, trying to be clearer so as not to further confuse him. "That was where we first met, remember?"

"First time Kholka see girl in river. Kholka hide in water. Girl fight with boy."

His words were confused, but he said them with such conviction that Gretchen began to doubt herself. That was where they had met, when she had first risen from her sickly stupor in his home. They had not met by the river. And the only boy she fought with recently was . . .

"This boy," she said. "What color was his hair?"

Kholka hooked his thumb and gestured skyward without looking. "Sun."

Trent. Gretchen cast her mind back, slowly recalling bickering on the riverbank after ambushing the Lionguard in the Dalelands. Gretchen had been taking a moment, her toes dangling into the chill waters of the Redwine, her mind running away with itself. Looking up, she had glanced at something in the water. She had thought it a rock until it blinked, and then it was gone, disappearing beneath the surface.

"That was *you*, Kholka? In the river? Watching me?"

"Kholka's river," he replied defensively. "Kholka fishing."

He wasn't lying—the Redwine was his as much as any

man's. In the past weeks, she had seen him at work, stalking through the swamps with his hunting javelin, spearing the smaller fish in the shallows where marsh became lagoon. She had followed him as far as she could before he left her behind, diving into the water and disappearing from view. Gretchen would then head back to his hut, to Shilmin and Khilik. Kholka would return much later, dripping with water, bigger, meatier fish skewered on his spear, captured in the most dangerous depths of the Redwine. She had not wondered how he had been able to swim and hunt so successfully. Until now.

"How do you get to be such an expert hunter, Kholka? How do you catch the big fish, swimming underwater with a spear? Could you teach me?"

He shook his head, the possibility out of the question. "Phibians live by river. On river. In river."

It wasn't much of an explanation, but it was all Gretchen was going to get from him. She walked on a while longer without saying anything, the sun beating down overhead, turning mud to dried-out clay. Birds chirped, taking flight when Shoma led the hunters through their territory, nesting waders making haste on their long, spindly legs. The substantial splash of water-bound mammals sounded on occasion, as they escaped toward deeper water. The phibians might have been fishermen, but they wouldn't turn down the opportunity to snare an otter or beaver. The meat was tasty enough, but the pelts were even more valuable. Summer wouldn't last forever.

"Where are we heading?" asked Gretchen eventually. It felt like they were moving to higher ground, away from the water.

"Shoma's father," replied Kholka. "Lives marsh's edge, alone."

"Kind of like an outpost?" She couldn't imagine a lonelier life, eking out a solitary existence in a swamp. "He's expecting us?"

"No."

"You know, whenever you're ready you can let me go on my way. You can see I'm better now."

She walked with a limp now thanks to the wound she had taken in the leg, but she felt as fit as she'd ever been. Caused by the claws of one of Lucas's Wyld Wolves, the injury was as stubborn as one delivered by silver. However, a few weeks outdoors with the Marshmen, grafting, hunting, helping where she could, had been good for her. And all Drew's speeches about aiding the weak, the hopeless, the helpless, the have-nots: they made perfect sense to her now.

"Not safe," said Kholka. "Leave when safe."

She grabbed him by the forearm, his leathery flesh cold to the touch. "You don't understand, Kholka. It will *never* be safe. There's a war out there. I'm needed, I can help."

She stopped speaking as she watched his smooth brow rise high and he looked down at her hand on his arm. She released her grip and those big, bulging eyes leveled on her.

"You could help," she said. "All of you. Everyone has a part to play."

"Not phibian. Not our world, your world."

"This is *our* Lyssia, Kholka. Not just the Werelords and the townspeople—the drylanders, as you'd call them. Phibians, therians, and drylanders—we *all* share this world. We should fight for it, together."

It was the sort of speech she'd heard Drew make countless times, the kind of talk that got her heart racing, the blood pumping, the hairs on the back of her neck standing on end. But coming from Gretchen, or delivered to this audience, it didn't have quite the same impact. Kholka turned away and continued walking.

Gretchen snapped the reeds around her as she reluctantly trudged after the Marshmen. Were they simply scared of what was out there? Did they fear further persecution? She was about to ask when a terrible wailing ahead pulled her from her thoughts. Kholka was already running, pushing past the phibians in front of her as he burst through the bulrushes into the clearing ahead.

Shoma's wailing continued unabated as the rest of the hunting party staggered into his father's plot of land, his sobbing joined by the cawing of a crow. The hut was built on drier land than Kholka's home. Gretchen figured they were still a good many leagues from the Dymling Road where it skirted

the Dalelands. Still far from civilization—but close enough, apparently.

The hut was a burned-out shell, the grass roof long gone and its blackened walls crumbled. Two wooden stakes had been driven into the ground at right angles to one another, crossing to make a large X. The body that hung from the frame might have once been human, but looking at the desiccated, misshapen form, it was hard to imagine it. She looked away in disgust, her eyes finding a discarded shield on the floor. Even covered in mud and blood, the roaring lion head was clearly visible.

As a child growing up in Hedgemoor, she had once seen a toad pinned out in the grass, shriveled in the sun, by the cook's sadistic young son. She bent, picking up the shield, and brought her eyes back to the corpse on the frame. Drained of fluid, its limbs were freakishly long, and its hands and feet had been lashed to the timbers. The large, sloping head slumped forward, a constantly shifting swarm of flies buzzing around it. A lone black crow sat upon the back of the head, pecking away at the threadbare flesh.

Shoma stumbled forward, wailing, shaking his spear at the bird until it took flight, squawking. The other horrified Marshmen stood staring at the body of their leader's father, disbelieving. Kholka turned to Gretchen as his distraught friend dropped to the baked earth, curling into a fetal position. He took the battered Lionguard shield from her hand.

Gretchen saw Kholka's throat suddenly balloon, heard his

chest cracking and popping as it shifted shape. That low-sunk head dropped a little lower, stubby neck vanishing altogether as body and skull seemed to merge into one. His eyes grew bigger, his mouth wider, his flesh rippling, toughening, turning from pasty gray to a murky mottled green. Before she had had time to think he was two feet taller, the thighs atop his powerful legs the thickness of her torso. He tossed the helmet to the ground and stamped on it with a huge, webbed foot, buckling it in an instant.

"Now," said the Werefrog, his voice a low croak and dripping with anger. "Phibians fight."

2

QUILLS AND ILLS

"**HOW CAN YOU** be sure he's telling the truth?" asked Drew, staring down the sea marshal of the Bastian navy where he stood chained to the brig wall. There was little room for maneuvering within the cell, just enough space for a jailer to step in to feed and tend to the prisoner. A cage of dark metal bars surrounded him, the door shut but unlocked, the Werefish posing no threat in his current predicament. A chain of iron links looped about his wobbling throat, pulled taut around his jutting jaw.

"I could keelhaul him, but I think he might enjoy that," said Count Vega, smiling as Scorpio snarled at him.

"Why would I lie to you, Wolflord?" spat the Werefish. "My war's over, my life, too, for that matter. When the Catlords get

wind of the *Bastian Empress*'s fate, my neck'll be for the block."

"You shouldn't be so negative," said Vega. "Perhaps we can find an opening for you in the Lyssian navy. I know of a poop deck that needs mopping. Come to think of it, the privy could do with a good scrub, too."

Scorpio laughed.

"I'd heard so much about you, Vega, but now I see most of it was just rumor of your own creation. Has there ever been a Werelord more in love with his own voice?"

The Sharklord only grinned wider. "But it's such a wonderful voice, don't you think, Scorpio? This voice has inspired a thousand sailors and broken as many hearts. It would be a crime to hide it away for fear it might make lesser therians such as yourself feel somehow unworthy."

Scorpio leveled his hateful gaze on Drew, ignoring the count's mocking words. "You should have killed me when you had the chance, Wolflord."

"I'm no murderer."

"This is war, boy. No such thing as murder. We're all just doing our job. Happens to be that job's killing, something I'm very good at. Don't shed a tear for my well-being. I wouldn't waste one on yours. If the roles were reversed you'd be scooping up your guts from your lap and shoveling them back into your belly right now."

"So long as you're our prisoner, I'll allow you to live, Scorpio. I won't see you killed."

"You won't, eh? I'll remember that. You can't possibly win against the Catlords, Wolf. Tell me, what is it about these Lyssian Werelords that makes you take a stand against Bast?"

"That's where you and I are different. This isn't just about theriankind. My fight is also for humanity across the Seven Realms."

"Humans?" scoffed Scorpio. "Why would you risk your life for those pathetic bottom-dwellers?"

"You couldn't begin to understand, Scorpio. Nobody—human *or* therian—should spend their life in slavery. Being born a Werelord doesn't automatically make you better than your neighbor. I fight for a free Lyssia in every sense of the word."

"You fight for a lost cause," said the Werefish. "Even if you somehow won this war, the Werelords of the Seven Realms would never stand for such change. Therians rule over humans. That is the way the world over. Your talk of freedom will bring a knife to your back."

Vega interrupted, drawing the Fishlord away from his rant. "You say the Red Coast's impenetrable?"

Scorpio shrugged, jangling his chains. "I didn't say that. You can certainly land there. That said, chances are that you and Tigara's henchmen will be cut to ribbons in no time."

The Werefish had seen the soldiers of the Tigerlord aboard the *Maelstrom* when a handful of the Furies had joined Vega while the Sharklord interrogated the Bastian sea marshal.

"Because of this mighty force you tell us is stationed

along the coastal road, correct?" said Vega, suspiciously.

Scorpio's eyes lit up. "I do hope you'll land there, Shark-lord, and find out for yourself if I'm telling the truth."

"Why such activity along the coast? How are such numbers gathered there?"

The Werefish sighed. "For starters, the remains of my fleet are anchored intermittently throughout the shallows. If you navigate your way past them somehow, you'll make land at the Pashan Road. This links the Doglord city of Ro-Pasha with the gateway to the west, the Bana Gap."

Drew and Vega glanced at one another, the look not missed by Scorpio.

"You mean to aid your friends in the Gap?" he asked.

"What do you know of our allies in Bana?" said Drew.

"That they're as good as dead if they aren't already. Join them, by all means: land along the Red Coast and make haste to the afterlife."

"This Pashan Road," said Vega. "You haven't explained why it isn't safe for us to travel."

"With the Bastian army concentrating on snuffing out what resistance remains in the Gap, the road provides a direct supply route for Field Marshal Tiaz's army. Bastians and Doglords alike traverse it in huge numbers, and the route is dotted with settlements, barracks, and oases of civilization. It's one giant war camp."

"There has to be another way in," said Drew, "some way of

avoiding direct entanglements with Tiaz until we really can't."

"If you're searching for a back door, there isn't one, Wolf," said Scorpio triumphantly. "Tiaz is a master tactician and the land of Omir is his until he concludes his campaign in Bana. The desert realm is inaccessible."

"You underestimate the fortitude of the Hawklords," said Vega.

"*You* underestimate the stranglehold Tiaz has over the Gap. Your friends have been imprisoned there for months, throughout winter and spring. Those who aren't already dead will have been driven mad by hunger." Scorpio grinned. "Bana is a tomb."

"So they haven't surrendered?" said Drew, keen to seize any morsel of good news.

Scorpio grimaced. "Apparently not. Seems your Hawklords and their Omiri friends would rather die free than live in shackles." He rattled his manacles as if to emphasize the point.

"Then there's still hope," said Drew, turning to Vega. "If the Red Coast is closed to us, where else can we get ashore?"

"The River Robben," replied the Sharklord. "We'd need to be wary, mind. The Great West Road is under Catlord control, and the river runs parallel to it."

Scorpio snorted. "Do you really think we would've left the Robben unguarded?"

"That leaves only Roby," said Vega quietly.

"Roby?" said Drew as the Werefish grinned. "I've never heard of it."

"Why would you have?" interrupted Scorpio. "It's a ghost town, isn't it? Razed to the ground by Leopold when the Lion first took hold of Sturmland, a message to all in the Whitepeaks."

"It was burned by the king?" asked Drew.

Vega explained as the Werefish giggled manically against the wall. "The Sturmish provided stiff resistance to Leopold, especially in the east. That land was home to your mother's people, of course, the White Wolves of Shadowhaven. Leopold made an example of Roby, near enough erasing the port off the map. That soon broke their resolve, and Duke Henrik bowed the knee. Reluctantly, of course, but bowed nonetheless."

"Roby it is! Haunted by the dead," said Scorpio, laughing uncontrollably. "Land there! Die there!"

Drew stepped up to the bars, his hand gripping the barred gate. "Haunted? What do you mean?"

But Scorpio's laughter cut off as abruptly as it had begun. "I'm done answering your questions," he sneered, eyes narrowing. "You'll *allow* me to live, little Wolf? You don't get to choose who lives or dies!"

He slipped where he stood against the wall, his legs going from under him as his body dropped toward the deck. The chains went tight suddenly, throttling him around his hideous, bloated throat. Scorpio's feet writhed against the floor as he allowed his full weight to fall against the shackles, welcoming the agony that followed. His eyes strained from their sockets,

a sickly grin spreading across his face. Drew moved forward toward the brig door, only for Vega to seize him by the bicep. The young Wolf glanced down at the Shark's hand, the count's face stern.

"Let go of me, Vega. He's choking in there."

"By his *own* volition," said the Sharklord. "If he wants to kill himself, let him."

Drew yanked his arm free, lifting the handle of the grated door to step into the brig. With his one sweat-slicked hand he reached down, hooking it under Scorpio's stinking armpit as he tried to haul him up. The Bastian's feet lashed out, trying to keep the Wolf back as his neck crunched within his chain noose.

"Stop fighting me," Drew snarled, trying to find a hold on the suicidal sea captain.

Scorpio's flesh was changing color now, not the strangulated hue of a hanging man, but bright flashes of yellow and orange fluttering across his throat. His clothes, already tattered from the prolonged interrogation at Vega's hand, tore loose as he welcomed the beast. Bright red spines with purple tips emerged from his head and shoulders as his body ballooned before them. Drew took a step back now, wary of the shifting Werelord.

The Sea Marshal of Bast spied the Werewolf moving back to the brig door. His legs kicked out again, one foot swiping Drew's legs from beneath him, the other kicking the barred

door and sending it slamming shut. The metal hand clapped down, snapping into place as the young Wolflord fell against it.

Vega moved quickly, seizing the door and lifting the mechanism, looking to shove it open. To his horror he found Drew's prone body blocking the brig's threshold, stopping him from entering.

"Move, Drew!" Vega shouted. "The quills!"

Drew looked up in horror as the burbling, bloody Scorpionfish now materialized before them, the chain about its enormous, bloated throat almost decapitating it. Its hands and feet snatched at the air, sharp talons that swiped at an invisible foe as it approached death. Pulling himself to his knees, Drew snatched at the door, trying to open it and squeeze through while avoiding the monstrous Werefish.

"Forrrrr . . . Bassssssssst . . ." were the last words out of its still grinning lips as they peeled back, revealing tiny razor-sharp teeth that studded the jaws. Its body was almost spherical now, pockmarked flesh still undulating with color, mottled yellow, purple, and black. The poisonous quills rattled as it spun about, turning its spine-covered back Drew's way. A spine shot from the Scorpionfish's shoulder blade, hitting the deck at the youth's feet with a resounding *thunk*.

"No!" screamed Vega, kicking open the door, the bars smashing into the Wolflord as the Shark rushed in. His rapier was out, lunging through the air and finding the back of Scorpio's head. The blade went through, embedding in the brig wall

on the other side, causing the Sea Marshal of Bast's struggling to instantly cease. The air in its swollen body began to dissipate at that moment, as if escaping a punctured wineskin, the monster's death rattle sounding with it. The quills that adorned its back went limp, falling flush against its hideous flesh as it hung suspended from the groaning timber wall, the chains still taut with the Scorpionfish's weight.

Breathing a sigh of relief, Vega turned to look at the young lycanthrope where he sat on the floor, arms crossed, sandwiched between the caged door and the barred walls of the brig. His face was pale, his eyes wide as he stared up at the dead sea marshal.

"Shocking, what some souls might do," said Vega, nodding, as he held his hand out toward his friend on the pitching deck. "Here, let me help you up."

Drew didn't move, hand and wrist stump holding his waist, horrified eyes still trained on the body that hung from the wall by chain and blade. Vega reached down, taking the youth's hand, attempting to haul him to his feet. His own face drained of color. There it was. Stuck in the lad's stomach was one of Scorpio's spines, its bloody base standing proud from Drew's flesh, its poisonous tip buried deep in his guts.

3

FATHER AND SON

HIGH LORD OBA closed his clawed hand around his son's throat, lifting the other's jaw until their gazes met. Onyx's own hand came up, seizing his father's neck, feeling the Adam's apple bobbing in his grasp. The two partially transformed Pantherlords held each other there for a moment, teeth bared, paws gripping, green eyes locked upon one another. Oba's jaws yawned open, a roar emerging that sent spittle showering his son's face. Onyx's eyes narrowed before Oba's show of strength. Then it was his turn. The younger Beast of Bast suddenly towered over the Lord of Braga, growing a further foot in height, leaving his father in his shadow. He bellowed back, his canines snapping as he shook Oba.

The snarls were suddenly replaced by smiles as the two

Werepanthers embraced, hands moving from throats to backs as they patted one another. The hug was bone-crunching, each threatening to crush the other in his arms, Oba's splinted left arm trapped between them where it rested in a sling. He pulled his son away from his chest and held him before him, right hand on shoulder.

"It's been too long, my boy," said the Lord of Braga.

He released Onyx, clapping his arms, before stepping past him. The son turned on his heel, following his father through the command tent. Oba paused by the two enormous black jaguars that lounged before the fire pit. The two rolled onto their backs like kittens as the old felinthrope crouched to scratch their bellies.

"It's good to see you, too," said Onyx, stepping over to the table and pouring a goblet of wine for his father. "I'm pleased you got here in one piece. I was beginning to worry."

"You received my message, then?"

"Sending the Vulturelord Ithacus struck me as a decidedly serious thing to do. I thought he was dead, or at the least you'd put him out to pasture."

"He was enjoying his retirement when I called upon him. Old as we are, he's still my most faithful lieutenant. There's nobody I'd trust more with important news. Nobody more than yourself, that is."

Oba straightened from the big cats and turned to his son, accepting the golden cup. He took a hearty swig, watching the

other all the while. Onyx noticed the cuts on his father's face, awful furrows that had been carved through his cheek.

"We encountered Staglords on the road from Highcliff," said Oba. "You know about them?"

"I know they've been striking our smaller camps. Brave of them to launch an ambush on your party, though, Father."

"Brave indeed. There was one of their number whom I'd dearly love to meet again, on my own terms." He lifted the broken arm in its sling. "I've the Wolf Knight to thank for this."

"One of the Staglords did it?" asked Onyx. "They're a thorn in my paw. Lord Reinhardt leads them, perhaps it was him."

"This was no Staglord. He let me know his name as we fled. Tell me: does Drew Ferran have any siblings?"

"You know as well as I that they were slaughtered by Leopold when he took the throne, Father. He's the sole surviving child of Wergar."

Oba stroked his jaw. "He said his name was Trent Ferran."

"Ah," said Onyx. "This brother, Trent Ferran, isn't related by blood. It was Trent's father who raised Drew as his own. In fact, Trent was once a Redcloak, working closely with my cousin Lord Frost, until he betrayed us. His ferocity has Muller's men running scared. And if he could do this to you . . ."

"He's strong for a human," muttered Oba, glancing at his slung arm. "Unnaturally so, I'd say. But he is, at the end of the day, a mere human, no?"

Onyx nodded. The Beast of Bast was quiet suddenly, step-

ping up to look at Oba's face. He traced a thumb over his father's ripped cheek.

"These injuries: from the Wolf Knight also?"

"Yes," replied Oba with a snarl. "As I said, our business is unfinished."

"It hasn't healed yet? When were you ambushed?"

"Five days or so ago," grunted the Lord of Braga. "I'd like your magister to take a look at it, actually."

Onyx peeled his lips back, his growl deep and rumbling. "It should be healed by now if a human did this. Which can mean only one thing."

He stepped away, pouring his own goblet of wine and polishing it off in a swift swig. Oba stepped up to a polished mirror that hung from the tent wall, turning his face so he could better see the livid wounds.

"What's that?" said Oba.

"That Ferran is no longer human."

"Explain yourself, Onyx. Do not test me with riddles. I am weary after a long journey. That you didn't bother to send anyone to meet me when I landed in Highcliff is something that I haven't yet raised with you."

"We're preoccupied here, if you hadn't noticed, Father. Sturmland has proved a tougher nut to crack than expected. A necromancer has taken up residence in Icegarden, just as it looked like the city was ours."

"What necromancer?"

"Blackhand they call him. He's a Boarlord from the Dale-lands, an old friend of the Wolf's before he immersed himself in dark magistry. My men are fearful of getting too close to the frozen walls of Icegarden: they say he can raise the dead."

Oba laughed. "Men will say many things when they're gripped by superstition. This Blackhand is an illusionist, a trickster, no more. Send your army to Icegarden at once. Tear down the walls and drag the Boar out into the open. Let's see how his dark arts help him then."

Onyx's eyes narrowed. He knew better than to challenge the old man. Blackhand was no trickster; Onyx had seen first-hand the kind of power the magister wielded. Rather than argue with his father, he chose another tack.

"Blackhand isn't the only danger we face in Sturmland. The White Bear of Icegarden's forces remain in the foothills—we cannot turn our backs upon them. They're led by Duke Bergan, the Lord of Brackenholme. If I could have spared an escort to meet you in Highcliff, don't you think I would have?"

Oba sneered at his son. "You mentioned this Trent Ferran being 'no longer human' earlier. Explain what you mean."

Onyx paced around the fire, crouching on his haunches to look into the flames.

"Lucas has been consorting with a Wylderman shaman named Darkheart."

"What are Wyldermen?"

"Wild men of the woods. They're bloodthirsty cannibals."

"A shaman, you say? Their version of a magister?"

Onyx picked up a steel poker and stoked the fire, sending a shower of sparks up toward the hole in the command tent's ceiling.

"The magicks that our magisters use are a world away from the Wyld Magicks of a Wylderman shaman. This Darkheart has taken the severed limb of Drew Ferran and brought about a new wolf creature, something neither human nor therian."

"A new breed of Werewolf?" gasped Oba from across the burning pit.

Onyx shook his head. "It's a mockery of a therian lord, Father—more beast than man. Around twenty wild men took part in Darkheart's ceremony, with Lucas's blessing, and each transformed into one of these 'Wyld Wolves.' I've seen what happens to those who survive their attacks. If they live and the disease doesn't kill them, they also go through the change."

"And you believe this Trent Ferran is one of these diseased Werewolves?"

Onyx pointed the poker at the old man's face through the flames. "If the Wolf Knight delivered those wounds to your face, then I believe that to be the case. Those are therian wounds, Father. They'll scar."

Oba angrily threw his goblet into the fire.

"All thanks to that foolish young Lion, Lucas? All the more reason why he, and his kind, have to go. You know why I'm here, Onyx?"

128

"Word travels fast across the Seven Realms."

"The union of the Catlords is broken. Panthers, Lions, and Tigers have all gone their own ways, and their allies with them."

"It seems impossible. How did this happen?"

Oba glowered. "Your sister."

"You're wrong," growled Onyx. "I know Opal. She would never betray the union. She's one of us."

"She was once, but no more."

The Beast of Bast's eyes narrowed. "What did she do?"

"She sailed to our homeland, brought the Wolf to Leos, right to the heart of our most sacred meeting place, the Forum of Elders. And that's where she chose to . . . clear her conscience."

"Her conscience?"

"I think you know what I speak of, my boy. Cast your mind back."

Onyx stared at his father, unblinking. "Taboo?"

Oba smiled grimly at the mention of the young Weretiger who had been framed for the murder of her Cheetah lover. The murder committed by Onyx.

"There are no more ghosts in Bast, son. It all came tumbling out in the forum: the death of Chang, the banishment of Taboo, and the complicity of the Lions in the whole sorry affair."

"How has this resulted in the Lions now being our enemy?" said Onyx. "High Lord Leon has been our staunchest ally

since you, he, and Tigara first carved up Bast. That we stand against the Tigers, I can stomach—they were always a breed apart, disapproving of our methods in cowing other therians. But the Lions?"

"It seems once your dear sister started speaking, she couldn't stop herself. She told Leon that Lucas killed his own father, Leon's son—because of you."

During his reign, Wergar the Wolf had been feared but respected by the people of the Seven Realms; Leopold the Lion, who stole his throne, was feared, hated, and ridiculed. When the young Wolf, Drew Ferran, rose to prominence as a claimant of the throne, Onyx, Opal, and a Bastian war-force had sailed north to Lyssia to seize back the lands in the name of the Cat-lords. After that disgrace, Leopold couldn't remain in power; he was insane, unstable, and utterly unreliable. Onyx felt sure he and Opal had done what anyone would've in their shoes: pointed out Leopold's shortcomings to his proud—and equally unhinged—son. Lucas had done the rest, slaughtering his father and seizing the crown in his place.

Oba continued. "So now the old Lion has sailed to Lyssia in his son's name, as I sail in yours."

"Mine?"

"Of course. You're no longer just fighting the Wolf and his allies, among whom the Tigers now count themselves—you also have Leon and Lucas to contend with. Let's smite this whelp of a Lion and smear his carcass across the Seven Realms."

"I need to find him first. Lucas has run off with his Wolfmen, searching for Lady Gretchen, the Fox of Hedgemoor to whom he was betrothed. I've sent Count Costa to look for him. Hopefully the Vulturelord can track him down and bring word back to me before Lucas gets wind of what's happened back home."

"You trust Costa?" asked his father.

Onyx arched an eyebrow. He rose to his full height before the fire, striding back to the table where his map was laid out, marking the shifting whereabouts of the Bearlord's forces. They grew fewer every day. Could he really be so close to victory only for his own felinthropes of Bast to arrive and spoil everything?

"This army of Leon's skirts the Dyrewood presently, marching north via the Talstaff Road," he said, jabbing the map with a thick forefinger. "How many do they number?"

"I couldn't say for sure," said Oba, stroking his damaged cheek. "His is a hastily prepared army, as is my own."

"So he's ill prepared?"

"I wouldn't go so far as that," said Oba. "He brings his greatest Redcloaks from Leos. These aren't Lyssian Lionguard, the fools who served Leopold. These are Bastian warriors."

"Please tell me the army you've brought is a match for him."

"The small force of Goldhelms who accompanied me today is the first wave. More come—they were in the process of securing Highcliff for us, dispatching or imprisoning what Redcloaks remained there."

Onyx's eyes widened as High Lord Oba continued.

"You need to weed out those who are loyal to us and those who stand against us, be they human or therian. Who's the one they call the sheriff?"

"That's Muller. He's the Lord of the Badlands."

"They make a human a lord in Lyssia?" sneered Oba, nose curling in disgust.

"It's a self-proclaimed title, Father. The sheriff is an ambitious man."

"The sheriff doesn't know his place," replied the High Lord, "like so many other pathetic humans in the Seven Realms. They're only fit for slavery. That he should rise to such lofty position makes a mockery of the natural order. He's the first one you should make an example of when this war is won: hang him from the highest rooftop for all humanity to see. Remind them of their place."

Onyx nodded, knowing all too well his father's opinion of men. The old Panther continued.

"Decide which Werelords on your war council are with us. It doesn't matter where their allegiance used to lie. Bastian or not, there can be no gray areas: they're either with us, or against us. If they say they're loyal to Lucas and Leon, then consider that their death warrant."

Onyx turned and looked into the flames. His war council numbered folk whom he had trusted, regardless of their origin: Count Costa the Vulturelord, the Werehippo General Gorgo,

General Skean the Cranelord. And what about Vanmorten, the tricksy Wererat who had considered himself Lucas's right-hand man until the arrival of Darkheart and his Wyldermen? Onyx had never trusted the Rat, but Vanmorten always knew which side his bread was buttered on, and they certainly agreed about the foolhardiness of Lucas's involvement with the Wyldermen. Where might his loyalties lie now?

"Well, boy?" said Oba, taking Onyx's empty goblet from the table and filling it with wine for himself. "What are you standing there gawping at? You've work to do. Show me why they call you the Beast of Bast."

Onyx set off toward the tent flap, his mind raging with ideas, many of them grim. *Gorgo first*, he reasoned. *The old Hippo can surely be trusted. But then who?*

"And don't forget, my boy," called Oba as Onyx paused at the threshold, "if you see your dear sister again . . ."

"Yes?"

"You kill her, of course."

4

BAD DEBTS

OPAL STOOD IN the shadows of the balcony, watching the Jackal king at play with his children. She wore a sheer black dress of the finest Omiri silk, its shimmering surface clinging to every line of her graceful body. Her green eyes blazed with envy, each burst of laughter from Faisal grating her nerves. She yearned to be in the Jackal's position, loved ones in her arms, but knew that day was distant, should it ever come. The Panther's own children were far from their home, in the safekeeping of High Lord Tigara of Felos, since she had turned upon her fellow Catlords. The Tiger would protect them while Opal fought overseas. She prayed they would remain safe from those who wished to harm her. That list grew daily.

She would stand by the young Wolf and see this grisly war through to its end, on her word. She and the Wolf were allies for now against the twin might of Lions and Panthers—her own kind—and she trusted the young lycanthrope as she hoped her trusted her. But the Sharklord who stood at his side? Opal owed him no such courtesy. It was Vega who had threatened the lives of her children, and for that he would one day pay.

Faisal's courtiers burst into a chorus of laughter as he lifted his eldest daughter, Kara, into the air, roaring at the ten-year-old and gnashing his teeth as if he might transform and eat her before their very eyes. His younger children surged over him like army ants. They clambered up his torso and, tugging at his toga, threatened to topple him. He let out a yelp as he tumbled onto a pile of cushions, lost beneath the giggling mass of tiny limbs. More guffaws came from the surrounding onlookers at the royal horseplay. Opal turned up her nose and looked away, out into the night over Azra.

"The king's antics offend you, my lady?"

Opal recognized the man's voice as he joined her on the balcony. It was Djogo, the human warrior who had earned a place by Faisal's side.

"I don't begrudge a man's play with his offspring," replied the Werepanther with a scowl. "It's the simpering sycophants that make my blood run cold, all desperate to please His Highness."

135

"Is that not the way of lesser men when in the company of the powerful?"

"It's the way of lickspittles," sneered Opal. "The actions of greater men speak volumes. They are the ones who rise into their master's sights."

"It's hard for any man to reach his master's attention, if society keeps him firmly beneath booted foot."

She turned to look at Djogo now, the tall human remaining a respectful distance from her. She knew from his coloring that he wasn't a man of the Desert Realm, his build and features reminding her of her homeland.

"You're Bastian, Djogo?"

"Of a sort, my lady," he said. "I was born on Talon."

"That would make you Bastian, then," she said. "Last time I checked that lump of rock was still under the control of the Lions of Leos."

"The nationality of an occupying force doesn't necessarily dictate the nationality of the people."

"Spoken like a politician," she said. "Or perhaps a separatist."

Djogo shrugged. "It's been a long time since I called Talon my home. While I'm sympathetic toward my people's struggle, I'm no freedom fighter. Talon's far in my past, my lady."

"So what's in Djogo's future?" she asked. "And you can stop calling me 'lady.' That's the talk of sycophants, and you know my feelings about those."

"As you wish," he said with a nod. "My future is tied to the Wolflord. That's where my loyalty lies."

Opal smiled. Since she had been Faisal's guest in Azra, her talks with the king had revealed plenty of this human's colorful backstory. He had been a slave, then a gladiator, until the Goatlord, Count Kesslar, had purchased him. In service to Kesslar, Djogo had traveled the world with his master, enslaving men, women, and children from both Lyssia and Bast. When the young Wolf was captured by Djogo and Kesslar, he was sold to Lord Ignus of Scoria, but not before Drew had cost the lean warrior an eye. Drew had been forced to fight in the arena for the amusement of the Lizards and their guests, much as Djogo had once done. But Drew had led a rebellion, freeing every slave and gladiator on the volcanic isle, including Djogo. From that day forth, they had been allies, and Djogo had sworn an oath of loyalty to the Werewolf and his crusade for equality and justice in the Seven Realms.

"You've made quite the impression on King Faisal, Djogo," said Opal.

"I've simply done my duty. When Drew left me here with Lady Shah he explained that we were to fight on in his name until he returned, and do whatever the king asked of us."

Drew had told Opal of Djogo's adoration of Shah, the Hawklady he'd known since they'd both been in the employ of Count Kesslar.

"I can't help but notice that there is no sign of Lady Shah

or the Hawklords," Opal continued. "I'd have expected at least some of them to have remained here in Azra. Did they all fly to the Bana Gap?"

"Every one of them," replied Djogo, his hard features struggling to hide his misery. "Count Carsten and Baron Baum, the Eaglelords who rule over all the Hawks, were sent north by the king upon their arrival. They took some of my friends with them—Krieg, Taboo, the Behemoth—in addition to King Faisal's finest Jackal warriors."

"So Shah went with them also?" asked Opal, knowing full well the answer.

Djogo cleared his throat. "Like I said. Every one of them."

"You must be keen to hit the road, then? Head to the Gap and see if your friends—and Lady Shah—are still alive?"

"When King Faisal is ready to ride, I shall be at his side. If he says we'll depart in the morning, I've no reason to doubt him."

"Do you truly think they've survived up there, locked away from the rest of Omir, surrounded by Field Marshal Tiaz's army? I know what the Tigerlord took with him along the Great West Road, Djogo. There are Vulturelords in his service, more than a match for your Lyssian Hawks. He has Werelords of Bast at his side as well, complemented by the finest Redcloaks and Goldhelms."

Djogo stared at Opal defiantly. "Then it's a good thing

you've brought the Furies of Felos with you, isn't it? And there may well be therian lords of Bast among Tiaz's number, but I doubt any of them are as deadly as the three I mentioned earlier—Krieg, Taboo, and the Behemoth. Each of my friends survived the Furnace, the gladiatorial arena on Scoria, and I reckon they're worth ten of your Werelords who sided with the Cats."

Opal nodded and smiled. "You've spirit and fire in your belly, Djogo. I can see how a lady could grow rather fond of you."

"As I am fond of you, Opal," said Djogo, unable to resist bowing. "You did, after all, save my neck from the executioner's blade. You freed the people of Azra just when all appeared lost. I'd wager you're as loved here as the king is."

"You're quite the charmer," she said, batting her lashes at the lean warrior. "Wherever your wife is, she must be very proud of you."

"I'm unwed," replied the one-eyed former slaver, turning his face away to stare down at the myriad lights of Azra.

Opal loved to play, and this was a most enjoyable game. *It's too easy, though,* she thought, watching Djogo as he stewed uncomfortably under her questions. *It seems almost a shame to put him through this, but then again . . .*

"I fear Lady Shah will be in for a shock if she's survived the siege of Bana," said Opal, instantly drawing Djogo's attention.

"That awful Vega is on his way there, intending to take her for his own."

"The Sharklord?"

"Indeed. Loathsome, cruel creature. Claims he left her with child in her youth—he gloated about it—and now reckons he'll take her again, this time back to the Pirate Isles. He described her as his 'work in progress,' whatever that means. Do you know anything of the Shark?"

"Only his reputation on the high seas," growled Djogo, his fingernails catching the marble as he gripped the banister. "He's betrayed a host of folk, from sea captains to kings. Even Wergar, the old Wolf, was double-crossed by Vega. I know he did business with Kesslar back in the day."

"So what he says might be true?" asked Opal, green eyes wide with mock shock.

"Shah knows him, for sure. They have a history, but she could never bring herself to tell me about it. I sensed it was hurtful and painful to her, so I tried not to pry. To hear him speak of her in this way . . ."

Opal spied his scarred hands trembling where he gripped the banister, the muscles of his forearms knotted with anxiety. The rage was coming off Djogo in waves. *Oh this is good,* mused the Pantherlady.

"He considers Shah his property," continued Opal. "With Kesslar and the Hawklady's father both gone, he said nothing could stand in the way of his claim upon her."

"He said that?"

"With a smile," lied Opal. "I've never met a viler, more cor-rupted soul. Who knows what possesses the Wolflord to trust one such as Vega among his council. Every word he whispers is poison in Drew's ear, every plan he puts in place a means to his own selfish end."

Djogo said nothing, his jaws grating, the marble balustrade almost crumbling beneath his trembling grip.

"Somebody needs to stop the Shark, before he can harm anyone else." She stepped up to Djogo and whispered in his ear, "Vega's a danger to us all."

With that she walked away, a spring in her stride, passing the king and his companions as they frolicked in the court-room on the eve of their march north. Faisal smiled from be-neath the pile of children, and she returned the greeting, black silk robes fluttering behind her. She glanced back before she exited the opulent chamber, catching sight of Djogo punching the balcony banister with balled fists.

A shame to use the man, she reasoned. *But some debts need re-paying.*

5
RUINED

THERE WERE NO fires to see, and no sounds drifted downhill from the tor's darkened, rock-strewn summit. He had the half-moon to thank for alerting him to the ruins, the site invisible until the clouds had parted overhead. Leading his mount from the trail, the young horseman had ridden ever closer, unable to resist investigating. He had been following his quarry for two days now, trying to remember what he had learned from his childhood lessons. His own father had schooled him well in the art of therianthropy, of controlling the Brenn-given powers that were at his fingertips, but it was his uncle who had shown him what it took to track a beast—or man—over field and fen. It was his late uncle Mikkel's lessons

that he had drawn upon of late as he pursued his prey through the wilderness.

Milo kept his horse's progress slow and steady, swinging out of Sheaf's saddle to lead her on foot. The young Staglord had ditched his armor when he first took flight from his brother and the Knights of Stormdale; no doubt Reinhardt had discovered the carefully assembled pieces of plate mail beneath the spare cloak the following morning, but by then Milo was long gone. The only thing he had kept was the breastplate, the same one their father, Duke Manfred, had worn in his youth. Like the young Staglord, it had been beaten and battered in the previous weeks, but it remained a lifesaver and a constant reminder of where Milo had come from.

Finding the gnarled remains of a dead tree, the boy from Stormdale lashed Sheaf's reins about the twisted trunk. The horse snorted, unnerved by something out there: his prey perhaps?

"Hush, girl," Milo whispered, running his palm over the gray mare's sloping head, trying to calm her. "It's probably nothing."

The horse calmed at his touch, dipping her head and nudging his chest gently. He ruffled her mane before pulling his soot-gray cloak across his chest, concealing the leaping buck emblazoned beneath it. With shortsword trailing at his side, blade hidden from the moon's light within the cloak, he set off

up the tor toward the tumbledown tower that crested its peak.

Why are you doing this again, Milo? Are you trying to get yourself killed?

He couldn't answer instantly, finding himself questioning his reasoning, and not for the first time. The moments of doubt came often for Milo as he considered what life might have been like if he had remained safely within the walls of Stormdale Keep. But how safe had he truly been there? How safe was anyone in the Barebones? The Rats and the Crows had demolished the city walls and almost reduced the keep to rubble. It was Drew Ferran's timely arrival that had motivated the Staglords and the men and women of Stormdale, and it was with the Wolf guiding them that they finally turned the tide. And Drew Ferran would never have known their plight if a headstrong young Staglord had not raced to Windfell to seek aid. That buck had been Milo.

That's why you're here, he reminded himself. *You're a man of action, Milo. You get things done; you make things happen!*

Milo felt reassured with every step that his reasoning was sound, that he was doing the right thing. He felt partly to blame for the fact that his quarry was on the run, alone in the wilds with nobody to turn to. Milo's petulance had led this poor soul to leave the Knights of Stormdale and strike out alone. That didn't sit well with the young therian, not least because this was the brother of Drew, Trent Ferran, a human as brave, bold, and awe-inspiring as any Werelord he had ever met.

144

Well, he was *human. Brenn only knows what he's becoming now . . .*

Milo feared what Trent might become when the moon was next full in a fortnight. The Wolf Knight, as he had become known, had set off east in search of revenge against King Lucas and the Wyld Wolves, last seen in the Dalelands. But Milo still harbored hope that he might make Trent see sense, persuade him to head north to the Daughters of Icegarden. The Bear-lady magisters might be able to help him reclaim his humanity. Surely that was more worthy than vengeance?

Milo stepped around a great chunk of fallen stonework, the crude blocks held together by ancient, crumbling mortar. The fortification had once been a beacon tower, used by the men of Redmire who had first settled in the Dales, a means to stay in touch with their neighbors and warn of the Wylder-men threat. Moss covered the entirety of its north-facing side. The young Buck reckoned he was maybe twenty feet from the summit now, the curving tower wall a jagged outline against the indigo night sky.

Milo welcomed the Stag to the fore, his nostrils flaring as he took in a lungful of air. He caught the scent of predators on the breeze, the unmistakable musky odor of hunters all about him. They could have been days or even weeks old, the ruins no doubt frequented by all manner of creature, but there was one scent in particular he was searching for, one he had picked up frequently in the past few days as he tracked Trent Ferran: the

beast. The bitter smell of urine soaked the stones, some animal having recently scent-marked the ruins. But was there something else there? Blood perhaps? Milo edged forward, clearing the remaining distance and creeping over the ramshackle wall's jagged edge.

Besides the lofty remains of the southern wall, an ancient fireplace told of the tower's past life, its wooden lintel still embedded within the ruins. The hearth and broken chimney stack were overrun with ivy, exposed to the elements as nature reclaimed the stone from mankind. Jutting steps rose up the curving wall, sticking out like rotten teeth in diseased gums. Bones littered the bare earth, snapped and splintered, the marrow long gone.

It was the sheep carcass in the center of the ruins that caught Milo's eye, its torso torn wide-open, innards gone. He had found Trent's campsite the previous night, the tidy remains of a skinned hare all that was left behind. What he had discovered here was an altogether more horrific, violent kill. The flies hadn't even found the corpse yet, steam rising steadily from its exposed rib cage. *Steam?* With sickening dread, the young lord from Stormdale realized this was a fresh kill.

He glanced high up above the fireplace to where the broken steps circled the southern wall. Slowly the shadows began to move, a shape disengaging from the stonework, emerging from the darkness, yellow, lupine eyes glowing as it looked down upon the boy.

146

"Trent?" said the lad, stumbling along the ruined tower's edge, unsure of why fear had gripped him so. "It's me, Milo!"

Had the poison already run its course, transforming Trent into one of Lucas's Wyld Wolves? Was Milo too late? He backed away from the fireplace as the yellow eyes followed him, narrowed and measured. Hungry. Milo shivered, his antlers tearing free from his brow.

Ferran—or the creature that had *been* Ferran—growled, sending a fresh bout of nerves jangling through the young Buck's body. Milo spied the point in the wall where he had clambered over the ruins, perhaps his best means of escape if he were to make it back to Sheaf. Milo leapt forward, aiming for the rubble.

The boy's trailing foot caught on the exposed ribs of the slaughtered sheep, sending him to the ground. He hit the dirt with a crunch, lip splitting and skull rattling. He rolled over, his world upside down. Through the darkness he caught sight of two blinking amber lights as the monster on the wall suddenly leapt away from the ruins, bounding to the ground.

The grotesque lycanthrope towered over him, its clawed feet gripping the earth on either side of Milo's head. He tried to rise, only for his foe to place a foot on his antlers, holding him in his place. Bloody spittle dribbled from the young Staglord's trembling mouth as his eyes scanned the beast's body.

The fur that covered Ferran's body was filthy. His head was utterly malformed, unrecognizable from the wild-eyed,

blond-haired warrior who had fought by Milo's side a matter of days ago. The lips of the beast's ruined jaws peeled back, jagged canines dripping hungry slather down onto the boy pinned below. Milo's eyes focused on the swirls of blue woad symbols that adorned the monster's body, just about visible beneath the matted fur.

This isn't Trent! It's one of the Wyld Wolves!

A sudden movement in the darkness caused the monster to look up, its attention torn from the helpless young therian at its feet. A blurred shape hit it in the midriff, lifting it off its clawed feet and launching it through the air. Milo felt the weight instantly removed from his antlers as the monster was driven into the fireplace. Stones were dislodged in a shower of rubble as the Staglord crawled onto his belly and looked up.

Milo's heart soared as he recognized the gray-cloaked warrior, battered wolf helm reflecting the moonlight as the Wolfman launched a flurry of blows to the knight's head. Trent fought back, butting the monster in the face and flattening its twisted muzzle. Clawed hands reached up, catching the Gray-cloak's helmet and ripping it from his head. The two brawlers spun, the monster taking its chance to drive Trent into the crumbling fireplace. More stones were dislodged through the onslaught, clattering onto the pair as they raked, punched, and kicked at one another.

The boy from Stormdale saw the beast's filthy fingers around Trent's throat now, his friend's face contorted as the

Wolfman squeezed his airways shut. He raked at the monster, his fingers falling short of his enemy's face as the beast locked its arms, burying the suffocating youth within the chimney stack.

Milo's antlers tore into the Wyld Wolf's back, causing it to release a howl of pain. The Staglord tried to drive his stubby tines deeper, twisting his head to cause maximum damage, but the beast released a hand from Trent to slash at him. He felt claws rip at his scalp, tearing out hair as he was yanked free from the monster's back and tossed against the wall. That was the opening the Wolf Knight needed.

Trent punched up at the arm that held his throat, his fist striking the monster's extended elbow from below. There was a *snap* as the arm twisted, hold instantly lost, and the Wyld Wolf roared once more. Then it was spinning, back in Trent's embrace, smashing into the fireplace again. The Wolf Knight's clawed hands were buried in the beast's woad-daubed chest, driving it repeatedly into the bricks as more ancient masonry collapsed about them. There was a splintering wail as the timber mantel gave way, twisting in its housing, the entire southern wall of the ruined beacon tower groaning above them. One more mighty punch from Trent sent the Wolfman into a heap upon the hearth before he leapt clear of the collapsing wall. Timber and wall descended upon the stricken monster, sealing it within a tomb of rubble.

Trent stood in front of the ruined wall, surrounded by

a billowing cloud of dust, before turning to Milo. His chest was heaving, his gray cloak now red about the throat where the Wyld Wolf had found his neck. Stepping up to the boy he extended a hand and hauled Milo to his feet. Milo felt Trent's clawed fingers catch his palm.

"You're the last person I expected to see out here, little lord," said Trent. "Why aren't you with your brother? Reinhardt will be worried sick about you."

"I came after you," said Milo, dusting himself down, his antlers already beginning to recede. "It's my fault you left the Knights of Stormdale, isn't it?"

Trent smiled. "I couldn't have remained there. I was a danger to all with each passing day. Baron Hoffman was right to demand I leave."

"But Trent, you're surrendering yourself to fate, to the transformation into . . . into one of those creatures," said Milo, pointing at the ruined wall and the settling dust.

"I'm going after those responsible for my fate, Milo," snapped Trent. "I'm stopping them before they can cause more harm. Starting with this one here," he added, following Milo's gaze toward the rubble. "How did you know this Wolfman was here? I picked up his trail earlier. Couldn't quite believe it when I found your horse down the way."

Milo felt a little foolish now. "I thought it was you. I wasn't expecting that monster when I ventured into the ruin."

Trent laughed, kicking a few bones across the ground. "Then it's a fine job we found one another when we did, eh? Looks like he'd been using this as his lair, or at least as a base for moving around the western Dales. I wonder what Lucas is up to . . ."

"You think he's still in the Dalelands?"

"I'm sure he is, as are the rest of his Wyld Wolves."

Trent made his way to the ruin's crumbling walls, hopping over the tower's broken base. Milo followed, sticking close to the Wolf Knight.

"Come with me, Trent," said the boy. "Let's head north, to Sturmland, see if we can find the Daughters of Icegarden. They can help you!"

"I can help myself," said the Wolf Knight, marching down the hill toward where Sheaf had been tethered. His own horse stood nearby, chewing at the bank of grass, its coat slick with sweat.

"How?"

"By killing Lucas and his Wyldermen."

"You'll be killing yourself in the process, even if you defeat him! Don't you see that? You heard what Magister Wilhelm said, Trent. When the moon becomes full, you *will* change, and this time there'll be no coming back! You'll become one of them!"

Trent turned angrily on the boy from Stormdale. "Don't

you think I know that? I don't care what becomes of me! I just need to *stop* the rest of the Wyld Wolves, prevent them from doing this to anyone else!"

"There has to be another way."

"There is none," snarled Trent, snatching at his horse's reins. "Now run along back to your brother."

"I don't know where he is now," replied Milo.

"Then run along back to Stormdale," said the Wolf Knight, straightening the riding blanket on his horse's back.

"I can't go back to Stormdale, not while there's a war to be fought in the west."

"Then just run along!" snapped Trent as he turned to the boy. "You can't do any good here."

"I beg to differ," said Milo from where he sat high in Sheaf's saddle, ready for the road.

"What are you doing? You can't come with me."

"I can do exactly that, Ferran. I won't be letting you out of my sight."

"You can't help me, Milo. I need to do this alone, and I can't be responsible for your well-being. It's going to be dangerous where I'm heading. There's no road back."

Trent gulped as he spoke the words, at peace with his terrible fate. He stared up at Milo who gazed back with sad eyes.

"You don't have to be responsible for me. I can look after myself."

"Like in the ruins up there?" said Trent. "You'd have died if I hadn't come for you."

"As would you if I hadn't gored the Wolfman with my antlers. Admit it, Ferran: we work well together."

Trent sighed and shook his head. When he looked back to Milo his voice was a low growl.

"I'm going to deal horrors upon the Wyld Wolves like you cannot imagine, my lord."

"And I'll be there for you, Trent."

"For me?" he whispered.

"Indeed," said Milo solemnly. "Because if you do succeed in slaying Lucas and his monsters before the full moon rises in two weeks, that'll leave just one monster that needs killing."

"You'd do that?" asked Trent as he clambered up onto his mount alongside the young Buck's horse.

"I'll kill you myself, Trent."

"Be sure you do," said the Wolf Knight, "or you may die trying."

6

THE PORT OF LOST SOULS

STANDING ON THE DECK of the *Maelstrom,* buffeted by the chill northern winds, Drew clutched the rail with his one hand. Summer it may have been, but Sturmland still found a way to grip one's bones with its frigid fingers. Somewhere, far along the Whitepeaks to the west, was Icegarden. Hector was there, mystery hanging over whether he was good or bad, alive or dead. Likewise, a mist hung over the port, so thick that the water was obscured from view, the ship floating on a sea of fog. Drew's hold was weak, his footing unsteady, as he took a moment to compose himself. Placing a foot on the gangway he set off toward the pier. Vega stared up as Drew descended, his look utterly disapproving.

"I can't believe you're coming," said the Sharklord with a shake of the head. "You're unwell. You need bed rest."

"I can't believe you thought I'd stay behind," wheezed Drew as he stepped unsteadily toward land. "What kind of leader would I be if I sent others to fight in my place?"

"A leader who lives to fight another day," replied Vega as the young Wolf joined him on the stone jetty. "A stiff breeze could snap you in two."

Vega's concerned face confirmed what Drew already knew: Scorpio had won, even in death. Drew's skin had a horrid, gray pallor, slick with sweat. It had been an hour since he had last been sick, but he knew another bout of vomiting was on its way soon enough. How was there anything still left in his stomach? *I fear the next time I heave it'll be my intestines coming up.* The wound in his guts itched within and without, the flesh yellow and puckered, refusing to heal. In spite of his injury, he had to continue, could not let his men see just how ill he had become.

The Furies of Bast were assembled before them on the deserted, fog-bound pier, resplendent in their brown leather cuirasses. Blades were sheathed on either side of their armored hips. A hundred of the Tigerlord's warriors remained with them, the others having sailed on to Azra with Opal. Drew prayed that the Pantherlady had succeeded in her mission. The odds were hardly stacked in her favor with the Hyena's forces surrounding the Jackal's city. A handful of sailors from

the *Maelstrom* and the *Red Dog* had followed them onto the pier, but there were plenty more seamen who remained aboard their vessels, refusing to come ashore.

"Why don't they join us?" asked Drew, noticing the rows of worried-looking faces aboard the ships. *Are those looks meant for me or the city at my back?*

"You didn't hear them?" said the count, looking inland, down the pier's length toward the city hidden in the mist.

"Hear what?"

"The dead," said Vega, his voice a whisper.

It was a blessing that the Lions and Panthers feared the port as much as the Lyssians. The piers and jetties were utterly deserted, bar the two vessels the Wolf's forces had arrived upon. Drew had heard the talk aboard the *Maelstrom* as they'd approached Roby. The pirates were as superstitious a folk as one could encounter across the Seven Realms. As if the warning words of the late sea marshal hadn't been enough, other grim portents had dogged their progress: terrible storms, spells of sickness aboard the *Red Dog,* plus an albatross that had collided with the *Maelstrom's* main mast, falling broken-necked to the deck. For any one of those things to have happened would have made the crew grumble. For all three to happen confirmed their fears. The port of Roby was cursed. It belonged to the dead.

"I heard nothing," said Drew with a shiver, turning away from the fearful faces of the sailors toward those pirates who had joined them. They looked awkward, shifting nervously,

their eyes flitting along the pier toward the ruined city ahead.

"Still," continued the Wolflord, aware of the seamen's unease, "it wouldn't hurt us to start moving, clear out of the city before nightfall. How far are the fishing villages along the northern banks of the Robben?"

"If we march out now we should reach one of those wee towns before midnight," said Florimo, the Ternlord stepping lightly down the gangway to join them, Casper and Figgis at his back. "I scoured the coast just this morning at first light. There were all manner of fishing boats beached along the banks that we can use to get across. Far less conspicuous than sailing up the Robben in a pair of pirate ships."

Looking past Florimo, Drew could see Casper had a pack across his shoulders, his shortsword tucked through a loop of leather on his belt. The lad's eyes were wide and serious as he remained behind the old navigator, seemingly hiding from his father. Figgis was glowering at the boy disapprovingly.

"No, lad," said Vega. "You won't be coming."

"I'm staying by your side, Father," said Casper, the term still new to his lips as he stepped around the Ternlord.

"Not this time, son," said the count, kneeling before the boy. "I need you to remain here, with the *Maelstrom*. With me gone, the ship needs a skipper."

"That'd be Figgis, though," exclaimed Casper, glancing up at the old sailor. "He's the first mate. Surely command should be his?"

Vega ruffled the cabin boy's head and smiled. "Ordinarily, aye, but not when the son of the pirate prince is aboard ship. Figgis, can I assume you'll remain alongside 'Skipper' and assist him in any way required?"

"Certainly, my lord," said the pirate, clapping a hand on Casper's shoulder protectively.

"I don't like it," grumbled the boy.

"You don't have to. I'm your father, and more importantly your captain," said Vega, winking affectionately. "Just do as I say, Casper. I'll see you again soon enough, and when I do I'll have a surprise in store for you."

The two embraced, Vega kissing the boy's forehead before reluctantly releasing him. This was a side of the count that few people ever saw. Drew couldn't help but feel a touch envious, seeing the two together. His own family was gone, and fond though he was of the Sharklord he wasn't about to hug him anytime soon. Not for the first time he found himself wondering how Whitley was faring. The girl from Brackenholme was frequently on his mind.

Drew gritted his teeth as the pirate prince and son concluded their good-byes, the stump of his left arm held against the wound in his belly. The wind whipped across the stone jetty, catching Drew's cloak and threatening to blow him off his feet. A howl was carried along the breeze, a ghostly, eerie wail that caused all from the *Maelstrom* to turn and stare into the mist. But the haunting sound was the last thing on the

Wolflord's mind. He was counting the days that had passed since Scorpio's quill had found his guts. The spine had been swiftly removed by a panicked Vega. But the damage was done; the powerful poison of the Werefish was working.

Drew was dying.

The Sea Marshal of Bast hadn't lied: Roby was a ghost town. The Wolf and his allies prowled along the dusty, cobbled avenue, eyes fixed upon the surrounding mists. The occasional building loomed through the cloudy curtain. Each bore the wounds of war, age-old scorch marks staining their crumbling facades. An eerie chill rolled off the ruins in waves, washing over the quick-moving troop as the fog swirled about them.

Drew kept the hood of his cloak about his face, shielding his fevered flesh from the wind. Again, the mournful wail sounded from the ruins, alarm spreading through the group and causing some to call out prayers. Others kissed the holy symbols they carried about their necks, calling upon their gods for favor while they made their way through the dead city. Florimo was out of sight, flying overhead, scouting the land about them. The Ternlord's wings were Drew's secret weapon, and the mind of the old navigator was just as crucial to winning the war in Lyssia. He understood the night sky better than anyone, and Drew had confided in him his crazy idea about harness-

ing the power of the moon. Florimo said it could work, if the heavens were in alignment. A lunar event was approaching, but time, alas, was against them.

Drew glanced to Vega at his side, the Sharklord's demeanor outwardly calm, though the hand on the basket pommel of his rapier told a different story.

"You mean to bring her back to him?" asked Drew, his voice threadbare.

Vega looked to him quizzically. "Who?"

"Shah."

Vega winced at the mention of her name. "I already regret promising him something I may not be able to deliver. The boy deserves to know his mother and that's all I want for him. But what if we arrive in Bana and—"

The count couldn't complete the sentence, but Drew knew his implication. Shah and the rest of them—the Behemoth, Krieg, Taboo—might all be dead, like so many of their friends in this bloody war. But Vega, scourge of the sea and devil of the Cluster Isles, was a sentimental fool at heart. Even with the odds stacked against them, he still sought redemption, trying to be a hero in the eyes of his own child. To reunite mother and son would be the Sharklord's greatest victory ever. Drew prayed he might live long enough to see it.

Once more the howls echoed through the city, causing the Furies who marched up front to falter and come to a halt. The wind whipped up the dirt on the road, blowing it from the cob-

bles and sending it whirling about the company. Hands went to faces, arms across eyes, as men shielded themselves from the blinding dust storm. Drew dropped to one knee, tugging his hood tighter about his head, bringing his chin down to his chest. Even over the howling wind and now frantic shouts of his men, he could hear his lungs rattling, struggling to work. He spluttered, coughing, a glob of blood splattering on the cobbles by his knee.

The awful wailing kicked up a notch suddenly. Some of the men were running now, breaking rank. Even a few of the fearless Furies were bouncing into one another, colliding with the pirates from the *Maelstrom* and the *Red Dog,* all composure lost. Drew looked up from where he crouched, spying Vega still at his side. The Sharklord gripped his head in his hands, hair caught between knuckles, pressing his palms over his ears. He glanced down at Drew, trying to comprehend the power within in the dread noise as their comrades dashed past them.

Those Furies who remained closed ranks around Drew and Vega, their twin swords sliding free of their sheaths as they readied for whatever was out there. Drew wanted to speak but found his throat now constricted, more blood gurgling up. He keeled over, collapsing onto the cobbles. Quickly, the count was beside him, cradling Drew's head in his hands as he trembled and twitched. Drew's vision blurred, the world turning red. He was vaguely aware of the bloody tears as Vega screamed into the howling wind.

"Help me!" shouted the Sharklord. "Somebody, help me! Sweet Sosha, save him!"

From where he lay in the street, Drew could see the sinister mist swirl and eddy, parting down the avenue ahead of them. The Furies who had remained stoic in the face of the terrible chorus of wails now backed up, staggering, some dropping to their knees. Even with his failing eyesight, Drew could see the ghost as it shimmered to life, stepping through the fog, drifting ever closer. The haunting howl was emanating from the specter's awful yawning mouth as it raised a clawed hand toward them. Then another materialized behind it, joining the first as they closed in on the cowering crowd in the street.

The last thing Drew saw before the world turned dark was Vega's stricken face, unable to cry out, his own voice lost as he shared the horror of the humans around him.

7

THE MIDNIGHT MEETING

"DOES NOBODY ELSE think this unorthodox?"

General Skean looked for support from his companions but received nothing in return. There were six members of Onyx's war council present, huddled within the ruined farmhouse. Baron Overmeir, the Buffalo of the Blasted Plains, stood behind him, fingering the dreadlocks of his thick-maned beard. The group's number fluctuated, having originally stood at a dozen before the ravages of war had whittled down their members. Other generals and noblemen were elsewhere in Lyssia, carrying out the Werepanther's orders.

"If the Beast of Bast says we're to meet him here, then we meet him here," said General Gorgo from where he leaned against one of the crumbling walls. "But if you want to

challenge Onyx's command, don't let me stop you."

In the distance, the lights of the Bastian war camp lit up the Badlands, the settlement more sprawling than ever as it had spread into the foothills of the Whitepeaks. Skean was proud of the army's handiwork, the war in the north all but won. The pile of rocks where they had assembled had once been the childhood home of Sheriff Muller, the only human member of Onyx's council. The Cranelord disliked the man, who was always seeking positions above his station. That the self-proclaimed Lord of the Badlands had been spat into the world in this miserable spot came as no surprise to Skean.

"I simply feel there should be a touch more consultation, Gorgo," said the Crane, irritated as ever by the Hippo's demeanor. "You'll have heard the rumors, no doubt? Oba isn't the only high lord who's sailed north: Leon's here in Lyssia."

"What would you propose we do, then, Skean?" chimed in Muller, right on cue. "We have the remaining forces of the Bearlords on the run, hiding within the Badlands and the Whitepeaks. Should we leave them be while we stare at our navels, hoping the Catlords can come to a compromise?"

"Oba and Leon need to speak, human," sneered Skean. "Keep whatever passes for a beak on your withered face out of this. Can you not see your betters are talking?"

"Hold your tongue, Skean," said Muller, straight back at the Crane, turning upon the general. "Your place is no higher at Onyx's table than mine. I'm a member of the war council, and

the Badlands are *mine*. You'd do well to remember that."

"My lords—" said Baron Overmeir, but Skean simply spoke over him.

"Is that an attempt at a threat, Muller? Where did you find a backbone all of a sudden? Was it beneath the rubble in this deity-forsaken pile of refuse that was once your home?"

Muller snatched at the sword handle on his hip, but Skean's daggerlike beak was already emerging from his fine face, glinting sharp and deadly in the starlight.

"Go ahead, *sheriff*, it would be my pleasure."

As Overmeir stood before Skean, General Gorgo seized Muller by the elbow, yanking him back a step and pulling his hand from the pommel.

"Leave it be, Muller," said the Hippo. "You're letting my countryman get under your skin. Save your squabble with him for another day."

"That's right," said Skean. "Be a good boy and listen to General Gorgo. For once his words have made some sense."

"Quit your squawking, Birdlord," rumbled the Hippo.

Muller and Gorgo were little more than lackeys for Onyx, reflected Skean. Neither ever stepped out of line, challenging the Panther's wisdom or authority. And who could blame them, thought Skean. The Pantherlord was a ferocious fellow, as mighty in battle as any Werelord ever known. Gorgo had shadowed Onyx across every inch of Bast, following him from one campaign to the next. He was a prize idiot, but a tremen-

dously capable warrior. But muscle could only ever get one so far. Brains were needed to direct the killing blow in any fight, and Onyx was presently without his.

"Birdlord, Gorgo?" said Skean. "Is that the best insult you can muster? I'll remember that the next time I cross words with the Vulture."

Count Costa, the Vulturelord, was the wits behind many of the Panther's greatest victories, and he was presently occupied with seeking out King Lucas. Skean had his concerns about what might happen if and when Costa found the Lion. The boy was, after all, still the King of Westland and Lord of the Seven Realms. Lyssia was his, not Onyx's, and any justice the Panther wanted to dish out upon Lucas had to be carefully considered. Skean, for one, would not sanction any action. It simply wasn't their place: a Lion ruled Lyssia, and if mistakes were to be made then the risks and consequences were his alone.

The other human in the war council's number was Major Krupha, survivor of the fall of Redmire to the rebels. A good chap, reasoned Skean, and a capable soldier. Unlike the talkative Muller, the Bastian commander remained silent, wary of voicing his opinion in such lofty company. At his side stood the ever-calm Lady Giza, the Weregazelle, keeping her big doe eyes fixed upon the men around her. She was the most level-headed member of Onyx's council, as Skean saw it, which meant she kept quiet unless she had something thoughtful to add to the discussion.

"My lords, we should put a hold on all military decision-making," said Overmeir, the Buffalo-lord, trying to defuse the tension. "At least until we get Oba and Leon to sit down together and hammer out some kind of agreement. It curdles my guts to see our masters at one another's throats."

"Agreed," said Skean. "There must be a way of having the Panther and the Lion sit down together, to work out their differences."

"Hammer out differences?" scoffed Gorgo. "Onyx will likely hammer your brains from your skull, Skean, to hear such talk. Do you really think his father will be amused by your suggestions?"

"I owe it to my liege lord to at least try," said Skean. "It was the Lions whom the Cranes of the Flooded Plains originally swore fealty to. We all serve the Catlords and Bast, but certain alliances run older and deeper. We should all tread carefully before making any rash decisions."

Overmeir nodded, grunting his agreement.

"We can speculate all we like about how to proceed," said Lady Giza finally, "but it's all pointless until Onyx gets here. Let us wait to hear what the Beast of Bast has to say, gentlemen."

"Sage words, my lady," came the Pantherlord's voice out of the darkness, causing all to start with alarm.

Each of them bowed at Onyx's arrival, the giant appearing from the back of the ruined farmhouse and stepping over the broken wall.

"I apologize for my tardy arrival," he said, his voice weary. "I found myself in need of fresh air. The camp can be so suffocating, don't you find? A walk in the dark can really clear one's head."

Skean glanced beyond the ruins into the wilds from where the Pantherlord had come, the land swallowed by the night. *Where has he been?*

"Anyway. To business. It seems you've started without me."

"Apologies," said Skean before anyone else could speak. "We found ourselves with an opportunity to discuss our present . . . conundrum."

Onyx sighed, as if tired of life itself. "So it seems news of our homeland has trickled through to the camp?"

"Indeed," replied Lady Giza. "The union is broken, is it not?"

"Where do we now stand?" asked Baron Overmeir.

"We stand here," said Muller. "There's a war still to be won, an army to command."

"But if the union is no more, what's holding that army together?" asked Skean. "I'm not looking to be divisive, my lords, but I can only see one path to resolution. High Lords Oba and Leon need to meet upon neutral ground and decide what to do."

"You think?" said Onyx quietly.

"I do," said Skean, pleased by the sound of his own voice. He'd given this serious thought and knew his reasoning was

sound. "You and I are kinsmen through our love of Bast, my lord. Each of us who sailed here to Lyssia shares this, forged over decades in service, side by side. We may come from different realms and regions, but we are Bastian brothers first and foremost. Whether our allegiances were originally to Panther, Lion, or Tiger matters not one jot in my eye. Our friendship supersedes any differences."

Onyx turned to Skean and smiled. "Honorable and heartfelt words, old friend," said the Werepanther, reaching out to rest a hand on the Cranelord's shoulder. He gave him a gentle squeeze. "One cannot fight alongside brave souls such as yours without a special bond growing. You truly think our camaraderie can trump the High Lords' difference of opinions?"

"I do indeed," replied Skean confidently. "Surely there are no disagreements that can't be remedied by discussion?"

"So you would speak with Leon? Seek him out and bring him to the table with my father?"

Skean nodded as Lady Giza stepped forward also. "And I wish to seek counsel with my masters in Felos. The Tigers are as much a part of this as anyone."

While one of Onyx's hands remained on Skean's shoulder, the other reached out and patted Giza's shoulder affectionately. "You would do that, my lady?"

"Truly I would, my lord, if I thought it might repair the fractured union," she said.

"And at the end of the day," said Onyx, nodding, "we each remain loyal to our masters—to Panther, to Lion, to Tiger? We forge a new brotherhood, a fresh understanding between the High Lords?"

"Indeed, Onyx," replied Skean as Giza smiled. "Let us return to our respective High Lords, with our retinues, and arrange a meeting at the soonest. Leon's force has already gathered in northern Westland. I could be there before dusk tomorrow if I fly to him tonight."

"Can I not persuade either of you to remain here, trust *my* judgment on how we proceed?"

Giza winced at his words. "I'd be a little uncomfortable continuing as we were."

"Agreed," said Skean. "The Wolf's forces are all but destroyed. Let Oba, Leon, and Tigara resolve their differences and then we may conclude our business in Lyssia."

"And you, Baron Overmeir?" said Onyx, looking between his two friends toward the Buffalo. "Where do you stand upon this matter? Would you follow General Skean to High Lord Leon and await the Lionlord's word on how to proceed?"

Overmeir snorted and shook his dreadlocked beard, Muller sidling up beside him.

"I came here to fight the Wolf and his allies," said the baron. "Point me where you want me to go, Lord Onyx. I'm your weapon to direct until this war is concluded."

The Beast of Bast brought his smiling gaze back to Skean

and Giza, his eyes moving from one to the other. He squeezed the Crane's shoulder again, while stroking the Gazelle's cheekbone tenderly.

"We've done great things together," said Onyx, his voice heavy with pride and something else. What was it, wondered Skean: regret?

"And we could have done so much more."

In his next breath, Skean's world was an explosion of bright light and searing pain as his head crumpled against Giza's. Their temples clashed with an awful crunch, Onyx having driven one into the other like a pair of cymbals. Even with his skull split, blood erupting from his battered brow, Skean embraced the beast. The avianthrope's face began to shift, beak emerging from his wet, red face and stabbing blindly at the Pantherlord. His wings broke free, arches of white-feathered cartilage rising from his spine through the back of his purpose-crafted breastplate.

Onyx released the stunned Gazellelady, concentrating on batting away Skean's rapierlike beak. He beat it one way and then the other before snatching it before it could strike home. The Cranelord felt his beak splintering beneath the Panther's grip, the Catlord's hands shifting into paws as he held Skean firm. He beat his wings, attempting to take flight and tear himself free. His feet came up, taloned tips raking out, the Beast of Bast's hold on his beak beginning to slip. The Panther let loose a growl as it jumped up, reaching past the Crane's head and

seizing a handful of white feathers at its shoulder. The claws went in, tearing tendon and breaking bone as it savaged the general's wing. Skean's beak came free at last, a screech of horror escaping the Crane's narrow throat as an elegant wing was torn away from its back.

With its means of escape gone, the crippled Cranelord was tossed into the rubble, landing unceremoniously against the broken wall. It spluttered and gasped, vision still shot, back aflame, the once deadly beak now battered and busted. Survival instincts were taking over, compelling Skean to rise again, not remain on the ground to be stamped underfoot. A line of figures emerged through the darkness to the front of the broken-down building, their golden helmets shining in the starlight, black horsehair plumes fluttering in the breeze. As the Goldhelms closed in, Skean saw Muller approaching, blade in hand, a smile upon his face. The Crane was suddenly running, hurdling the rocks at the rear of the farmhouse. It caught sight of a slack-jawed Lady Giza. Major Krupha stood behind her, his sword through her belly. Overmeir watched, stunned. The Buffalo's dark face was now pale, his ragged beard trembling as he gritted his teeth. Gorgo stood beside him, a thick hand resting on Overmeir's shoulder.

"You do right, dear Baron," grunted the Hippo as Skean stumbled away from the ruins, shifting back to human form, the sheriff hot on his heels.

"Leave him, Muller," shouted Onyx. "Let him run! See what awaits him in your Badlands!"

Where do I go? Where can I run? The Crane could feel the blood weeping freely down his back, streaming down his flesh, spattering the earth in his wake. If he could make an arc back to the war camp, perhaps he could find his brothers where they rested, awaiting his return. *Strength in numbers, Skean: that's the solution.* He glanced back as he ran, seeing nothing, hearing only his heart pounding, beating like a drum through his battered head. Had Muller truly let him go? Where were they? Were they following?

The Cranelord looked forward just as his foot struck a rock, propelling him skyward into the night. He was cartwheeling, hitting the ground in a shower of stones as he went into a tumble. The world was tilting as Skean bounced down an incline. When he finally came to a halt at the base of the slope he raised his weary, crumpled face and blinked the blood from his eyes. Crows took to the air around him, cawing as they went. The breath caught in his dust-choked throat.

Onyx had been busy. The bottom of the ditch was littered with the butchered bodies of his enemies, heaped on top of one another. Skean spied red cloaks on most of them, and judging by their insignia these were officers of the Lionguard, high-ranking soldiers. The odd Werelord lay among them, the horns, tusks, or twisted wings rising from the mass of corpses. Dark

figures stepped among them, Blackcloaks of the Vermirian Guard putting the occasional survivor to the sword. Their master stepped among them—Skean instantly recognized Vanmorten's cowled form as the Ratlord strode through the slaughtered toward him.

Vanmorten crouched before the fallen Cranelord as Skean spluttered in the dust. The cowl fell back, and the stars shone over Vanmorten's grotesque visage. The left side of his face was burned to a blackened crisp, while the right was bare of flesh, the skull glowing in the sickly light. He reached out, scarred flesh already transforming into the clawed hand of the Wererat. By the time he'd seized Skean by the scalp, he'd completely shifted, daggerlike teeth twitching with anticipation, pink eyes wide with delight.

"The Beast of Bast keeps me terribly busy," hissed Vanmorten. "A loyal ally's work is never done."

Skean tried to speak, tried to beg for mercy, but his throat was clogged with blood and dirt. He could only whimper as the Wererat closed its jaws about his neck, finishing the job that Onyx had begun.

PART III

FIRST BLOOD

I

Passing Through

THE ROOM WAS almost as she'd remembered, but like everywhere in the Seven Realms it bore the scars of war. Trailing lace curtains still hung draped from the four-poster bed, ivy and leaves delicately embroidered throughout their length. The adjoining dressing room's door was ajar. When she was small it had been a treasure trove of gowns, but now only a handful of dresses hung within, plain and more practical affairs than befitted a lady of Lyssia. Jewelry boxes and gem-encrusted bottles had once sat atop the vanity table, containing bracelets, bangles, and perfumes from across the Seven Realms, none of which the tomboyish girl had ever used. They were gone now, casualties of the Wyldermen's occupation of Brackenholme. The

balcony doors were wide-open, the sound of the city rising up from way below, lifting her spirits. Summer's rays illuminated the chamber all around. Flowers stood in a plethora of china vases, gifts from the household to celebrate her return. But for all the beauty of the bouquets, Whitley's eyes were fixed upon the hand-me-down quilt of her childhood, and the selection of weapons that were spread out upon it.

A pair of hunting knives lay side by side, their newly sharpened blades catching the sunlight. Her shortbow sat beside them, its freshly lightened bowstring taut as cheese wire. A fully loaded quiver hung from the chair back, a score of arrows crowded together, their feathered fletching bristling. Her quarterstaff was last, placed along the bed's length, running from foot to pillow, iron-shod ends dark and oiled. She sighed as she appraised them, the items a world away from all else in the bedchamber. This was a room fit for a princess. That was what she'd been once. Of course, she was still a Werelady, the daughter of the Bearlord of Brackenholme, but the path she had taken had left the fancy things behind. She was a scout of the Woodland Watch—a damned fine one at that—and she had no need for trinkets and tiaras. The knives, the bow, and the staff: these were the tools of Whitley's trade now.

A knock brought her round, her head snapping up as she turned to the door.

"Enter."

To her surprise, it wasn't her mother who entered the room. Duchess Rainier had spent the previous two days trying to encourage her to remain in the city, to stay in the Woodland Realm. What mother would truly want her child to march to war, possibly never to return, especially the sole surviving off-spring? But Whitley couldn't concede. Her brother had been murdered at the hand of the Catlords, and her father was lost—possibly dead—somewhere in the wilderness. The girl was the only ursanthrope from Brackenholme left standing. She was the next in Bergan's line. Her people looked to her for direc-tion, and she wouldn't let them down. She managed a strained smile as her visitors entered the room.

"So keen to be away again?" said Yuzhnik, leading Baba Soba into the bedchamber. The Romari giant was the blind el-der's eyes, always close to her side, a tower of strength for the frail old woman. Whitley and Yuzhnik had become firm friends since they had first met in Cape Gala so long ago: he was one of the few people in the Seven Realms she would trust her life to, as well as those of her loved ones.

"I've already stayed too long," said Whitley, reaching down and snatching up the knives. "The men and horses are rested and fed, and we've taken on provisions for the journey. The Dymling Road awaits us."

Since the city had been reclaimed from the Wyldermen after the tribes' blistering attack, the itinerant Romari people had put down roots in Brackenholme, something unheard

of for the traveling community. One of the five Great Trees, the Queen Beech, had succumbed to the fires that had raged through the city. However, the Romari craftsmen had transformed a burned stump into a piece of art, carving the heroes of the Battle of Brackenholme into the scorched trunk. Upon returning home, Whitley had been heartened to spy the likenesses of the lute-playing Stirga and the fallen Hawklord Red Rufus chief among them. Working alongside the people of the Woodland Realm, the Romari had set about rebuilding the city, patrolling the ancient roads that cut through the Dyrewood, making the world that bit safer. The threat of attack from the wild men still lingered—they were still out there in the great forest, nursing their injuries—but for the time being, Brackenholme felt like the safest place in Lyssia for allies of the Wolf.

"Must you go? Cannot another go in your place?" asked the man.

"Did my mother send you?" said Whitley, securing the daggers in place on her weapon belt. "I might have guessed she'd call upon those closest to me."

"That was the worst side step I've ever seen," said Yuzhnik. "I ask you again, is there not someone else who can go instead?"

"No, there isn't," she said, unhitching her green cloak from a bedpost. She wrapped it about her shoulders, snapping shut the Wolfshead brooch beneath her chin. "The Woodland Watch needs me, old friend. They need a ruler of Brackenholme to lead them to war."

"I've said my piece," grunted Yuzhnik, and Whitley allowed a relieved breath to gently escape her clenched jaws. *Good. Perhaps I can be on my way, now?*

Soba's hand shot out suddenly, seizing Whitley's and pulling her close. Her face was worn and weather-beaten, a mass of deep lines and wrinkles that made her look like a dried apple. The baba's eyes suddenly appeared from within the folds of skin, a pair of pale sightless orbs. Whitley flinched, unnerved by the way the wisewoman seemed to stare straight into her soul.

"Death awaits you in the north, child. A battle like no other shall come to pass. Whether the Wolf will live or not, I cannot say, but many will die. Those that the Wolf loves will perish before the final ax falls."

"Those the Wolf loves?" asked Whitley, her voice thin and scratchy, riddled with alarm. "All of us?"

The Romari woman sighed. "Those the Wolf loves shall die. Brother shall cut down brother. Death will find Drew Ferran."

"I know what you're doing," said Whitley angrily. "You and my mother have conspired against me, to keep me here. You're trying to get inside my head, to stop me from going. It's not going to work, Baba. I rode here with the Werelords of the Longridings to gather Drew's allies, while he raises an army in the east. Drew needs me. I—"

"*You* need *him*," interrupted the baba. "Your mother's con-

cerns are her own, child, and I come to you of my own volition. I do not attempt to dissuade you. I left Yuzhnik to make his clumsy overtures in that regard." She squeezed his hand, the giant wincing at her bony grip.

"So why tell me these things?" gasped Whitley, taking up her quarterstaff.

The baba smiled on. "You were always going to go to him. Love is a powerful thing, is it not?"

Whitley shivered, feeling utterly exposed before the wise-woman. Soba's words seemed to break down all her barriers, cut through the childish fears that had dogged her relationship with the young Wolflord all this time. Whitley had never been more aware of her true feelings for Drew, the sensation both nauseating and overwhelming.

"Oh, it is, Baba," she whispered, finding tears in her eyes. "I do love him and I'd tell him as much if I ever see him—" She shook her head with frustration. "*When* I see him again. Brenn see us safely to each other's arms once more."

More figures appeared in the doorway suddenly, Duchess Rainier looking in disapprovingly, a middle-aged Greencloak at her back.

"You still intend to leave?" Whitley's mother asked.

"I must go, Mother," she said, turning to the woman. "I'm a commander of the Woodland Watch, and the heir to Bracken-holme. It has to be me."

"But your uncle Redfearn—"

"Will stay by your side and protect the city. Although if he can spare his best warriors I won't say no." Whitley addressed the Greencloak commander. "General Harker, please send word to our allies within the city: Duke Brand, Lord Conrad, Baron Eben, Captain Ransome, and the rest—Romari, Woodlander, Furies, and friends all. Tell them to ready their warriors. We ride within the hour."

"As you wish, my lady," said Harker, bowing before turning and disappearing into the palace. Whitley watched him go before turning back to Rainier. The duchess wept freely, unable to keep back the tide of tears.

"Do not go, Whitley."

Daughter stepped up to mother, resting her staff against the bedchamber wall momentarily.

"I must," she said, stroking her mother's cheek. "Drew needs me."

Whitley felt Baba Soba's hand upon her shoulder, through the material of her cloak. She gave her a comforting squeeze, bony knuckles creaking.

"Come, Yuzhnik," said the baba. "Let us leave mother and child alone."

The Romari giant led the old soothsayer out of the room, closing the door behind him to leave Whitley in Rainier's arms. She held on tight, burying her face in the nook of her mother's

neck, fearing that if she let go she might meet death that bit sooner.

"Come back to me," sobbed Rainier.

"I'll try, Mother," whispered Whitley, her breath warm against her mother's throat, Rainier's red hair plastered to her teary face. "Brenn help me, I'll try."

2

More Edge

REDMIRE HALL HAD seen some unlikely occupants in recent years. Initially the home of the Boarlord Baron Huth, the manor house had been seized by his youngest son, Vincent, after his father's grisly demise. That tenant hadn't lasted long, fleeing Redmire in a cloud of controversy, bad debts chasing him from his ancestral seat. Next had come the Ratlord Vorhaas, taking the hall in the name of King Lucas and commanding the Lionguard throughout the Dalelands from within. His occupancy was cut short by Lady Gretchen and her Harriers of Hedgemoor, Trent Ferran among their number. The two and their band had remained in the manor for a brief while before taking to the road once more. Then Lucas had come with his Wyld Wolves, seeking out the girl who had once been betrothed

to him, burning all he found on his insane crusade. Two of these monstrous men were now the masters of Redmire Hall, far removed from the noble Boarlords who were the rightful occupants. These were lords of a different kind, their subjects death, decay, and destruction.

Their nest within the shell of the manor house was a grotesque affair, littered with splintered bones and shrouded in flies. Human remains lay alongside those of animals. A couple of crows hopped, pecking at what morsels they could scavenge. The beastly Wyldermen lay in the deepest, darkest shadows. Whatever dark magicks had transformed them into these monsters had changed them irrevocably. They were creatures of the night now, shunning the light and hunting beneath the moon.

Trent stood a distance from them, the sun high overhead, Wolfshead blade in hand. He and Milo had picked up their scent days ago, following them to Redmire. They had given the Wyld Wolves time to settle after the previous night's exertions, waiting until they were convinced they slept. One lay against a wall, a shredded bearskin thrown over it, the pelt alive with maggots and grubs. The other was curled up atop a nest of bones beside a hole in the floor, oblivious to the precarious nature of its bed, the drop leading to the cellars below.

Feelings of revulsion coursed through the Wolf Knight as he stared at the disfigured Wyldermen where they lay, having feasted on Brenn only knew what. Was this what awaited Trent? He felt a slowly building rage at the hand fate had dealt

him. He looked across at Milo and nodded, the boy moving gingerly closer as Trent shifted the Wolfshead blade in his grip. Each had their own target. With a nod, they were off.

Trent proceeded carefully, dozens of bones littering the path between them and the sleeping beasts. A quick glance to Milo and he could see the boy closing in on the Wolfman beside the wall, shortsword held out before him in both hands. Focusing on his own route through the debris, Trent took two more tentative steps, a few yards from his enemy now. Again, a look to Milo. The Staglord's progress was a touch slower, caution his watchword against these bigger, more deadly foes. The boy looked to Trent and managed a nervous smile, but it was clear from his pale, glistening face that he was terrified. A movement at his feet caused Milo to jump suddenly, lashing out instinctively. The crow hopped clear with a squawk, landing upon a pair of crossed bones, sending them rattling across the floor.

Time slowed.

The monster beside the wall was up and leaping toward the young Stag. Its brother was slower to stir, leaving Trent to make a snap decision: dispatch his own foe or jump to the aid of the boy. His mind was made up before he'd drawn breath. Before the beast could strike Milo, it found itself hammered into the wall, Trent's left shoulder having blocked its charge. The sword tumbled out of his hand with the impact as the two grappled one another to the ground. The young Wolf Knight

tore the creature's face with his clawed fingers, channeling his attack toward its head.

His hands found its eyes, the beast squinting them shut, struggling to resist the Graycloak's blinding onslaught. As he dug his claws in, it raked its own down his forearms, attempting to shake him loose. The skin tore away, bloody trenches plowed through his flesh as quivering muscle was revealed. The two rolled, the beast trying in vain to dislodge him, bones crunching and skittering beneath them.

The second monster was up now, leaping at the young Staglord, but Milo was ready. Fool he might have been in the first instance, but he wasn't about to make the same mistake a second time. The boy roared as he met the monster across the ruined hall, his antlers having emerged. The Wolfman tried to parry Milo's shortsword, a couple of dirty fingers flying loose in the process. But that was enough, the hideous Wolfman finding a way past the blade to bowl into Milo's chest. The two tumbled into their own melee, each searching for a telling blow.

Trent's assailant screamed as the youth's claws finally dug into its eyes. The beast stumbled back, blind and stricken, sending bones bouncing across the flags. Sightless though it was, the Wyld Wolf still had other senses to call upon, pouncing upon the wounded Graycloak on the floor. Eyes, however, would have been handy. As the beast landed on Trent, claws outstretched, it found the Wolf Knight's feet braced against its breastbone. Trent had been ready, his raised feet meeting the

creature like an acrobat might catch a tumbler. He straightened his legs, launching it back into the air, the monster vanishing into the cellar's black pit.

Trent looked up to see Milo and the other Wolfman wrestling with one another. The boy went to butt the beast, the hideous lycanthrope punching him in the jaw before his antlers could strike it. The boy's head went back, hitting the flagged floor as the Wolfman moved its attention to his throat. Before its teeth could strike home, Trent's hands had seized it by the shoulders, hauling it up and away from the young Buck. The beast threw an elbow back, striking the Wolf Knight in the solar plexus and causing him to fold like a house of cards. Trent couldn't breathe, the wind knocked from his body, leaving him paralyzed where he knelt in the filth.

The monster glanced back at him, a smile of yellow, razor-sharp teeth zigzagging across its misshapen face. Its fur was clotted with blood and excrement, the remains of feathers hanging from its matted mane the only hint that it had once been a Wylderman. Chuckling, it returned its attention to the young Staglord, preparing to finish off the boy. The awful laughter ceased abruptly. The Wyld Wolf grunted and shuddered, dropping to its knees before the young Stag as Trent's breathing began to level out. The monster slumped forward, hitting the cold stone floor, a human femur buried deep in its belly. Milo stood there, hands open where he'd relinquished his hold on the splintered bone, his face a mask of disbelief.

"Good lad," whispered Trent, as he recovered his senses.

A gurgling growl came from the cellar's entrance, rising up from the darkness below. The two looked at one another warily, Trent struggling to his feet. Milo dashed across the chamber, snatching up their swords, passing the Wolfshead blade to his friend. Trent took the weapon and turned to the pit.

"Stay back, and be ready for anything," he said to Milo before advancing warily. He peered over the edge.

The blinded Wylderman didn't look quite so monstrous anymore, crumpled below in the darkened basement. If anything it looked less beastly and more like the human it had once been. It lay in a pathetic heap, its neck twisted at an awful angle, a burbling whimper emanating from its throat. Even through the gloom Trent could see its neck was broken. He stood over the hole before dropping through, landing astride the crippled Wolfman. Its bloodied sockets stared into space as Trent knelt down beside it, moving his face until they were inches apart.

"You were human, once," said the youth from the Cold Coast. "Tell me what I need to know and I'll end your misery."

The beast moved its mouth, muzzle twitching as it tried to make words.

"You . . . like me . . ." The monster managed to laugh, a wheezing rattle escaping its horrid lips.

"Where's your master? Where will I find Lucas?"

The laughter continued, growing fainter as the Wolfman's

life began to fade. Trent shook the beast by its shoulders, the crooked head lolling, the grotesque giggle continuing. Its gums smacked, the words guttural.

"More . . ." it spluttered. "Edge . . ."

"What do you mean? More edge? My sword?" Trent held the Wolfshead blade against its neck. "You want my blade?" he screamed angrily.

The tormented soul that had once been a Wylderman uttered one more word as it took its last breath.

"More . . ."

The monster was still, dark tongue lolling from between its daggerlike teeth. Trent punched the beast's chest angrily before crying out in frustration. His scream became a howl as he emptied his soul, cursing the Wyld Wolf's riddling words.

"More edge," said Milo from above, his voice quiet and scratchy. "Edge more."

Trent sniffed back the tears, lifting his face up to the light and the bright-eyed young Stag who crouched over the hatch.

"Edge more," he said again, this time more confidently. "Hedgemoor, Trent. Lucas is in Hedgemoor."

3
GRAY SON

WHERE DREW WAS, he had no idea. He lay upon a pile of animal skins, the fur soft and warm beneath him. A chill wind rushed over his body, the unmistakable whiff of salt in the air. He knew he'd been asleep, his dreams haunted by the ghosts of his loved ones. *Am I still dreaming? Does my mind play tricks on me?* The world was fog-shrouded and impenetrable to his bleary eyes.

Sitting up, Drew was surprised to see a figure moving toward him through the gloom. Her ivory skin glowed like the moon, and her gray eyes sparkled, studying him keenly as he scrambled to his feet. Her face made her appear a touch younger than he was, but she had long white hair braided down her back, with tiny shells, beads, and feathers twined

throughout. She wore a mottled brown animal-skin cloak with a ruff of dark fur around its hood that hung loose, revealing her pale shoulders.

In one hand, she carried a staff of bleached wood that reminded him of driftwood like one might find along the Cold Coast, with more feathers and small bones adorning its head. Her other hand reached out toward his face before descending over his torso. There it paused, fingers fluttering a hair's breadth from the wound in Drew's guts. Then they connected, their touch electric against his abdomen.

"I see you're feeling better, Gray Son," she said.

"Better?" He glanced back at the bed of animal skins upon the rocky ground.

"You were calling for Brenn's embrace when we found you by the river. But now your strength is recovered. The corruption is removed." Automatically, Drew ran his hand over his stomach, pulling open his shirt and looking down. The wound was no longer discolored, the flesh already scarring over.

"You're a healer, like my friend Hector?"

She arched an eyebrow. "I am *nothing* like your friend Hector."

Drew sensed her displeasure at mention of the Boarlord. It appeared his sordid reputation had reached Shadowhaven.

"You're a magister, though?"

"No, Gray Son. I am a seer."

"What happened to my friends?"

The white-haired girl cocked her head to one side and stared quizzically at him. "You ask a lot of questions, Gray Son."

"Why do you keep calling me Gray Son?"

"There's another question."

Drew shook his head. There was something familiar about this girl that he couldn't quite place, and it nagged him as much as her peculiar behavior.

"You're not at all what I expected," she said. Her big eyes looked a little less innocent now, and more mischievous. "I expected the Gray Son to be a giant, such are the stories told about him."

"You keep saying 'the Gray Son,'" he said. "What do you mean?"

"You are the child of Wergar, are you not? The last son of the Gray Wolf of Westland. As kings go you're rather small in the flesh, and a little rough around the edges."

Drew was taken aback.

"Look, little girl, I don't know who you are or what your business is, but I'm tired of your talk. Am I your prisoner? Where are my men? Whom must I thank for healing my wounds? If you won't answer my questions, then fetch me someone who can!"

The girl's eyebrows rose, a smile spreading across her pale face.

"And such a temper, too! You get that from your father, I expect—"

His hand shot out, seizing her by the wrist, his other arm at her waist. Her staff clattered to the ground as Drew pulled her in close. He snarled, showing his teeth. But if he had hoped to intimidate her into quitting her childish play, it didn't work. She stared back at him, cold and unblinking.

"Release her or lose your other hand."

Drew turned to his right as a figure emerged from the fog. A good head taller than he was, the stranger wore a cloak similar to the girl's. His white hair hung loose and shaggy about his face, his lantern jaw set in a grimace. At first glance Drew assumed he also carried a staff, lowered and pointed toward him. As the man stepped closer the spear's shining, metal head caught the light, leveled at the young Wolflord.

"You going to lower that spear?" asked Drew, his eyes never leaving the stranger, his arms still wrapped tightly about the girl.

"Will you release her?" He was a few summers Drew's senior, his voice deep and baritone, booming from his barrel chest.

"What have you done with my friends and belongings? Am I your prisoner?"

"You're no prisoner, Gray Son," said the giant youth. "And your belongings are safe."

"Show me my friends!"

"Show us some trust," growled the warrior, twirling the

spear in his grasp, its blade shining white. "We are your kin, after all."

Drew's eyes flitted into the mist, looking for a sign of where he might be. He backed up, finding the beginnings of an incline. How was he to suddenly trust this peculiar duo? He had been with the Furies and the Sharklord in Roby; that was his last memory. And what was the man talking about?

"Kin?" said Drew, stumbling farther down the slope.

The girl suddenly raised her head from his chest. The snarling muzzle of a White Wolf met his alarmed face, causing him to instantly release his hold. His foot stepped back into thin air and he threw out his arms, losing balance. Glancing over his shoulder, he spied churning water and jagged rocks through the mist.

The girl's claws caught his flailing hand, the two joined once more, both heading over the cliff to the waves below. Her other hand reached back, snatching the man's spear as he thrust it through the air beside her. The three hung there for a heartbeat, a suspended chain of interconnecting limbs, before gravity and momentum seized the moment. Drew felt himself swing through the air, watching with amazement as he was suspended helpless in the grasp of the White Wolf. The warrior roared, every muscle straining as he swung them all about, depositing them back onto the solid ground of the cliff top.

Before Drew could catch his breath the female lycanthrope

had rolled clear, the man's spear point jabbed into the hollow of his neck below his Adam's apple.

"Mikotaj, no!" shouted the girl, appearing behind the towering warrior. While she had returned to human form, the other was changing. Drew could see the young man's face twitching, white stubble bristling over his jaw as his muzzle began to emerge. His gray eyes clouded over yellow, focused on Drew with deadly intent. He felt the spearhead prick his flesh, the unmistakable white metal of enchanted Sturmish steel capable of killing him in an instant. The girl's hand landed on Mikotaj's broad shoulder as she brought her face down to his lupine ear.

"No, brother," she whispered.

"You don't want to upset the White Death, Drew."

All three turned to look across the rocky precipice as Count Vega approached through the thinning mist. The Sharklord was smiling, arms open.

"The White Death?" asked Drew as the giant lycanthrope snarled.

"That's what his enemies call him," continued Vega. "Perhaps we can just take a moment, my lords and lady. Especially you, Mikotaj. It seems we've all gotten a little hot under the collar, no?"

Mikotaj snarled once more before yanking the spear from Drew's throat, his features slowly shifting back. The count stepped between them, bending to help Drew to his feet.

"I owe the Gray Son an apology, Count Vega," said the girl, her big eyes flashing with something that might've been shame. "My playful nature can often get me into trouble."

"Call me Drew," said the young Wolflord, brushing himself down. "And I'm sorry, too. I fear I lost my sense of humor some time ago."

"Better to lose that than your head," grunted Mikotaj, turning his neck as his jaw and spine realigned with a resounding *crack*. "Apologies aside, never touch Miloqi again."

"You're awfully protective of your sister."

"As would you be if there was someone so precious in your life."

Drew found himself thinking of Whitley again. *What would I do to keep her safe from harm?* The list was endless.

"Mikotaj and I are the only remaining White Wolves of Shadowhaven," said Miloqi, by way of explaining her brother's passionate words.

"How can you be sure of that?" asked Vega. "I've heard rumor of others roaming the Whitepeaks."

"We've found none," said Mikotaj.

"The Lion broke the will of our people many years ago," added his sister. "Those who once called Shadowhaven home are flung far across Sturmland. Leopold left deep scars behind, turning our once great city into a pile of ashen ruins."

"My mother, Queen Amelie, hails from Shadowhaven,"

said Drew, unable to hide his excitement about telling them his news. "You're not alone."

"We are now," said Mikotaj bitterly.

Drew didn't understand what he meant. He looked from the giant warrior to Vega, who dipped his head and avoided the Wolflord's gaze. Miloqi was the only one who would look at him, her big gray eyes now full of sadness.

"I'm sorry, Gray Son, but the queen is dead."

"We truly are alone," said her brother.

"Dead?" said Drew, his body motionless while inside he was reeling. "How?"

"We don't know the details, but we fear she met her end in Icegarden," said the girl. "Her howl was heard as far east as Shadowhaven."

"How can that be? That's hundreds of leagues away!"

"There are ancient magicks in this world, Gray Son, many particular to each Werelord," said Miloqi. "The Werewolf's call can come in many ways, shapes, and forms. It can be the howl that heralds battle and rallies an army. It can be the blood-chilling wail that strikes fear into the heart of the mightiest warrior. And it can be the mournful death cry carried upon the wind, racing across mountains until it finds its way home."

Drew shook his head, struggling to accept Amelie's death. There had been so much he had hoped they could do together, so many things he wanted to tell her. Now it had been snatched away from him, like so much else.

Vega cleared his throat. "Come. Let us talk while we walk." He set off along the cliff, finding the path down that he'd taken up, the other three following him as he descended.

"You know these White Wolves?" whispered Drew. "You speak like old friends."

"I knew their father, but these two were infants the last time we met. No, I've had a few days in their company while you convalesced. They've been generous, if peculiar, hosts. You've been ill, Drew; terribly sick with Scorpio's poison. Miloqi's the only reason you still draw breath. Her magick saved your life."

Drew glanced back at the following White Wolves, irked by the healer's mischievous ways and her prickly brother.

"Please tell me you've some good news from the wider world?"

"Morsels," said the count. "Mikotaj has heard of Icegarden's survivors making their way east."

"Survivors?" Drew hated asking the question. His old friend Hector had taken the city for himself, with the help of the Crows, seizing it while Duke Henrik and Onyx had warred with one another. To learn of bloodshed by the Boarlord's hand was utterly unfathomable, but he knew it to be true.

"Many, it would appear," added Mikotaj. "Word has carried our way that they left the city in droves, aided in their escape by Blackhand, of all people, the villain who had imprisoned them in the first place."

Drew seized the small sliver of hope. In recent months he had been horrified to hear of his dear friend's descent into wickedness, fearing the innocent young Boar from Redmire was forever lost. Could he truly have turned away from his dark path? He prayed it was so.

"Hector helped them escape? Then he's come to his senses?"

"I fear not. He didn't join them in their exodus. He directed them into the catacombs beneath the Whitepeaks and left them to find their own way out. They joined with the remnants of the Bearlord army once they reached daylight. Blackhand remains within the frozen walls of Icegarden."

Drew stepped down the cliff after Vega, the sea captain's steps deft and sure on the mist-slicked rocks. The white-haired siblings followed close behind. Through the mist Drew spied the twisted mast of a ship poking out of the churning waters.

"This stretch of water," said Drew, gesturing with his stumped wrist as they climbed closer. "The River Robben?"

"Indeed," said Miloqi.

"And beyond, across the neck, is the entrance to the Bana Gap, and our imprisoned allies," said Vega. "These cliffs are on either side, making it almost impossible to bring an ocean-going vessel in. This part of the Robben's a graveyard to many a good ship."

"We still need to find a way across," said the young Wolflord.

The sea mist cleared as they reached the bottom of the incline. A long shale beach stretched out, jagged, outcroppings of rock reaching into the fast-flowing tide like clawed fingers. At least three dozen long rowboats rested on the slate pebbles, surrounded by men loading gear onto them: shields, spears, swords, and saddles. Horses were led across the gray stones, the beasts whinnying nervously as they boarded the larger skiffs. Furies worked alongside northmen, Bastians beside Lyssians, as they prepared the fleet of vessels. Florimo strode toward their party, the navigator's arms loaded with Drew's weapon belt and breastplate.

"Thank you," said Drew as he took his sword and studded leather from the Ternlord. His eyes lingered upon massed ranks of northmen along the shore, axes and spears strapped to their animal hide armor. The warriors easily outnumbered his own force, yet the White Wolves had said they were alone. If so, where had this army come from?

Drew turned back to Mikotaj and Miloqi. "I thought you said you were the sole survivors of Shadowhaven?"

"Of the White Wolves, aye," said the warrior. "But the humans who lived alongside us? They still heed our call."

"Come, Gray Son," said Miloqi, slinking past him toward the waiting army. "You've friends to free."

4
THE FARM AND THE FIRE

IT WOULD HAVE been the perfect picture of a Dalelands idyll. The sun hung high overhead, casting summer rays over the picturesque land below. A few cotton clouds drifted lazily in the azure sky, meandering through the heavens. The warm wind caressed the hills. If it were not for the spiral of black smoke that rose from the burned-out farmhouse to the north, Gretchen's heart might have soared.

"Smoke bad," said Kholka, the king of understatement.

The phibian war party was spread out through the meadow, hunkered low, peering through the tall, shifting grasses. They numbered thirty, the strongest and most able-bodied men the village could offer.

"Carry on," said Shoma, pointing east with his spear.

"No," said Gretchen. "We need to investigate."

Shoma frowned at her, an expression he favored frequently whenever the two conversed.

"We must go and look," clarified the girl. "There may be clues there, something that points us toward their whereabouts."

"Carry on," repeated Shoma, now shaking his head and jabbing his weapon eastward. "Redmire. Redcloaks."

He wasn't wrong. Redmire was the biggest settlement in the western Dalelands; if the Lionguard were anywhere, then that was surely the place. Shoma's desire for revenge was clouding his judgment, though, since the Lionguard had butchered his father on the outskirts of the Bott Marshes. His rash actions could lead them all to their deaths.

"Listen, Shoma. You're in *my* world now. If we're to attack the Redcloaks, half the battle is gaining as much information on our enemies as possible. If we go in unprepared we'll be cut to ribbons!"

"Carry on," said the phibian stubbornly, moving to strike at her feet with his spear butt.

"No," she snarled, seizing it before it could hit the earth.

Now they had the attention of the rest of the war party, all eyes on the girl and their elder. Shoma's throat ballooned as he grew in stature, legs extending, enormous thighs rippling with muscles. Gretchen stood her ground, a deep growl emanating from her chest.

"Girl mad!" hissed the Werefrog, his eyes bulging, skin mottling green and brown.

"Let's make a deal, Shoma," she said, keeping hold of the spear. "We investigate that farm. If there's nothing there that can help us, I won't challenge you again. This war party is yours to do with as you will, and I'll do as you command. But if there's information to be found there," she went on, pointing north to the tower of black smoke, "well, I think we need to reevaluate who leads this group, don't you?"

"Fair words," said Kholka, a chorus of agreeable croaks coming from the other phibians. All eyes turned to Shoma, awaiting his response. The elder's huge eyes narrowed, lids stretched over pale yellow globes.

"Fair words," said Shoma, snatching his spear back from Gretchen's hands. "Lead on, girl. Then Redmire."

The farm was typical of those in the Dalelands, a cattle baron's homestead. Built on one floor, its roof had once acted as a hayloft, the hall below open and housing the farmer, his family, and his workers. The people who worked the land in these parts were a communal bunch, living in one another's pockets and sharing good and ill fortune. Those who had made this farm their home had encountered the latter variety of fortune, and to grisly effect.

On approaching the farm, the Marshman war party had discovered the male farmers staked into the ground, in the same

manner as Shoma's father had been killed. Of the women and children there was no sign, which caused Gretchen's blood to run cold. The old hayloft that had run the length of the house was gone, devoured by the inferno, the building a burned husk like so many throughout the Dalelands. *Is fire the answer to every invading force's problems?* The corpses of the farmers weren't the strangest things the band of phibians found there, though. Nor was the blackened farm and its crackling, still smoking timbers.

The bodies of two dozen Lionguard littered the ground in and around the smoldering farmhouse. Slumped over barrel and wall, lying in ditches, battered and broken in the rutted road; the slaughtered soldiers were everywhere. Throats were slit, stomachs slashed, limbs severed, and lives snuffed out. Swords remained in the scabbards of many of the Redcloaks, the men butchered where they stood before they could even defend themselves. The phibians moved among the dead, poking them warily with their spears, unable to comprehend the bizarre turn of events in the farmhouse. Gretchen's frown was so deep she could feel the approach of a headache. *Who would do this? Are my* friends *responsible for this?*

She should have felt joy to see the Lionguard cut down to size in such dramatic fashion, but other feelings clouded her mind: pity, shock, and disgust. This was a victory against the Redcloaks, but the manner of it was horrific. If her people had been responsible, they had moved on since she had led them. She

doubted prisoners had been taken, and it seemed clear no mercy had been shown. She shivered, unease welling in her guts.

"You ill?" asked Kholka.

"With worry," said Gretchen as Shoma strode up to the two of them.

"Good work," said the elder, casting his spear around them and pointing out the slain Lionguard. "Many dead."

Gretchen held her tongue. She wasn't about to begin another argument with Shoma, not so soon after their last altercation. She walked away from them, closer to the burning ruin. A horse lay slaughtered on the cobbled forecourt, still harnessed to a tarpaulin covered wagon. The decapitated body of a Redcloak sat propped against one of the wagon's wheels, head in lap, face frozen in a ghastly death mask. No, this couldn't be the work of her friends.

Behind her, a whimper sounded from within the wagon. She glanced back, spying the bundle of tarpaulin in its back. Whipping out her hunting knife, she waved back to Kholka, catching his eye. She pointed at the wagon and raised a finger to her lips. Before he could move, Shoma had already reacted, leaping forward from where he stood and landing atop the open wagon. Gretchen cursed, jumping up the back of the wagon as Shoma reached down, snatching the tarpaulin and yanking it back.

A Redcloak lay beneath the sheet, curled up, holding his

belly in his bloody hands. His face was drained of color, auburn hair plastered across his wet brow. His eyes were bleary as he stared at the phibian and Foxlady. Gretchen saw Shoma draw back his spear, about to strike home.

"No!" she yelled, jumping in front of the Werefrog and pushing his weapon aside.

"Shoma want revenge!"

"Shoma can wait for revenge!"

She looked back to the young Lionguard who trembled at her feet. "How old are you?"

"I seen fifteen summers," he whispered through bloody teeth.

"And they let you take the Red?"

"Conscripted from my village on the Cold Coast," said the boy, wincing. "They ain't fussy about age since the war started. Oh, Brenn, my guts. It hurts so bad. Please make it stop!"

Her hatred of the Lionguard waned, looking at the wretched boy close to death. The lad was a victim of the war as much as the phibians.

"The dead farmers," she said. "You're responsible for this?"

"Not me," said the lad. "The others. I didn't do nothing. Just followed orders."

Gretchen shuddered at his last comment. She knew only too well what that might mean. Even the most rational peacetime folk could commit atrocities during wartime when

following orders. The phibians had all gathered around the wagon now, their big eyes trained on the lad, spears waving like reeds in the river.

"What happened here?" asked Gretchen. "Who killed your troop?"

"Our own," said the soldier, moaning again as he rolled into a fetal ball.

"What do you mean, 'your own'? Redcloaks did this?"

"Goldhelms," spluttered the boy. "Them Bastians, weren't it. Welcomed them into our camp with open arms and look what they did!"

Gretchen turned to Kholka. "Goldhelms turning on Redcloaks? Panthers against Lions?"

"Means what?" said the Marshman, trying to follow her train of thought. She shook her head, forgetting that hers wasn't his tongue.

"Sorry, Kholka. It seems our foes have made enemies of one another. Catlords of Bast fighting those who rule Lyssia."

"Good thing?"

"I hope so." She turned back to the Redcloak. "Where did the Bastians go after they did this?"

The boy wheezed where he lay and then managed a chuckle.

"What's so funny?"

"They're going to Hedgemoor."

Gretchen's ears pricked at the name of her home.

"Why Hedgemoor?"

"Because that's where King Lucas is," said the boy, coughing up blood as he laughed. "And the rest of them!"

"Lucas is in Hedgemoor?"

"Aye. He's made it his home in the Dalelands while he searches for . . ." the lad's words trailed off as he looked hard at her. "It's you, ain't it? You're his bride: the Foxlady!"

"I'm no bride of Lucas's," she snapped. "Why do you laugh, though? Who are the rest you speak of?"

Even as she asked the question she knew the answer. Her mind went back to the terrible night in Bray, where she'd seen her friends butchered by the young Lion king and his awful twisted lycanthropes. Trent had been killed that night, murdered before her eyes by the monsters.

"The Wyld Wolves, my lady," said the boy. "If the Goldhelms think the king's going to roll over and show them his belly, they're in for a shock. Just wait until Darkheart and his brothers get ahold of 'em!"

Darkheart, the Wylderman shaman. The man was a monster, and with this terrible transformation had become so much more.

"You'll help me?" the boy begged, rocking on the timber cart as Gretchen turned to Kholka.

"We need to go to Hedgemoor. You want revenge upon the Redcloaks, that's where the true target of your ire resides. The Werelion, Lucas, has made the city his home. It was his men who killed Shoma's father—ordinary men like those who lie

211

dead here today. But it's his will they carry out."

She heard a sudden *thunk* from behind as something hard struck the timber base of the wagon. Looking back, she saw Shoma standing over the boy. The Redcloak no longer struggled, his fight instantly over. As the Marshman pulled his spear from the body, Gretchen stepped forward and slapped him hard across the face. "What in Brenn's name did you do?"

"Shoma help boy. Pain end. Now Redmire. More Redcloaks."

She brought her hand back to strike him again. "You cold-hearted son of a—"

He caught her wrist and snarled. "Girl say: *Shoma wait for revenge.* Shoma wait long enough. Shoma take revenge."

Gretchen tugged her hand loose and sneered at the elder. She reached down and pulled the tarpaulin over the dead boy.

"So you did," she said. "What a brave warrior you are, Shoma. And now to my terms. We've discovered plenty by coming here, including the whereabouts of our enemy. I'll be leading this war party henceforth. Agreed?"

She looked to the phibians as they all croaked their assent, many glowering at Shoma and his vengeful deed. Gretchen stared coldly at the elder as he looked away shamefaced.

"We don't travel to Redmire. We go to Hedgemoor. We've a Lion to hunt."

5

HEDGEMOOR

"YOU GO NO further, Milo. I mean it."

The two Graycloaks stood in the shadows of the gatehouse, looking across the abandoned courtyard. One wore the soot-gray of Stormdale, the other the pale gray of the Wolfguard, but each served the same man: Drew Ferran, last of the Wolves of Westland and rightful king of the realm. They had made their way through the city, expecting to encounter signs of life along the way, but there had been none. The streets were empty, the city silent and uninhabited. It was as if the entire populace had simply pulled up stakes and scarpered. And now they stood before the stately Hedgemoor Hall, laden with gloom and choked by a thick veil of ivy.

"I've come this far with you, Trent. You remember the deal we struck?" said Milo, hand resting on the pommel of his shortsword. "I need to be there for you."

Trent shivered. The lad was right: should the Wolf take control, the young Stag would do the necessary deed and put him out of his misery. That is, if Milo wasn't killed in the process. The beast that lurked within Trent was getting stronger day by day, struggling for dominion over his mind and body. He looked back down the road they had approached the mansion along.

Gretchen had told him of Hedgemoor, how the city was widely regarded as the Garden of the Seven Realms. In his more fanciful moments, Trent had looked forward to the chance of visiting the city one day with her, should Lyssia ever know peace again. Perhaps it had been a beauty once, but no more. The entire city was tired and weary, the flowerbeds that lined the avenues overgrown, their plants dead or overrun by sickly weeds. Severed heads sat atop pikes and spears along the walls, a remnant of General Krupha's reign over the city. The rotten skulls faced outward, picked clean of flesh, a warning to all. Bray burned, Redmire razed, and Hedgemoor abandoned, the Dalelands were a cursed realm.

"Please, Milo. Stay back here. Don't come with me. If Lucas is in there—"

"We'll face him together," cut in the boy. "We're a team, Trent. You and me, against all odds, shared kinship and shared

foes. It was Brenn who guided me to you on the banks of the Redmire, back in Bray. He's kept us together ever since."

"It's all part of Brenn's grand plan, eh? Very well," said Trent. "But for pity's sake, if all looks lost, if it seems Brenn has taken his eye off our welfare, get gone, Milo. If I'm done for you start running and you don't stop until you find friends. Understand?"

The boy didn't acknowledge him either way. His mind was clearly set.

"Come," said Trent. "Let's discover what's in there. Tread carefully, Milo. Tread silently."

The two set off into the courtyard, hugging the shadows that shrouded the walls, drawing ever nearer the foreboding Hedgemoor Hall.

Signs of the Wyld Wolves were everywhere. The air within the mansion was thick with their scent, and the remains of many of their victims littered the once fabulous corridors of the stately home. The carpets were painted dark with all manner of terrible stains; tapestries and paintings had been vandalized and torn down. Around each corner a fresh abomination awaited, acts of mindless violence that were the handiwork of the monstrous Wyldermen. Trent and Milo moved stealthily, making no sound with their passing. Occasionally, the Wolf Knight glanced back, pleased to see that the boy was focused

on the task at hand, eyes on their dark path, ignoring the horrors that surrounded them.

The main hall of the house had clearly once been a breathtaking affair. Dark chestnut panels clad the walls up to the pitch-black vaulted ceiling, reminding Trent of a grand hunting lodge, but the notion ended there. The hall was a disgrace, now taking the breath away in a quite different manner. An enormous fireplace dominated the far end of the darkened room, the fire crackling and spitting within the sole source of light. Choking black smoke swirled out of the blocked chimney, spilling into the chamber and rising into the ceiling where it gathered in clouds. Those once splendid walls were now adorned with terrible trophies, the body parts of the occupants' enemies hammered in or rammed onto the splintered wood.

An enormous table ran the length of the hall, every seat taken by a golden-helmeted Bastian soldier. At first glance, Trent feared they had walked in on some kind of military council, until he realized none were moving. As his eyes adjusted to the gloom, he spied the blood on their pitted armor. Many sat in their chairs, or were rather fixed there, swords having been driven through them into the wooden backs of their seats. Some had fallen free of their positions, slumped onto the table facedown in empty tin plates. There were perhaps two dozen Goldhelms propped about the dining table like mannequins at a feast. Flies buzzed, making homes in the corpses, the only meal that was under way.

"Come out of the shadows."

Trent had never heard him speak before. He had served him, sworn an oath to the speaker's father back in the day when he'd foolishly taken the Red. He had joined the Lionguard under the misguided belief that Drew Ferran was a monster; Trent had needed vengeance for his mother's death, and becoming a Redcloak outrider had given him a stab at that.

How wrong he had been. The Lions were the monsters, all of them, and they'd been the cause of Trent's mother's murder, committed by a Ratlord at the behest of King Leopold. And now that monster's son sat before them, alone at the head of the grisly table, fire at his back, iron crown sitting flush upon his brow.

"Would you disobey your king? Come forward so I may better see my subjects!"

Trent looked around the room, behind the chairs that held the dead Goldhelms. Of the Wyld Wolves there was no sign. Were they out hunting? It was late in the day, approaching dusk. Did they still sleep in a pit somewhere, shunning the light like the others they had encountered? He could feel his heart rate quickening, sudden and terrifying. Alone with the king, now was their chance. The Wolfshead blade slid silently from its sheath as Trent looked to Milo, a frightened smile passing over the boy's face. He had been right: this was Brenn's doing. He watched over them. He wanted this deed done.

"You're no king of mine, Lucas," said Trent as he strode

forward, Milo following behind. The boy from Stormdale was already beginning to shift, his antlers emerging from his brow.

"You dare to walk into my country retreat, unannounced, and speak to me this way?" exclaimed the young Lion, his voice thick with outrage, though his body language told a different story. He sat slumped, every bit as lifeless as the dead Bastians at the table.

"I dare do a hell of a lot more than that, you mad fool."

Trent leapt up onto the table at its bottom end, setting off between the assembled corpses, kicking plates aside as he went. As he ran, he felt the months of pent-up anger coming off him in waves, rage speeding him toward his enemy. The Wolfshead blade trailed at his back, ready to strike when he reached the Lion. His mother and father dead, Gretchen taken from him by the Wyld Wolves, his brother Brenn only knew where—all because of Lucas and his family. Now was the time to strike back for the last of the Gray Wolves and Westland.

"Be careful, Trent!" shouted Milo.

As Trent leapt into the air, sword now high over his head, ready to come down and split the king in twain, Lucas was already rocking back in his chair. At the last moment, Trent spied the crossbow in the Werelion's lap, heard the twang of the bow, and felt the bolt hit him in the chest. The king was out of his chair by the time Trent crashed into it, timber frame collapsing, the young Graycloak landing in a heap of kindling before the fireplace. He cried out as he reached up, finding the

bolt embedded through his leather, buried in the right side of his chest.

"Trent?" said the Lion. "As in *Ferran*? Can it really be?"

The Wolf Knight rose, ignoring the pain in his chest. Lucas was smiling, jabbing a finger at Trent's torso.

"You can thank me for that. It could quite easily have found your heart, Trent. I was going to kill you until your little friend back there alerted me to your name."

Lucas slapped his thigh and laughed, tossing the crossbow aside as Trent circled him. The boy king looked bedraggled and unkempt, a shadow of the shining prince that Leopold had shown off to all and sundry back in Highcliff. His yellow hair was greasy, plastered against his filthy face, a patchy beard around his neck and jaw. Livid scars marked his cheek: Trent knew Gretchen had left them there. Spots and sores covered his skin.

"You look ill," said Trent.

"It might be my diet," said Lucas. "I suspect I need some fresh meat."

"Reckon it's the company you're keeping," replied Trent, knuckles straining as he gripped the sword, weighing his chance to strike. Lucas seemed distracted, animated, almost enjoying the conversation.

"Well, Brenn help us, Trent Ferran. Who could have imagined this? A family reunion, if you will, eh?"

"You're no family of mine."

"Ah, but we share a brother, do we not?"

"Your brothers are the devils, those Wyld Wolves. I'll be killing them once I'm done with you."

"Brave words for a man who's slowly bleeding out." The king gestured to Trent's chest. "That looks like it smarts. Am I right?"

"I've had worse," Trent lied, the pain sickening, his breastplate filling with blood.

Lucas's laugh became a growl. "Don't be silly, Ferran. Of course you haven't. But you will. Oh my life, you will."

As the Werelion began to change, movements caught the Graycloak's attention above. From out of the thick cloud of black smoke that boiled at the ceiling, dark shapes began to fall, landing all around the room. Their clawed feet hit stone flags and timber table, their bodies thick with dark fur, hackles bristling malevolently. Yellow eyes shone all around him in the darkness as the Wyld Wolves materialized from the gloom. Lucas backed away, swallowed by the shadows as the monsters took his place.

"You return to the pack," said one of the beasts, the only one of their number that appeared vaguely human. It wore a headdress of capercaille feathers, and two serrated flint daggers hung from loops of leather about its waist.

"You're not my pack," snarled Trent, Wolfshead blade in one hand, claws open in the other. The beasts growled and snapped at him. He spun, slashing, stabbing, and biting, trying to ward them off.

"Milo!" he shouted, suddenly terribly aware of his young friend's plight.

"Looking for this little chap, are we?" asked the Werelion, returning to allow the fire to illuminate his prisoner. The Catlord dragged the young Stag by one of his antlers, the boy's head trapped by a pawlike fist. The Lion shook him, bringing the lad up before its maned face.

"Let him go," begged Trent. "He's only a boy."

"I'll release him on one condition," said Lucas. "That sword you carry. I've longed to have it for some time, Ferran. It was your brother's, was it not?"

"It was our father's," corrected Trent. "He carried it as a member of the Wolfguard when he served King Wergar, before your old man stole the throne!"

"Isn't it wonderful when a weapon has such a story to tell, handed down from father to son? Throw it here, Ferran, and I release the boy."

"I'm no boy, Lucas! I'm Lord Milo, son of Duke Manfred, Staglord of Stormdale!"

"And a proud little Buck you are, too," Lucas said, smiling briefly, the Lion's face momentarily benign before it turned back to Trent. "The Wolfshead blade, Ferran. Give it up."

Trent grimaced, watching the beasts as they circled him. With the Wolfshead blade and its silver-blessed steel he had a chance against the Wyld Wolves, no matter how remote. But if he gave it up, he was sure to die. Then again, if it bought Milo

his freedom, it was a small price to pay. Putting his faith in Brenn, he tossed the sword across the hall where it clattered onto the floor at Lucas's feet. The Lion bent down and picked up the sword in its free hand before straightening.

"Good dog," it said, turning the weapon one way and then the other in the light of the fire, inspecting its craftsmanship as the Wyld Wolves drew closer to Trent. "And now we can release the little Staglord."

The Wolfshead blade vanished into Milo's stomach in one smooth fluid movement. Trent's scream came out as a howling roar as he watched Lucas unhand the boy's antlered head, his young friend sliding off the blade and onto the fire's hearthstone. The Wyld Wolves were already striking Trent, their claws tearing at his back, his shoulders, punching and slashing. He heard Lucas's voice as he sank to his knees beneath a hail of blows.

"I'm hungry all of a sudden," said the Werelion, crouching over the dying boy. "I think venison's on the menu."

6

THE BATTLE OF THE BANA GAP

THE NORTHERN BAREBONES rose out of the desert, a menacing curtain of towering rock that separated Omir from its neighboring realms. From Riven in the west to the Red Coast in the East, the black mountains were impassable; only the mad and suicidal chose to traverse them. Even at the height of summer, the temperature dropped in the Desert Realm, and sparkling frost formed over the region. The moon and stars shone, reflected across the sand in shimmering crystal fields. There was only one safe route through the Barebones, one road that cut through the mighty pillars of dread, dark rock: the Bana Gap. The city from which it took its name was carved out of the cliffs, an impenetrable fortress left over from a bygone age.

223

The army of the Catlords sat camped below the sheer walls of jagged stone, reinforced by an immense force of Omiri. The tents of the elite Goldhelms and Redcloaks took the higher ground at the base of the opposing cliffs, in fine sight of the city. Above them, the Vultures of Bast roosted on the rock face, in total command of the sky, their fellow countrymen's command tent below.

The Weretiger, Field Marshal Tiaz, kept one eye on Bana, his other on the camp of Omiri that massed to the south. He stood outside his tent, glowering at the unruly horde, their fires burning in the night. Could a Cat ever truly trust a Dog? In this case, they had no choice. These were not the proud Jackals of the Desert Realm but their violent, covetous neighbors, the caninthropes of Ro-Pasha. They wanted Omir for themselves, to carve up King Faisal's land with Lady Hayfa, the Hyena of Ro-Shan. Since they had sided with the Bastians, the job was almost done. With Azra surely fallen to Hayfa, all that remained was to put that gaggle of fools who hid within the fortress city of Bana, the allies of the Wolf, to the sword. They had been locked within the mountains for months now, humans and therians alike, Jackals and Hawklords, doomed to die together in the ancient tomb.

Tiaz's army watched the city, faint fires burning within the slatted windows of the rock face. The enormous stone doors, scores of meters tall, remained closed to the outside world, the mechanisms within ensuring none could pass. Hundreds of

feet up the cliffs, the occasional balcony, tower, or turret sat proud, carved out of the black stone. These were barricaded and barred, fortified from within. There'd been no movement up there for weeks, the besieged defenders hiding away like vermin behind their defenses. The Tigerlord suspected they were on their last legs now, their provisions gone, nerves shredded, and will broken. Any day now, he would give them his final terms. He might even show clemency, allow some to live. All but the Hawklords who commanded them; Count Carsten and Baron Baum needed to be made examples of, as well as the Bastians who were said to fight alongside them. There had been a rumor of a Catlord among their number, but Tiaz scoffed at the notion. What felinthrope in his right mind would battle against his brethren, so far from home?

Old and tired though he was, there was nothing weary about Tiaz's eyesight. He called out now, pointing skyward, causing all about his command tent to stir. The shout went up, spreading like wildfire, Vultures taking to the wing as they heeded the field marshal's warning. There it was, flitting down the cliffs from high above the city, wings folded as it plummeted. Even from this great distance, the Tigerlord could see white feathers and a slender frame, with a rapierlike beak trained earthward as it descended through the Bana Gap. The Vultures were already closing in, rushing to intercept but caught quite unawares. The Birdlord had landed upon a balcony, taloned fists hammering the barricades as it called for the attention of

those within. The Vultures were almost upon the white avianthrope when lights appeared on the balcony, torches lending their glow to the jagged rocks about them as the defenses were briefly opened. Arrows flew, showering the Bastian Werelords and scattering their attack before the barriers were brought up once more. The lights were snuffed out and the messenger bird was within the city.

"Ready yourselves for anything," snarled Tiaz, storming into his command tent as his men rushed to purpose. "And fetch me my armor. The night just got interesting."

Field Marshal Tiaz had only just donned his breastplate when the first attack came, through the heart of the Bana Gap itself. With the only resistance gathered in the black mountain, Tiaz had collected his might around the fortress city, foolishly neglecting the road north. The lands between the River Robben and the Barebones had been all but forgotten, long ago conquered in the earliest days of the war, the entire Great West Road under the command of the Catlords. The battle was in Bana: what could possibly come from the north?

A bloodcurdling howl heralded their arrival, as if an army of the dead charged between the mountains. The Catlord army wavered, fear and trepidation gripping Lyssian and Bastian alike. Some Redcloaks turned and ran, while the Goldhelms

steeled themselves before the mournful wail. In that moment of doubt, the Wolf's forces struck, stampeding over the first line of defense. Channeled through that narrow corridor of rock came a tide of shield and sword, bow and spear. The Furies of Felos—men who had *trained* under the watchful eye of Tiaz—ran alongside pirates of the Cluster Isles and warriors of Shadowhaven.

Drew led the way, Moonbrand singing as it sought out his foes. His jaws clapped and the sword struck out, cracking limbs and snapping bone. Miloqi's terrible howl, though unnerving, was no longer something her allies feared. The strange magicks that she channeled, unique to the White Wolves, were a gift as powerful as Bastian blasting powder. The Catlord forces crumpled beneath their charge, rocking back on their heels before being trampled underfoot.

Vega and Mikotaj fought either side of Drew, bringers of doom that escorted him ever deeper into enemy territory. The Sharklord's monstrous head was slick with gore. His rapier darted in and out, striking men standing upright, their hearts suddenly punctured so they were dead before they fell. The giant White Wolf laughed as he fought, eyes wild with mad delight, enormous spear tossing enemies aside as his fur turned red and dark with death.

The second wave came from the black cliff itself, the great steel doors of the fortress city yawning open as the force

within made a final, frantic bid for freedom. While the army who camped in the Bana Gap had safely bided their time for the passing months, awaiting the siege's inevitable conclusion, those with the mountain stronghold had become steadily more desperate. When Florimo had arrived at that late hour, the Ternlord's message was simple: it was do or die. The brave but weary souls inside the fortress had readied weapon and armor and shared their farewells. Gathering before the doors, they had waited for the signal, their hearts racing with anticipation, their torment soon to be over one way or another. Therian lords had stood beside human friends, the bond of the besieged having broken down all station and standing. As Miloqi's dread howl sounded in the Gap, the mechanism cranked into life, cogs turning, bars unlocking as the steel doors swung outward. Ragged Jackals leapt forth as half-starved humans charged, Hawklords taking to the air in a shower of faded feathers.

Momentarily stunned, the Catlord army found itself torn between two enemies. While the Vultures swooped down to meet the Hawks in the sky, the Goldhelms clashed with those who escaped the city on foot. Jackals and therian lords of the jungle continent met across the front line as men of Bast and Lyssia crossed swords. The proud Werelords of Omir were not alone, joined by the survivors of the Furnace—Krieg, Taboo, and the Behemoth—alongside falconthropes too frail to fly.

Field Marshal Tiaz led the Redcloaks up the Gap, directing the vanguard against the greater force. Whatever happened

in the coming battle, there was still a means to retreat, not that the Tiger liked to consider such things. That useless rabble the Doglords called an army covered their backs in the desert, waiting to be called upon should reinforcements be necessary. As for the enemy, those who emerged from the city were a wretched, ruined lot, destined for the long sleep at the end of Bastian blades. The onrushing mob from the north, however, was a quite different beast. This was clearly the main threat to Tiaz, an army of fresh, fit, and fully prepared foes to face. Over the sea of helmet, pike, and sword he could see the enemy command leading the charge. Dark and gloomy though the Gap was, the Werelords were well illuminated among the Lionguard, a Sharklord in a kill-soaked frenzy while a berserk White Wolf went wild nearby. The light that shone on them came from the white sword that glowed in the clawed hand of the Gray Wolf—*the Gray Wolf.* There was only one that yet lived, realized Tiaz, a surge of excitement gripping him as he understood whom he faced.

The Tigerlord ripped his sword free from its scabbard, vivid stripes of orange and black appearing across the fur that flooded his flesh. He turned, calling out to his senior officers. General Primus, cousin to Onyx, strode to his side, the young Panther wielding a wicked scimitar, its crescent-moon blade blessed with silver runes. Lord Urok, the Red Ape of World's End, beat his chest with excitement, hefting a mighty pick from a loop of leather on his back.

"With me, brothers," said Tiaz. "We end this war tonight, and so cover ourselves in glory."

As the Tiger, Panther, and Ape pushed through the Lion-guard, drawing ever closer to their enemy, they were unaware of the chaos that had erupted beyond the Gap in the sand. The Doglords, those thieves of the Desert Realm and unlikely allies to the Cats, had been stirred from their tents. Jackals swept through their encampment, led by King Faisal of Azra. He was not alone, his brothers and cousins fighting at his side.

The Furies under the command of Opal cut a merciless swath through the oblivious Doglords alongside them, living up to their names as their twin blades saw red. The Beauty of Bast danced before them, claws and sword seeking the canin-thropes of Ro-Pasha. Djogo followed behind her, sticking close to the Pantherlady, in awe of her might and keen to reach the Gap. And there were others, the richest merchant fighting alongside former slaves set free at the behest of Drew Ferran. Humans with something to fight for: their city, their country, their freedom.

The third force had attacked.

Drew chanced a look to the heavens as he strode forward on long, lupine legs. Hawks and Vultures swooped and spun, clash-ing and crying, shrieking and stabbing. The dark sky was alive with aerial combat, every bit as deadly as what played out be-

low within the Gap. A Lyssian falconthrope was plucked from his fight with one of the foreign Birdlords, the talons of a second Vulture seizing his back and tearing his shoulders apart. As the Bastian released the broken-winged warrior, he swiftly followed in a downward spiral, a Hawklord arrow thrumming through his throat.

Bringing his attention back to his own battle, Drew found himself firmly in the thick of the fiercest fighting. Vega and Mikotaj were nowhere to be seen, the only allies nearby the occasional huddle of Furies and Sturmlanders. The Furies were more calm and composed than any humans he'd seen, working as a unit. When enemy weapons approached, the twin blades crossed and parried, every bit as effective in defense as attack. With the blows deflected they struck out in deadly waves, cutting back the Lionguard like a field of scarlet wheat. And then there were the men of Shadowhaven. Like barbarians from the storybooks, they roared and bellowed as they battered their way through the Redcloaks, axes and spears scything and jabbing.

Brave though his allies were, they were horribly outnumbered, their progress through the Gap stuttering to a stumble. The tide of Redcloaks before them had now reinforced after the initial attack. Though the Wolf's force had struck a heavy blow with their surprise assault, the hundreds of Lionguard who'd died in those earliest moments hardly seemed missed, rank upon rank standing before them. While some were the

soft-bellied Lion's men of Lyssia, sworn first into Leopold's service and then Lucas's, many had sailed to the Seven Realms from Bast. These were the authentic Redcloaks from Leos, sent in recent months to swell the Catlord army.

The front line of the battle was a terrible press of desperate souls, pushed on by the weight of numbers at their backs. Some dropped their swords, switching to dirks and daggers or feet and fists, struggling for dominion over their enemy in grisly embraces. Screams and roars filled the air, joining the cacophony of clashing steel as the din of battle filled the Bana Gap.

Moonbrand came down and across a row of Redcloak weapons, transforming spears into splintered staves in an instant. The Werewolf stepped forward, pushing the useless weapons aside with his shoulder, and bringing his sword back along the line. With the distance between them now closed, the white Sturmish blade found the Redcloak torsos, ripping a terrible cut through them. The men went down as the Wolf advanced, inspired to greater deeds by Miloqi's terrible wail ringing in his ears. The lady of Shadowhaven was back behind their lines, howling her heart out, chilling the blood of their foes and testing their resolve. To those who enjoyed her allegiance, the song was haunting and beautiful, another weapon in the Wolves' arsenal.

"Wolflord!"

It came out as a roar that shook the black walls of the Bana Gap. The fighting slowed as heads and helmets turned in the

direction of the voice. The cry might have been for Mikotaj, but Drew knew better. The challenge was meant for his ears alone. The sea of scarlet capes parted, Lionguard drawing back from the Wolf of Westland, shields and swords held up defensively. His opponent stamped toward him on heavy, pawed feet, the plain, metal breastplate the only nod to armor. His broad head was fixed in a terrible frown, flashes of black running through the fiery orange face. White furred lips peeled back, whiskers quivering like steel needles as he bared a monstrous set of canines.

"So you're the little lycanthrope that's got my kinfolk in a fluster?"

Two more therianthropes appeared on either side of the Tigerlord. One was an enormous Wereape with massive, powerful arms covered in thick, red hair. The other was a Pantherlord, his black skin coated with a sheen of sweat despite the chill air.

"And you'd be Field Marshal Tiaz," said the Werewolf, lowering Moonbrand as the Tiger prowled closer.

"I'd pick that up if I were you, pup," snarled Tiaz. "Be a shame if your death went down in the history books without a little dance first."

"There needn't be any fight, Tiaz," said Drew, shaking his shaggy gray head. "Your fight isn't with me. It's with him and his kinfolk."

Drew gestured toward the Panther as he weaved through the Lionguard. Tiaz growled.

"My fight's with Primus, is it? You've mistaken my general for one of your mongrel friends, boy. The Panthers are my allies, Bastian brothers through and through."

"You hear that, Primus?" shrieked Urok the Apelord, laughing. "Apparently you and Tiaz have bad blood!"

"That might be the case if he doesn't get on and skin this Wolf cub," snapped the Panther of Braga, twirling his scimitar in a dark fist. "Let's get this over with, Tiaz."

"Listen to me," said the Werewolf, eyes trained upon the enormous Tigerlord. "The Panthers are not your friends, nor are the Lions. This war has reached Bast and it is greater than you could imagine. Your union's broken, the Forum of Elders dissolved."

"You expect me to believe your babble?"

"I'm the closest thing you've got to an ally here, Tiaz. These Goldhelms and Redcloaks you command: they serve your enemies. You just don't know it yet."

A murmuring ripple passed through the Lionguard that surrounded Tiaz, as the Weretiger eyed them suspiciously. His eyes suddenly narrowed as he lifted his sword.

"You'd say anything to save your hide," he snarled, dropping to his haunches, preparing to leap forward.

"Stop!"

The cry came from above, causing all to look up. Half a dozen Hawklords came down fast, a handful of their fellows still fighting overhead, keeping the Vultures at bay. Drew rec-

ognized the Eagles, Count Carsten and Baron Baum, the lords of the falconthropes. Florimo flew between them, the Ternlord's bright eyes frantic with fear. But all eyes were upon the Hawklady, and the slender figure she carried in her arms.

Lady Shah's wings beat hard, great downdrafts lifting the sand off the ground and sending it whipping through the crowd. Drew lashed out with Moonbrand, roaring at the Lionguard, clearing a space for her to land. A lithe woman dropped from Shah's hands, the Tigerlady landing deftly beside the Werewolf. The two regarded one another—not a look of hate or suspicion, but one of relief and respect to be side by side again. She turned her gaze upon Tiaz.

"Father," she hissed as the Hawklords and Florimo landed behind them. Baum and Carsten looked weary, the count's head bandaged with a rag around eye and beak. Baum seemed more able, the baron resting a reassuring hand on his brother's shoulder.

Upon hearing his daughter speak, the fur that covered Tiaz's body receded, all his rage and aggression dissipating in an instant. He shrank before them, losing a foot in height, transforming from field marshal to father in the blink of an eye.

"Taboo? Can it be you?" His lips trembled as he shook his head, forgetting where he was. The sword was limp in his hands.

"Tiaz," said the Panther Primus. "I don't like this. Do not trust her."

Taboo growled at the dark furred Catlord, and he yowled back, spitting.

"Let them speak," said Drew, pointing Moonbrand threateningly at the Panther.

"Or you'll do what?" said Primus.

"We'll do plenty."

It was Vega, pushing his way through the Wolf's soldiers, Mikotaj at his side. Each was awash with blood, spear and rapier wet, teeth stained dark.

"How can you be here, in Lyssia?" said Tiaz.

"It's good to see you, too," she replied. "Scoria fell, as did the Lizardlords you sold me to."

"You were not sold, Taboo. The Elders had you banished for your crimes."

"Not *my* crimes," she spat, angry now, years of her life lost in the Furnace as a plaything of the Lizards.

"It was Onyx who murdered the Cheetahlord, Chang, and it was Taboo they framed," said Drew.

"They lie!" shouted General Primus. "Kill the Wolf and be done with this talk."

"I heard the confession from Opal's lips," said the Werewolf, "as did the Elders. *That* is how the forum fell apart. Your three houses have gone their separate ways. Tigers, Lions, and Panthers: you look after your own from now on. You might want to start with your daughter, Tiaz."

The Red Ape, Urok, grabbed one of the Redcloak com-

manders, whispering into his ears before sending him on his way. The captain was gone into the crowd in an instant as the chorus of murmurs continued again.

"Kill the Wolf, Tiaz, or stand aside and I'll do it," said Primus.

"You'll have to go through me," snarled Taboo, hackles rising as she raised her spear.

"We talk," said Tiaz, raising a hand to silence his daughter and the Panther. "A parley between myself and the Wolf, each with a second present. Lower your weapons, all of you!"

More therian lords were emerging through the crowd now, each gravitating toward those with closest allegiances. Another Ape joined Urok, while a Buffalo arrived at Primus's side, snorting and lowering his horned head menacingly. Already, Drew could see the Goldhelms and Redcloaks moving apart, a delineation appearing through the Catlord army.

"Join me, Tiaz," said Drew. "But do it quickly. Your friends seem to be cooling to the idea of Bastian brotherhood. Do you not see who fights by my side? I call the Furies of Felos my friends, sent here by your father, High Lord Tigara."

Tiaz saw them now for the first time, the southern warriors—his own people—stepping through the crowd, bowing briefly to their lord and master. It was all becoming painfully clear and obvious to him.

"Father," said Taboo, pointing at the black mountain with her spear. "I've been imprisoned within Bana with the Hawks

and Jackals while you tried to starve us out. The Forum of Elders was built on lies, lies that stole me, your only child, from you. Do right by me, where you failed me before."

Field Marshal Tiaz, high commander of the Bastian army, glanced back at Urok and Primus. His doubting look was all it took.

Primus lashed out at Drew with his scimitar. Tiaz jumped forward, taking the blow across the chest. Sparks flew as the blade cut through his breastplate, which came away in pieces as the Tigerlord hit the floor. Taboo leapt between them, clawed foot striking Primus in the chest. The Panther fell to the ground, bringing the scimitar back up to parry the Weretiger's spear. Meanwhile Urok, the Red Ape, attacked the nearest Hawklord, his mighty hands seizing the falconthrope by the wings. It was Baron Baum, the battered Eagle too weary to evade the stronger, fitter Wereape. Feathers flew as his terrible hands and teeth set to work, Count Carsten leaping onto Urok's back, desperately trying to haul the beast from his brother.

Taboo found herself in the middle of the Goldhelms, their swords slashing at her as she tried to find Primus on the ground with her spear. She was exhausted from malnutrition, the fight quickly draining what energy she had left. Primus dodged this way and that, the Panther's agility saving his skin, before he struck out with his scimitar, the blade flying across her. She tumbled back as Primus jumped up, looking to strike the kill-

ing blow. Instead he found the Werewolf had replaced her, his white sword sweeping out and leaving a trail of fresh wounds across the Goldhelms. The enchanted white steel narrowly missed the young Panther's neck, causing Primus to stagger back with alarm.

The battle raged on three sides. Redcloaks surged into Goldhelms, the second Apelord ripping limbs from those humans who stood in his path. The Buffalo who had stood beside Primus charged, trampling Sturmlanders as his head connected with Mikotaj's broad torso. The White Wolf howled as horns punctured flesh, driving him back and into the earth. A wing of Vultures swooped down, ripping faces, severing heads and causing Redcloaks and Sturmlanders alike to duck. With their allegiance to the Panthers confirmed by their actions, they descended upon the Hawklords, one giant among them seizing Shah and yanking her into the air with a talon about her throat. It didn't go unnoticed. Count Vega leapt, rising high to seize the avianthrope's other leg, the three of them careering into the heart of the battle, Shark and Vulture stabbing and raking at each other as they went.

Drew and Primus traded blows, swords and teeth clashing as they circled. The occasional sword swiped their backs as Furies and Goldhelms found a way in, but the two dueled on regardless. The Panther was upon Drew suddenly, its great flat head butting the Wolf in the face. His muzzle on fire, Drew

went down, kicking to topple at the Catlord's legs. Blades were dropped as claws found throats, Drew's single hand struggling to match the damage the Panther dealt out, the gray fur of his chest wet with his own blood. His stumped wrist struck out, its steel cap catching Primus sweetly across the jaw and sending him rocking back. Drew's claws left red trenches in the dark flesh of the Catlord's belly, and as the Panther came forward once more it held Moonbrand in its grasp, turned down to strike.

The Panther was illuminated by the white brand, face contorted with gory glee, the world darkening about it, drowned out by the night. Only it wasn't the night that had plunged them into shadow. A shape had appeared behind the Panther, through the melee that raged about them. The Catlord turned to see what had caused the blackout. A pendulous bone-splintering body-blow from a great stone mallet caught Primus. The Catlord's torso crumpled as the giant hammer pulverized its body, dislocated limbs jangling like a rag doll and launching the Werelord through the air. Drew watched the Panther's corpse hitting the distant black cliffs with a terrible, rattling splat. His eyes came back to the figure with the mallet, the Weremammoth dwarfing all around.

The elephantine therianthrope's gray hide was hatchmarked with scars, peppered with arrows, flapping ears torn and tattered. His head moved suddenly, a savage thrust catch-

ing a cluster of Goldhelms with his tusks and sending them sprawling. He looked back at Drew.

"They said you wouldn't come." When the Behemoth spoke, his great sad voice was so sweet to Drew's ears that it near broke his heart.

"They were wrong."

7

BROKEN HOME

GRETCHEN SAT ON the steps of Hedgemoor Hall and wept. In her hands she held the small splintered tine from a broken antler. A shortsword was plunged into the earth at her feet. She had left the Marshmen in the building, searching for any sign of survivors, but she knew that was a waste of time. And she knew for certain that she couldn't cross the threshold again, not as things stood. Her home had been defiled, no corner untouched by Lucas and his Wyld Wolves. The entire estate showed signs of their hideous handiwork, half-eaten human remains littering the halls and corridors, their effluence marking every corner and chamber. Memories of her childhood, those precious moments in the company of her late parents, had

been soiled and sullied, the dark specter of the Lion looming large over all. Now he was gone, leaving Hedgemoor Hall used and abused, a filthy shadow of its former self.

Worst of all had been the boy. The main hall had been left dressed like some freakish theater. They had found the Goldhelms that had been tracked into Hedgemoor. Their butchered bodies had been arranged around the banquet table like puppets, strings cut as they slumped in their seats. But the boy's body—what remained of it—was left in the earl's old seat before the fire, antlers snapped from his disfigured face. None of the phibians had been prepared for this, some hunching double and vomiting, others wailing mournfully. Somehow the sight of the child's remains had pushed them beyond the breaking point. Gretchen had taken the boy's sword, fully intending to return it to his father if he still lived, for she loved the old man dearly. She turned the tine in her hands and shook her head. Without a doubt she knew this had been Milo, the son of Duke Manfred. She had seen the boy on occasion throughout his brief life. And now he was gone, and in such horrific fashion.

"Perhaps he didn't suffer."

Gretchen looked up and saw nobody. Pocketing the tine, she sniffed back a tear and rose to her feet, pulling the shortsword from the earth in the process.

"Who's there?"

The town was shrouded in the half-light of dusk, turn-

ing the once colorful city and stately home into a grim, gray graveyard. She looked back through the doors into the building, hoping she might spy one of her Marshman companions, but there was no sign of them.

"Brave lad to walk into Hedgemoor like that, to certain death. Then again, it's not like he was alone."

Gretchen detected from the accent that the hidden stranger was with the Catlords. Her eyes flitted across the once elegant grounds as she stood, seeking out movement in the many shadows and finding none. She stepped away from the house, turning as she searched her surroundings.

"You seem to know an awful lot about what happened here, Bastian. Show yourself. Don't be shy."

The stranger laughed, his voice echoing around the courtyard's four walls. "So you might try to put a blade in me, Foxlady? I know who you are, and you seem to have surmised my allegiances well enough."

"You're scared of me, then?" asked Gretchen, craning her neck to search the crenellations that crowned the walls. The severed heads of her kinsmen dotted the ramparts on spears.

"I said you might *try* to stab me," corrected the stranger with a chuckle. "Hardly makes me afraid."

"So again, show yourself."

"The fellows you arrived with," said the Bastian, changing the subject. "Who are they? Half-naked, with fishing net

cloaks; freakish company for a therian lady to travel with, no?"

"Just more poor souls your brethren have wronged. I take it you're aware of the Goldhelms who sit dead within my hall? You were with them?"

"No, but I knew a few of their number. Good men all."

"Killers all," said Gretchen, making her way to the staircase that ran up the wall's edge. His voice was coming from above, there was no doubt. "They slaughtered their own kin at a farmhouse a day's ride away. We tracked them here."

"They weren't kin, if you're talking about Redcloaks," came the stranger's echoing voice. "It seems there's been something of a . . . splintering among the Catlord union of late."

"Splintering?" Gretchen arrived on the top of the walls, treading carefully through the detritus and debris that littered the terrace.

"The Goldhelms are Panthers' men, while the Redcloaks serve the Lions. For them to be butchering one another bodes ill for my work in Lyssia."

"So you're with Onyx?"

"We go back away, you could say. I assume you knew the dead boy?" His words were cold and unfeeling, causing Gretchen to shiver.

"The Staglord Milo. He's the son of Duke Manfred."

"Of course he is," said the stranger, as Gretchen heard the sharp snap of his fingers. She kept her head fixed forward,

but she'd now placed where the sound had come from. It was Hedgemoor Hall itself. But where? The roof or one of the upper floors?

"As enemies go, you're very chatty," she said.

"I've missed talking to a lady, especially one as fine as yourself. We don't have to be enemies."

"You said he wasn't alone," she said, ignoring his charming words, "but his was the only body we found in there, if you disregard your slaughtered friends."

"That's right," said the man. "They took the other Graycloak with them, the king and his Wyld Wolves. An odd-looking thing he was, too."

Still facing forward, along the wall, Gretchen's eyes were now trained upon the second floor of the house, scouring each empty window for signs of life and finding nothing.

"A Wolfguard?"

"More Wolf*man* than guard, in all honesty. A bedraggled-looking beast with filthy blond hair. He was going the same way as those monstrous Wyldermen."

Gretchen could see he wasn't on the roof: *Where in Brenn's name are you?*

"Explain yourself," she said, trying to keep the hidden Bastian distracted as she searched for him.

"Lucas's Wyld Wolves," said the foreigner. "Sorcery created the beasts, a combination of wild man and lycanthrope."

"That isn't possible," said Gretchen, realizing with a sigh

she was still alone, with no sign of the phibians in the courtyard below.

"I'd have said as much myself before I witnessed it with my
sharp eye. Darkheart his name was, a shaman from your Dyrewood. The corruption is passed on through the bite. Amazing
what you can conjure up when you've the severed paw of the
Wolf of Westland to play with."

Gretchen blanched as the stranger continued.

"Lucas was certainly keen on the other one, so much so
he spared the young fellow's accursed life. A sword to the guts
would've been the kindest thing. They'll all die in the end,
these Wolfmen. That's bad blood coursing through their twisted veins."

"You saw plenty, then?"

"I had a fine vantage point," replied the man. "Surprising
what one can see and do when everyone's eyes are trained on
the ground."

"You like surprises?"

"The greatest surprise was Lucas sparing the Graycloak's
life. Perhaps the sword the blond chap carried was the deal-
breaker. It certainly caught the king's eye. Not often one sees a
Wolfshead blade these days."

Gretchen's heart skipped a beat at mention of the weapon.
It couldn't be Trent, could it? He'd been killed in Bray, butchered by the Wolfmen. She'd seen it with her own eyes. Or had
she? He'd gone down beneath them, bitten and brawling.

Could he have survived? And could that bite have turned him into a monster? That he might have lived was joyous news, but if he was now diseased by dark magick, perhaps his death was unavoidable. Could a human *ever* survive a therian transformation?

"And with Lucas and his Wolfmen gone, you lingered here?" she said. "You didn't think to be on your way, try to get back to your master, the Beast of Bast? The roads aren't safe; there's a war on, you know."

"Don't worry about me, my lady," said the man, the smile creeping into his voice. Her eyes went to the front of the house as he continued. "I can be on my way back to Onyx in no time at all. And I've no fear about traveling by road, but thanks for your concern. I thought it best to wait till a few days later, see what crawled out of the woodwork before reporting back to the Pantherlord. Good thing I hung around, eh? I've so much more to tell him now."

Hedgemoor Hall was a bizarre-looking structure, its face adorned with nooks and crannies, balconies and balustrades. A mass of vines and ivy covered the walls, windows nestled among the dense, tangled vegetation. Gretchen's eyes narrowed as she advanced along the stone walkway, drawing close to the house, her heart quickening. *Where* are *you?*

"Perhaps I may return home sooner rather than later. Wouldn't it be nice to have us out of your hair, Lady Gretchen?"

"You can all be on the way as soon as you like. You're not welcome in the Seven Realms," she said angrily. "None of you."

"Your passionate words aside for a moment," said the stranger, "I'm afraid I don't take orders from the young Lion's plaything."

Gretchen found herself shocked by his words. He'd gone from polite, almost charming, to insulting and insinuating. The idea that she might be a toy for any man, most of all the despicable devil that was Lucas, enraged her. She snarled, flicking her hands out on either side of her, claws and red fur emerging from them.

"Then perhaps you'll take a beating instead?"

"Perhaps, my lady, I'll just take you!"

The ivy that adorned Hedgemoor Hall erupted suddenly. Emerald leaves exploded outward as a winged shape launched from within, flying toward the girl on the battlements. Gretchen turned, claws out, just as the figure landed upon her. Black wings arched from its back, its feet clutching the Werefox tightly by each wrist. A ruff of white feathers encircled the avianthrope's throat while its disjointed neck bobbed, crooked beak clapping menacingly in Gretchen's face. She snarled and snapped back, but the monster simply pushed her back with its legs, talons keeping her out of reach.

She writhed in the grotesque Birdlord's grip, but it was no good; she was held fast. The Werefox's jaws snapped at the

avianthrope's ankles, but the monster yanked her arms farther apart, clawed toes tightening about her elbows.

"Struggle all you like, Lady Gretchen, but we're going for a flight," said the monster, its wings cutting the air in powerful, sweeping motions. "If I were you I'd make myself comfortable and try to relax. The Badlands are quite a distance and—therianthrope or not—a fall would be most unpleasant."

A couple more wing beats and Gretchen felt her scrabbling feet lose purchase upon the wall. She was kicking out at the air now, dangling helplessly in the Birdlord's talons.

Something whistled through the air, puncturing black wings and hitting the avianthrope's back. The monster shrieked, feathered appendages instantly folding as it tumbled from the air in midflight. Girl and beast landed on the mossy cobbles of the courtyard in a crumpled embrace.

Gretchen rolled off the Birdlord's body, spying the splintered arrow that was buried in wing and shoulder. The monster shuddered, the wind crushed from its lungs, distorted neck twisting as it gasped for air. The Fox of Hedgemoor looked up toward the gatehouse as she heard footsteps. A hooded figure was walking delicately forward from the shadows, bow raised, fresh arrow nocked and trained upon the pair of them. Gretchen's heightened sense of sight allowed her to see through the twilight past the archer. Other figures moved through the darkness behind him, the city streets slowly coming to life. She spied just a few movements initially, but within moments the

road beyond the gates was teeming with activity, troops of soldiers rushing forward toward Hedgemoor Hall.

More noise drew her attention to the mansion as the Marshmen rushed out of the building, alerted by her earlier screams. They hurried into the courtyard, loping and leaping, spears and torches raised before them. The hooded figure swung the bow their way as the phibians brought their weapons back, ready to launch them at the bowman.

"Don't!" shouted Gretchen to the Marshmen. "He saved me!"

As the phibians halted their attack, the Foxlady turned back to the archer, the torchlight now illuminating the green cloak in the gloom. Shoma stepped up to Gretchen and, using his spear, prodded the Birdlord where he lay, moaning in agony. The girl from Hedgemoor ignored him entirely, her eyes still fixed upon the slender Greencloak archer who stepped steadily closer before tossing back the emerald hood.

"He?" said Whitley, her smiling face a sight for Gretchen's sore eyes. "A girl might take offense."

8

UNEASY ALLIES

THE JOYOUS SOUNDS of merrymaking rose between the rocks of the Bana Gap as the victory celebrations reached heady heights. Even though the morning sun was up, the corridor through the mountain was still dark but for the fires the Omiri danced around. Music played, people sang, games were played, and loved ones embraced.

For all the rejoicing, though, the festivities were laced with sadness. Those who had been imprisoned within the city by the Catlord army had all but given up on freedom until the events of that night. For many, the reunions were bittersweet, friends and family having been lost to the war that had gripped the Desert Realm. Humans and therians alike were bereaved,

Jackals comforting their subjects as they toasted the brave dead together.

High above the Gap, Drew Ferran stood on a stone balcony and admired the view. Here was a victory on the battlefield at last, a reason for them to cheer. He was under no illusions: one fight did not mean the war was won, but it was a start. Each triumph was another notch on the weapon belt, a step closer to the ultimate goal of a free Lyssia for every soul. It was good to see all sides mixing below, the men of Shadowhaven standing with the Omiri, Furies of Bast among their number. The vanquished enemies were long gone. The Redcloaks and Goldhelms had fled north, still fighting with one another, while the Doglords had been scattered by Faisal's charge. Their ragtag encampment that had covered the northern desert had been ripped up by the Jackals, the Pantherlady Opal adding her fury to the Doglord misery. Their provisions had been shared out, food and wine passed to every poor, hungry soul who had been starved within the city. The Dogs had fled back to their home in Ro-Pasha, licking their wounds. Drew hoped they remained there, forever regretting their choice of ally in the war that had seized Lyssia.

A hand clapped upon his shoulder, causing him to start.

"You've the look of a lemming there, lad," said Krieg. "Don't be jumping now, after all we've been through!"

Drew smiled at the Rhino, his old friend from the arena on

Scoria. "Until I grow a pair of wings I can't see that happening."

Behind Krieg stood the other gladiators from the Furnace, Taboo and the Behemoth. To find they had survived the siege of Bana had pleased Drew beyond words. Along with the Hawklords, the three had traveled to the city in the mountains to help free the imprisoned Jackals, instead finding themselves locked within the rock alongside them, their foes gathering beyond the gates. Their willingness to fight for someone else's freedom, a world away from their homelands, was a credit to the trio's bond with the Wolf, forged out of pain and suffering.

"Come," said Krieg. "You're missed at the table."

The victorious lords and commanders remained in the hall within the mountain, enjoying a victory feast. Omiri, Sturmish, and Bastians shared food and drink, picking the night's battle to pieces and plotting what their next step might be.

"If it's all the same to you, I'll stay out here a while longer," said Drew. "It's a fine morning."

"Can't say I blame you," replied the Rhino, taking a great breath. "After being cooped up in this black rock for months, this air tastes mighty fine!"

"Besides," added the Behemoth, his voice a low rumble, "there's only so much food and drink a fellow can stomach."

"You jest, my elephantine friend," said Krieg. "Your guts are cavernous enough to eat an army's rations and still have room for pudding."

Drew noticed Taboo's reluctance to join her friends' ban-

ter. The Tigerlady stood apart from them on the balcony, resting her elbows on the stone balustrade. Her face had a look of thunder, as if she might explode at any moment. Drew gulped, always wary of her temper. One had to choose words carefully when speaking with Taboo.

"You're not in the mood for company, Taboo?"

The woman growled. "Breaking bread with turncoats and traitors doesn't come easy to me."

Drew flinched, knowing full well whom she spoke of. "There's nothing simple about the world we live in and the war we fight."

The list of those Taboo considered enemies was extensive. She had enjoyed putting the Lizardlords of Scoria to the sword, but it was the Catlords who fed the flames of her wrath. It was the conspiring felinthropes of her homeland—her own kind— who had delivered her to the Lizards in the first place. They had plotted and schemed, condemning her for the death of the man she had loved when it had been Onyx, the Beast of Bast, who had done the deed. So deep ran their manipulations that even she had believed in her guilt until the truth had been revealed. Drew had set her straight, as gently as was possible, explaining how she wasn't alone in being deceived. Her own father, Tiaz, had been duped by the Lions and Panthers. She had lived her life thinking she was insane, a danger to those she loved, but now she knew better.

"Two who sit in there are responsible for what I've become."

"What you've become?" said Krieg. "You've become a strong, loyal, and redoubtable friend. I can think of few others, bar the Behemoth, whom I'd rather have at my side in a tight fix."

"I've become a killer," growled Taboo. "I would've been a lady of Bast. I could've had a future back home, until they discarded me, tossing me to the Lizards and the arena. That's all I can do now. I'm a weapon, nothing else. Perhaps I should thank Opal and Tiaz the only way I know how?"

Drew saw her claws leave furrows in the stone balcony as orange hair bristled over her hands.

"Taboo," he said, keeping his voice calm. "He's your father."

"*Was* my father," she corrected him. "He lost all right to call himself that when he turned against me in my hour of need."

"You called him Father down there, in the Gap, and he listened."

"I do what's asked of me if the need's great enough," she said with a shrug. "Plucking at his heartstrings seemed to do the trick, don't you think?"

She wasn't wrong. Her words had made the difference, persuading Tiaz to side with them and finally driving a wedge into the Catlord forces. The hope that Tiaz might be able to repair his relationship with his wronged daughter had been what had driven him on.

"You mean to say he can never find a place in your affections again?"

"He's no longer welcome to my affections."

"Regardless, I doubt that'll stop him from trying to find his way back there," sighed Drew. "He's your father. He loves you. He was a victim of your enemies' trickery also, remember?"

Taboo bristled with annoyance. "Tiaz was duped by the Lions and Panthers. He's an idiot to have believed their words above those of his daughter, but the other one in there—Opal—she knew full well what she was doing. She helped her brother frame me for Chang's murder. She set it up so that I paid for Onyx's crime. I'll have my revenge against her."

Drew groaned. *Here we go again.*

"You'd best get in line," he said. "There are a few who'd have vengeance upon the Beauty of Bast, not least my friend Whitley, whose brother was killed at her command. But you'll need to go through me first."

She turned her head to face him, green eyes wide. Drew lifted his jaw, staring her down. Her surprise turned to a glare, two thin emerald slits of distrust fixed upon the Wolflord.

"You'd side with her against me, after all I've done in your name?"

"That we were able to come to your aid is thanks to Opal. She broke the Forum of Elders apart, exposing the lies that had been committed by the High Lords against one another. Chang's murder, your wrongful banishment, Leopold's being killed by Onyx's command—every dark and dirty deed carried

out by the Lions and Panthers was brought to light by her. The Furies of Felos—*your warriors*—fight by our side as a result of Opal's actions."

"She's a monster."

"She's *our* monster," replied the Behemoth. "Save your fight with her until after this war's won, Taboo."

Taboo snarled at the Weremammoth, but he paid her no heed, staring past her placidly as others joined them on the balcony. King Faisal led the way, the Eagle Count Carsten at his side. The Hawklord's bandaged face was grave, his loss one of the greatest of all. Brave Baron Baum had died in the Gap, torn apart by Urok. The Apelord had subsequently died at Carsten's hand, but there was no bringing the count's brother back. Emaciated though he was, he could not yet bring himself to eat, his hunger a dull pang compared to the heartache of a slaughtered sibling.

"Let us not fight among ourselves," said the Eagle. "Leave that for the Cats and Dogs. We must stay strong, stay together. This was but a small victory. One realm has been taken back from the Bastians, but there is more work to be yet done."

"My friend's words are sage," added Faisal. "We must put aside our differences in the face of the greater good. If it's any consolation, Lady Taboo, Opal has proved herself time and again since she set foot in the sand. It was she who led the attack upon Hayfa, turning her out of Azra and putting the Jewel of Omir—and the Hyena's many cannons—into our hands.

She also led the charge into the Doglord lines down there, surrounded by your brave Furies of Felos. Just like Djogo, she has righted past wrongs. Don't question her allegiance. She fights for the Wolf. She fights *with* us."

Drew looked for Djogo, the former slaver, among the crowd at Faisal's back but couldn't spy him. Drew and Djogo hadn't found time to properly catch up yet. No doubt the soldier would want to speak with Shah, the Hawklady. Drew knew well enough the feelings Djogo had for the woman. She was presently in the House of Healing, with Miloqi, the White Wolf of Shadowhaven, looking after Vega. The Sharklord had picked up his fair share of wounds in the Battle of the Bana Gap. Miloqi was an able enough healer to coax him back to health in quick time.

"So," said Faisal, content that Taboo's complaints had ceased. "Azra is safe, our enemies' war machines now trained out from the walls and onto anyone who dares approach. The Doglords have scarpered, tails between their rotten legs. And the Redcloaks and Goldhelms are on the run along the Great West Road. What next, Lord Drew?"

All eyes landed upon the young Wolf, the weight of expectation as crushing as always. *When will their demands cease? Will I ever have anything that resembles a normal life again?* He longed for a simple existence, away from the trials of kingship. The Dyrewood: that's where he wanted to be, away from the world and its worries. Again, he found himself wondering about Whitley's whereabouts. So many reunions with old friends, but the

one he really wanted back in his arms was the girl from Brack-enholme, the scout's apprentice. *Does she even live?* Drew cleared his throat, suddenly choked by the emotion of the thought.

"Where's Florimo?" he asked, looking past the group and back into the hall. The crowd parted as the Ternlord made his way through, his usually elegant gait a little worse for wear after indulging in the Redwine claret.

"My lord," he said, bowing clumsily. "Do you have another service you'd like me to undertake? Say the word and my wings are yours, dear chap."

Drew found his smile. Florimo never ceased to amuse, and since he had delivered word the previous night to the prison-ers within Bana, he had reveled in the adulation that followed. Despite the fact that he had played no part in the actual battle, the old navigator was still a key player in its outcome. Without that brave, frantic flight into the city, arrows and Vultures at his back, those within would never have opened the gates to attack the enemy. He had even heard a cousin of Faisal's refer to the Tern as the Hero of Bana, something Florimo would surely enjoy writing into his next bawdy song.

"I need you to look at the stars again, my friend."

The elderly sailor looked confused for a moment.

"The stars, Florimo," he said again.

The navigator suddenly clapped his hands, tapping his beaky nose and winking. "I hear you, my lord. Of course, of course."

Inwardly, Drew sighed. He and Florimo had an understanding, born out of long nights in one another's company aboard the *Maelstrom,* talking about the moon and its cycle. From these conversations the two had devised a plan that could have a huge bearing upon the outcome of the war. It could be terrible, it might fail in dramatic, deadly fashion, but it appeared to be the last throw of the dice for the young lycanthrope, when facing a monster like Onyx, the Beast of Bast. It seemed that the red wine had addled the Ternlord's mind, forcing Drew to be a touch more direct with him than he would have wanted. It was too early to reveal their intentions to the others.

"I hardly see how stargazing will help us defeat my brother," said Opal, slinking out of the shadows, Tiaz close by. Drew didn't enjoy seeing the two of them together. That they had sworn allegiance to him was one thing, but these were two of the lords of Bast who had sailed to Lyssia to aid the Lion. Not so long ago the pair had been his mortal enemies, and now they were working together?

"We need to march at the soonest," added Tiaz, his voice subdued as he addressed the throng. He clearly appreciated the fact that he was the newcomer, the proverbial cat among the pigeons. It would take time before Drew's friends finally accepted him as one of their own, if ever. His eyes lingered upon Taboo as he continued.

"Those Redcloaks and Goldhelms who broke rank will be scurrying back to Onyx as we speak. We shouldn't be wasting

time eating and drinking. We should catch them on the run."

Count Carsten turned and glowered at the Tigerlord, his haggard face barely visible beneath the bandage. "In case you didn't notice, some of us have been starved to the point of death over recent weeks within this city. Your army saw to that. Many of us have lost those closest to us, loved ones and family. If it's all the same to you, Tiaz, we'll take a moment. We'll eat. We'll drink. We'll prepare our dead for the long sleep. Then we'll march west."

Tiaz growled. "Now isn't the time for sentiment or blame."

"It's the perfect time for sentiment," retorted Carsten, taking a step toward the hulking Tiger. Faisal placed a hand on the Hawk's shoulder while Opal moved between the two therian lords.

"Each of you makes fair comment," said Drew. "Let's not fight over this. We'll work as quickly as we can to organize our departure, but we don't scrimp on ritual with our dead. In the meantime, those who are able-bodied should prepare for the road. Send word to every commander down there to ready their troops for the journey into the west. Duke Bergan and the people of Icegarden were sighted heading toward Robben, according to Mikotaj and Miloqi. That's where we're going, because you can bet your life Onyx will be hot on their heels. Count Carsten: this isn't a question I relish asking, but how soon will your brothers be ready to take to the air?"

"Some are already out there, Drew, having gone after the

Vulturelords. A handful remain here, less than ten of them. But we can be ready to fly tonight. A bit of shut-eye this afternoon, prayers for our fallen, and we'll be good to go."

"Good," said Drew, seizing the count's forearm as the two shook hands. "I hate to burden you again, but we'll be needing you to carry a handful of us. Demeaning, I know, but needs must."

"Consider it our honor," replied the grizzled Eagle.

Drew set off into the hall where they had banqueted, the crowd falling in behind him. The enormous table that they had sat at still had the remains of the feast littering it. The hulking Mikotaj, barbarian White Wolf of the frozen north, had his pack open, emptying slabs of half-eaten meat and whole poultry into it. He looked up as they entered, giving them an unapologetic shrug.

"Well, nobody was eating. I didn't think you'd mind."

9

THE SHARK AND THE HAWK

"**YOU KNOW, YOU** could be gentler with me."

Count Vega winced as Shah yanked his arms high in the air. Miloqi, the white-haired seer from Shadowhaven, passed the bandage about the Sharklord's chest, binding it tight around his torso. The handful of medics in the House of Healing were down below in the Bana Gap, working their way through the many wounded survivors of the battle. As Vega's injuries were not life threatening, it had been left to Miloqi to stitch him back together.

"I could be a lot of things with you, Vega, but most of them would put you closer to death's door," snipped the Hawklady. "Quit your whining and keep still."

"Don't confuse my words for misery, my dear," said the count, his smile briefly transforming into a wince before those perfect teeth flashed once more. "Rough though your touch is, I'd still brave every demon of the sea in order to feel it upon my flesh once more."

"He has a way with words, doesn't he?" muttered Miloqi as she worked the dressing into a knot below his breast.

"Oh, he's all charm." Shah nodded, glowering at the smiling Pirate Prince of the Cluster Isles.

"I never mentioned charm," said the seer, coaxing a chuckle from the Hawklady.

Faced by the twin scorn of the therian ladies, Vega's smile slipped. "Ganging up on a defenseless old sailor? Hardly fair."

"Calling yourself old, now?" said Shah. "Are your misspent years catching up with you? Regretting your past?"

"I regret some things, certainly," said Vega, the humor gone from his voice now. He placed a hand on Miloqi's wrist as she finished up on his bandage. "Lady, could you perhaps give us a moment alone?"

"You rest up—while you can—and don't do anything strenuous," said Miloqi. "I'm no magister, but I know herbs and medicines like few others. Who needs magicks when Mother Nature blesses us with her rich bounty? The dressing stays on for at least a day—you can thank Brenn that you heal quicker than most."

She stepped away from the two, leaving them alone in the darkened room. A candle sat in a pool of wax on the bedside table, the flame flickering and sending shadows dancing over the Hawklady's face. Vega lay back upon the cot, looking up at Shah as she stood over him, arms crossed.

She was every bit as beautiful as he recalled. Her long black hair was braided, piled atop her head, great gray eyes trained upon the convalescing count. Slender though she was, that gentle frame hid the fiery strength of the Werehawk. Her late father, Baron Griffyn, had been the heir to the city of Windfell, home of the Hawklords of the Barebones. Yet here was his daughter, playing nurse to the Shark. He couldn't resist teasing her.

"You know, you could always fluff my pillows," muttered the Sharklord, shifting awkwardly as he settled. "It's not too much to ask, is it?"

"It most certainly *is* too much to ask," said Shah. "I'm not even sure why I'm here making sure you're all right."

"I get under the skin, don't I? Even after all these years you still love me, don't you? It's fine, I get that. You're only therian."

Shah ignored his playful words, sticking with her anger. "You abandoned me, Vega. You left me in Kesslar's hands in Ro-Shan. What happened to taking me with you?"

"I was a guest of Lady Hayfa," replied Vega. "She was courting me, wanting my hand in marriage—"

"Hayfa courting *you?*" scoffed Shah.

"Believe it or not, little bird, I'm quite the catch! Anyway, her agents got wind of our friendship—"

"Friendship?" said the woman, interrupting him again. "Is that how you'd describe it?"

Vega sucked his teeth. "Our *affair,* then. She didn't take kindly to the news, was going to have me killed, such was her rage. I had to get out of Omir quickly, and besides which, Kesslar had already set sail with you aboard the *Banshee.* There was no way I could go after you without endangering the lives of you and your father."

"You could've come for me," said Shah, her voice hard but her face soft, tears rising in her eyes.

"You belonged to Kesslar. The Goatlord would never have released you from bondage, or dear old Griffyn for that matter." He reached forward to take her hand. "I heard what happened to your father. I'm so sorry, Shah."

She pulled her hand away. "If you were any kind of man at all you'd have come looking for me, and my father."

Vega's head dipped, ashamed. "Back then I wasn't the man I am now. I was more selfish, more cowardly. I'm different now. I've learned that some things are worth fighting for."

"A little late in the day for an epiphany, isn't it?"

"You can blame Drew Ferran for my change of heart. If I was any kind of noble beast back then I'd have come looking

for you, searched the oceans and turned the seas red until I'd tracked down Kesslar."

Shah arched an eyebrow. "Yet you didn't, did you? You disappeared, back to the Cluster Isles, your reputation intact."

"Hardly! The Cluster Isles were no longer mine—Leopold had given them to Ghul, the Squidlord. The only home I had was the *Maelstrom,* the only family the lads who worked her decks by my side."

"My heart bleeds for you, Vega," snapped Shah. "You poor, poor wretch! What a life you were left to live!" She leaned in close, her breath hot in his face as he flinched before her fury. "You left me *with child*! I was pregnant, and that infant was yours, Vega! You had your fun and were on your way. That baby was taken from me, Shark; taken by my own father and spirited away so that Kesslar never got wind of it. If he'd had that child, he'd have sold him or done worse. So my father gave him to a merchant friend. Brenn only knows what became of my beautiful baby."

Vega cleared his throat as she slowly pulled away, picking his words carefully. He didn't want to mention Casper's whereabouts, not here and now. The lad was aboard the *Maelstrom* with Figgis. The count had to pick his moment to introduce son to mother, and vice versa. Better to wait until he knew they were close.

"You have to hope Griffyn placed the child into safekeep-

ing. You father will have done right by you and the baby. I'm sure it's fine."

"*It?*" Shah slapped him hard, propelling his head back into the pillow. "*He* was a boy, a beautiful boy and I'll never know him! He was *your* son, Vega. Show some compassion, you cold-hearted swine!"

She went to strike him again, but Vega caught her wrist in his hand. He faced her, cheek still smarting from where she had struck him. There was little he could say that would make her feel any better. He let go of her wrist.

"Hit me, if it helps," he whispered. "Peck, rake, and kick me if it takes the edge off your pain. But don't remain angry at me, I beg you."

He lay back, waiting for the blows to rain down, but none came.

"I'll remain angry at you until I close my eyes for the long sleep," said the gray-eyed woman. "I hate you, Vega. Dear Brenn, it feels good to say that to your face," she gasped, sniffing back the tears and laughing.

"How can you say that?" gasped Vega, horrified to hear her words. He had loved her all this time, yet had been unable to tell her, to find her.

Shah's laughter was gone in an instant. "Kesslar may have crushed my spirit and bruised my body, but strength of spirit can be found in others, and bruises always heal. You broke my

heart, Vega. You ruined me, as sure as the Goatlord ever did."

Shah turned her back on the weary Sharklord, leaving him alone in the dark room once more, only the candle for company.

Leaving the Count behind her, Shah stepped through the doorway, her head and heart in turmoil. Despite all that had happened, a part of her still loved the man, but she would be damned if she would let him see it. Her child remained gone, her father still dead, her life in tatters. She could well imagine what he had been through when he had been chased out of Ro-Shan without even being able to say good-bye. She didn't doubt that every word he had said had been truthful, that he regretted what had happened so long ago. But was he truly a changed man? Could she allow him to get close to her again? Just seeing him again had rekindled that fire that had burned within her. She wanted to hold him in her arms, but now wasn't the time or the place. The Shark still had penance to serve.

Pulling the door closed behind her, Shah turned, instantly jumping with alarm when she spied the figure in the shadow-strewn corridor. It was Djogo, fellow survivor of the Furnace and another soul who had been abused by Kesslar. For a long time she had depended upon him, and he had been there for her through her darkest moments. They had been close, that bond born out of the trials they had faced. It had not been love, though; not like with Vega. The farther they had traveled away

from the hellhole that was the Furnace, the more t[...]
had cooled, but she would forever consider him he[...]
embraced him.

"You gave me the fright of my life there, Djogo," she said as
he hugged her back. They separated and she looked him up and
down. "It's good to see you again. I feared I would die in this
Brenn-forsaken city without seeing those dearest to me again."

Djogo flinched at her words, a peculiar smile appearing
upon his lips. "You're much loved by us all, Shah. I feared we'd
never be reunited." He held her hands in his own, giving her
fingers a squeeze. She withdrew them, though the former slaver was reluctant to release his grip.

"We have so many people to thank for our good fortune,"
she said. "Perhaps we *can* defeat the Catlords after all." She
looked over her shoulder at the door to Vega's chamber, then
back to Djogo. He'd been out here when she left the room. *How
long had he been standing there? Was he eavesdropping?*

"Have you been out here a while?" she asked.

"I came looking for you. I thought you might want to eat:
it's been an awfully long day, and I put some food aside for you."

"That's very sweet of you, Djogo."

"You've been crying," he said, raising a hand to wipe a tear
from her cheek. She flinched. He looked past her to the door.
"The Sharklord." It was a statement rather than a question.

"Yes," she replied, annoyance still evident in her voice.
There was something odd about Djogo and she couldn't quite

place it. He seemed outwardly calm, but his eye—that one good eye that Drew hadn't taken from him ages ago—remained fixed upon the door, unblinking.

"Come," she continued, disturbed by her friend's mood and keen to lead him away from the House of Healing. "This meal you've spared for me. I would eat it, and hear about all that you've done since we've been apart."

Djogo blinked at last, as if waking from a trance. He held a hand out before him in the corridor.

"After you, my lady," he said, as the two set off down the carved, stone corridor, leaving the sickbeds and Sharklord behind them.

PART IV

THE DIE IS CAST

I

RED MEAT

AMID THE CHORUS of snarls and growls, the merchant could be heard crying out for kindness, for mercy, for his sorry, luckless life. His pleas fell on deaf ears, his scream rising to a terrifying pitch before suddenly being cut short, alongside his life. Trent felt relieved for the poor man, his torment finally over, and more than a little jealous, too. Such a release would be a blessing for him.

Lucas and his Wolfmen had stumbled across the merchant and his caravan that evening. They had killed the guard in short time, but the trader's death had been drawn out, the Wyld Wolves taking great delight in torturing him while Lucas rifled through the wagon like a common highwayman. He

was in there presently, getting roaring drunk on a cask of Haggard ale. For the merchant's sobbing to have ceased was music to Trent's ears, but the noises that now followed made his blood run cold. Even lashed to a caravan wheel, some distance from where the man was murdered, he could hear the wet tearing as the Wolfmen ripped his warm corpse apart. When the rending ended, the monstrous lycanthropes scattered through the makeshift camp, body parts in clawed hands, finding quiet spots to devour their meals.

Trent retched, straining against his ropes, but nothing came up, his stomach as hollow as the Werelion's soul. He looked up as he saw a figure prowl forward on dark fur-covered legs. It was Darkheart, the one Wolfman who still appeared slightly human. The dirty black feather headdress remained entwined through the matted hair that covered the creature's head. Its distorted jaw was slick with blood, shining black in the moonlight as the Wyld Wolf slurped back a strip of skin that hung between its canines. In one hand it carried a large piece of flesh, bone protruding from it. With another bile-coated heave, Trent recognized it as a femur.

"Not hungry, Wolf Knight?" asked the hideous shaman.

"Go away," said Trent, looking away as the Wolfman crouched on its haunches before him. He heard teeth seize the meat and tear a chunk loose before gulping it down.

"You need to eat," said the other.

Suddenly, the meat was in Trent's face, thrust toward him. He could smell the blood, the raw aroma overpowering. Human or not, the flesh was enticing, causing his stomach to growl and his mouth to salivate. Trent hadn't eaten for days, not since the awful events in Hedgemoor. He snarled, pulling his face clear as Darkheart swung the leg's remains beneath his chin.

"Suit yourself," growled the Wolfman. "I look after my pack. And I'll look after you."

"I'm not part of your pack, and I'd rather starve than eat anything you give me," said Trent, facing the monster now.

While the other creatures feasted around the camp, their shadows moving in the darkness, it appeared this one— Darkheart—preferred the companionship of Trent.

"You don't mix with your brothers, I see," said Trent. "You think you're better than them?"

"Of course I do. They're blinded by the beast, utterly surrendered to it. They don't realize that they could have had the best of both worlds if they'd just fought the change that little bit harder."

"Like you did?"

"Like I did."

Something toppled over and shattered within the caravan, heralding a string of curses from the drunken young Lion within.

"For how long do you plan to serve Lucas?"

"The king and I understand one another. He can help me reclaim the Dyrewood from the Bearlords. And I can help him seize Blackhand from the throne of Icegarden."

"What's his obsession with the Boarlord magister?"

"Blackhand killed the king's mother. He's nothing if not sentimental."

"He's mad."

"That may be, but for the time being I'm happy to follow his commands, do as he wills. It gives me pleasure to see the humans and therians of Lyssia cower before our bloody work."

"So that's it? Revenge? You travel to Icegarden just to kill the Boarlord?"

"Perhaps," said the Wyld Wolf. "Maybe he's more useful alive. Rumor has it the dead roam the Whitepeaks, and it's Blackhand who pulls their strings."

Trent sneered. "If the Boarlord killed Queen Amelie, the Lion will want him dead. He'll have the magister killed. No ifs, no buts."

"Perhaps the Lion and I will reassess our arrangement at that point," said Darkheart. "I can be persuasive when needs be."

Right on cue, the beast gulped down another piece of flesh, red droplets spattering his fur. Trent found himself transported back to Hedgemoor, witness to the awful butchery of Milo at the hands of Lucas. It wasn't just the lad's death, it was the

horror that followed that would haunt Trent to his dying day.

"The boy," said Trent, his anger rising again as he remembered the foul deed. "The Staglord. What Lucas did—"

"The king was hungry," shrugged the Wolfman, "as must you be. Eat."

Again Darkheart thrust the meat Trent's way, and again he recoiled against the wheel's wooden spokes.

"You'll change, Wolf Knight," said the shaman, crunching his teeth on the femur's end, dark tongue trying to poke the marrow from the bone. "You'll be like us soon enough. Not now, not tomorrow. But when the moon comes . . . then you'll change."

"I'll die before I change," said Trent defiantly.

"That could yet happen," said Darkheart. "One of my brothers died during the final change. When the moon is next full, *that* will separate the wolves from the men. Then we'll see if you're truly worthy to be one of us. Then we shall all be equal."

"You're not like them, though," said Trent. "They're animals. You're not. You retain your humanity whereas they've stripped theirs away. You and your brothers are not equals— you're the one with the power, Darkheart. You're the one with the brains."

"Clever, Wolf Knight." The monster smiled, more human than ever as he dabbed the blood from his jaw with the back of a dark furred forearm.

"Why? Why do you not throw yourself into the change like the others?"

"I have lived my life in the shadows of others, Wolf Knight: my father, my mistress Vala the Wyrm, even the Lion," he added, glancing to the wagon at Trent's back. "It is time I make my own shadows, Trent Ferran, brother Wolf. They shall follow me, and I shall bring about a new dynasty in the Dyrewood. The woods will belong to *my* wolves, the Wyld Wolves, and I shall return there once I've had my revenge."

"Against Drew," said Trent. "The one who you've to thank for your hideous 'gift'—you would kill him?"

"The Gray Wolf murdered my father and slew my mistress Vala. I will have vengeance and then return to the Dyrewood to make it my kingdom. You may join me at my side."

"I'd rather take death," said Trent, spitting at the shaman.

The Wolfman rose, tossing the half-eaten piece of meat into Trent's lap where it landed with a soft *plop*. Trent wriggled instantly with disgust, bucking his groin until the bone tumbled into the leaves beside him.

"You don't get a choice, Wolf Knight. You change under the moon and you *become* part of the pack. You'll become a Wyld Wolf like the rest of my brothers. You don't have the strength to resist."

"You're wrong, Darkheart," said Trent. "I may not be a Werewolf like Drew, but my heart pumps with the same pride

and determination that makes us Ferran boys. If you think I'll roll over and join you, you're mistaken."

"I do, and you will," said the beast, picking up the meat again and tearing a morsel off it with his clawed fingers. "You'll be in the dirt at my feet like the rest of them, seeking my approval for every pathetic deed, soiling yourself and rolling about in your own filth. You'll do all this, because at the end of the day you're human. You're nothing like Drew Ferran."

"You survived the change," said Trent, a hint of desperation creeping into his voice. "What makes you so special?"

The monster dropped before him, one hand seizing Trent's mouth and prizing it open. He felt like his jaw might tear off as the shaman's filthy fingers worked the piece of raw human flesh into his mouth. It gripped his face, shaking it one way and then the other before releasing its grip. Trent spat the flesh out, choking, sobbing, retching all over as the monstrous Wolfman towered over him again.

"What makes me so special?" said Darkheart. "I'm strong, Wolf Knight. I'm strong."

2

OUT OF THE MOUNTAINS

THE ABSENCE OF snow was taking some getting used to. Having spent what seemed like an eternity in the Whitepeaks, first climbing the mountains and then hiding in their shadows, Duke Bergan had given up the notion of ever seeing grass again. Months ago, he and his small band of companions had traveled to Icegarden, hopeful of finding his cousin the White Bear, Duke Henrik, in a charitable mood. As luck would have it, Henrik took them in, only for the united Bearlords to find themselves crushed between two foes: beneath them in the foothills was the Catlord army, while at their backs the city had been seized by Baron Hector, the traitorous Lord of Redmire. When the time had come, the Sturmish survivors

had fled deeper into the Whitepeaks, away from their enemies, to face their toughest foe yet: the weather.

Even by Sturmish standards, the winter had been grim. The winds flayed flesh and battered bodies, breaking the spirits of humans and therians alike. Having had the foresight to bring provisions with them in their flight had been the only thing that had kept Bergan and the Knights of Icegarden from the long sleep.

Bergan looked back up the mountainside toward the long train of people who trailed down the barren slope. Though below the snow line, they were still a distance from anything that resembled proper vegetation. The odd withered tree stump or shrub clung to the slopes, talonlike roots gripping the rocky inclines. The Bearlord turned, facing downhill. A staggered tree line weaved along the slope perhaps three hundred yards below, pines swaying in the breeze like lonely emerald sentries. Black Crag rose up at the head of the valley, a steeple of ugly volcanic stone that had stood there since time began. Beyond the crooked mountain, the vast expanse of green countryside rolled out before them, enticing and hopeful, promising better than all they had endured. There would be food down there aplenty, enough to feed his ragged army.

My army. Bergan chuckled, his laughter grim and humorless. These weren't Bergan's people. They were the men, women, and children of his slain cousin, Duke Henrik, a people dispossessed, forced into a nomadic life. Bergan's people were back

home in the Dyrewood, safe—he hoped—within the walls of Brackenholme. *Keep my wife and daughter safe, Brenn. I beg you.*

"We're perhaps a two days' hike away," said Reuben Fry suddenly, the Sturmish general standing on a jagged outcropping and facing toward the sunrise.

"You can see Robben from here?" exclaimed Bergan, stepping up to the rock and squinting into the distance.

"I see the lake, of course. The Wildcat's town sits upon the island at its center. Can you not see the sunlight catching upon the water? It's like a sliver of silver, my lord."

Bergan scratched his ragged beard before shaking his head. "I swear you've some Hawklord blood in there somewhere, Fry."

"It has been said," replied the man, hopping down from the ledge and joining the Bearlord upon the scree.

Fry had been one of the first to swear loyalty to Drew Ferran, having served the boy's father before Wergar's death, and he had risen to become the highest-ranking soldier in the Wolfguard of Westland.

"Enjoying the view?"

Bergan glanced back up the slope as the bald-headed Lord of Thieves, Bo Carver, stepped gingerly toward him. Pick followed, skipping lightly down the slope, the young pickpocket having no trouble finding her feet on the uneven, shifting surface. Carver fared less well. The stones slid underfoot as the old rogue approached, the sweat glistening off his pate, trickling down the serpent tattoo that adorned the left side of his face.

"Enjoying the exercise?" replied Bergan, reaching out to catch the reformed thief by the elbow before he stumbled. "My dear old mother's more agile than you, Carver, and she's been dead for twenty years."

Carver tugged his arm free, grinning at the Bearlord. Though a war still raged throughout the Seven Realms, and they had endured all manner of hardship in the Whitepeaks, it was hard not to feel joyful with blue skies overhead and the summer sun kissing their faces. Pain and heartache no doubt awaited them in the green hills below, but for that brief moment the three men and the young girl stood in silence and breathed in the unspoiled air.

They numbered a few thousand, the majority being civilians who had escaped Icegarden. Hector had allowed them to escape, much to the surprise of the Wolf's Council. According to Carver and Duke Manfred, the young magister had appeared to turn a corner after the awful death of Queen Amelie. Coming to his senses, he had banished the phantom of his dead brother, Vincent, who possessed him. The Wolf's Council had caught a glimpse of the old Hector that evening as he plotted their escape from beneath the noses of his allies, the Crows of Riven. For the first time since Hector had accidentally killed his brother, Vincent's evil spirit hadn't been in control of the once gentle lad. Hector hadn't followed them, though, leaving Bergan to fear the worst: he might well be dead at the hands of

the Crowlord Flint. Who knew what had become of the Boar-lord and the frozen city?

Bergan once more inspected the refugees. Here and there, a knight of Icegarden rode among the people on a stocky-legged Sturmish warhorse, bolstering the spirits of the surviving infantrymen. There were around eight hundred warriors left, each as weary and weather-beaten as the next man. Their mistress, Lady Greta, was still farther back the way they had come, descending the Whitepeaks with Duke Manfred and her young lady-in-waiting, Bethwyn, for company. The girl from Robben had lost her queen, but in Greta she had found a saddened substitute. Greta's brother, Duke Henrik, had been killed by Lucas, and Greta carried her brother's gauntlet down from the mountains, the White Fist of Icegarden bound in the slain Henrik's cloak. Bergan's old friend, the Staglord Manfred, shadowed her every step.

"Your Grace," said Fry, shifting his bow off his shoulder.

"What is it?" asked Bergan as the archer plucked an arrow from his quiver. He followed the man's line of sight. Fry was looking up, toward the sun. With horror the Bearlord spied the shapes in the sky. They were dark, distant blurs, impossible to spot if it hadn't been for the Sturmlander's keen eyes.

The Lord of Brackenholme's heart sank. They had been lucky as they had traversed the Whitepeaks, leaving the Cat-lord forces behind them in the foothills, seeking the bleaker,

more desolate places within the mountains. Yet all this time, one constant threat had hung over their heads, a shadow from above: the Crowlords.

"Take cover!" shouted Bergan, waving his arms frantically at the line of people who trudged down the ridge. Carver bounded down the slope, Pick staying close by his side. The last thing they wanted to do was cause a panic in the mountains, with sheer drops all around them, but if ever there was a cause for alarm it was the Crows of Riven. Lord Flint had seized leadership of his many siblings and cousins, unifying them against all opposition, carving out a new future for his brethren alongside Hector in Icegarden. The mountains of Lyssia were to be his, and those who had once been his neighbors—the Stags of Stormdale—would feel the full might of his wrath.

The cries of children sounded across the scree-covered incline before mothers stifled their sobs. The healthy helped the elderly and infirm to hide behind walls of rocks, ducking behind boulders. Many soldiers lifted their shields or dug them into the loose stones, ushering civilians beneath them. The Crowlords favored death from above, dropping missiles or firing arrows upon their ground-dwelling foes. Out here on the mountainside, the refugees were utterly exposed, easy pickings for Flint and his brothers.

"How many do you see?" asked Bergan, as Fry loaded his longbow.

"I count nine, possibly ten."

Carver rejoined them around the edge of the rocky outcropping. "With no Birdlords to protect us, even one Crowlord could cause havoc among our number. But ten? This could be our undoing."

The Bearlord couldn't bring himself to respond to Carver. Their people were exhausted, their provisions long gone; they had been surviving on whatever they could forage in the wilderness for the past few weeks. They had little hope of defending themselves. As Bergan saw it, there was only one option.

"I need to draw their attack," said the Bearlord, turning to the others. "Once I have their attention, you need to get moving. Lead the people down the mountainside, and head around Black Crag and on to Lake Robben. Go!"

With that, Bergan was off and running, not waiting to hear the men's dissuading words. Their voices called to him, but he didn't turn from his path, staggering across the sliding stones, pebbles tumbling underfoot. Coming from the east, no doubt these Crows had come from Riven itself as opposed to Icegarden. Bergan couldn't help but feel cheated. They'd covered the Whitepeaks, dodging the avianthropes only to encounter them so close to the safety of the Robben Valley where Lady Bethwyn's father awaited them, their only hope. But now Bergan would never see the old Wildcat one last time. He would never see his wife again, nor his daughter, dear Whitley. Would the Wolflord, Drew Ferran, that brave boy from such humble beginnings, triumph against the Catlords? He prayed to Brenn it would be so.

Bergan tore his filthy jerkin open, limbs thickening, black claws splitting the skin as they burst from his fingertips. He dropped forward as he ran, pawlike hands tearing up the scree as the beast swiftly emerged. His skull groaned and creaked, a splitting sound reverberating through his spine as the Bear's head let loose a mighty roar. Birds took flight from the mountainside as the giant ursanthrope, Lord of Brackenholme, thundered toward a cliff top. He skidded to a halt, back on two legs again, the Bear's bellow sounding across the valley. Spittle flew from his cavernous mouth as he snatched his ax from the loop of leather on his back.

Already the dark avianthropes were heading straight for him. They carried others in their arms and talons, no doubt the Ugri warriors who had fought by their side in Hector's name. A quick peek over the shoulder downhill revealed the first of the refugees disappearing into the tree line. *Good.* His death would buy them time. Besides which, he didn't intend to go alone. If the Crows dared approach him, they could expect their wings to be torn loose and thrown to the wind. *See how you fare without your foul black feathers,* thought Bergan, chuckling to himself as the Lords of Riven drew nearer. The humor vanished as the dread moment approached. *Dear Brenn, watch over my wife and child.*

Pebbles scattered as others joined him on the cliff top. There was Carver, long knives in hand, one raised and ready to be flung skyward. The girl thief, Pick, had been replaced at his

side by Ibal, the mute killer who had once worked for Hector. The rotund rogue was a different man now, looking to do some good in his final days before the long sleep. A snort on Bergan's other side made him turn to see the transformed, antler-adorned head of Duke Manfred. The Staglord's eyes rolled as steam billowed from his flared nostrils.

"Always running off to have fun without me, Bergan," said the Stag, swinging his greatsword before him in both hands. "You never change."

Bergan's heart sparked with hope. So long as there were folk like these still fighting the good fight, the Seven Realms might yet survive the madness of war. He hefted his ax into the air as the avianthropes swooped down, out of the sun.

"For Lyssia!" bellowed Bergan.

Carver was about to launch a dagger skyward when he halted, and with good reason. The dark silhouettes of the Bird-lords suddenly shimmered as colors shone on their wings. Feathers of red, gold, and gray could be seen as the weary heroes realized these weren't Crows they faced.

It was the Hawklords, returned. One by one, they dropped their passengers onto the cliff top as Bergan, Manfred, and the thieves stepped back.

The strangers were all shapes and sizes, and each one eyed Bergan and his friends warily. A heavyset warrior carried a spiked mace, spinning its haft in his hands. A pair of falcon-thropes released a giant onto the rock behind the first man,

the cliff rumbling with his impact. Then came the first of four women, all grace and sure-footedness as she rolled and came up with a spear. The next was a shaven-headed warrior, her skin so black it shimmered with shades of blue and purple beneath the sun. *A Werepanther?* She was carried by a Hawklady, the falconthrope landing alongside her while her brothers remained on the wing. The final woman was little more than a girl, with delicate, pale skin and white hair. Her eyes instantly locked with Bergan's. There was something familiar about her. *A White Wolf?*

But it was the final passenger's arrival that made the appearance of the others all fade into insignificance. Count Carsten carried the last fellow, but Bergan's reunion with the Eagle of the Barebones would wait. As the duke strode forward, the young man hit the rugged rock and stumbled forward into the Lord of Brackenholme's bear hug.

The lad had grown up a lot since the Bearlord had last seen him a lifetime ago in Highcliff. He had the beginnings of a beard, had lost a hand, and had found the strength in his young limbs to rival that of an ursanthrope. The Bearlord wheezed as the youth released his hold, allowing him to breathe again as the two stared at one another, eyes flooded with tears.

"You're a sight for sore eyes and then some, Drew Ferran," choked Bergan, shifting back to human form. "Lyssia's missed you, my lad."

Drew smiled and nodded. "Fear not, old man. I'm home again, and I'm going nowhere."

3

AT ONE ANOTHER'S THROATS

THE GREAT WEST ROAD, once the avenue by which traders had traversed Lyssia, was now the route home for a battered and beaten army. Legions of Lionguard traipsed west, the Omiri desert an all-too-vivid recent memory. Since they had abandoned their fleet of ships in the mouth of the River Robben and had no time to return to them, land was their only means of escape. They had never suffered a defeat of such magnitude before, but their own allies had turned upon them as the siege of the Bana Gap became a bloodbath. With Goldhelms attacking Redcloaks, the forces of the Wolf became the least of their concerns. With the Gap lost, their battle had raged on, each army trading blows with one another as they fled the Desert Realm. They had eventually parted north of

Bray, the Panther's force heading into the Badlands along the road to Icegarden. The war camp of Onyx was their destination, and the Lionguard could expect a frosty reception should they be foolish enough to venture there.

Cranelords glided high above, scouring the terrain ahead as they escorted their troops home. The occasional melee had broken up their journey, with Vultures engaging them in aerial ambushes. But in time, the attacks had diminished. The farther the Lion's army progressed along the ancient road, the more of their kind they encountered, picking up the first deserters of the battle in the desert, as well as those who had never left the west. Gradually their numbers were increasing, and with each passing league their anger was growing: anger at their betrayal by the Panther's forces, and anger that victory in Lyssia was slipping away from them.

The Battle of Bana Gap was but a skirmish. The true Battle for the Seven Realms lay ahead.

Whitley stood in the center of the rutted road, staring west. Redcloak campfires danced in the darkness, both on the thoroughfare and beside it. It was hard to judge the distance at night, even with the waxing gibbous moon hanging in the heavens like some monstrous eye. She could hear the occasional faint peal of laughter or angry shout, suggesting the encampment was perhaps three or four hundred yards away. Close enough.

Beyond the settlement, more fires shone in the distance, the Lionguard army having bedded down on the road.

She turned and looked back. More fires pockmarked the Great West Road, trailing far into the east. No doubt the Lionguard were alert, eyes fixed upon the north where their enemies were gathering. The union of Catlords was in tatters, the hopes of Onyx and his cohorts dashed by division and betrayal.

To the south, the Badgerwood loomed, the largest forest of the Dalelands. It was tiny by the Dyrewood's standards, but compared to any other woodland in the Seven Realms it was a sprawling affair. She glanced at the dense mass of trees, the shadows between each gnarled trunk concealing all manner of danger. To the north lay the Badlands, Icegarden, and Robben, the home of the Wildcat Baron Mervin. It was the latter she was heading for: a little bird had told her all she needed to know regarding the whereabouts of her allies. The land here was blanketed in mist, leaving an anxious feeling in the pit of Whitley's stomach.

"It's quiet."

Whitley turned as Gretchen emerged through the darkness. The girls wore matching green cloaks of the Woodland Watch, the perfect camouflage in the wilderness.

"Too quiet," said the Bearlady, pointing east and then west. "That's quite the gap between campfires. The Redcloaks have left this part of the road unguarded."

"All the better for us, Whitley. Don't go wishing for a fight when we can avoid one."

"What if we head off toward Mervin's land and find ourselves marching straight into the heart of the Lion's camp?"

"Then we force our way through until we get to the shore of Lake Robben," replied Gretchen. "We'll fight soon enough, Whitley. Let's cross that bridge—and that lake—when we come to them."

"It's times like this that I wish we had an avianthrope with us, someone who could scout the land ahead. It feels like we're walking blind."

"We do have a Birdlord, remember?" said Gretchen, glancing back to the Badgerwood.

"I can't see Count Costa being especially sympathetic to our plight. We need to keep the Vulture's wings clipped: he's valuable to us in many ways, not least as a source of insight into how Onyx's mind works."

"It's nearly full," said Gretchen, staring up at the moon. "Two or three nights, do you think?"

Whitley understood her friend's anxiety about the moon now that she knew where Gretchen's heart lay. The pair had spoken plenty since finding one another in Hedgemoor. From the way Gretchen spoke of Trent Ferran, she was hopelessly smitten with him—not that she would admit it. Poor Trent had been bitten by one of Lucas's awful Wyld Wolves, and the corrupted lycanthropy that coursed through their bodies was

now taking over his. Count Costa had spelled out the rest: once the moon was full, the boy would be lost to them forever, his body changed irrevocably into that of a Wyld Wolf.

Whitley reached out and squeezed Gretchen's shoulder. "He'll be all right. We'll find him in time."

"Hands in the air!"

The man's voice came out of nowhere, causing both girls to start. Whitley winced. *How could we be so foolish?* There was the twang of a crossbow and a bolt hit the packed earth at her feet, fired from within the mist to the north of the road.

"In the air," repeated the man. "Now!"

Reluctantly, both Gretchen and Whitley raised their palms, turning toward the side of the road as figures appeared through the fog—first a couple, then more, materializing like phantoms from the gray mist. Within moments she counted more than twenty of them, a handful with crossbows trained on the girls, the rest advancing with swords and shields.

"I should've changed, I could've sniffed them out," cursed Whitley, shaking her head.

"Me, too," agreed Gretchen, muttering under her breath.

"Quiet," said the Redcloak spokesman, stepping closer. The insignia across the shoulder of his scarlet cape told them he was a captain, and the grin on his face confirmed that he was mighty pleased with himself. He was the only one unarmed. The commander reached out with both arms and yanked the Wereladies' hoods away from their faces.

"Well, well," he continued, looking the girls up and down. "I thought for a moment we'd found us some Greencloaks who'd wandered out of their stinking forest, but look at this, lads! A couple of wenches, wandering the Great West Road."

A series of lewd jibes followed as the girls stood there nervously, the men circling them like a pack of wild animals. Therianthropes though each of them were, they were vastly outnumbered by the Lionguard, who had crossbows primed and swords and shields at the ready. Even the mightiest Werelord would have been in a fix against these odds.

Whitley flinched when one of the Redcloaks reached out, brushing his hand through her hair. She spun about, back-to-back with Gretchen, her hands lowered now and curled into fists. The soldiers laughed at her show of resolve, which only angered her further.

"Keep calm, cousin," whispered Gretchen. "They see you shift and those crossbows will sing!"

She was correct, of course. So long as the Lionguard were dismissing them as a pair of harmless girls, they still had a surprise up their sleeves should they need it.

"So tell me, pretties," said the captain. "What are you doing on the road at such an hour, so far from home?"

"How do you know we're far from home?" asked Gretchen.

More laughter from the men as their commander nodded approvingly. "You got a homestead nearby that me and my boys have somehow missed?"

"I bet they've got food there, Captain!" shouted one of the men excitedly.

"Aye," added another as he walked past them. "Fresh meat or some such. I'm fed up with these foul trail rations. Does your old man have any ale?"

"Better still, does he have any more daughters?" said another, leering at the girls as he passed by the other way.

"You take another step toward me and you'll know pain," said Whitley, her hands open, nails poised to lash out.

Both girls had allowed their therian sides to rise to the surface, simmering behind their human appearance. While Whitley was ready to tear strips from any of the Lionguard who came too close, Gretchen was sniffing at the air, eyes scouring the fog, ears searching for a telltale noise. She reached back, taking Whitley's hand in her own, and pulled it down to her side, her grip tight and insistent. Whitley fought it at first until she also heard the sound. There it was—the unmistakable croak in the darkness.

"Let us go," said Whitley calmly. This brought about another bout of laughter from the Redcloaks.

"Did I hear you right?" scoffed the captain.

"You heard her well enough," said Gretchen. "If you had any sense in that tiny, cramped skull you'd be running now, fleeing to your master's skirts."

The men continued to laugh, but their commander wasn't amused. He sneered as he stepped up to her, eyes narrowed,

filthy fingers brushing her hair and running through her ringlets.

"I know you, little red," he said quietly, balling her hair between his fingers and curling them into a fist. She winced as he gave her head a violent shake. "Where've I seen you before?" His eyes went wide suddenly as he realized Gretchen's identity, his face draining of color.

"You should be running," repeated the Werefox.

Spears flew, finding the crossbowmen first. They went down under a hail of hunting javelins. Figures leapt and loped out of the Badgerwood's edge, bounding out from between the trees on powerful legs. The Lionguard turned, raising weapons at the dark, darting shapes, but all too late. The soldiers were flattened or bowled off their feet, carried off into the mist with spears through their guts. Shields buckled and swords were knocked aside as the phibian warriors of the Bott Marshes rushed their enemy.

The captain spun as his men cried out, dragging Gretchen by the hair, shoving her before him into the way of the Marshmen. The green-and-brown-skinned spearmen were making short work of the Redcloaks, bringing spears and knives down on them and stifling their screams.

"Stay back!" the captain shouted at the phibians as they leveled their wide eyes upon him. He held a dagger to Gretchen's hip, its tip pressed beneath her ribs. Each of the Werefrogs rose to their full height, some as tall as eight feet,

flicking the blood of the commander's men from their spears. Whitley stepped in front of them as the captain watched in horror, ranks of soldiers and horsemen emerging from the Badgerwood at her back. Greencloaks and Graycloaks, Romari and Furies, all led by a host of colorful Werelords. Archers took position on the flanks of the approaching force, bows trained upon the fires to the east and west. Still they came, the forest now alive as the hidden army revealed itself, spilling out of the darkness as they crossed the old road, making their way toward Robben.

Whitley continued to approach the captain, demanding his full attention, every step measured and confident. Each of them ignored the seething mass of marching soldiers at her back, only the phibians following her as the Redcloak officer backed up into a tree. He could retreat no farther. He couldn't take his eyes off Whitley as the dark fur of the ursanthrope began to shimmer across her flesh. It was only Gretchen's growling voice that stirred him from his horrified, fascinated reverie.

"I said you should've run."

Her hair was coarser now, the captain's fist entangled as she whipped about. His wrist snapped, cracking like celery. Gretchen twisted her body, trying to contort out of reach of his blade, but the dagger still scored the skin on her hip. She felt the burning touch of the silver-blessed steel as it parted the flesh. Enraged, her claws and teeth found the captain's

301

face, tearing it away and sending him to the ground. Kholka bounded past her, his spear finding the Redcloak's chest and silencing his gurgles.

Gretchen winced, clutching her wound with bloody fingers as the procession of soldiers rushed across the road, a fast-moving river of swords, shields, and spears.

"I can stitch you up," said Baron Eben, the young Ramlord parting from the ranks of soldiers to rush to her side.

"Not here, not now," said Yuzhnik, the giant Romari ushering the magister on his way and back into the line. His eyes were fixed on the campfires as torches began to waver in the darkness. "Seems the Lionguard heard the death rattles of their brethren."

Yuzhnik went to help Gretchen, but she knocked his hand aside. *Same old Gretchen,* Whitley thought, smiling. *Stubborn to the end.*

"I'll be fine," said the Werefox, grimacing. "We need to keep moving."

"And if you stumble, you'll be carried," said Yuzhnik gruffly.

Whitley was relieved that the strongman had joined them on their journey. Baba Soba had charged him with leading the Romari warriors into the approaching battle. There were zadkas among the travelers who were more experienced when it came to diplomacy and conflict, but there were few who inspired the people as much as Yuzhnik.

"She won't stumble and you won't need to carry her," said Whitley as one of the Greencloaks brought her horse over. The two of them helped Gretchen into Chancer's saddle, Whitley patting her mount's neck affectionately.

"Onward, Chancer," she said, his ears flicking at his mistress's voice. "Don't let up until your hooves hit Lake Robben."

4

An Unexpected Hand

DREW STARED UP into the sky, the summer sun hot on his face, watching a circling shape high above him. It might have been an opportunistic raptor from the Whitepeaks, a Sturmish Kite perhaps, scavenging for pickings in the valley, but somehow he knew better. It dipped in and out of the clouds, getting a good look at the Wolf's ramshackle war camp that had made the shores of Lake Robben its home. Others had spied it, too, ceasing their tasks to call and point. There was a clapping sound nearby as the two remaining Hawklords shook their wings from their backs, crouching for a moment before launching themselves into the air. The falconthropes had never been busier since they had arrived in Robben, constantly

in flight, marshaling the skies above the camp and trading skirmishes with the avianthropes who fought for the enemy. With a few powerful beats they were climbing into the heavens.

"Fly along, little bird," whispered Drew as he saw the distant Vulturelord suddenly switch direction, peeling away to head off eastward.

"They know we're here now," said Duke Bergan, walking up the shale slope to join him on the grass bank. Behind him the pitched gray canopy of the command tent rose from the beach, its canvas stretched taut over stakes driven into the earth. "There were a couple of Cranes spotted this morning, too. If the divisions within the Catlord ranks are as you say they are, then both Onyx and Lucas will be aware of our movements."

"Onyx and Lucas?" said Drew. "It's Oba and Leon who've now made this war their own. They set sail for the Seven Realms once they knew the Forum of Elders was sundered."

"Why they couldn't have had it out back in Bast, Brenn only knows," muttered the Bearlord.

"Because Lyssia's the prize, Bergan. The entire Seven Realms stands to be won. They had it once, with Leopold, but they lost it. He wasted his victory over Wergar, his cruel reign alienating the people against him."

"Spoken like a king," said Bergan.

Drew shook his head. "I don't want to be a king, old man.

I want to see the Catlords and their allies sailing south, never to return. There's little I want in life, and a crown and throne don't appear upon that list."

"Yet king you are, Drew."

Drew sighed as he cast his eye over the camp. Smiths had set up their workshops, having had the foresight to bring their grinding stones and tools with them when they had fled Icegarden. Lars Steinhammer was their most senior, master smith from beneath the Strakenberg mountain and keeper of the secrets of Sturmish steel. Fletchers worked feverishly, preparing arrows by the crate-load to be sent to the front line. Beyond the hills at the head of the Robben Valley were their defenses, makeshift and ramshackle, but better than nothing. General Fry had marshaled the troops, ensuring they made the best of the natural defenses, seizing the higher ground and digging in. Presently, that force consisted of the remaining soldiers of Sturmland, knights and infantrymen stretched to their limits. And there they awaited the inevitable, eyes constantly peering back behind the lines, praying for the arrival of reinforcements.

"How long until Tiaz's force from Omir arrives?" asked Drew. He had left the Tigerlord in charge of the strange army that had triumphed in the Bana Gap. Some had been wary of the appointment, but it was the only one that made sense. Tiaz had turned his back on the Lions and Panthers, siding with Drew like his father and his daughter. If his words were to be believed, he would do anything to repair his relationship with

Taboo. Besides, Drew had left Djogo with Tiaz as the Tiger's second. At the first sign of betrayal, the former slaver knew exactly what to do. Vega was there also, as a second pair of eyes and ears.

"Four or five days' march, so your friend Florimo reckons. It's quite an army, but I fear they may arrive here too late. A damned shame. We're down to our bones now."

"I'd hoped that Whitley might have gotten through to Brackenholme. She planned to gather an army and march north. Your daughter's a . . . remarkable girl."

Drew stopped short of telling Bergan what he truly thought of her—that he loved her, that he wished beyond words that he might see her again. To think he might die without holding her one last time left him weak of spirit.

Bergan nodded grimly. "Come, the Wolf's Council awaits you," he said, leading him off the embankment and across the beach to the tent. "It's grown somewhat since we last sat down together."

The two therians stepped under the canopied awning, the canvas keeping the worst of the sun's heat off them. There were no chairs to sit on, no table to stand around. The assembled commanders of the Wolf forces sat on boulders, lay on the pebbles, or paced about within the shade. Manfred appeared to be holding court presently, but he was mired in an argument with Taboo.

"The Lions and Panthers are our greatest threats," said Ta-

boo, wagging a clawed finger at the Staglord. "We should strike out now, before they have time to assemble an assault. Let me and the Hawks hit them in the night. Krieg and the Behemoth will accompany us. Waiting here for them to arrive? That's madness. Sitting on a beach never won a war, horned one."

Manfred snorted angrily, recoiling at the nickname she'd thrown him. "Listen, Catlady: you may think your enemies are your kinfolk of Bast, but they're the least of our concerns. The greatest threat to the safety of the Seven Realms remains in the mountains. So long as Baron Hector remains unaccounted for, I fear for what has befallen him."

"You're worried about one little Boarlord?" exclaimed Taboo.

"I'm worried about his state of mind, and the power he can harness. The Lord of Redmire has garnered a terrible reputation through his Dark Magistry. He can raise the dead and command them to do his bidding. You think an army of Catlords is something to fear? Imagine an army of the dead!"

"Alarmist nonsense!" scoffed the Weretiger, waving a hand dismissively at him. "The dead cannot rise. Illusions of some kind. Parlor tricks."

"Enough," said Drew. "The dead *can* rise, Taboo."

"We saw it ourselves in Cape Gala," added Lord Conrad. Duke Brand snorted approvingly beside him.

"I've witnessed Hector's communing firsthand," said Drew.

"But he could only control one spirit, Manfred. I imagine holding more than one in his thrall would be beyond my friend's powers."

"I hope you're right," said Manfred.

"As do we all," agreed Bergan. "The thought of that sweet lad from Redmire becoming some ghoulish necromancer baffles me. I'd need to see it with my own eyes before I believed it."

"I pray you don't have to," said Drew. "It's not pretty."

"Hector's power is somehow connected to his hand, Drew," said Manfred cautiously. "It's a withered, shriveled thing, utterly unnatural. I don't doubt for a moment that's the source of his wickedness."

Drew nodded, although inside he was in turmoil. He didn't want to imagine what Hector might have become. Instead, he clung to the hope that his friend had indeed experienced an epiphany and turned away from his dark path. The greatest question in this entire war was who awaited them in Icegarden; Drew prayed it was Hector, and not Blackhand.

"So we attack the Catlords, then?" said Taboo, keen to talk of the fight closer to home, her eyes burning with vengeful delight.

"With what?" Bergan laughed. "Taking our best fighters out on some half-brained mission and leaving the camp weakened hardly seems like a sound plan."

"Don't worry, old man. You can remain here with the

women. I only want the strongest by my side when I find Onyx."

The Bearlord continued to laugh. "You're a spirited Cat, aren't you?"

"You can have an army by your side, Taboo, and it won't matter."

The sultry voice came from outside the tented area. Drew looked past the others, finally spying Opal where she lay on the rocks, basking in the sun.

"You will not defeat Onyx," said the Pantherlady, purring as she spoke.

Taboo hissed at the Beauty of Bast. "You think your brother is that strong? Invincible? His reputation is built on myth and folklore."

"His reputation is built on an extensive series of campaigns across our homeland, little Tiger. In each case he was victorious. And in each case my brother took his share of kills. Therian kills."

"He's not invincible," said Bergan, his grim humor subsiding. "If anything, from what I saw, he's overconfident. I witnessed Duke Henrik bringing him to his knees. The White Bear would've killed him on the slopes of the Strakenberg if the Lion hadn't interceded. Henrik had him, Drew."

Each of them shared the same regret that the White Bear had been stopped, so close to defeating the Pantherlord. Lucas had darted in, murdering the old duke while he was engaged in a duel.

"You'll hear from him shortly," said Opal, eyes opening now as she turned her face their way. "My brother will issue a challenge: mortal combat with a champion, that's his way. Defeat him and the war is won—his generals understand the terms."

Drew looked across at Florimo, the old seabird staring back at him knowingly. They were all quiet, considering her words as she went on.

"Tempting, isn't it? One duel and it's all over? That's how he draws them in. Unarmed, my brother has faced opponents of all shapes and sizes, wielding blade, bow, and battle-ax, but it doesn't matter. It always ends the same way. This is how he's earned the moniker the Beast of Bast."

"So we find a champion?" asked Krieg, the Rhino joining the debate. "I'll fight him."

"He's fought Rhinos before," said Opal, stretching on the rocks.

"Not like me."

"Just like you, armored to the hilt with horn and hide. He's killed them all with his bare hands."

"Then I shall fight him," boomed the Behemoth, tiring of the Pantherlady's dismissive nature.

"Too slow," she said, before waving a finger at Taboo. "And you're too headstrong."

The Tiger hissed at her cousin, who simply grinned and closed her eyes again.

"Perhaps you should fight him, Opal?" said Manfred. "Or are you afraid?"

The Pantherlady didn't reply, but her smile vanished instantly.

"If anyone fights him, it shall be me," said Drew grimly. "His quarrel's with the Wolf. That's what he'll get."

Drew faced the Ternlord who had been watching on nervously.

"Florimo, how did you and Lady Shah fare on your visit to Robben town? Is Baron Mervin joining us on the mainland?"

The old navigator scratched his jaw, pink feather wilting from his bandanna in the heat. "The Hawklady and I delivered his daughter, Lady Bethwyn, back to him."

"And?"

"And he directed us to depart. Shah has remained there, trying to persuade him to see reason. Alas, he's proving most intractable."

"What?" exclaimed Bergan. "Mervin's an ally! He was a founding member of the Wolf's Council in the wake of the uprising in Highcliff."

"How can he not join us now?" asked Manfred. "Has he betrayed us?"

"Did he give you any reasoning?" said Bergan.

"None, my lords," said the Tern. "It's something benign, I suspect."

"What are you talking about, man?" said the Staglord, irritated.

Drew raised his hand to calm the duke, nodding as he understood the navigator. "He's afraid isn't he?"

Florimo nodded sheepishly. "Can't say I blame the old chap. Things do look rather bleak, all things considered."

"Stirring words, Ternlord," said Taboo. "You're an inspiration to us all."

"We can't all be bloodthirsty monsters like your kind," said Bergan, clearly sympathetic to Mervin's decision.

This prompted a heated exchange from the Werelords as they shouted one another down. Meanwhile, Drew could see that Miloqi and Lady Greta were deep in conversation, their heads together while the others bickered. The elderly White Bear, heir to the throne of Icegarden, spoke in an animated fashion. Drew stepped over to the pair, keen to hear what they had to say.

"Can I see your wrist?" said Miloqi as Drew came near. He raised his hand. "Sorry, I should've been clearer. Show me your other one."

The girl reached forward and took his handless forearm, lifting it so that Greta could see it. The metal cap that he wore over its end was bound with dirty rags, securing it in place.

"May I?" asked the Lady of Icegarden, tentatively taking the bindings between her fingers. Drew nodded as the argu-

ment raged on at their backs. Her hands worked quickly, peeling the rags away before gripping the metal cap gently. It was wedged on tightly. She pulled and twisted, and the covering came away with a satisfying sucking sound. Drew felt the air on the scarred stump, the sensation peculiar. It was at that moment that he realized the cap had been in place for weeks. He couldn't remember the last time he had taken it off, the young Wolf happier to ignore his amputated limb rather than dwell upon it.

"Please tell me there's a point to this?" said Drew forlornly, staring at the scarred flesh where it had been stitched together long ago. He had bitten off the hand, choosing life over death and accepting the disfigurement. To look at it now sent shivers racing down his spine, despite the heat.

"Could it work?" said Miloqi, the question directed at the White Bear magister.

"Possibly," said Greta. "My great grandmother was the last to carry out such an enchantment. But I'll need to speak with Steinhammer first. He'll know. I can't do it alone. We need to do it together."

"The smith?" said Drew, recognizing the name.

"You know his workshop?" asked Greta, and Drew nodded. "Seek him out. I'll meet you there."

With that, Miloqi seized him by the arm and led him from the tent. Her brother, Mikotaj, remained with his army of

northmen, heading west with Vega. Miloqi pulled Drew up the beach and onto the grass bank.

"What in Brenn's name's going on?" asked Drew.

"I am a seer, Gray Son," said Miloqi, a hint of irritation in her voice for having to explain herself. "As such, I often 'see' things. Like it or not, you feature in my dreams and visions frequently of late, fighting some unseen, shadowy foe."

"Unseen, shadowy foe? What does that mean?"

"How should I know? That's the joy of being a seer. Little ever makes sense. But I do know this: in these visions you appear with two hands."

"Two hands?"

"This is going to get dull very quickly if you just keep repeating what I'm saying, Gray Son."

Drew caught sight of Steinhammer, clanging away at a white-hot piece of steel before plunging it into a large bucket of water. There was a loud hiss, steam erupting around the smith, before the metal reemerged, a perfectly fashioned black short-sword. Steinhammer looked up as they approached.

The man dropped to his knees before the Wolflord, causing much embarrassment to Drew.

"Please don't. I should bow before you, Steinhammer. It's your steel that's kept half of these men alive on the battlefield throughout the winter."

"I'm not the only smith, my lord," said the man, his droop-

ing handlebar mustache glistening with sweat. He wiped his hands on his leather smock and reached out to shake Drew's.

"No, but you're the best, Lars," said Greta, pushing her way through the approaching Werelords and striding up to the smithy. In her arms she carried a bundled gray cloak, its ermine edge coiled about it like a sleeping snake.

"You flatter me, my lady," said Steinhammer. "How can I help you?"

Greta unwrapped the bundled cloak. Drew's eyes widened when he spied what was within.

It was an elegant gauntlet fashioned from the same white metal as Moonbrand, the sword of the Gray Wolves of Westland. Greta turned it over in her hands, holding it reverently as she brushed her fingers over its broad palm. It resembled a bear's paw, only with tiny hinges, plates, and joints covering it entirely. The way it was being handled, Drew might have expected it to groan or creak, grate or clang, as the many minute moving parts rubbed against one another. To his surprise, the gauntlet remained silent.

"This was my brother's, and before him my father's, and his father's before that," said Lady Greta as the others gathered around them. All were silent as she stared at the shining steel, lost in thought for a moment. She blinked and turned to the Wolflord.

"The White Fist of Icegarden is yours now, Drew."

The young lycanthrope was taken aback. "You're too kind,

truly, but I can't wear that. Remember?" He shook his stumped wrist at her and shrugged.

"That's why we've come to see Lars Steinhammer," replied the White Bear.

"We'll need to do it tonight, under moonlight," said the master smith, nodding sagely.

"Do what?" asked Drew, perplexed.

"Tonight's your lucky night, Gray Son," said Miloqi, giving him a dig in the ribs with her elbow.

"How so?"

She smiled. "Tonight you get your paw back."

5

THE LORD OF ALL LIONS

THE WHISPER WENT through High Lord Leon's war camp like wildfire: the king was returned. Soldiers scrambled from their billets, rushing to line the route Lucas took as he made his way to his grandfather's tent. But their smiles slipped as the Werelord they served shambled up the rutted road through the camp's heart. He was disheveled, emaciated, his blond hair wild and filthy, matted with burrs, blood, and bone. His eyes were fixed straight ahead toward the tall red tent that was home to Leon. The Redcloaks gave the young Lion and his pack of Wyld Wolves a wide berth, the monsters snarling as they passed through. Lucas wasn't greeted with cheers or hails, handclaps or heralds. Instead, he was met with looks of disgust and fear. The return of the king was an inglorious affair.

A chain was fastened about Trent's throat, the other end wrapped about Darkheart's clawed fist. The links rattled as Trent stumbled along, legs weary and vision hazy. He hadn't eaten in days. He had seen what they killed, knew well enough what food they favored. His dreams were haunted by memories of poor, sweet Milo and his last moments. Lucas was the worst of them. The Wyld Wolves were more beast than human, but the king was supposedly a therian lord, with a mind that was his own. Trent would sooner starve than become like him.

Besides, Lucas may have been nominally the leader of the Wyld Wolves, but it was clear to Trent who pulled the strings. Darkheart was behind every decision the Lion made, whispering in his twitching ear, pointing him where he needed to go. The shaman seemed to have mastered the best of both worlds. He still had the cunning mind he had always had and was able to communicate as before, unlike his brethren, who now resorted to growls and barks. Added to this was the physical might of the lycanthrope's body, every inch packed with brutal, bloody brawn.

They were heading to Icegarden. The king had business to attend to with Blackhand, the dark magister who now ruled the frozen city. And Darkheart was keen to witness just how powerful the magister actually was.

A figure emerged from the enormous red tent before them, seven feet tall and almost as broad. His large skull was sloping, heavy brow overhanging, eyes twinkling in the dark spaces be-

low. His jaw jutted out, casting a shadow over his broad, bare chest, stubby yellow teeth rising from an ugly underbite. The man's arms were enormous, almost trailing to the ground as he approached. His pale skin was devoid of hair and hatch-marked with old war wounds. His bowlegged gait came to a sudden halt before the king's procession as he rose to his full height, gaining at least another foot on top of his towering frame.

"All hail King Lucas," the giant said, more than a hint of derision in his voice.

"Ah, the Naked Ape!" exclaimed the king, throwing his arms out and admiring the fellow as if he were a beauty to rival Opal. "How are you, Lord Ulik? That hair not grown back yet?"

Ulik sneered. "You were a child when we first met. I see some things don't change. Your grandfather will see you now."

Lucas jumped forward and growled at the hulking Apelord. "I didn't come here seeking an audience with High Lord Leon. He should be awaiting *my* arrival! Out of my way, you ugly buffoon."

The young Werelion shoved past Ulik, his Wyld Wolves following as he stormed into the tent. The Apelord watched them pass him by, ignoring their snarls. Trent's eyes met with Ulik's for an instant, the giant nodding imperceptibly. *An acknowledgment?*

The interior of the tent was a world away from the sprawling chaos outside. The finest velvet drapes hung from the ceiling, sweeping down in great, looping arcs, tied in place by ropes

of spun gold. A circular table sat at the tent's center, covered in a huge chart and models. Even from a distance, Trent recognized the chart as a map of Lyssia, the playing pieces representing the various sides in the war. The red pieces would be the Lions, the gold the Panthers. Gray would have to be the Wolf: there were Drew's forces, gathered around Lake Robben. And another collection of pieces were clustered to the north. These were black, in and around Icegarden in the mountains. *Blackhand.*

A pair of knights in burnished red plate mail stood on either side of a wooden throne, their swords standing point down on the rich carpeted floor, gauntleted hands resting on the pommels. Only their faces were uncovered, their steely-eyed gaze fixed upon those who entered. Their blond hair was tied back, the Lions of Leos unmistakable with their angular features. No doubt these two were cousins of Lucas, pure-blood felinthropes of Bast, the personal guard of the High Lord. Red-cloaks stood around the outer edge of the chamber, forming a circle of sword and shield around the table.

Leon leaned over the round table, examining a scroll, a rakish general at his side. The officer had a lean, hungry look about him, his eyes widening as the dozen Wyld Wolves entered the command tent with the young Lion. Trent spied his hand hovering over the saber on his hip, ready to withdraw it at any moment. There was a rustle of steel around the chamber's edge. Finally, High Lord Leon looked up from the map, rolling up the scroll and handing it to the general.

"Grandfather," said Lucas, strolling casually around the table toward the old man. "It's been far too long."

The frail old Lion's face was a mess of old wounds, punctures pockmarking it where his enemy's teeth had exposed skull. His mouth was disfigured on the right side, a jagged scar zigzagging up to his ear where the flesh had been torn. He'd been stitched together by the best magister Bast could offer, no doubt, but the injuries would remain: these had been dealt out by a fellow Werelord.

Leon reached out and grabbed the young Lion about the throat, his bent back suddenly straightening as he lifted Lucas off the floor. Instantly the king was shifting, but so was Leon, his arm thickening, hand transforming into a terrible paw. He squeezed tighter, holding back his grandson's metamorphosis until the youth clawed miserably at the arm, tongue lolling from his gasping jaws. The Wyld Wolves began to move to Lucas's aid, but the Redcloaks and knights pointed their silver blades menacingly. The officer beside the king shifted instantly, the Cranelord whipping his saber from its scabbard. Trent glanced back to spy Lord Ulik standing at the tent's open door, blocking the exit.

"You little worm!" shouted Leon. "You backstabbing, cretinous worm!"

Lucas whimpered, his face turning purple as Leon roared, spittle showering the king.

"Lion does not bite Lion! Son does not slay father! Or per-

haps the old rules no longer apply, boy? Maybe a grandfather can kill his own grandson, eh? What kind of half-wit do you have to be, to turn upon your own?"

Lucas's mouth worked, but only a reedy croak came out. Leon tossed the haggard felinthrope to the floor and stood over him.

"Well?" shouted the High Lord, booting the youth in the ribs with a well-placed kick. "Speak!"

"The Panther, Your Grace!" whimpered Lucas. "It was Onyx's doing . . . he and his sister . . . made me!"

"They *made you* kill your father? You expect me to believe that?" The old Lion flexed his claw, glancing to the Cranelord at his side. "You hear this, Clavell? The Panthers put the poor kitten up to it. Rotten beasts."

"It's true!" gurgled Lucas, nursing his throat. "I was not myself. I fear they poisoned or bewitched me! If my mind was my own that would *never* have happened. I loved my father . . . "

He collapsed into a bout of tears, curling up at Leon's feet. The High Lord looked from the pathetic king to the Wyld Wolves, his eyes lingering on Darkheart. Trent saw a look pass between them. The wizened old Lion then turned to Trent.

"Who is this, and why do you have him on a leash? He's not like the others, is he?"

Lucas glanced up from where he lay, sniffing back sobs and snot as he saw who his grandfather was looking at.

"This is Trent Ferran, Your Grace!"

"Ferran? As in—"

"The very same," said the young Lion, rising from the carpet. "Only he isn't a Wolflord like his brother. This one is human. Or was, I should say."

"Was?" said Leon, stepping closer to Trent to examine him. He looked him up and down as Darkheart wrapped his clawed hand around the chain that bit more. Darkheart yanked Trent away from Leon, ensuring he was beyond striking distance of the High Lord.

"These are the Wyld Wolves I told you about, Your Grace," said Clavell the Cranelord. It was clear to Trent that Leon's airbound spies had been watching them as they made their way to camp. "Monstrosities conjured by whatever foul magicks these Wyldermen channel."

"And this Ferran boy is blighted by the same . . . disease?" asked Leon, eyeing them all suspiciously.

"My lord," said Trent, his words catching in his throat. Darkheart tugged him back, growling at him.

"Let him speak," said Leon.

Reluctantly, Darkheart allowed the chain to go loose. Trent smacked his lips. The sensation was strange, as if his teeth were too big for his mouth.

"Please, my lord, I beg of you. Remove me from the company of your grandson. He is . . . *ill.* His mind is riddled with madness. He's not fit to think for himself, let alone rule Lyssia."

Lucas and the Wyld Wolves growled at him, but Trent

ignored them, the young Graycloak searching Leon's eyes for reason and sense. The High Lord raised a withered hand to silence them, before taking the chain and unwinding it from Darkheart's hand.

"I should have you all killed," whispered Leon, leading Trent away from the Wyld Wolves and securing the chain about the tent's central pole. "You've carried out an unholy act, taking a therian's blood and gifting it to humans. But this Ferran lad may be of use to me. Perhaps family ties can break the Wolflord's resolve. Clavell, get this wretch fed. And washed. The rest of your Wolfmen may leave, Lucas. We can arrange for some kind of camp to be set up for them away from the other men. Perhaps even a kennel in the wilds."

"You would dismiss my personal guard?" exclaimed the Lionlord.

"*Personal guard?*" shouted Leon incredulously. "They're abominations. Look at them: pathetic mockeries of a therianthrope, each and every one."

Darkheart spoke at last as the Lionguard began to usher the Wyld Wolves from the tent.

"Your Grace," said the Wolfman. "I have Ferran on a chain for good reason. The full moon approaches. When this occurs, a change will take place: he'll either live and become something bigger, stronger, like my brothers and me. Or he shall die, too weak to survive the Wyld Magick."

Leon's eyes narrowed as he looked at the shaman. "You

would nursemaid this one? Be there to hold his paw when the change takes place?"

"I'm intrigued to see what happens," said Darkheart. "He is the first bitten by one of my brothers that I know of to have survived this far. Most die of the wound they receive. But Ferran seems stronger than that."

"Most?" hissed Leon, craning his neck to look at Lucas. "How many humans have these Wolfmen of yours bitten? More important, what number survive, carrying the same corrupted disease in their blood?"

Lucas had no answer, his eyes large and pale as he stared back at his grandfather.

"Take them away," snapped the High Lord as Ulik seized Darkheart by the scruff of his neck, leading him from the command tent. Lucas watched them disappear. Trent could see immediately that the king looked fearful.

"Clavell," said Leon, taking his place on the throne. "Show the scroll to my grandson."

The Cranelord, now shifted back to human form, handed the parchment over to Lucas, who unrolled it and began to read.

"What is this?"

"It's a challenge, Your Majesty," said Clavell. "Onyx proposes a contest among himself—champion of the Panthers— and a champion of the Lions and of the Wolf, at an appointed time. The three warriors are to fight one another at the same time until only one remains standing—the death of the de-

feated is entirely at the whim of the victor. The winner takes all. The winner takes Lyssia."

"I've seen him send these challenges before," said Lucas. "He did the same thing to Duke Henrik in the Whitepeaks, called him out to fight him."

"Yes, we heard all about that," said the Cranelord with contempt.

"My intervention hardly tipped the scale," said the young Lion defensively. "Onyx never loses."

"Interesting you should say that," said High Lord Leon. "You've returned to the fold just in time, grandson. You have a chance now to reclaim a shred of dignity after the string of woeful deeds you've carried out this past year."

"Reclaim my dignity?" said Lucas.

"Indeed," replied his grandfather with a smile. "Prepare yourself, child. You're the new champion of the Lions."

6

THE SMITH AND THE SURGEON

DREW STARED UP at the heavens from where he knelt unblinking, focusing on the moon. So often the root of his power, it was now a source of calm as Lady Greta and Lars Steinhammer manipulated his arm, outstretched across the boulder beside him. He felt the jostle and jabbing of fingers and blades as both magister and smith worked on his flesh, connecting white steel gauntlet to scarred skin. Occasionally he felt a hard tug, as the pair discarded caution in favor of force, peeling back the flesh to attach metal to bone. Scalpels opened muscle, needles binding threads of the finest Sturmish steel to muscle and tendon.

It should have hurt like hell, the procedure carried out without any anesthetic—he needed to be awake throughout,

to respond to the commands of the Daughter of Icegarden. But somehow, the pain was just a dull throb, as if Drew were watching from above, suspended in the cool night air, removed from the ordeal.

Florimo stood nearby on the hillock, an arm around Miloqi. Not only a seer, she was also an accomplished healer, but this operation was beyond the realms of her expertise. Magistry was a specialized form of healing, and the magicks Greta and her kind channeled were beyond the comprehension of normal humans and therians. The navigator had blanched as Greta's scalpel had made its first incision. *Some folk will never get used to the sight of a bit of blood*, thought Drew. It was strange to think that the hopes of all Drew's allies depended upon the wisdom of this gnarled, eccentric Tern. It remained to be seen whether his plan would come to fruition.

"My work here is done," said Steinhammer.

Drew was pulled away from the moon by the metalsmith's words, and turned to look at his arm. The boulder was stained dark, the White Fist of Icegarden fitted over the stump where his hand had once been. Beneath the pooling red liquid, Drew could see the runic symbols that Greta had painted upon the rock, tiny swirls of white metal paint. The ground around the boulder was encircled by a thick line of brimstone, the same yellow powder that his old friend Hector had used to summon departed souls. *Hopefully we won't be encountering the dead tonight,* Drew thought, fearful of what had become of the young Boar-

lord. As he ceased his moon-inspired meditation, he could feel an itching, irritating discomfort shooting through his arm. He made to move, and the discomfort became white-hot pain.

"Wait!" said Greta, placing firm but gentle hands on his shoulder, fingers wet with Drew's blood. "You mustn't move!"

"But I feel nothing but pain," gasped Drew. "It's like there are a thousand fishhooks buried in my flesh." At that moment he felt something metallic grate against the severed bones of his forearm, deep within the limb. He heaved, overcome with nausea, afraid he might throw up.

"The job is only half-complete," said Steinhammer, wiping the blood from the gauntlet with an oily rag. He stood and stepped back, out of the circle of brimstone, his face beaded with sweat. "The rest is in the hands of Lady Greta."

"It's in the hands of Brenn," said the magister, closing her eyes and beginning her incantation.

Her words were different from Hector's. Drew's recollection of the Boarlord's communing consisted of a series of archaic, unintelligible utterings. To Drew the words had sounded ugly and dark, not meant to be spoken by therian or human mouths. In contrast, Greta's voice was musical, the words beautiful, escaping her throat in a singsong fashion before lingering in the air. It reminded Drew of the wind chimes his mother had placed in his room as an infant, sending him back to happier times on the Cold Coast, lazy summer evenings and the welcome approach of slumber.

Greta rose from where she knelt beside him, opening her arms and looking up to the heavens. Drew felt something hum on his hip, a vibration that coursed through his body. It was Moonbrand, the sword of the Gray Wolves of Westland. He grabbed the handle in his right hand and gave it a gentle pull, finding that the blade now glowed at his touch. He unsheathed it as Greta sang her ethereal song. The runes that marked its edge were now dancing with sparks of white fire, the light slowly consuming the blade. Drew looked from the sword to the magister, shocked to see that her eyes also shone with the same cold blaze.

The White Fist glowed like Moonbrand, vibrant and full of life. Tiny specks of light disengaged from the metal, rising into the air and drifting on the breeze like unearthly spores. They twirled through the air around Wolflord and magister, caught up on the strange currents that seemed to carry Greta's song about them. More and more of the light particles rose on the current, casting a sparkling light over the faces of the onlookers. The lights were a spiraling twister, reaching for the moon overhead.

Greta's face shone, hair billowing about her. The hilltop was now awash with light, as others from the Wolf's camp began to climb the slopes to see the spectacle. Through the sparkling storm Drew could make out their vague silhouettes materializing from the darkness, caught in the thrall of the magister's enchantment.

Suddenly, the wind was dying down, its intensity dropping as Greta's voice diminished. The white lights slowed, dropping from the air, drawn back into the gauntlet that was attached to Drew's arm. The White Bear's head slumped against her chest, eyes closing, as she wavered where she stood. Steinhammer caught her as she collapsed, the smith laying her gently onto the grass as the last sparks of white fire returned to the glowing gauntlet.

It started with a tiny spark in his left bicep, a minuscule bolt of lightning that shot up his arm along dormant nerves. Drew turned to the White Fist of Icegarden as the metal began to hum, its cold glow sending waves of strange heat over him. Another spark raced up his arm, this one reaching his shoulder. *Did the gauntlet just twitch?* Drew blinked, staring intently at the metal glove, his eyes bleary in the face of its glow. He could feel the heat in his fingers now, radiating up the limb and through his body. *My fingers? What am I thinking? I don't have any fingers!*

His arm was alive now with shooting pains as long-lost digits came back to life. Drew watched with wonder as the gauntlet suddenly became animated, metal fingers twitching in time with his thoughts. He concentrated, willing them to close. The hand made a fist. Drew gasped. He looked up at Florimo and Miloqi. The old Tern's jaw was slack and useless, while he could see tears of hope in the White Wolf's eyes. Greta's eyes fluttered open where she lay in the smith's lap, and she nodded weakly as she witnessed the Wolflord's joy.

Slowly, Drew rose to his feet, fearing the gauntlet might separate from his arm as he lifted it from the boulder. It didn't. It remained in place, fixed firmly to bone and tendon, as weightless as Moonbrand and as real as his own flesh. Sword and White Fist continued to glow in the moonlight as the crowd of onlookers around the hill's summit grew.

"Does it hurt?" asked Greta.

"It feels . . . like my own hand," he replied, his voice frail with awe. "How can this be?"

The magister of Icegarden and Steinhammer both smiled knowingly.

"It's not something that can be explained, Drew," she replied.

"Equal parts magick and metal," added Steinhammer, "with a bit of blood, sweat, and tears thrown in for good measure."

"Your own blood?" said Drew.

"Yours," said the smith, "although you're welcome to my sweat and tears."

Drew returned Moonbrand to its scabbard and then compared his hands to one another. The White Fist was bigger than his other hand, but he imagined that when he was transformed, the gauntlet would match the Werewolf's claw. Its lightness was incredible, its movements instinctive and completely in tune with his mind. He lifted it to his face, turning it one way and then the other as he inspected its intricate craftsmanship. When he lowered it, he saw Bergan at the edge of the hilltop,

stricken with wonder. Behind him, the other members of the Wolf's Council had gathered.

"Send word to Onyx," said Drew. "Tell him I'll face him."

"You're sure about this?" said Bergan. "Onyx has faced a foe wearing that weapon before, and it did Henrik no good. He was ultimately unable to harness its true power, and it cost him his life."

"Perhaps Onyx is unaware of the weapons I have at my disposal," said Drew, brushing a hand over the white orb pommel of Moonbrand on his hip.

"Regardless," said the Bearlord, "he won't risk finding out. I guarantee you, Drew, he won't face you at night. Not as near to the full moon as we are. He's no fool."

Drew glanced at Florimo, who was smiling back.

"I'm counting on that," said the young lycanthrope, drawing puzzled expressions from the onlookers. "Send my reply to the Panther. I'll fight him under the terms of his challenge. I'll meet him, and whomever the Lions send, on Black Crag at noon, the day after tomorrow."

"Are you sure you won't reconsider?" asked Bergan.

For an answer, Drew turned to Count Carsten, one of the few falconthropes who wasn't presently patrolling the skies around the war camp.

"What distance is Tiaz's army from Robben? How long until they're with us?"

"Four days, I'd guess," said the count. "A mighty force that

army may be, but it can only march so fast and must make camp at night. We will be without some of our greatest warriors for the time being—Tiaz, Faisal, and Vega—not to mention their amassed force."

"If the Lions or Panthers attacked us now, weakened as we are, the consequence would be dire." Drew turned back to Bergan. "We can't afford *not* to send someone to answer Onyx's challenge—not when it could mean the end of this war."

"I just don't see why it must be you, Drew. Send someone else, a born fighter, an experienced warrior, an older man who's lived his life."

"A practiced soldier who's long in the tooth," said Drew with a smile. "Where on earth might I find such a character?"

"I don't mean just me, although I would gladly face Onyx on your behalf. There are others who would fight in your place."

Echoing the Bearlord's sentiments, a host of therian warriors stepped forward from the crowd behind him: Krieg, the Behemoth, Taboo, and Count Carsten. Even Manfred offered his services, the old Stag nodding to Drew.

"You can pick any one of us, my boy," said the Lord of Stormdale. "You know we'll do you proud."

"I don't doubt you would, Manfred, but this fight's mine. If there were any other way, don't you think I'd have taken it? This war is between the Wolf and the Catlords. It's only right that I take the challenge."

Grudgingly, the Werelords accepted Drew's words. Only Bergan shook his head, still disapproving.

"Then we waste time," said Taboo haughtily. "You've grown soft, Wolf cub. When was the last time you trained for battle?"

Drew stared at the Tiger incredulously as some of those gathered grinned at her humorless comment.

"I beg your pardon? I've been fighting a war!"

"You're about to face the greatest battle of your life, not some gaggle of clumsy Redcloaks or bumbling Goldhelms," Taboo snapped. "You'll be fighting two opponents. The prospect of Onyx alone should be enough to make you soil your britches, and you can be sure that the Lions aren't going to send a weakling."

"What would you propose, Taboo, that might toughen me up?" Drew asked, the intended sarcasm growing less the more he thought about it. There was a hint of truth to her words. This was no ordinary fight. Krieg spoke up.

"You, Taboo, the Behemoth, and I shall depart to a . . . quiet place. Somewhere with no distractions. There, we shall prepare you. Think back to Scoria, lad. Back to the Furnace and the heat and the whip. We'll break you and put you back together: harder, tougher, meaner. We will prepare you to face Onyx like no other Werelords could."

Drew nodded. He couldn't argue with them, and he knew their regime would be brutal.

"One more thing," rumbled the Behemoth. "We received

word from the Catlords. The Lions have chosen their champion to enter the arena with you and Onyx. It is to be Lucas, Drew. You'll be facing your brother."

Drew momentarily went weak at the knees. The young Lionlord was the last person he expected to face. Some monster, perhaps, dragged out of a steaming Bastian swamp and fed nothing but Lyssians for the past thirty days—that was more the Catlords' way of playing. But Lucas? He was a year or two Drew's junior, but just as ferocious in battle. If reports were to be believed, he had grown some since they had last met one another, back when Lucas was a mere spoiled brat prince.

"Lucas is blood," said Drew, flexing the metal hand once more, sending steel claws springing from the fingertips. "And this war was of his making. It's down to me to stop it. Lead on, brothers—and sister—of the Furnace."

Bergan stepped in front of him and placed a hand on Drew's chest, stopping him from following the trio of gladiators.

"Is there nothing I can do or say that can sway you from this path?"

Drew sighed. "Believe me, my friend. I wish there was." He caught a twinkle in the duke's eyes. "Just what are you up to, old Bear?"

Bergan nodded slowly and stepped to one side. He reached back with his other hand and beckoned into the night's darkness. Drew squinted as he saw a group of figures step closer. He spied familiar faces there, Greencloaks of the Woodland Watch,

including his old friend General Harker. Yuzhnik, the Romari strongman stepped up, ax upon his shoulder, smile across his face.

But it was the two girls who were with them who caused Drew's heart to skip a beat. He rushed down the slope to them, throwing his arms out wide, White Fist of Icegarden and trembling hand of flesh and blood gripping each of them in his embrace. Words could wait. For the moment the three young therians held one another and wept.

7

THE SIMPLEST CHOICE

THE LAKE WAS calm as a mill pond, the distant lights of Robben town reflected off its placid waters. The three friends sat on the shale beach, shoulder to shoulder, the young man in the middle. Food had been eaten, drinks had been downed, and tales had been shared of all the exploits they had endured. Theirs was not the only reunion; therians and humans from across the Seven Realms enjoyed one another's company. Duke Bergan had finally surrendered his daughter back to her friends after nearly crushing her with one of his infamous hugs. He had taken great delight in reuniting the three, and would return to them in time. Presently, the Bearlord of Brackenholme mingled joyfully with his men from the Woodland Realm. The noise might have woken the dead.

The Wolf's army had swelled with the new arrivals, but it was still small compared to the massed ranks of the Panther and Lion. A group of rangy warriors had set up their own camp farther along the shore, apart from everyone else, the odd-looking fellows gathering around a fire. Drew watched with interest as one of them raised a skewered fish to his wide lips, tearing the steaming white flesh from it.

"These are your Frogmen?" he asked Gretchen, as one of them stared their way, his eyes luminescent in the dark.

"They're phibians," she replied, twirling something pale and hard in her hands. Drew had seen her pull it from her boot and now wondered what it was. "They're good men, too. Well, most of them, anyway. Their leader was a pain in the rump until I put him in his place. They follow me now, not him."

"You put their leader in his place?" Drew laughed. "What happened to the girl from Hedgemoor who only mixed with the great and not-so-good?"

"She grew up." Gretchen smiled, not bothering to argue with him.

How could she? She knew what kind of person she had been, back in the day, and the transformation that had taken place in her was remarkable. Drew hardly recognized her. She was still a striking, beautiful creature who caused the hearts of most men to quicken as she passed, but there was a toughness to her now that hadn't been there before. She was a better per-

son than the one he had known. Their smiles slowly subsided as each of them stared at the twinkling horizon.

"What's that you have there?" asked Drew, indicating the object in the girl's hand. She lifted it to show him: a splintered tine from an antler. Milo's antler. Drew had liked the boy: the young Buck had shown great bravery on numerous occasions, winning the Wolf over with his heart and heroism. The lad had epitomized all that was great and good in the world, standing up to the Catlords, determined to play his part. Determined to make a difference. Drew had heard the horrific details of the boy's death at Lucas's hand. Milo's father, Duke Manfred, presently mourned his lost son, wandering the night somewhere on the war camp's edge.

"I must return it to Manfred," she whispered, sliding it back into her boot. "I'd forgotten I had it until now. It should return to Stormdale, with his sword."

Drew nodded, unable to find the words.

"It's late," said Whitley, trying to change the grim subject. "Hadn't you best get your rest? Your friends from Scoria sounded keen on putting you through the wringer."

Drew sighed. "You can tell I'm itching to get to that, can't you?"

"They seem like a hardy bunch," said Gretchen.

"What they endured in the Furnace at the hands of the Lizardlords . . . well, it beggars belief," said Drew. "Many of their

friends died there when we escaped, and others have died since. They're as close to me as family."

They were quiet again.

"You know there are only three more nights until the full moon," said Gretchen.

He nodded. Before Drew had spent time with his friends, he had insisted on meeting Count Costa. The Vulturelord had been carried, bound and gagged, from Hedgemoor. Costa had been able to shed light on Onyx's and Lucas's plans, as well as the Wyld Wolves and the horrible sequence that had been set in motion for Trent—the bite, the change, the capture. Time was running out for Drew's brother. Come the full moon, the disease would work its dark magick completely. He would be a Wyld Wolf, just like Darkheart and his monsters.

And if that happened, Drew wouldn't be the only one grieving. Incredible, he thought, that his brother and the girl who had both enchanted and enraged him had somehow found one another while the war raged around them.

Now, Drew reached out and took Gretchen's hand. "Try not to worry. I fight Onyx and Lucas soon enough. Only then can we negotiate Trent's release back to us."

"You can't negotiate with Lucas," snapped Gretchen. "He's blinded by vengeance and consumed by madness. He won't let anything stop him from reaching Icegarden. It's Hector he wants."

Drew shook his head. "He has to fight me and Onyx first,

Gretchen. He won't reach Icegarden if I defeat him in the contest."

"Lucas is a loose blade, Drew," said Gretchen, her voice trembling as she bowed her head. "After what he did to poor Milo, Brenn only knows what he'll stoop to next. I fear Trent is doomed."

Drew watched a tear roll down her cheek and bead off her chin. He stifled a smile as he thought of Trent. His brother's fuse was shorter than his. He could only imagine how heated early exchanges between the Lady of Hedgemoor and the Redcloak outrider must have been. For their friendship to have blossomed in spite of those initial differences led Drew to think there must be something quite remarkable between them. The tear that fell from her jaw convinced him as much.

"As long as I live and breathe, I won't give up," whispered Drew. He squeezed her hand. "I give you my word, Gretchen."

Drew turned to Whitley, catching the girl watching him. She rose to her feet, avoiding his gaze.

"I'm going to turn in," she said. "I'd advise you do the same, Drew. A busy day awaits you."

"Good night, Whitley," said Gretchen, smiling at her friend as the Bearlady set off back toward the tents. Drew watched Whitley go, wondering what had rattled her.

Gretchen's voice was in his ear suddenly. "For all your wisdom and wits when it comes to war, you really know very little about women, Drew Ferran."

"What do you mean?" he replied, his face flushed with color.

"Go to her."

Gretchen was smiling sweetly, her eyes sparkling as she nodded. Drew gave her a quick peck on the cheek and then he was up and running down the beach, feet churning up the pebbles as he went after Whitley.

"Whitley, wait up!" he shouted, the girl turning as he stumbled up to her. "You walk away with no good night? What's all that about?"

"I figured you wanted some time alone with Gretchen. You've a lot to catch up on, no doubt." She made to walk away again, and Drew reached out and grabbed her arm.

"Hang on," he said, trying to catch her evasive gaze. "Are you angry with me?"

"Why would I be angry with you?" Her posture was stiff, her voice scratchy.

Drew pulled Whitley closer now, turning her so that they were face-to-face. The White Fist held her by the elbow and his other hand came up to lift her chin.

"Then why do I feel such distance between us?"

"What do you want me to say, Drew?" replied the girl from Brackenholme. "I understand. Gretchen's a princess; any man in his right mind would want to be with her. I won't stand in your way. I know it'll be different now. Lyssia needs you for its

king and Gretchen for its queen. You and she . . . you're meant to be together."

Drew laughed. It wasn't harsh and mocking at his friend's expense, but happy and heartfelt. He shook his head.

"If that were true, Whitley, why would I do this?"

Before she could ask what he meant, he leaned in, planting a kiss upon her lips. She softened in his arms, as the kiss became an embrace. His hand went to her cheek, warm skin against cool. Drew kept the White Fist behind her back, but Whitley's fingers still found his, flesh and metal intertwining. The moon shone down, casting its magical glow over the therians. "What does this mean, Drew?" Whitley whispered. "How can this ever work?"

"Why shouldn't it?" asked the youth from the Cold Coast. "I choose you, Whitley. Not just over Gretchen or any other lady from the Seven Realms. I choose you over Westland, over the crown and over the throne. If I can't make you my bride, then I'll turn my back on it all. I ask you, when did I ever want to be king? Westland doesn't need another Werelord on the throne, and I certainly don't need a palace. I could live in a hole in the ground: I'd want for nothing if I had you by my side."

She reached up and brushed a trembling hand against the stubble of his jaw, his gray eyes twinkling from beneath that mop of unruly dark hair.

"Drew Ferran, you are a fool."

"A lovesick one, perhaps, my lady," he said with a crooked smile.

He was off and running then, pulling her along behind him, the girl from Brackenholme giggling as they ran.

"Where are we going?" she gasped.

"To your father." Drew laughed. "There's something I must ask him!"

8

SCRAPS FROM THE TABLE

THERE WERE A handful of meals Trent had enjoyed throughout his life that had lived long in his memory. Birthdays and solstices as a boy back on the farm, rare trips into Tuckborough when he had stayed over after market day. The roast dinners in the Plum Dove were the stuff of legend, hog with all the trimmings and giant rinds of crackling.

But they all paled in comparison to the meal he currently enjoyed. The steak didn't last long, ripped apart and devoured within moments, the young Wolf Knight almost choking in his eagerness to feast. When that piece was gone, High Lord Leon had tossed him another slab of red meat from his plate, Trent snatching it out of the air and going slower this time. He

thought the growling was his own belly until he felt it reverberate through his throat.

"Don't worry, boy," said Leon. "I don't intend to take it from you. Believe me, I can spare a cut from the Lion's share."

His silver platter was piled high with choice cuts of steak, each one rare, barely touched by flame. The High Lord of the Werelions watched Trent intently, the youth feeling his eyes burning into him, studying every mouthful.

"I can't say I blame you," said Leon, his knife slicing through a steak. "I'd rather starve as well than eat another soul, human or therian. That my grandson partakes in that hideous pastime gives me no pleasure."

He popped a bite of meat in his scarred mouth and leaned back in his throne, savoring the flavor. Trent remained chained to the central tent pole to the side of Leon's great wooden chair, but the High Lord had brought cushions from his own bed for the young Graycloak to lie upon, as well as a pitcher of water from the table. Prisoner he may have been, but he was no longer being abused by the king and his monstrous Wyld Wolves. The hour was late and the chamber was shrouded in darkness, shadows dancing by candlelight all around the velvet walls.

"What do you intend to do with Lucas?" asked Trent, finally finding his voice.

"Chances are, he'll be torn limb from limb by the Beast of Bast in his upcoming fight," said Leon. "Onyx was never one for showing mercy in a fight. But my grandson has shown remark-

able resilience in recent years and a knack for the unexpected. I wouldn't be at all surprised if Lucas had a trick up his sleeve when the time comes."

"So if he lives, then what?"

"He will step down from his position as king once the war is won," said the High Lord. "It wouldn't do for him to abdicate in the middle of this war. An army needs a figurehead. It's bad enough the Panthers and Tigers have turned traitor on us. We need stability now. Once all our foes are defeated, he will be sent back to Bast."

"And then what, my lord?" asked Trent, remembering his manners.

Leon growled. "I am . . . undecided. But he shall answer for his transgressions. To kill his *father*—my son—as he did? Tell me, Ferran, what kind of man was your own father?"

Trent had to think for a moment, those earliest memories cloudy and waning. He saw Mack Ferran's face, jaw set, stern demeanor. Humorless.

"He was a hard but fair man, my lord. He fought in the Wolfguard before he became a farmer."

"Ah, the fabled Wolfguard. A proud band of soldiers, as I recall. A pity for Wergar that his greed and lust for battle was his undoing in the end. He made it all too easy for my son, Leopold, to slip into Westland and take the throne from under his nose."

Trent didn't respond. He had never known Wergar, had

no connection with the old king. It was Drew who held Trent's bond, the Wolflord who had grown up a shepherd on the Cold Coast, his twin brother in all but blood.

"Your brother Drew Ferran: he's not like Wergar. The old Wolf was reckless and selfish, easily drawn into conflict. This new Wolf is more cautious. And he thinks about others, his people."

"He was raised by the same folk as I, my lord. Good people, Mack and Tilly Ferran. Humans. That gives him a unique perspective compared to the rest of you . . . Werelords."

"A fair point," said Leon, nodding as he cut up another piece of meat. "You two are close?"

"We were, once upon a time."

"I'm sure there are regrets on both sides, Trent Ferran. But let me ask you this."

Trent looked up, swallowing down the last morsel of steak. The Lion went on.

"Is your brother a reasonable young man? Can he compromise when the need arises?"

"I suppose so." The captive Wolf Knight shrugged, his chains jangling. "He's always seen the shades of gray, the good and bad in people."

"This makes me wonder: what might he do to save your life?"

Trent was speechless. How could he answer that?

"It's clear he thinks the world of his family," said Leon,

raising his hand in the air. "I'm guilty of such indulgence, too. But in your brother's case, perhaps this can spell an end to the war."

"How?"

"You could be the bartering chip we need to make him stand down, him and his armies."

"He won't surrender just for my wretched soul," said Trent, even though a small, miserable part of him wished that would be so. "Sacrifices have to be made to win wars, my lord. I'm willing to play my part."

"That may be, lad, but those are *your* sentiments, not your brother's. What would he give to see you again, eh?"

"Once he knows I have the Wyld Wolf blood poisoning me, I imagine he'll speed me toward the long sleep. It would be the kind thing to do."

"You've given up hope of being human again?"

"Look at me," said the young Graycloak, lifting his hands. Dark fur coated their backs, his fingernails now thick yellow claws. His face remained human in shape, but the dirty stubble that had covered his jaw was now thicker, ranging down his throat to his chest and around his cheeks and brow. His teeth grated against one another as he ran his tongue over their edges, fully aware of how monstrous he appeared.

"There's always a way. It was magick that turned you onto this path. Perhaps magick can bring you back from it, too?"

"A magister?"

"Indeed," said the High Lord. "The Daughters of Icegarden are in the Wolf's company. I suspect they can do something to halt the Wyld Magick's progress."

A flicker of hope rose in Trent's heart. "You think?"

"It's worth finding out, isn't it?"

"How?"

Leon pushed his plate away, rapping his gnarled fingers on the table in thought. His scarred face was illuminated by the candelabra that stood at its center.

"I could ride out to meet with your brother tomorrow, before the contest the day after. If I can parley with him, perhaps I can make him see sense. In return for handing you back to the Wolf's fold, his armies step down, relinquishing Westland and Sturmland to my Lions. Perhaps they bend the knee, and we combine our might against the Panthers," he said with a wizened smile.

"You want Sturmland also? You had Westland before."

"Yes, lad, but we all know where the true wealth of Lyssia resides." He pointed north, bony finger wagging, his voice colder now. "Beneath the Strakenberg, the White Bears of Icegarden have hoarded treasures for centuries. It's time they turned them over to their masters."

"But Blackhand reigns in Icegarden, alongside the Crows."

"And I shall break them upon the ground when I claim the frozen city for my own."

"Drew won't agree to this," said Trent, shaking his head wearily. "He won't risk everything he's fought for, just for me."

"That's not a decision you get to make, Master Ferran," said the High Lord of Leos, sitting back in his chair. "It's a conversation to be had between Wolf and Lion."

Trent leaned back against the tent pole. Was there a way of avoiding further conflict, some means by which the war could be concluded and Trent could claim his life back? *Can the Daughters of Icegarden truly help me? Do I still have a shot at redemption?*

He looked up at the High Lord just as a figure materialized through the shadows behind his throne. His blond hair, though wild, was clean now, shining like a golden halo as he reached around the wooden chair and seized his grandfather about the throat. Leon's eyes sparked open instantly, but it was already too late. Lucas's grip was like steel, his muscular arms locked about the chair, fingers squeezing the High Lord's airways closed.

"Your *personal guard* don't appear to be as effective as mine, Grandfather," whispered the young Lion into Leon's ear. "My Wyld Wolves are no doubt feasting upon their flesh presently. They've heard Bastian meat is the sweetest of all."

The old Lion struggled and fought, unable to change properly thanks to Lucas's claws around his throat. His claws raked at his foe's powerful, furred forearms, but they held fast. The chair rocked as Lucas hauled his grandfather back, the High

Lord of Leos releasing a hideous gurgle as his legs kicked out in vain. One foot struck the table, sending the metal platter tumbling to the ground, meat and cutlery clattering over Trent.

With a snarl, Lucas gave the old man's neck one final twist, and with a snap the struggle was over. He released his hold, letting the High Lord collapse back into his throne as if slumbering, the only telltale sign of his demise the open eyes and bloated tongue that lolled from his lips. Lucas craned about and, with a deft prod of a clawed finger, popped it back into his grandfather's mouth. Lastly he cast his hand over the Werelion's face, closing his eyes for one final time. He turned and looked down at Trent on the floor, the Wolf Knight spattered in blood and stricken with fear.

"I hope you've eaten," said the king. "We've a long walk ahead of us."

9

THE UNION

THE BETROTHAL CEREMONY was small, far removed from the typical pomp of a royal wedding. The skies were a bright, brilliant azure. The air was still, no breeze to speak of, and the hilltop was transformed from the previous night. The boulder remained, now scoured clean of blood, and the crowds had long gone. Alongside Miloqi, who carried out the blessing, there were only two others present. Duke Bergan stood behind his daughter, the proudest son that Brackenholme had ever sired. To his side stood Gretchen, honored to bear witness to the union of her dear friends.

Drew noticed everything. They held a garland of ivy in their joined hands, its tendrils bound about their wrists up to

their elbows. Miloqi's words, though foreign to them, dripped with love and affection, prayers of peace and a prosperous future. Tiny flowers of primrose and blue covered the crown of the hill, a joyous smattering of summer color. The same flowers had been bound together in links by Gretchen, entwined throughout the long braids of Whitley's rich auburn hair. It was piled on top of her head, revealing the clean, elegant lines of the Bearlady's neck. Slowly his gaze wandered up to her face, where her smile welcomed him, warm and inviting.

"You look gormless," she said, heralding a snorting laugh from Drew.

"I'm not allowed to look at you now?"

"It'll take some getting used to."

"You chatter too much," said Miloqi, drawing the two out of their playful squabble. She unraveled the ivy and took the garland from their hands. "Less talk, more kisses."

As Drew took Whitley in his arms and kissed her, Bergan and Gretchen clapped and hugged one another. The Bearlord couldn't resist a triumphant cheer, which turned into a glorious roar. Gretchen pulled her friend from Drew's hold and gave her a squeeze. Bergan pulled Drew close to pat him on the back. The Wolflord felt the air expelled from his lungs with each body blow, the old duke forgetting his strength in the moment. Finally, Drew turned to the seer from Shadowhaven.

"Thank you, Miloqi," he said, grinning. "It means the world that you could do this for us.

"You should smile more, Gray Son," she said, cocking her head. "You're actually quite handsome when you're not frowning."

"You'd frown if you lived my life," said Drew. He stepped forward and hugged her as Whitley and Gretchen continued their giddy banter. "Again, thank you."

"It is not a marriage, Gray Son. I'm no priestess, just a girl who sees strange things in her dreams. This was a blessing, a precursor to the actual event. This is a proclamation of your love for one another, a sign unto Brenn that you make a commitment this day."

Drew smiled, before Miloqi leaned in closer to him again. "Make the most of these moments, Gray Son," she whispered in his ear.

With that, she kissed his cheek and stepped away, retreating across the hilltop in the direction of the war camp. Drew watched her depart, both fascinated and puzzled by the White Wolf. He was stirred from his thoughts by a hearty clap to his back, as Bergan congratulated him once more.

"There will be a ceremony, son, back in Brackenholme. Or Highcliff, should you wish, although there's nothing quite like a wedding in the treetops."

"We've a war to win before that can happen," said Drew.

"I asked you before if there was nothing that could stop you from facing Onyx," said Bergan. He turned and looked at his daughter as she laughed with Gretchen. "I'm going to ask

you again, Drew, and think carefully on your answer."

It was a cheap blow, but Drew couldn't blame Bergan: he would have said the same thing under the circumstances. Things *had* changed now.

"You're a sly one, old man. Your sentiment's sound, but it has to be me. This war is between the Wolf and the Catlords. A fight to settle it should be fought by the very same. I'd never ask anyone to do anything I wouldn't do myself."

"This day, lad," sighed the Bearlord, "should be your day, yours and my daughter's. You shouldn't have to go and train in preparation for a battle. You had sure as Brenn's breath better return to her, do you hear me?"

Drew nodded and smiled wearily. "A bit more pressure. Just what I need." He winked before Bergan could object. "I wish to Brenn I could be with her, today of all days, but you know what must be done."

The Bearlord nodded reluctantly as a trio of familiar figures advanced up the hill toward them. A fourth person stood apart from them, staring up at the sky.

"Are you ready, boy?" shouted Krieg. "We're wasting time. You've had your fun, now there's work to be done."

The Behemoth nodded beside him before adding three words of his own: "What Krieg said."

"You're nothing if not punctual," said Drew. "Can a fellow not have a moment with his loved one?"

"Congratulations," hissed Taboo to Drew and Whitley. Try

as she might, every word the Tiger uttered always sounded like a threat.

"Thank you, Lady Taboo," said Whitley, which prompted a couple of chuckles from Krieg and the Behemoth. The Tiger scowled at them before returning a smile to the Bearlady.

"There's been a change of plans," said Taboo. "Seems there's been an uproar in the Lion war camp. You won't be facing Lucas now. The little Lion's gone missing. You'll be fighting some Apelord instead, Lord Ulik."

"I know Ulik," said the Behemoth. "Distant cousin of Arik and Balk who fought in the Furnace. They call him the Naked Ape, a giant like myself without a hair on his body. A monster in battle."

"I met him once before also, on the battlefield, before I was sent packing to Scoria," said Krieg. "Of all the Apes he's probably the most noble, but a more humorless Werelord you'll never meet."

Drew nodded, assailed by fresh waves of nausea. With the Lion missing, Brenn only knew where, he was beginning to feel stretched thin. He turned to Whitley, who now hugged Gretchen.

"I'll see you later," she said simply.

"I have to go, Whitley. I'm so sorry, but—"

"Drew, I completely understand. I know more than anyone what duty means to you. Go. Work hard with the gladiators and give them as good as you get." She lifted a hand and

brushed his cheek. "Do your duty, Drew. You have my blessing."

"Did I ever tell you I love you?" said Drew.

"You know, I think you might have mentioned it." She smiled. "Good-bye, Drew."

He set off down the slope, the gladiators falling in around him.

"We've prepared a ludus of sorts," said Krieg.

"An area to train in," added the Behemoth, his voice making Drew's bones hum.

"All those happy memories of Scoria will be flooding back in no time," replied the Wolflord. "I'll catch you up."

Before they could object, Drew peeled away from the group, bounding down the slope toward the fourth figure he'd spied from the hilltop. Florimo stood stock-still, legs slightly apart, head tipped back and facing the sun. His black bandanna had been tossed to one side, the pink feather still wedged into its dark folds. The navigator was at work.

"Well, Florimo?" asked Drew. "Have we timed it right?"

The eccentric Ternlord turned to him, his usually cheery face bereft of humor. It was odd to see the old sailor so serious, but the future of the Seven Realms hung in the balance, dependent upon his answer.

"We have, my lord," he said, reaching out a thin hand and squeezing Drew's shoulder. "The heavens are in alignment."

Whitley and Gretchen looked down from the hill's summit, alone now as Duke Bergan set off after the rest of them. Whitley's fixed smile slipped a little as the Foxlady of Hedgemoor turned to her. Gretchen's own face was set hard as stone, her back to the others as they vanished down the slope.

"Well?" asked the girl from the Dalelands. "You know where Lucas is heading, don't you?"

"I'm friendly with one of the stable lads from Brackenholme," said Whitley. "He can have Chancer and Bravado ready to ride within the hour."

"Are you going to say good-bye to Drew?"

"I already have," replied Whitley, setting off hurriedly down the grassy slope, trampling the flowers of primrose and blue underfoot. "Come, the ride north's treacherous. We've a lot of ground to cover, and the foothills are still teeming with Bastian troops. We need to be swift and silent."

"You're sure you want to accompany me?" said Gretchen, halting her friend for a moment to squeeze her hands. "I can do this alone. You shouldn't have to risk yourself for Trent. You don't even know him. I'd hate to put you in danger."

"After what we've been through, Gretchen?" replied Whitley. "He's Drew's brother. How could I *not* help? Plus, Hector's still up there. Between us, you and I just might help him see sense. Come. We all have our duty to attend to."

PART V

THE BATTLE ON BLACK ROCK

I

WELL MET AT LAST

DREW STOOD ON the plateau of the volcanic peak, the sun hidden in the heavens at his back. The weather had changed, and not for the better. Dark storm clouds gathered across the sky, plunging the dark spire of Black Rock into shadow. The pockmarked stone sent Drew back to the hell of the Furnace, fighting for his life alongside his fellow gladiators. He glanced over his shoulder. There stood Krieg, his eyes burning holes in Drew's back. Florimo stood beside him with Opal, Bo Carver, and Duke Bergan, the Tern looking up to the gloomy sky. Drew caught his eye. The look he gave the Wolflord didn't inspire confidence.

Preparations that morning had not been ideal. Having trained until sundown under Krieg's punishing schedule,

Drew had collapsed onto his cot, assuming Whitley would be nearby. The girl was nowhere to be seen and after he had fallen into a brief but intense slumber, he was stirred at first light by Taboo. He had half expected to find Whitley then, standing over him, but the Bearlady wasn't present. Heading back to the makeshift ludus—the gladiator school in which he'd learned his "craft"—Drew had sent word to Bergan, hoping to discover her whereabouts. The Bearlord hadn't seen her. Nobody had, and Gretchen was missing from the camp, too. The anxiety that gnawed at the pit of Drew's belly had since intensified.

Wing beats told them they were no longer alone. Four Cranelords came in to land, two of them carrying a hulking figure between them. He landed dead center on the jagged rock's plateau, rising up to his full height. The Behemoth hadn't lied about the Apelord's size: he had to be eight feet tall and hadn't yet transformed. The final two Cranes and a pair of blond knights in suits of red plate mail landed on either side of him. One of the Cranelords stepped forward to introduce their warrior.

"Lord Ulik of World's End, my lords, champion of the Lions of Bast."

"The Naked Ape," said Krieg with a grunt. "We've met before. The Battle of Umbar's Crossing."

Ulik nodded slowly. "Bad day for the Rhinos. You were one of the few who survived?"

"No thanks to your kin," replied Krieg, spitting onto the dirty rock.

"War is business," said Ulik, unblinking. "Try not to take it personal."

"What happened to Lucas?" asked Opal. "I thought he was supposed to be your champion?"

Ulik remained silent as the Cranelord stepped forward, his epaulets bristling in the breeze. "Lady Opal. How's life now that you've turned against your own kind?"

"Surprisingly liberating when all's said and done," said the Pantherlady. "How's life as a simpering lickspittle, Clavell?"

The Crane ignored the Panther and instead turned to Drew.

"I am General Clavell, commander of the Cranelords of the Flooded Plains. The king was indeed due to fight today. Sadly there was . . . an incident in our camp. High Lord Leon is indisposed, and King Lucas is otherwise engaged. Our hopes rest upon the vast and able shoulders of Lord Ulik."

"What do you mean, indisposed?" asked Drew.

"As of yet, we can't—"

"Lucas killed him," said Ulik, his voice monotone and emotionless as Clavell watched, horrified. "That's a father and a grandfather Lucas has dispatched now. It doesn't pay to be related to the king."

Bergan chuckled at the Apelord's deadpan delivery.

"If Leon's dead and Lucas is missing, who exactly are you fighting for?" asked Bo Carver.

Ulik glanced over his shoulder at the two red-plated knights, their feline faces cold and unblinking. He turned back to the Lord of Thieves.

"The Lions number many, human. Another will take the throne in Leos soon enough, and his gaze will fall upon Lyssia. He will look favorably upon those who remained loyal when none were left standing."

"You're a fool, Apelord," said Carver. "This is your chance to break the yoke that shackles you. You could be free again."

"Again? I was born in servitude to the Lions of Leos," said Ulik as noises over the cliff's edge heralded the arrival of the final combatant. "I was never free."

Drew took a step toward the plateau's edge, peering into space, as a sudden updraft caused him to stagger back. A host of Vultures rose before him. One after another they deposited their grim passengers on Black Rock's summit.

A Buffalo-lord landed first, his ruffled mane of dreadlocked hair and beard reminding Drew of Stamm, his old friend from the Furnace, now dead. There was nothing genial about this fellow, though, the Werelord's face already contorting, horns threatening to emerge from his skull. Next came Sheriff Muller, self-proclaimed lord of the Badlands.

"Bo Carver," said Muller, the two inextricably connected

through their work in the criminal underworld. "Odd company you're keeping these days."

The Lord of Thieves glowered back, shaking his head. "I could say the same of you, Muller," said Carver. "I always knew you were rotten to the core."

An old acquaintance of Drew's arrived next, the young Wolf's stomach lurching at the sight of the black-robed chancellor landing on the cliff. His face was hidden within the cowl, but Drew would know the Wererat Vanmorten anywhere. He was about to shout something, his composure almost lost at the sight of the monster who'd killed Tilly Ferran, when the final figure emerged over the plateau's edge.

The two Vultures worked hard, wings straining as they carried Onyx the last few feet through the air, finally releasing him onto the volcanic rock. Drew heard the therian lords behind him gasp, and his own breath caught in his throat. The Beast of Bast slowly rose, a tower of toned muscle and scarred skin. His flesh was spangled with old welts and cuts from a lifetime of violence. His yellow eyes shone when he spied Opal across the rocky platform.

"Sister!" he exclaimed with a smile. "So good to see you. Come, embrace me." He stepped forward, arms open wide, waiting for her to approach him. Opal's eyes narrowed as she glanced at Drew. He knew her well enough to see she was afraid. The young Wolf turned back to the Pantherlord.

"You can talk to me, Onyx, not Opal. You're not here for a family catch-up."

"A shame," said the beast. "We've much to discuss. Perhaps that can wait until later, eh, sweet sibling?"

"Leave her be," commanded Drew.

"My, my," said the Panther. "Well met at last, Wolflord. You're very quick to tell your betters what to do. I have to assume you're used to getting your own way. A shame that's about to come to a sudden and violent end this afternoon."

"Is this your means of defeating your opponents, Onyx? You bore them to death with bravado and bluster?"

The Pantherlord smiled. Even in human form he was utterly and frightfully intimidating.

"I see you've brought your trinkets with you," said the Panther, beginning to stroll around the plateau. As he set off, the crowd moved back, his progress prompting Ulik to start walking away from him. Drew in turn followed, and within moments the three combatants were circling.

"You mean the gauntlet and sword?" said Drew.

"The White Fist of Icegarden and Moonbrand, if I'm not mistaken. I've done my research, Wolflord, and I've faced the Fist before."

"I heard all about it," said Drew. "You got the Lion to finish the battle you couldn't."

"Wrong," growled Onyx. "That spoiled kitten jumped in

and ruined all that was honorable in that contest."

"I'm amazed that you care about honor, after what you did to Taboo so many years ago."

Onyx's eyebrows rose as he looked to Opal. "A bit loose with the tongue are we, little sister? Seems you need a lesson in discipline. Father can mete that out when we've concluded here and the war is won."

He snapped his teeth. Opal flinched, a rare moment of weakness from the Pantherlady.

"To me, Onyx," said Drew. "Talk only to me."

"Your trinkets," the beast repeated, "will do you no good, foolish boy. The moon will not help you today. I'll crush your Sturmish steel like it's a tin sheet. But tell me, how did they manage to fix the Fist to your arm? I thought I'd be facing a cripple today, not a warrior with a full complement of limbs."

Drew unsheathed Moonbrand. Ulik had nothing to say, the Naked Ape's eyes flitting constantly between Wolf and Panther, hand reaching behind his back to withdraw a thick wooden handle with a long chain of heavy silver links on its end. Drew eyed it with curiosity; what appeared to be an enormous cannonball was fixed to the chain's end, the kind the biggest Bastian guns would launch with blasting powder. Except this one shone, made of solid steel and shot with silver. Drew dreaded to imagine what damage it might do if it connected with him.

He had now completed the circuit of the plateau and was

almost back in his own camp again. Krieg was beckoning him, calling him over, while Florimo continued to stare at the dark clouds overhead, hopping from foot to foot. To all upon Black Rock, it appeared a storm was approaching.

"A shame Lucas couldn't be here, the patricidal maniac," said Onyx, his voice deeper now, full of booming bass. "I'm sure we'll catch up with one another soon enough."

Drew watched as a coat of smooth black fur emerged through Onyx's skin. His hands broadened, transforming into paws as his chest cracked and popped. More muscles appeared as the Werepanther gradually took shape in all its fearsome glory. Drew could hear Krieg's voice whispering at his back as he let the Wolf in. He closed his gray eyes for a heartbeat, the Rhino's words racing through his mind like a mantra.

"Remember, show no sentiment or compassion. Forgiveness is a weakness. It's kill or be killed."

When they flicked open again they were the yellow, baleful eyes of the Wolf.

2

THREE SIDES TO EVERY FIGHT

FROM HIS TIME fighting in the Furnace, Drew had learned that there was never anything as simple as a three-way fight. Understandably, brief partnerships often formed as the two weaker gladiators ganged up against the toughest opposition. Once, and if, the fiercest combatant was taken out, then the secondary contest would take place as former allies turned on one another. No such silent agreement was entered into on Black Rock that day. It was every therian for himself, and the odds seemed evenly stacked.

Transformed, Lord Ulik was a shuddering mass of bleached flesh and brute strength, pale arms knotted with sinew and muscle. The Wereape's sloping domed head, devoid of hair like the rest of the beast, made the creature look demonic, teeth

erupting from its jutting jaw like crooked yellow stalagmites. The trunk of its body was huge, the rib cage the circumference of a wagon wheel. Most dangerous of all was its reach, the Ape's mauling grasp well beyond that of Drew and Onyx.

The Panther had many natural weapons to call upon, but chief among them was agility. Its speed was like nothing Drew had ever encountered before, paws dancing lightly across the rough stone as it searched for the first decisive blow against its foes. As ugly as the Naked Ape was, Onyx was beautiful, as striking a therianthrope as Drew had ever seen. There wasn't an inch of fat on the felinthrope's shimmering, stalking body, every fiber honed on making it the perfect killing machine.

Drew glanced up at the sun, still partially obscured by clouds. The heat that had been in the air for the past week was gone, and the atmosphere on Black Rock was cool, almost autumnal. The wind whipped across the plateau, sending a cloud of fine dust whirling into the air. His own transformation was complete. He hadn't even felt the change, the pain of snapping bone and twisting tendon no longer registering for the lycanthrope. He could feel the muscles bunched within his powerful legs, ready to launch him forward at any moment. Moonbrand trailed beside him, pommel clenched in his hand, while the White Fist of Icegarden remained open, clawed fingers twitching with terrible expectation.

The Panther struck first, bounding across the rocky arena like black lightning. The Ape's arms and flail came up fast, but

nowhere near as quick as the felinthrope. All four of Onyx's paws struck Ulik in that great barrel chest, forcing the Ape to tumble back, ribs battered. The Catlord didn't waste the momentum, propelling itself back off the Ape's torso in the direction of Drew, its first foe already staggering near the cliff's edge. The Wolflord brought Moonbrand about, the Sturmish sword cutting through the air, straight for the Panther's face. Dark claws came up, catching the steel halfway up the blade and sliding down toward the hilt. Drew heard the metal cut through flesh and bone, threatening to saw the paw in two as it progressed down to the handle, but Onyx just gripped all the tighter. By seizing Moonbrand, he had slowed the blade's momentum at the expense of his left hand, thus managing to get in close to the Wolf. The two hit the deck, Panther on top.

Drew brought the White Fist about, striking Onyx's jaw, but before he could hit the beast again, the Panther's free paw had struck out, seizing the gauntlet midswing. Its face was crumpled where Drew had struck, right eye squinting and bloody, but Onyx paid no heed. The Cat's jaws came down, the Wolf turning his face sideways to meet it between them. Their teeth locked, grating against one another as each forced their mouths shut, trying to crush their enemy's face. Lips peeled back, whiskers twitched, as gums were torn and shredded. The Panther's greater body weight was bearing down on Drew, crushing the air from his chest and the fight from his limbs.

Moonbrand remained out of action, Onyx still clutching the blade in a bloody paw. Dropping the sword, Drew reached up and clutched the Panther's throat, claws digging in. The monster turned the blade in its tattered hand and thrust it down into the Wolf, searing pain hitting the lycanthrope in the guts as his own sword struck home.

The Panther's head suddenly flew to one side as something heavy impacted with the left side of its skull. A chorus of cheers and hisses went up from the onlookers as the felinthrope was blasted clear of the Wolf's body. The Apelord's flail whistled through the air overhead, having struck a staggering blow against the Werepanther, ball and chain increasing speed as the bald giant towered above its foes, recovered, the sky above gradually darkening, gloom descending as if his bulk alone could block out the light. Drew could hear something, ringing in his ears. It was Carver's voice.

"Move, Drew!"

He snapped to, just as the flail changed its direction, hurtling toward the ground where he lay. Drew rolled, and the silver shot ball smashed the black stone into dust where his head had been. Ulik's huge foot descended upon Drew, prehensile toes seizing the young Wolf by the arm and throwing him across the plateau toward the cliff. Clavell whooped, clapping excitedly as the Werewolf tumbled and skidded closer to the drop. The White Fist scraped and scrabbled at the ground to

slow his progression toward the drop, claws digging into the volcanic stone and leaving furrows in its wake. Drew came to a halt with his legs hanging over the ledge, death calling from below. Drew looked up, expecting the ball and chain to connect with him in a final telling blow, but the Ape and the Panther were once more engaged.

He hauled himself back onto the cliff top, chest heaving and the wound in his hip weeping blood. It was deep, not a mere scratch like others he had been able to fight through and ignore. This was Moonbrand's mark, the steel cutting him as indelibly as silver. He looked up to Florimo, the Tern's face fixed on the dark heavens. Drew spied the Ape facedown on the ground, the Panther now straddling it, having somehow wrestled the flail from Ulik's grasp. The silver chain was wrapped tight about the Ape's throat, the ball in Onyx's paw as he smashed it down repeatedly against its skull. Ulik's arms reached back, trying in vain to grab the Pantherlord, but Onyx wouldn't be caught. The huge limbs fell, the defeated Apelord close to its last breath, the fight gone from its massive frame. The Catlord had its foe trapped, and death was but a strike away.

The Panther's head was yanked back as the White Fist came down over the top of it, claws digging into its scalp and hauling it off the Wereape. A roar erupted from Onyx's throat as a flap of skin peeled away from the Beast of Bast's head, revealing bare skull plate beneath. The sky had darkened consid-

erably, as if a storm cloud had gathered above the mountaintop. The Panther turned to the boy from the Cold Coast. The young Wolf looked exhausted, the wound in his midriff turning his gray fur into a bloody mop. Onyx followed the lycanthrope's gaze to where Moonbrand had been flung into the melee, at the feet of one of the onlookers. It was Muller. The sheriff smiled as he kicked the sword across the arena to the Pantherlord.

Onyx snatched up the Sturmish sword as the Wolf wobbled on weary legs and the Ape choked on the floor, eyes bulging, chain locked tightly in place. Drew advanced. *Keep going, Drew. Just a little longer. You can do this.* He approached the Panther, trying to feign an attack and come in from another angle, but Onyx saw through the ruse. A hammer blow of knuckles sent Drew pirouetting in the air, his jaw almost dislocated by the punch. The lycanthrope dropped to one knee now, his right fist holding his side closed, trying to staunch the flow of blood. He tried to rise, attempting to find his feet again, but ended up on his knees.

The Panther roared triumphantly as the unearthly darkness continued to descend.

"Remember this moment well, those of you who live to see another day!" bellowed Onyx, stepping up to the Wolflord, who knelt in a spreading red puddle. "History is made. The future of the Seven Realms is decided with this blow!"

The sky changed in that heartbeat, the clouds parting as

the world was plunged into twilight. The sun, hidden from sight for so long, was now a great black disk, a halo of fire burning around it and sending waves of energy coursing through the lycanthrope's body. The moon had found its way across the heavens, blotting the sun from existence, projecting its lunar power over the world below.

This was the celestial event Florimo had known of and Drew had hoped for. Everything he and his friends had done over the passing weeks and days had led up to this. All their hopes had hinged not only on arriving in Robben when they did, but also on the Beast of Bast making his boastful challenge.

All who were gathered on Black Rock were distracted by the solar eclipse, even the Pantherlord pausing from dealing the Wolf the killing blow. A hissing roar erupted in Onyx's clawed hand as Moonbrand burst into life suddenly. It wasn't the fabled white fire that the enchanted steel of Sturmland brought forth beneath the moon's gaze, though. Instead, ghastly black flames raced up and down its length, taking the Panther completely by surprise. The weapon hissed and spat in Onyx's grasp, as if knowing the soul that wielded it was unworthy, showering sparks of un-fire and ancient energy over the Catlord's torso.

Whatever magicks were channeled through the moon by the sun, they had a profound effect upon the boy from the Cold Coast. The wound in his belly was knitting together as he moved, his accelerated healing intensified beyond any known

proportion. Not even Moonbrand's injury could withstand the moon's healing power, and the Werewolf of Westland enjoyed the moon's blessing as no other therianthrope ever could. He was gorging on its dark light, the raw lunar energy coursing through his entire body. By the time Drew leapt from the volcanic rock, Onyx's eyes coming down onto the terrible sight of a fully recovered lycanthrope, it was already too late for the Beast of Bast.

The White Fist of Icegarden was now a flaming gauntlet of black fire, its razor-sharp talons leaving bright red ribbons across the Pantherlord's belly, from right hip up to left shoulder blade, almost tearing Onyx in two. The crowd of onlookers gasped as the roles were reversed, the Panther of Braga now kneeling before the Werewolf. Moonbrand fell from Onyx's limp wrist to the ground with a heavy clang, as Drew stepped past him toward Ulik.

The Naked Ape's face was bloody and purple, lips bloated and one eye puffed out as it tried to disentangle the chains around its neck. The side of its face was smashed in where Onyx had battered it repeatedly with the flail's ball, the other eyeball all but destroyed in a crushed socket. Drew stood over Ulik, the black sun shining at his back. He saw the Ape mouth two words silently: *finish me*. The White Fist seized the chain, knuckles flaming against Ulik's throat. The Werewolf squeezed and pulled, the claws slicing through the silver links until the chain rattled to the floor in a dismembered heap of metal. The

Apelord took a shaky gasp of air as Drew rose and turned to the onlookers.

"It's over," said the Werewolf, his gray fur bristling stiff in the breeze as he paced around the summit of Black Rock, looking at each of them in turn, including Ulik. "It's over. Take your dead and take your injured. Take your armies and leave these shores—*my shores*—never to return. Lyssia and her people belong to Lyssia, not Bast. And should you ever return, I won't be so forgiving."

He came to a halt beside Onyx, the warrior lord barely upright. Another gust of wind whipped across the plateau. The monstrous Werepanther didn't look quite so terrifying anymore, the light fading from its eyes as the scourge of the Seven Realms, the towering Beast of Bast, toppled over, never to rise again.

3

TAKING FLIGHT

A DAY OF CELEBRATION was turning into a night to remember. The lake shore and meadows of Robben Valley blazed with life and laughter as the Wolf's victory was sung to the heavens. Drums and pipes sounded, fiddles sawed, voices were raised, both tuneful and tuneless. Bonfires blazed, sending sparks into the air that glittered and glowed, flittering like fireflies across the water. Women danced, men jigged, children ran, and old folk wept. Sturmlanders, Romari, Brackenholmers, and Longriders joined hands and clashed mugs as they cracked open the Redwine's finest wine barrels. What provisions had been stored for a forthcoming war were broken out and devoured. Impromptu songs were scribed, naming the heroes who had led the people to victory. Hawks and Horselords, Bulls

and Bearlords, Rhinos and Ramlords: all received mention in the bawdy ballads. But one name rang out louder than any other, higher in adulation than any Werelord had ever known.

The people cheered for Drew Ferran.

"I have to go," said Drew, pushing past Duke Brand.

"What do you mean?" said Bo Carver. "There are festivities to be enjoyed, Your Majesty. The troops want to see you. They *need* to see you."

"I'm needed elsewhere," said Drew, pausing for a moment to clap the man's arm. "Sorry."

"This is most unorthodox," grumbled the Lord of Thieves, sloshing the wine in his cup. "Who ever heard of a king leaving his victory celebration? What could be more important?"

"A husband going after his bride," said Duke Bergan, the Bearlord appearing beneath the canopy's entrance, his face hidden in shadow. "You couldn't find her?"

Drew pulled his weapon belt tight about his waist, tugging the leather through the buckle and securing it in place. He winced with discomfort, the stitches from Greta and Miloqi's handiwork straining across his belly wound.

"Could *you*?" He didn't mean to snap, but his irritation levels were rising. "Time's against us, old Bear. We all know where she's gone. Where *they've* gone."

Bergan nodded as other members of the Wolf's Council ap-

peared behind him, their smiles slipping as they saw the look of thunder on Drew's face.

"What in Brenn's name's going on?" asked Duke Brand, the last of the noblemen to push his way beneath the canvas awning. "Why the long faces? You look like a bunch of Horselords!"

He elbowed Conrad beside him, the blond Lord of Cape Gala groaning at the Bull's terrible humor. Brand was still grinning, his bald head gleaming with sweat, worked up by some excessive stomping that passed for dancing.

"Whitley and Gretchen are gone," said Drew, making no attempt to humor the Bull. "I'm going after them."

"What do you mean, gone?" said Conrad.

"My brother Trent is a prisoner of Lucas's. Tonight is the last night of the waxing moon: tomorrow it will be full, and then the Wyld Magick will change Trent forever. The Lion is dead-set upon traveling to Icegarden. He seeks revenge upon Baron Hector the Boarlord, for the death of his mother—my mother—Queen Amelie. It all points to Icegarden, and that's where I'm heading."

"You believe the Wereladies have headed to Sturmland?" asked General Fry.

"I know it, Reuben," said Drew. "I can feel it in my blood. Gretchen is . . . fond of Trent. She and Whitley won't leave him in Lucas's hands. I wouldn't have either if I hadn't been sworn to face the Panther and the Ape on Black Rock. The moment I heard that Lucas had gone missing, it was obvious where he

was heading. Whitley and Gretchen will have figured the same thing."

Krieg entered the canopied command tent from another direction, the Rhino out of breath from running. "Yesterday, not long after your ceremony, lad, the girls took two horses—yours was one of 'em—and headed out. The stable boy thought they were just off scouting."

Drew twisted the black leather breastplate around his chest, slackening the collar about his throat. He reached out the White Fist of Icegarden and hefted his gray cloak from where it was bundled atop a boulder.

"Count Carsten, I have need of your wings one last time," he said. "I'm sorry to ask this of you. I'm sure you'd rather be here celebrating with your brethren."

"It would be my honor to carry you to Icegarden, Your Majesty."

Drew smiled and then turned back to his oldest adviser. "I need you to stay here, old Bear. You're my voice in my absence, understand?"

"I'm coming with you," said Bergan.

"I can't allow that," replied Drew. "I need you here, Bergan. You and Manfred, both. I don't know what I'm heading into. At best, my old friend Hector is a prisoner of the Crowlords. At worst, Sturmland is now the domain of the risen dead."

"You can't ask me to remain here while you go and search for my child!" roared Bergan.

"I can and I am," said Drew, his voice quiet as he spoke. "I need you here, leading the people and looking out for Manfred, who still mourns Milo."

"This is Whitley we're talking about, son. She needs me."

"Your people need you, the Woodland Watch who are here as well as those who await you back in Brackenholme. Duchess Rainier remains in your hall, awaiting the return of both you and Whitley. She's already had Broghan robbed from her. Don't let her lose her husband and daughter, too, in one fell swoop."

"But she's in danger—"

"I know. Let me fetch her, Bergan. Please."

Bergan didn't nod, but he didn't say no. He simply stared at the Wolflord, red-rimmed eyes welling with tears. "Bring her back to me, son. One way or another."

Drew hugged the Lord of Brackenholme and kissed his bearded cheek. "I shall, father-to-be. You have my word."

He asked the next question to nobody in particular. "All our missing friends—do we know their whereabouts?"

"Shah remains in Robben town with Lady Bethwyn and her father," said Carver.

"Someone should send for the Hawklady," grunted Duke Brand, knocking back the last of his wine.

"Do we know how long until the army arrives from Omir?" asked Drew.

"By my reckoning they're still three days out of Robben," said Florimo. "Two days, at a push."

"Good," said Drew. "We'll all sleep a lot better when we know our ranks have swelled and our brothers and sisters are returned to our arms."

"What would you have us do while we await the arrival of Tiaz's army?" asked Brand, pouring himself another cup of wine.

"Well, you can start by sobering up," said Drew, provoking a derisory snort from the Bull. "The war is won, if we are to believe the agreement we entered into. The Catlord armies should be decamping by now, according to oaths sworn on Black Rock. But I will only truly be content when I know our enemies have departed Lyssia, each and every one of them."

Grunts of agreement went around the command tent. Ready to depart, the Wolflord turned back to Carsten, finding Krieg, Taboo, and the Behemoth gathered around him.

"We're coming with you," said Krieg. "I've already spoken to Carsten. He can spare a few more of his brothers to lend us a helping wing."

"I can't—"

"You can't stop us," said Taboo. "We're not your subjects like these Lyssians."

"We don't have family or loved ones to lose," added Krieg.

"And besides," said the Behemoth, "we've come this far already. I always wondered what the Whitepeaks looked like. Now I get to find out."

4

A Brave New Union

LORD ULIK WINCED as the magisters bound his head in herb-soaked cloths. He would never see through that eye again, the silver ball of his own flail having pulverized it during the fight. The bandage tightened, knotted behind the crumpled lump of flesh that had once been his ear. With High Lord Leon dead, his command tent had been turned into a field surgery for Ulik. Pains still shot through the Naked Ape's body, a dislocated shoulder humming where the Beast of Bast had tried to tear an arm from its socket. His entire spine felt as if it had been trampled upon by a horde of Weremammoths, twisted out of shape. *Perhaps my stoop's been straightened,* he thought. He might have managed a grim smile if it weren't for the meeting he was currently witnessing that left a cold,

hollow feeling in the pit of his bruised stomach. His one good ear twitched as the conversation continued.

"I'll admit, Your Grace, I wasn't expecting a visit from you," said General Clavell, seated on the slain Lion's throne. "If I were, I might have arranged for a more salubrious welcome."

"Think nothing of it, general," said High Lord Oba from the opposite side of the round table. He held one of the playing pieces that had been used by Leon during the campaign, a red lion. Oba looked up, catching sight of Ulik, the Wereape glowering at him. "I would've sent word, but these are unusual times. I thought it best to bypass decorum in lieu of urgency."

"A fine sentiment," said Clavell. "It's quite a party you've brought with you, I see."

They were all there. General Gorgo stood beside the Panther, the Hippolord's gaze fixed upon the hosts, unwavering. Behind Gorgo was Baron Overmeir, the Buffalo of the Blasted Plains, with the human Sheriff Muller, skulking at their back. Clavell's own close advisers and Lionguard were gathered around them, the two young felinthropes of Leos closest to the visitors. Nephews of the dead Leon, Lords Luc and Lex, were itching to show their worth, and both desperately disappointed that their war was over before it had begun. They held their swords in their hands, lowered but ready, not taking any chances in their present company.

"I'm in a strange land, General," said Oba. "Better to have

company who knows their way around, isn't that right, Muller?" He smiled at the human, showing his teeth.

"Very true, Your Grace," said the bandit lord, bowing nervously.

"You've done well to catch us," said Clavell. "We decamp presently. Tomorrow we depart for the coast."

"Then we've caught you just in time," said Oba. "I've a proposition for you."

Clavell arched a slender eyebrow and leaned forward in his chair. "I'm not sure what you've come here offering, High Lord Oba, but I'm already showing you and your company more respect than you deserve. My masters in Leos will not look kindly upon my entertaining you."

"Hardly entertaining," grunted Gorgo. "You haven't even offered us a drink, Cranelord."

The Lionguard shifted imperceptibly around the circular chamber, a ripple of tension running through them as hands gripped weapons. Overmeir and Muller turned around, facing the Redcloaks and a pair of Werelions at their backs.

"You always were a mannerless oaf, Gorgo," said Clavell. "Tell me, which one of you was it who killed my brother, Skean?"

Nobody replied. Oba looked away from the Cranelord, stroking the pommel of his sickle where it hung from his belt.

"Come, don't be shy," said Clavell, rising from the chair finally, staring them all down. He walked around the table, com-

ing to a halt before Oba. "We're all old friends, are we not?"

"It was Vanmorten who dealt the final blow," said the Panther, his voice rough as sandpaper, "but he wasn't alone."

"He couldn't be here now?"

"The Lord Chancellor is otherwise . . . engaged. He has business of his own to attend to."

"You would protect him from me when I seek justice?"

"This is war. There were many thorns that needed extricating from our paws that night."

"Thorns? Is that how you saw my brother?"

"Those that were in our war camp, yes," said Oba. "Things were done that I suspect neither side was proud of, but it's in the past now. Can we not move on?"

Clavell sneered. "You may be able to, but I—"

High Lord Oba's sickle went deep into the Cranelord's belly three times before any of the Lionguard could react. With the final blow he dragged it up Clavell's torso, opening the avianthrope's chest and letting him collapse to the floor in a gurgling heap.

"Birdlords can be such bores," he said, flicking the blood off his sickle before depositing it back on his belt. He looked up to find the Lionguard's weapons were all leveled upon him, including the swords of the twin Werelions.

"Tell me," said Oba, directing his question toward the brothers. "Since when does a Catlord of Bast sit back and take

orders from an avianthrope? Did I miss that edict in the Forum of the Elders?"

"The forum is no more," growled Lord Lex, whiskers emerging from his contorting lips as he bared his huge teeth.

"You saw to its demise when you had Leopold murdered," added Lord Luc, his red steel breastplate groaning as the Lion within emerged.

Overmeir and Gorgo had shifted now, Buffalo and Hippo snorting as they prepared for the worst. Only Oba remained in human form, the High Lord in a relaxed mood as he continued to reason with the Lionlords.

"Regardless of the past, we should be looking to the future, my cousins."

"Cousins?" hissed Luc.

"Let me finish before you rush onto our claws and tusks," said Oba, raising a hand to silence the young Werelord. "I've known you boys since you were kits back in Leos. I was there on your naming day, not that you'd recall. I said back then that you were both destined for greatness. And here we are," he concluded, casting his hand about the dark tent.

"I hardly see what's so great about this."

"Potential, Luc," said Oba. "It's all about potential. Tell me, who waits for you back home in Bast? A collection of uncles and cousins who have lived their fat, fruitful lives within the safety of Leos's walls?"

Luc and Lex watched the Panther as he continued, glancing to one another briefly.

"You travel here, risking your lives and legacies for them—for what reward? Should you die they'll write ballads about you. Should you live, they'll get even fatter upon your good fortune, while you remain a tool of theirs, to manipulate at their whim."

"Like Onyx was for you?" asked Lex.

"Onyx was a weapon for the whole of Bast. He lived and died for our homeland's glory," said Oba proudly. "But he didn't want a normal life, a throne. He wanted war. He wanted blood. Do you share those desires, or do you have your hearts set on a fine pair of crowns?"

"What's your proposal, Oba?" said Luc.

The High Lord of Braga's smile was wide and bright, lighting up his dark face. "We form an alliance once more, we reunite and take the Seven Realms in the names of the Lions and Panthers. Not the Tigers: they're our enemy now as much as the Wolf is. Bast will be ours again—jointly, my dear cousins—and we'll carve up the High Lord Tigara's lands between us."

"We entered an oath when we agreed to the contest on Black Rock," said Lex. "We each put forward champions, and swore that those defeated would relinquish their claims upon Lyssia. That oath was made under the eyes of our forefathers, Oba. Our word cannot be broken. That you seem so keen to

break yours raises the question of just how low you can stoop?"

Oba laughed as he leaned over the table, looking down over the map. "I made an oath for the Panthers of Braga. Leon, I should imagine, gave his word for the Lions of Leos. Those armies are effectively disbanded from the moment we agree on our union, cousins. There's a vacuum in Lyssia that we can fill. A new golden age of Catlords awaits, where the Wolf's friends are put in their place. As for the humans of the Seven Realms, they shall be put to work under whip and shackle. They've grown ambitious, spoiled by their masters. The Wolf and his allies allowed them to rise up: they need returning to their bellies in the dust."

Sheriff Muller shivered at the High Lord's words as Oba placed one hand around the pile of red models that represented the Lion's force. His other hand slid behind the golden pieces that marked out the Panthers. He scooped the two sets together, creating a jumbled pile of figurines, outnumbering all else on the table.

"A new army is forged—Lions and Panthers—in the name of Bast. No redundant oath—and no ragtag army that fights for the Wolf—could stand in our way."

That smile remained fixed on Oba's face as the two young Lionlords looked to one another, their eyes sparkling as they considered the possibilities. As one they slammed their swords back into their scabbards and stepped over Clavell's bloody

corpse. They extended their hands, and Oba seized them by the forearms, drawing them in close and hugging them as a father hugged his children.

"Greatness awaits us all, my boys," said the Panther, disengaging with them. "The reign of Leopold will be a distant memory before long, and the mad king Lucas a twisted growth on the Lion's family tree. One that we can prune when the time is right."

The two Lions moved among Oba's council, each shaking hands and swearing oaths of loyalty to one another. Lex turned to one of the Lionguard.

"Send word to all our officers. Cease preparations to decamp. And ready the men for battle," he snarled. "We came here to fight a war, and a war we're going to get."

Oba glanced about the tent as the others cheered the Lion's bold words. Something was amiss.

"My lords," said the Werepanther, clearly niggled. "That great brute, the Naked Ape. Where is he?"

Lex looked about, just as all of them did. "He was here but a moment ago, getting stitched back together."

"Find him, please, dear cousins," said the High Lord of Braga. "I didn't much care for the way he looked at me."

5

LONG WAIT OVER

THE PATH TO Icegarden was lined with the dead. Trent spied hands emerging from the snow on either side of the old road, fingers frozen, clutching skyward in a motionless grasp. Heads and torsos were partially visibly, half buried by drifts where they had fallen. The fallen weren't restricted to one particular army. They had found Redcloaks and Goldhelms farther down the valley, Vermirian Guard by their side, bodies picked clean of flesh by scavenging animals. Now, well above the snow line, the corpses were of Sturmlanders, their white cloaks and fur skins as hard as stone, bonded by ice to the land they had loved.

The sun had set on the third day of Trent's forced march up into the mountains, Darkheart's knives and Lucas's sword

constants at his back. The Wyld Wolves seemed unperturbed by the frigid conditions. As wild men, they had been used to stalking the Dyrewood naked. The filthy fur that now coated their misshapen bodies provided them with an additional defense against the elements. Trent was faring less well. Still human, at least until the moon rose, he could no longer feel his hands or feet, despite the torn cloth he had swaddled them in. The end couldn't come quickly enough for the Wolf Knight. He only hoped he could kill Lucas and the shaman in the process.

"Behold," said the king, pointing at the towering white walls ahead of them. "Icegarden." He turned to the Wyldermen and grinned. "Our new home," he added.

Lucas had little to say to Trent. He had spent the entire journey in fevered conversation with Darkheart, revealing his intentions in some detail. Their flight through the Lion's war camp had been frenetic and bloody, the Wyld Wolves tearing through anyone who stood in their way. Nobody had given chase, and why would they challenge a mad king and his pack of mongrel therianthropes? *Let the snow take them*—that would've been the Lionguard's thinking, Trent reasoned. As they climbed the ice-encrusted slopes, the full extent of Lucas's hatred of the Boarlord, Blackhand, had come to light.

That the magister had killed the king's mother was apparently only part of the story. The bookish young magister had served the prince throughout his teenage years as the apprentice to the old Ratlord magister Vankaskan. But the

moment Drew had come along, Hector had sided with him, betraying his master and helping the Wolf topple Leopold from the throne. In Lucas's wild eyes, killing Blackhand had become a quest as noble as that of any storybook hero.

"Where is his army?" asked Darkheart.

"Cowering within the walls, perhaps," said Lucas. "He has the Ugri warriors of Tuskun fighting for him now. They'll wet themselves when they see your brothers arrive at the gate."

"The gates are already open," said the shaman, pointing a clawed finger across the frozen meadows beyond the defenses. "Could it be that this Blackhand is expecting you?"

Lucas glared at the walls and open gates. As far as Trent could tell, the giant walls were unmanned, as was the gatehouse. The darkness of the approaching twilight made the gap in the enormous slabs of ice look like the yawning mouth of some monstrous beast, waiting to swallow any who wandered too near.

"The little pig always was an idiot," said Lucas. "What does he even know about defending a city? He won't have read about that in a book!"

Darkheart shoved Trent forward, the chain about his neck rattling as they continued to trudge toward the city. The Wolf Knight couldn't help but glance up at the sky beyond the Strakenberg, the giant mountain that towered above Icegarden. The moon beyond it slowly rose into the heavens. At some point in time it would crest the mountain's edge, casting its unearthly

glow over the city below. Casting its terrible spell over Trent.

"Go no further!"

The shout came up from ahead, causing the Lion's party to come to a stuttering halt. They searched the growing shadows for signs of life, but saw none.

"Who dares command me, the King of Westland?" shouted Lucas.

He turned to one of the ten Wyld Wolves who stood beside him. The Wolfman set off, bounding forward with a snarl. It got perhaps four yards away from the king when an arrow hit it in the chest, crunching through its gnarled breastbone and finding its heart. It landed on its back, limbs relaxing into the snow, as its dying breaths steamed from its open jaws.

"The next one's got your name on it, Lucas," came the voice, almost a growl. "Release your prisoner."

Trent winced as he felt a sudden, searing pain strike his guts. It was the worst kind of cramp, as if a knife had been taken to his insides and drawn across the wall of his belly. He cried out, drawing the attention of Darkheart, but the king continued.

"You work for Blackhand? I can pay you. Stand aside and let me pass. My argument's with your master."

"Blackhand isn't my master," said the stranger. "The prisoner: now!"

"And you'll let us pass?" No reply was forthcoming. Lucas turned to Darkheart.

"The Wolf Knight is turning already," the shaman said quietly. "I say we hand him over. This fool doesn't realize what he's letting himself in for if he means to take our friend from us."

Lucas grinned as the shaman unwrapped the chain from about his hand.

"On your way, *brother*," Darkheart whispered in Trent's ear before giving him a shove forward. Trent started running as the shaman called after him. "Watch the moon, Trent Ferran! Perhaps we'll meet again on the other side!"

Trent stumbled through the snow, ignoring the jeers at his back as the Wyld Wolves suddenly spread out into the snow on either side of the road, diving for cover. Already he could hear them snarling and barking to one another as they advanced. Another spasm of pain shot through his guts, almost sending him to the ground, but somehow he kept his footing, staggering on toward Icegarden. A figure suddenly rose from a snow-covered bank beside the road. It wore a cloak of woodland green and carried a taut shortbow, loaded arrow aimed at the road behind him.

"Run on," said the stranger, the voice softer now, feminine. He rounded the snowdrift to find another Greencloak standing beside a pair of mounts, one a handsome chestnut stallion, the other a powerful-looking white warhorse. The second figure tossed her hood back, ringlets of rich red hair tumbling around her face.

"Trent," gasped Gretchen, throwing her arms open to him. He wanted to run into them, to seize her, hug her, but he faltered. He looked at his hands, clawed, frostbitten fingers trembling through bloodied rags. The dark hair that coated his arms was covered in cuts and open wounds where Lucas and his Wolfmen had beaten him. He hadn't seen a mirror for weeks, but he knew all too well how hideous his face must now look, with the terrible lycanthropy riddling his body, changing him daily. He turned away, afraid for her to look upon him.

She brought her hand up to his face, turning him so that she could see him. If she was horrified by what she saw, Gretchen didn't show it. She hugged him hard, and he returned it tenfold, tears flowing freely from his bleary eyes. Again, a pain ripped through him, making him release her and drop to the snow. An invisible knife raced down his spine, causing him to twist and contort in the white powder as Whitley emerged around the drift.

"We need to go," said the girl from Brackenholme. "Now!"

The two girls helped Trent to his feet, just as a terrible wail sounded on the wind. Alien words of ancient, arcane power rolled out of Icegarden, crashing over the walls and washing down over the valley beyond. The three felt the words pass through them, chilling their blood. A terrible gurgling howl sounded beyond the drift, and Trent couldn't help himself. He pulled loose of the girls and scrambled up the slope to see what had happened. Cresting the snowbank, he could see one of the

Wyld Wolves, perhaps forty yards away, wrestling with a figure in the snow. The attacker's furs were encrusted with chunks of ice, and he appeared to be trying to bite the Wolfman. Other figures could be seen, too, materializing in the frozen fields, rising from the white earth.

"Enough," said Whitley, dragging Trent back and down the bank. "You're going on Bravado with Gretchen." She pushed the two of them toward the warhorse as she headed to Chancer.

Whitley grabbed her horse's reins just as the beast let loose a scream of its own. A man stood on the other side of Chancer, his fingers entangled in her faithful mount's mane. He was big, a northman by the looks of things, possibly one of the Ugri from Tuskun. His skin was withered, shrunken over his bones, and his mouth and chest were painted scarlet, a great chunk of horseflesh trapped between his teeth. The man's eyes glowed with a bright blue fire that sent the Bearlady back to "the Pits," the old prison beneath Highcliff where she'd witnessed Hector commune with a dead Redcloak. She remembered, too, the un-dead Lionguard who'd bitten her on the Talstaff Road, immune to all damage bar a blow to the head. Whitley cried out as the snow around the frantic Chancer suddenly flooded with blood. The dead warrior took another bite from her horse's neck be-fore falling onto the snow, pulling the beast over onto itself.

Gretchen pushed Trent into Bravado's saddle and seized the reins, pulling the horse up the slope as more of the fallen dead began to rise from the snow around them.

"Whitley!" she screamed. "Run, for Brenn's sake!"

The girl from Brackenholme watched in horror as her beloved horse kicked and snorted, the ghoul beneath still gnashing and gnawing at Chancer's flank. Her hunting knife was out in a flash, as she leapt over the fallen horse and drove the blade into the dead man's skull. His fight ceased instantly as Whitley moved to her horse. Trent watched from the warhorse's saddle as the scout whispered her good-byes to her steed before drawing the blade across its throat. She rose wearily, staggering after Gretchen and Bravado as they retreated up the road, away from the risen dead who now filled the snowy fields, slowly closing in on their party. Their moans, carried on the wind, struck terror into the hearts of the terrified trio. There was only one place they could head to: Icegarden. Within moments, the walls loomed about them. The moonlight broke over the Strakenberg and they were swallowed by the monstrous gatehouse.

6

TREMORS

HUNDREDS OF LEAGUES from his old home in Highcliff, stuck between Robben Valley and the Badlands, Bo Carver found himself in unusual company. Patrolling the perimeter of the Wolf's war camp, trading brief greetings with those few who remained on watch, he felt like a tongue-tied youth in the presence of such beauty. For Carver, the footpad who had turned from larceny to leadership, walked with Lady Shah, the Hawklady of the Barebones, heir to the seat of Windfell. They didn't come much loftier, or more striking for that matter. The conversation was made all the more awkward by the topic: his old friend Vega, the smooth-talking Sharklord who clearly still held a place in her heart.

"Vega's a good soul in a rather naughty body," said Carver.

"It's fair to say he courts controversy wherever he goes, but I tell you no word of a lie when I say he always spoke of his one true love."

"He paid you to say such words," said Shah, but she smiled, scuffing the ground as they strolled beneath the stars.

"He pays for nothing. If he remunerated all he'd promised me down the years I'd have a king's ransom with some change left over to buy the Strakenberg mines."

Shah's laughter was trilling and musical, sending a shiver down Carver's spine.

"You seem friendly with Duke Bergan," said the Hawklady.

"We've grown to depend upon one another, ever since we fled Highcliff together. Strange how adversity can bring two such very different souls together, isn't it?"

He chanced a look at her, but she wasn't biting. *Losing your touch, Carver,* he mused.

"He fears for his daughter," she said.

"As would any father. The girl's headed north to Brenn knows what horror. I pray Drew gets to her in time."

"My cousin Carsten will get him there, fear not. The loss of a child is something no parent should have to endure."

"Aye. Look at poor Manfred. The old Stag lost his youngest in Hedgemoor, half-eaten by that monster Lucas. If Drew does anything when he gets to Icegarden, he needs to send that Lion to the long sleep, once and for all. If ever a bad 'un had it coming, it was Lucas."

There was no argument from Shah. "You've a child of your own, I've noticed. The girl, Pick?"

Carver smiled. "You're not the first to say that. No, Pick isn't mine. She's a fellow survivor from Highcliff, a pickpocket from the docks who wanted into the Thieves Guild. She's a clever girl. I'd be proud if she were my daughter, believe me. You've none of your own?"

She looked like she was going to say something, then shook her head.

"Fear not, my lady. Perhaps you just need to find the right man."

"I thought I had," she whispered.

A couple more night watchmen saluted as they passed them by, the men struggling to remain alert after the tide of goodwill and celebration that had washed over the war camp. Carver spied a jug of wine beside a nearby boulder, the men clearly a little too relaxed. He bent and picked it up.

"I'll leave this in your billets," said Carver. "Remain alert, lads. You hear?"

Sheepish grunts and ayes came back as the two walked on.

"You're worried?" asked Shah.

"Cautious," he replied. "I've had too many dealings with thieves and therian lords down the years to think that anything's black and white. We can relax when the Bastians are truly gone. Until then we should be prepared for anything. If you think—"

Shah's hand came up and her fingertips brushed his lips, sealing them closed. Carver's heart rate quickened for a moment, the teenager inside expecting a kiss to follow. He was to be disappointed.

"Hush," she said, gesturing east in the direction of Black Rock. He followed her pointed finger, sure and straight like a hunting hound's nose.

"What am I looking for?" asked Carver quietly.

"Don't you see it?" said the sharp-eyed Hawklady. She shook her head. "Apologies, Lord Carver. I forget you're just a human."

Regardless of if she truly cared for Vega or not, how could she ever fall for a foolish old mortal like Bo Carver? He squinted into the darkness.

"You see something?"

"I see someone."

She stepped away from the Lord of Thieves and began to shift, wings emerging from the golden warrior's breastplate that she wore about her chest. Her face transformed swiftly, and even as she changed from beauty to beast, Carver found her no less alluring. She was about to take flight when Carver reached out, seizing her wrist.

"Where do you think you're going?"

"Out there, to investigate."

"Not without me you're not."

There was no argument from Shah, and the thief regret-

ted his pushiness when her talons dug into his shoulder blades as she lifted him off the ground. He reached up and grabbed her raptor legs, trying to ease the pressure where his great frame hung from those deadly feet. Then they were off, flying through the night, following the valley up toward Black Rock, grass speeding by below. As she slowed, Carver released his hold, flying through the air to hit the field, stumbling to a halt as he whipped long knives from his belt.

As Shah hovered above them, unhitching a bow from her hip, Carver instantly recognized the foe they faced. The Lord of Thieves had witnessed the fight on Black Rock, and had been certain the brute who fought for the Lions must have died of his injuries. Yet here he stood, Lord Ulik, the Naked Ape of World's End, his enormous head bound in bandages. He carried no weapon, and one hand clutched his hip as if he were crippled by a stitch from running flat-out for days. He raised the other hand out before him and waved it, shaking his head.

"I'm not your enemy," he grunted, short of breath. "They are." He gestured behind him with a nod of the head.

Carver and Shah looked past him whence the Wereape had come. From their own lines where they had been patrolling moments earlier, they had been blind-sighted to the vast horde that had rounded the volcanic spire of stone at the head of the valley. Yet there they were, a boiling mass of tiny shapes, the land undulating as a mighty army marched forth like a swarm of ants. They carried no torches, only the occa-

sional glint of moonlight catching the myriad weapons they carried with them to war.

"How can this be?" said Carver, his voice catching in his throat. "An oath was taken by all parties on Black Rock."

"One I abide by," said Ulik, "but others do not share my honor. The Lions and Panthers are reunited. Warn your people, warn the Wolf, and be quick about it."

There was a faint tremor now, just noticeable underfoot. The earth moaned beneath the steady progression of the advancing armies from Bast. Carver's head spun to think about their number, and their makeup: Redcloaks from Lyssia and Bast, Goldhelms from the jungle continent, the brutal Vermirian Guard, and Sheriff Muller's bandit army. War machines from the west and blasting cannons from the south. Vultures and Cranes, Buffalos and Hippos, Lions and Panthers as one again. Carver turned to Shah, their faces pictures of fear.

"Fly back, my lady. Tell Bergan, Manfred, and Brand of what comes. Then fly on to Robben. Plead with Baron Mervin for his help. We are greatly outnumbered by the enemy and need all the help we can get."

Shah was already flying, soaring away, as Carver threw his arm around the weary, wounded Wereape.

"Come, Lord Ulik," said the master of thieves. "You're with friends now."

PART VI

WAR OF THE WERELORDS

I

A Cold Welcome

DREW'S HEART LURCHED as he was carried high over the great frozen walls of Icegarden, the white roads and avenues rushing by below. Silhouettes shambled and shuffled through the snow-covered streets, drawing ever closer to the mighty monument at the city's heart. The palace of the White Bears protruded from the Strakenberg, towering flying buttresses holding it aloft, a cathedral to the glory of Sturmland. The figures that ambled through the city all headed in the same direction, to the great doors that marked the palace entrance, as if answering some ghastly call to prayer. They amassed on the steps, hammering at the threshold, clawing at the wood, wanting to enter and claim their prize. As Count Carsten swooped low, the dark wanderers looked up, the blue

fires in their eyes flashing as the Wolf and his allies sped by overhead.

Icegarden was lost to the dead.

A balcony ran the length of the walls over the grand entrance, some sixty yards above street level, no doubt a viewing deck from which the White Bears had once greeted their loving public. By the time the Hawklords deposited their passengers on the balustraded platform, the steps that led to the doors below were invisible, crowded with the ghouls who had claimed the city as their own. Drew saw something flash across the road before the Strakenberg Gate: a white horse, riderless, a mob of risen corpses clawing at it as it charged by. Even from this distance he knew it to be Bravado. With dread, he wondered if his warhorse was the only living creature in Icegarden.

The Behemoth stepped past Drew and peered into the open archways that provided entrance into the city. There were six openings in all, each leading onto a flight of steps down into the palace. Tattered drapes hung from the walls, their once pristine surfaces covered in frost and mildew. The smell that rose from the dark staircase beyond caused the Weremammoth to raise a giant hand to his mouth.

"Smells worse than Krieg's loincloth after a day in the ludus," snorted the Behemoth, shifting his enormous mallet off his back. His friend glowered as he unhooked his spiked mace from his belt. Taboo skipped past each of them as, spear raised, she entered the palace.

Drew was close behind her, Hawklords and fellow gladiators falling in as they descended the broad flight of steps. It opened into a great entrance hall, the carpeted staircase pitted and ripped, littered with detritus. Suits of armor lined the walls, the kind worn by the knights of Icegarden, back in Robben Valley. A pair of tall, ornate doors, fashioned in bleached white wood, suggested the way into the palace proper, while behind the staircase was the main entrance. The terrible moans of the dead were everywhere, finding their way into the ancient hall, stone and timber providing no defense against their wails.

Drew paused as the others passed him by, having spied something on the bottom steps that piqued his interest. He bent down, picking up an oily black feather from the stone, twirling it between his fingers. A growl behind the staircase made them all turn back toward the shadows that gathered around the threshold. A figure stood leaning against the doors, its chest and throat a bib of streaming blood, its clawed hands gripping the bar that held them shut. Drew recognized it instantly as a lycanthrope, but it was hideous and malformed, its muscles and bones distorted and twisted, the hair that covered its body patchy and sparse.

A chuckle from the ornate white doors beyond the stairs caused them all to spin as Lucas, surrounded by more of the Wyld Wolves, pulled the doors shut behind him, stopping Drew and his friends from continuing into the palace. The bang re-

verberated around the entrance hall, prompting the wounded Wolfman into action.

"No!" shouted Drew, raising the White Fist to plead with the monster, but it was too late. The wooden bar snapped back, the doors suddenly heaving open as the dead poured through. The Wolfman went down first, putting up little fight, his body torn to pieces by the mob in moments, while the rest lurched onward on spastic feet, arms grasping hungrily toward the Werelords.

Hawklords and gladiators closed ranks, those who hadn't yet transformed shifting swiftly, forming a wall of weapons against the tide of walking corpses. Once soldiers of Sturmland and warriors from Tuskun, the former enemies were allied in death in a war against the living. The Behemoth turned his back on the others, facing the beautiful white doors with a grunt. The Weremammoth braced his elephantine feet apart and lifted his giant mallet. With a trumpeting cry he brought the stone head about, striking the wood with timber-splitting might.

Lucas grinned as he staggered away from the white doors, Darkheart by his side. A handful of the Wyld Wolves remained with him, a couple of them gravely injured, snarling and snapping at one another as they held their guts in place. The king himself had a bite in his neck, his right shoulder shining dark with

blood as he backed into the grand hall of Icegarden. He spun, staggering forward, eyes staring up in wonder. High above, the jewel-encrusted ceiling sparkled, as if the heavens themselves had gathered within the enormous chamber. Enormous marble pillars stood to attention in elegant rows, each supporting the lofty roof, each one shrouded in shadows. A vacant throne sat on a dais at the end of the long hall, the red carpet that led to it soiled and stained.

"Where have you run to, my ladies?" laughed Lucas, his voice echoing around the vast hall. "Come out, come out, wherever you are!"

Darkheart followed the king, his eyes searching the darkness for any signs of life, his brother Wyld Wolves continuing to bicker and bite at each other. Whitley held her breath as the shaman's eyes passed over her hiding place in the recesses of the hall. He was the only one in their number who was untouched by the battle, the beast she had once known as Rolff showing no sign of wounds.

"How many?" whispered Gretchen. Her hand reached back behind her, resting on the crouching Trent's shoulder, his head dipped to his chest.

"I see five Wolfmen and Lucas," said Whitley, panting, trying to catch her breath. "Too many."

"Then we wait," said Gretchen. "Let them go on, deeper into the palace. When they leave the hall, *then* we find our way

out. We have who we came for. Let the dead have Lucas and his cronies."

"But what about Hector?" said Whitley. "Can we leave him here?"

"That's even assuming he's alive," replied the other. She reached out and squeezed her friend's hand. "This is a city of the dead. Nobody living could have survived here."

Whitley nodded, hoping in that moment that Hector's death had been swift.

"Your Majesty!"

The words echoed around the grand hall, causing all to halt what they were doing. Whitley peered around the pillar once more, watching as Lucas answered the disembodied voice.

"You have me at a disadvantage," shouted the king. "You know me, yet I do not know you. Could you be an old friend, happy to see me?"

"Oh, I don't think your relationship with your apothecary could ever have been described as that."

Whitley recognized the voice now: it was Hector.

"It sounds like you know your place, Boarlord. You accept that I am king!"

"I accept that you call yourself King of Westland, little Lionlord. But you're in my kingdom now."

Lucas laughed as the white doors at the back of the chamber began to shudder under great impacts.

"You would call yourself a king, Piglord? Lord of books, master of parchment, that's all you'll ever be."

"You always did mock Hector's books and scrolls, Lucas," said the Boar, his voice still echoing. "Yet you have no idea what those books and scrolls unlocked. You're weak, Lionlord. Pathetic."

It was Hector's turn to laugh now as the Werelion growled, snarling and snapping at the shadows.

"Show yourself, wretched magister! You'll pay for what you did to my mother!"

More laughter. "You don't care about what happened to that old witch!" Whitley was shocked by Hector's words as the Boarlord continued. "You've always been jealous of Hector, of that wonderful mind. You were always threatened by the weakling magister, unable to best him in a battle of wits. That the old Wolf died by my hand is but a justification for your mad little quest."

Whitley looked at Gretchen, both surprised by Hector's choice of words. What had gotten into him?

"The longer you hide in the darkness, the more drawn out your death shall be!" roared the Lion as the doors shuddered again, timbers beginning to fracture.

"I don't *hide* in the shadows, Lionlord," giggled the magister. "The shadows are my friends. . . ."

Right on cue the shapes began to appear in the darkness,

disengaging from the pillars and shambling toward the living. They rattled as they went, tattered wings hanging limp from their backs, taloned feet scraping the stone flags as they advanced. Most of them were making their way toward the Werelion and his companions in the center of the hall, where the monstrous faces were suddenly stricken with horror. Two of the terrible undead Crowlords, though, had spied the trio, and they turned their twisted faces toward their hiding place, blue eyes burning.

"We need to go," said Gretchen, reaching down to seize Trent by the shoulder. "Now!"

The Wolf Knight's head came up suddenly, almost biting the Foxlady's fingers from her hand. She shrieked as she pulled back, falling into Whitley's arms, as the boy from the Cold Coast began to rise to his feet. His chest cracked as it expanded, claws extending through bloody fingertips, muzzle tearing the skin of his face as his jaw groaned and dislocated. The foul yellow eyes of the Wolfman were fixed upon the two terrified therian ladies.

Fixed upon its prey.

2

PERSUASIVE WORDS

"LISTEN TO HER, Father, you know she speaks sense!"

Lady Bethwyn knelt beside her father's throne, holding Baron Mervin's liver-marked hands in her own as she pleaded with the old Wildcat. Behind her, Lady Shah stood, hands on her hips, her face a mask of frustration. She glowered at the other nobles in the room, each of them looking away, afraid to face her disgusted glare.

"I cannot do it," said the Lord of Robben. "The only hope for the people of this land is to stay out of the conflict."

"How can you say that?" asked Shah, tired of waiting for a daughter's gentler words to have an effect upon the baron. "You were a founding member of the Wolf's Council. To turn your back on them now, in their time of need, is utter cowardice."

"How dare you, Lady Shah," said the old man, rising from his chair and releasing Bethwyn's hands from his. "You have the gall to speak to me this way, after I risked so much to stand with the young Wolf?"

"Stand with him again, that's all I ask!"

"I stood with him last time, and what did it get me? Lucas and his Redcloaks treat me like a war criminal, the Redcloaks pillaged the Robben Valley and turned peaceful folk out of their homes. Did you see the tents and camps that cover this island? We are overflowing with refugees, Hawklady! Would you have me send farmers and woodsmen to war?"

"But what of your army, your soldiers? The Robbenguard could bolster our lines."

Mervin stepped toward her, spittle foaming on his lips. "I will not send my men to their deaths!"

Shah shook her head. It was Bethwyn who finally spoke up.

"What happened to the man I was proud to call my father?" she whispered, her face tearful as she addressed the baron.

"If you had been here when the Wolf's Council lost Westland back to the Catlords, if you had seen the bandits of Sheriff Muller riding roughshod over our meadows, you might think differently." Mervin sighed. "You may not judge me so harshly, daughter."

Mervin might have said more to Bethwyn, but the doors of the courtroom were suddenly flung open, clattering back on

their hinges. A number of the Robbenguard ran in, yammering their apologies, leather helmets flapping about their heads as a group of armed men marched into the hall. Scuffles were breaking out as the intruders wrestled with the baron's soldiers, forcing them back, drawing weapons of their own and coming close to blows.

Faisal brushed the guards aside, the Jackal King of Azra paying more attention to the room's decor than the effort of the resistance. Shah's old friend Djogo strode behind him, shoulder to shoulder with Field Marshal Tiaz, the former commander of the Catlord army. Florimo was also there, struggling to keep up with the fellow who strode at the front of the group. Their leader wore a black cape with red lining that hung from one shoulder, his pristine white shirt fresh for the occasion. Booted feet clicked across the flags as he closed swiftly upon the Lord of Robben, a wide smile spreading across his handsome face. Shah's heart skipped a beat. Even after all these years, the Pirate Prince of the Cluster Isles still knew how to make an entrance.

"Baron Mervin, my old friend," said Count Vega, clapping his hands before flinging them out on either side of him. "How in Brenn's name are you, dear fellow, and what in the Seven Realms are you doing hiding on your island?"

"My war's over, Vega," said the old therianthrope, wagging a finger and pulling a disapproving face. "I won't be drawn into further conflict with the Catlords."

Vega stepped up and slapped the baron across the face,

Mervin's head spinning as he tumbled back and collapsed into his chair. The audience gasped as the Wildcat looked back at the Sharklord, outraged. The count paused for a moment, straightening his cuffs before raising his hands by way of apology.

"I'm sorry, Baron Mervin. It's rude beyond words for me to appear in your court with my motley gaggle of acquaintances. Worse still to lay a finger upon you. Here's the thing, my lord."

Vega walked past Shah and Bethwyn, perching his leather-clad bottom on the arm of Mervin's throne as the old man looked up fearfully. The Sharklord continued.

"I've had a hell of a time since I last saw you, when we first turned Leopold off the throne and stuck a Wolf there in his place. I've been hunted, I've been betrayed, I've been stabbed, I've been killed—well, almost—and I've been a prisoner for a fine lump of that time, too, tied to a sea tower in the middle of the ocean. I've seen good men and women die, some too young to be taken from this world, and I've seen less noble folk than you and I give everything in the name of freedom."

Vega reached down and patted Mervin's trembling knee.

"So, when I hear that you've been . . . shall we say, reluctant, to join the fray, to help our comrades in their time of need, well . . . it rather makes my blood boil. It makes me want to shift, Mervin, just like in the old days, when you and I fought alongside Wergar. You remember that time, don't you? I could be terribly wild in battle couldn't I? Frenzied, you might say? I'd just lash out, willy-nilly, striking all kinds, be they friend or foe."

Vega looked down at the old baron. Shah was astounded by the silence in the courtroom.

"Am I forgiven?" asked Vega, tilting his head and pulling a sad face. The Wildcat nodded as the count went on. "More importantly, will you be sending the Robbenguard out to aid our brothers and sisters upon the mainland? This is the final battle, Mervin. You could help, also. You may be long in the tooth, but I know you've still got it in you."

The old man nodded as his daughter rushed to him, crying and smiling as she hugged him. Vega turned to all in the room.

"You can all do your bit—there's a place for each and every one of you out there, should you find the backbone to help your fellow Lyssians against these vile invaders." He pointed toward the doors. "If you're fit and healthy, if you can swing a sword, throw a spear, or fetch and carry arrows, get yourself out of that door and head to the beaches. Take a boat, take a skiff—swim if you must—but head to the western beach at the foot of the Robben Valley. Your neighbors need you."

Shah strode through the streets of Robben, surrounded by Vega and his companions. Field Marshal Tiaz was in deep conversation with Baron Mervin, who carried his armor and sword and was followed by his entourage. Soldiers and sailors held torches and lanterns aloft, bells ringing through the town, calling the people to arms. Each building they passed provided more bod-

ies, men and women, young and old, running out of their doors, gear in hand. They all fell in line, making their way down to the harbor.

"I don't think your cyclopean friend is very fond of me," Vega whispered to Shah, smiling and waving at Djogo where he marched along close by.

"Djogo's a good man," replied Shah. "He has trouble trusting folk is all."

"Not sure what reason I've given him to distrust me," said the Shark with a shrug, tossing back his dark hair. "Perhaps it's my comfort with my feminine side he dislikes. Some chaps are threatened by a fellow with long locks."

"Perhaps he finds you arrogant," said Shah, rolling her eyes. "He wouldn't be the first."

Shah walked on ahead of him, equal parts exasperated and excited. The Sharklord still cast a spell over her, no matter how hard she tried to fight it, and the more time she spent in his company, the greater the enchantment became. She smiled as she progressed down the cobbled road toward the harbor, making sure the boastful count couldn't see her joy.

"Captain!"

The boy's voice rang out over the noise of Robben preparing for war, as the lad came running up the cobbled street toward them. He had tousled dark hair, and a confident spring in his stride that reminded her of Vega in his pomp.

"Excuse me, ma'am," said the boy in an altogether quieter

voice. The two locked eyes with one another. Shah cocked her head, as the boy did the same. There was something familiar about his big, gray unblinking eyes.

"Ah," said Vega, catching up to them and tousling the lad's mop of hair. "You've met Casper, then?"

"I'd hardly say met," replied the Hawklady as the boy fell in line beside the count. "Ran into, perhaps."

They turned the corner in the road and looked out over the bay. Shah thought she might stop breathing when she spied the armada that crowded the harbor. She had seen those ships before, out to sea in the Desert Realm. Thirty Bastian warships, used by the Catlords to deposit troops on the shores of Omir, floated side by side, waiting to set sail. Their decks were crowded with soldiers. Furies of Felos stood shoulder to shoulder with men of Azra, while barbarians from Sturmland waved axes and spears in the air, keen to do battle. The great White Wolf, Mikotaj, waved from the deck of the *Maelstrom*, beckoning for them to hurry. The pirate prince's fabled vessel was dwarfed by many of the dreadnoughts around her, but there wasn't a sleeker, more handsome ship in the fleet.

"Well," said Vega, patting Casper's shoulder as the lad stood between him and the Hawklady. "They were just sitting there at the mouth of the River Robben. Nobody was using them."

Vega crouched beside the boy as the others continued to walk past, taking Shah's palm in one hand and the cabin

boy's in the other. The smile he gave Casper was unlike any the Hawklady had ever seen. It was gentle. It was loving.

"This is the lady I told you about, son," said Vega, turning from the boy to look up at Shah. Casper followed the count's gaze to face the shocked Lady of Windfell, his big gray eyes widening with wonder.

"This is your mother."

This time, Shah stopped breathing.

3

THE CRUELEST BLOW

THE TALL WHITE doors of Icegarden's great hall shattered, sundered by the final hammer blow from the Behemoth's stone mallet. Drew and his companions rushed over the threshold, hurdling twisted timbers, the dead shambling after them. The Weremammoth was last to climb through, the Hawklords covering his retreat, striking out with sword and spear, helping the giant to safety. At their backs, the Werewolf raced ahead through the cavernous hall, Moonbrand in hand, Krieg and Taboo close behind.

A melee had broken out before the stone throne at the head of the chamber, where the Werelion and his Wyld Wolves were surrounded by a group of terrible, dark ghouls. Drew's progress slowed as he recognized the awful figures as Crowlords,

who sought the Lion out as he clambered atop the granite chair, lashing out with sword and claw, trying to keep them at bay. There were maybe a dozen of the rotten monsters, their wings hanging loose and useless from their backs, raking, pecking, and biting the Wolfmen and their master. Dead though they were, it was clear the creatures still retained something of the therian strength with which they had been blessed, as one of the Wyld Wolves went down beneath talons and beaks.

An eerie laughter echoed around the hall, a terrible, sick gurgle that sent shockwaves of fear through each of the gladiators. Drew felt as if his insides had been scrambled, the Rhino vomiting at his side while Taboo hissed at the shadows. Blue eyes shone in the darkness as more of the risen Crowlords sought out the living, slowly shimmering into view. A woman's scream from the cloisters made Drew's head turn. There, in the distant recesses, he spied torchlight, dancing between the pillars. Lucas had heard it, too, and leapt off the throne, disappearing between the columns.

Drew and his companions found their way blocked, four corpses shambling toward them. Two were Crows, the others Ugri, and all hungry for flesh. Sword, mace, and spear struck out, breaking limbs and smashing ribs. Hands were severed, but still the dead advanced, clutching the Werelords with rotten stumps, mouths tearing at armor and snapping at the air. Drew felt his cloak caught in the grip of one of them, the monster's stinking jaws yawning open as it hauled the Werewolf in.

The White Fist grabbed its chest, crushing the right side of its torso, but the creature paid no heed. Moonbrand came down, taking its left arm off at the shoulder, but Drew remained entangled, the bite a moment away.

"You go on, lad!" shouted Krieg, lowering his head to charge the group. He lashed out with his spiked mace, catching the ghoul that held Drew and dragging it clear as he battered them. The Werewolf's cloak was ripped away, and for a split moment he had his opening, diving through the gap. He caught sight of Taboo roaring as she dove into the scrum, her spear running a corpse clean through the head.

At every turn, Drew found more of the walking dead, staggering out from behind columns and snatching at him. What was it Hector had called them? *Children of the Blue Flame.* If this was all Hector's handiwork, then he had been busy. What had possessed his friend to take such a dark and demonic path? And were they under his thrall or simply attacking out of instinct, seeking the warm flesh and blood of the living? Manfred had warned Drew of what had happened to the Boarlord, but he had struggled to believe it. Witnessing the fate of Icegarden now, he knew the Staglord's words had been true.

Leaping between the columns and bounding over the dead, Drew arrived at the area that was flooded by torchlight. Flaming brands were fixed in brackets on either side of an open doorway, a breeze from the portal causing the fires to splutter and spark. The first few steps of a spiral staircase

caught the light, the rest shrouded in darkness. A figure stood in the opening, a giant of a man with an ax in each hand. He could have been a statue; his chin was resting upon his chest, as if he were asleep upright, and his skin was as pale as the snow beyond the walls. The frozen barbarian was the least of Drew's concerns, though.

Lucas held Gretchen by the throat, up against the wall, his sword point to her belly. *The Wolfshead blade.* That had been Drew's once, lost long ago along with his hand during the battle in Cape Gala. How had it come to be in the Lion's possession? Whitley stood a few yards from him, both hands up, pleading with him. She saw Drew skid across the flags and quickly turned to him, raising her hand.

"Stay back, Drew!" she shouted, the Werewolf instantly staggering to a halt.

"But he's got Gretchen!"

"And I'll cut her up if you take one step closer, brother," snarled Lucas. "Show yourself, Boarlord!" he yelled up at the ceiling, but to no avail. There was still no sign of Hector, only more sickly laughter echoing around the hall.

Drew glanced over his shoulder as something large and dark dashed by, too fast-moving to be one of the risen Crows.

"Let go of her, Lucas," begged Whitley.

"She's my bride, Beargirl," snapped the king. "I'll do with her as I please."

"I never married you, you mad fiend!" said Gretchen, the

Fox's features coming to the fore as the Lion squeezed her throat.

She choked, clawing at him, but Lucas only jabbed the Wolfshead blade deeper between her ribs, threatening to open her up. He heard the growl behind him drawing closer, the beast's feet padding on the floor, and called back.

"Stay back, Drew Ferran, or I swear to Brenn you'll see my bride's insides. I came here for vengeance. I'll take the Fox with me, too."

"I didn't move, Lucas," replied Drew.

The Lion craned his head about, coming face-to-face with the advancing Wolfman. Drew looked at the monster as it stepped between the columns, snarling at the Lion. Unlike the Wyld Wolves he'd seen earlier, this one looked fresher, cleaner, more human. Its features and limbs were transformed as theirs were, but the fur that covered it was paler, almost golden. The grotesque lycanthrope turned to look at the Werewolf, a flicker of recognition crossing its snarling face. *You know me?* wondered Drew.

"I'm telling you one last time, Lucas, release her!" said Whitley.

The king laughed nervously as he looked from the Werewolf to the Wolfman. "Oh this is too good to be true! Drew Ferran facing not just one but *both* of his brothers."

Drew blinked in confusion as the monstrous Wolfman brought its hate-filled gaze back upon the Lion. It raised a

clawed hand, pointing at Lucas, its voice a low gurgle.

"Grrrrr . . . cherrrrrrn!"

Gretchen.

Suddenly, it was all blindingly clear to Drew: *Trent*. On every level, the creature that had been Trent Ferran knew the Lion had to be stopped. But did it understand the danger its actions might put Gretchen in?

It was about to leap at Lucas when Drew reached out, snatching the monster in his claws. He yanked the lycanthrope back, standing in front of it as it scrambled forward again. The Wolfman snarled at the Werewolf, but Drew stood his ground.

He couldn't stand back and let his brother cause harm to Gretchen. Nor could he get drawn into a fight with him. Who knew how such a contest could end?

"Trent, I know you're in there. Stay back, I beg you. Don't attack him, or he'll hurt Gretchen."

"This is too wonderful!" said Lucas. "Keep the foul beast away from me, there's a good Wolf. "

The Werelion dragged Gretchen along the wall, away from the frozen warrior with the pair of axes, watching the pair of lycanthropes. The Werefox brought her jaws down around Lucas's forearm, daggerlike teeth sinking deep into the flesh. The Lion wailed, keeping hold of Gretchen and raising his sword to strike her. The Wolfman hurled itself into Drew's broad gray chest and knocked him crashing down to the flags before bounding on toward the Lion.

The Wolfshead blade scythed out, Lucas changing its direction, letting it fly toward the Wolfman. The blow hit home with such force, the beast spun about on the spot, as Lucas brought the longsword back for a second swipe. Drew heard Whitley roar, the Werebear diving forward and tackling the lycanthrope, her pawed hands seizing its claws, as she threw the beast clear of the fight. Simultaneously, the Wolfshead blade sliced through the air behind her, and she tumbled to the floor beside Drew. The wounded Wolfman bounced off the frozen warrior that blocked the stairwell, its claws digging into the stone flags as it tried unsuccessfully to steady itself.

Drew stared into Whitley's eyes where she lay beside him, her body shifting quickly back to human form. She looked terribly shocked, shivering. Drew looked past the fallen girl as Lucas staggered away, his grip on Gretchen lost in the melee, the Foxlady falling to her knees beside the stricken Wyld Wolf that was Trent.

The frozen warrior suddenly looked up at last, as if stirred from its slumber. The dead Ugri looked down at Gretchen and the Wyld Wolf. It took a couple of steps forward, raising its twin axes and turning them in the air. The disembodied voice sounded again, dripping with malevolence.

"Kill them, Two Axes. All of them."

The Lionlord took his chance, darting along the wall's edge and diving through the gap the dead warrior had left at its back. An ax scythed back, sparking off the brickwork, but the

king was already past it and gone. The risen giant leveled its flaming blue eyes back upon the broken lycanthrope at its feet, the Wyld Wolf snarling back.

"Drew!" cried Gretchen.

But the Wolflord was reaching out to the whispering Whitley and lifting her into his arms. Her lips were turning blue, her teeth rattling now as she trembled. The Bearlady's back was wet, even through the thick material of her cloak. Drew brought his hand round, finding it slick with blood. Whitley's eyes fluttered as Gretchen screamed. Her breathing was stuttering now, erratic and desperate, catching in her throat.

"No," Drew whispered, the chaos around him muted and distant. He was just the boy from the Cold Coast, holding the girl from Brackenholme, for one last time. And then she breathed no more.

4

A Tide of Hope

"TO ME!"

Bergan's roar sounded and Greencloaks came. Men of the Woodland Watch from Brackenholme and Darke-in-the-Dyrewood heeded their liege's call, running between bush and tree, dashing over the battlefield, finding their way through the troops to where they were needed. The Bearlord stood as the last line of defense in the bottom of the valley, knee-deep in meltwater, surrounded by the dead and the dying. A handful of phibian warriors were with him, led by Shoma, with Kholka by his side. It was along the mist-covered riverbank where the fighting had been fiercest, the Wolf's army trying to prevent the Catlord force from following the river down to where it

became Lake Robben. The river was the weak point, and the felinthropes had seen this.

The battle lines were drawn out, rising up the valley and beyond the hills on either side, the Bastians striking from numerous positions and harrying the Lyssians in every quarter. The Horselords and their brothers from the Longridings were out of sight; Bergan hoped Brand and Conrad had not deserted them, prayed to Brenn that they were defending the northern flank, keeping position as promised. The Furies who had accompanied Whitley north from Calico were also lost from view. Could they join forces again with their former allies? Would they be so treacherous?

Other great, noble Werelords stood around the Bearlord, forming a line in the water alongside the Frogmen, stopping the enemy from sneaking through. His brother, Baron Redfearn, stood to one side, while Duke Manfred of Stormdale presently waded upstream, his greatsword arcing about his antlered head, scaring those about him, both friends and foes. The Staglord was fighting with the blind fury of a berserker, seeking vengeance for the deaths of his brother, Mikkel, and young Milo. A skirmisher, one of Muller's odious warriors, tried to swim past the Bearlord, taking advantage of the opening the Stag had left in the river. Bergan's ax came down and the man floated on, dead.

"Manfred!" he screamed from the top of his ragged lungs. "Return to me! We need you here!"

Bergan could have wept when he saw the Stag glance back, bloody face smiling, before returning to the fray. Manfred was gone, and just when the Bearlord needed him by his side more than ever.

"We go with him," shouted Kholka, bounding through the river on great, powerful legs. His chieftain, Shoma, shouted after him, reluctantly falling in line as the other phibian warriors followed Kholka. Swords and spears rained down upon the Frogmen as they struggled to keep up with the Staglord. Those Greencloaks who could be spared elsewhere had now appeared upon the bank, bows loaded, arrows finding Bastians. General Harker led the way, never out of earshot of his liege lord, his sword cutting a path through the enemy ranks. They were not having it easy, though. Crossbow bolts were returned, puncturing leather and finding flesh. This was the last line of defense, the tattered row of battered and beaten souls who stood between the Catlord army and the refugees on the western shore of Lake Robben. They were done running: where else was there left to go? The Seven Realms were surely lost.

A roar to Bergan's right was cut short as a bolt buried itself in Baron Redfearn's throat, the Bear collapsing back through the rolling mist with an almighty splash. Bergan instantly rushed to him. Redfearn snarled, the flights poking from his neck, blood spreading between great, bared teeth. The bolt appeared to have missed his windpipe, buried in the surrounding

muscle. The ursanthrope waved the duke away, rising out of the water.

"Worry about yourself, big brother," Redfearn gurgled, fishing his ax back out of the current, and taking his place once more by Bergan's side. "We make our stand here, tonight."

The Lord of Brackenholme managed a smile. Here, at the end of their fight, far from home, he had his brother by his side. That meant something.

"For the Dyrewood!"

As if carried on a tidal surge, a fresh wave of Goldhelm warriors from Braga suddenly rolled forth through the river fog, shortswords and shields held before them as they charged the Bearlords. Steel cut in downward strokes, silver-blessed and deadly to any therianthrope. The ursine brothers felt their bitter kiss upon their flesh and fur. On the shore the Greencloaks were engaged, Pantherguard storming their weary line, the Woodland Watch buckling under their might.

Another crossbow bolt whistled past, nicking Bergan's thick brown ear. A second hit his thigh. His ax blows split men in twain, his jaws tore faces, his free paw ripped off limbs. Blood was trickling into his eye, half blinding him. Between swings, he bent low, scooping up a pawful of water, throwing it in his face. As he moved to rise, a great shape exploded from the river in front of him, showering everyone in frigid water as it crashed into the Bear of Brackenholme. Redfearn lashed out,

catching the monster's flank, but he was immediately drawn away by the Goldhelms who maneuvered between the brothers. The duke and his therian assailant went under the surface into a dark and murky world.

Bergan felt his stomach gored open, a horn or teeth slicing his pelt apart. He could feel his flesh and innards flowing loose in the water, wanted to poke them back in and fight on. He needed to breathe but just saw bloody bubbles before his face as the beast on top of him crushed the air from his chest. He reached down, having lost his ax, and grabbed the enemy about its huge head. He twisted with all his might, turning its jaws away from his stomach as it advanced to wound him again. Somehow he twisted, rolling over and rising to his knees in the river, as the monstrous Bastian Werelord erupted from the water once more, Bergan's ax in its hand.

"The river is ours!" bellowed General Gorgo, the Hippolord shaking the Bear's half-moon blade skyward in triumph. A great mountain of a figure, the flabby gut and fat arms hid an enormous strength. Tusks rose from the Hippo's broad, wobbling jaw, stained yellow with age and decay.

"The river, the mountains, the air we breathe," said Bergan, spitting blood. "They'll never be yours. The Seven Realms will be forever Lyssian. You'll never own these lands."

"Enjoy that air, Bearlord," said the monster, weighing the ax in both hands as it prepared to strike Bergan down. "It's the last you'll ever savor."

Cries from the Bastians all around them caused the Hippolord to look up suddenly, past the kneeling Bearlord, downriver, as something huge appeared through the water. Bergan glanced over his shoulder at the ship looming into view, cutting through the mist as its hull splintered and buckled against the riverbed. The timber screamed from the rocks tearing into it, the river water rushing into the ship's belly. The *Maelstrom* shuddered to a halt, its crew leaping overboard on ropes and nets, rushing to the water to meet with the enemy. But it was the captain who caught Bergan's eye, leaping off the prow, whirling rope and anchor about his head as he flew toward the two Werelords. His skin was gray, rows of teeth on show as those dead Shark eyes focused upon the Hippolord.

Bergan flinched as the anchor tore into Gorgo, almost tearing the general in two, the mangled body splattering into the Goldhelms as they stood stunned in the river. Count Vega landed beside the Bearlord, ripping the anchor out of the Hippo's corpse and sending it into the air once more. This time he struck a pair of Bastians in the face before yanking it back into his hands.

A great noise rose from the lakeshore behind them as more ships hit the beach, an army disembarking and rushing into battle. The great White Werewolf, Mikotaj, leapt into the Goldhelms on the shore, tearing them off Harker and tossing them into the river. Miloqi's terrible howl suddenly rose from the beach, racing up the river like a tidal surge and striking fear

into the heart of each of her foes. The Tigerlord Tiaz marched forward, flanked by the Furies, cutting all in his path like wheat before the sickle. Djogo followed, staying close to the Weretiger, while Lord Chollo raced ahead of them, the Cheetahlord a blur of tooth and claw.

"Into them, boys!" shouted the Pirate Prince of the Cluster Isles wading up the river, deep into the heart of the Catlord army. "Let's see how these lads handle a fair fight!"

5

BLOODY TEARS

THEY WERE IN the woods, running. She was ahead of him, laughing, just out of reach, teasing him as he gave chase. She wore the cloak of woodland green, but her staff and bow had been left behind. They were barefoot, the soil warm beneath their feet, the smell of bark and bracken all around them. He reached out, fingers brushing her flowing auburn hair as it swished by, just beyond him. He laughed, called to her, and she looked back, smiling. And then she was pulling away from him, faster, swifter, losing him in the forest. Again he shouted her name, called for her to wait, come back, but she was gone, a shadow flitting between the trees before being swallowed by the darkness.

He was alone in the woods. He was alone. . . .

"Drew!"

Gretchen's scream coaxed him from his daydream, rising in pitch and panic. Whitley's head lay in his lap, her eyes closed, his fingers brushing her cheek. He was human again, the beast having receded, his skin against hers, still warm. She looked asleep, happy. How had it come to this? How could they have come through so much, endured such hardships, only for the girl he loved to have been taken from him? She had tried to save Trent from Lucas's blade, pushing the Wyld Wolf clear of the Werelion's attack and taking the brunt of it in the process. *Why did you do that, Whitley? Brenn, help me understand why?*

"Drew!"

This time, Drew looked up. Through tears, he could see shapes moving in the gloom, the firelight reflecting off the pale flesh of the frozen warrior. Did it matter that he chose to kneel here, with the girl from Brackenholme in his arms? Would anyone truly miss him if he lay down beside her and gave in, waiting for death? His family was all gone: Mack and Tilly, Amelie, even Trent was damned, turned into a twisted version of himself. *What's left for me?*

"Drrrrroooooo!"

It was a growl, low and gurgling, coming from the Wyld Wolf's throat as it lay wounded on the floor. The Werefox stood before it, protecting it from the twin-axed corpse. Drew looked across, his eyes locking with the beast. His brother. *Are you truly*

still in there, Trent? The eyes that stared back were yellow, lupine, not the sparkling blue ones that had charmed all the girls from Tuckborough into his arms. Whitley had given her life so the brothers could be reunited. So that Gretchen could live. So others could go on.

Go on.

Drew gently laid Whitley on the floor, delicately, as if not to wake her. Then he picked up his sword and rose. He dragged his forearm across his face, wiping the tears away. He moved forward, unsteady at first before finding his feet, finding his anger, shifting with each step.

The Werefox defiantly guarded the wounded lycanthrope, struggling to hold the dead Ugri back. The two axes remained in the ghoul's hands, as if frozen there, impossible to remove. The monster forced her to the ground, her back bending beneath its undead will. She kept her arms locked, preventing the axes from striking her, but the corpse's teeth worked, gnashing, drawing ever closer. A white light illuminated the dead Ugri momentarily. One of the arms sagged loosely, lopped off at the shoulder. Gretchen tossed it aside as a further blow from Moonbrand took off the other.

The risen corpse of Two Axes, champion of Tuskun, warrior chieftain of the Ugri, turned to face its assailant. Another blinding white flash. Its torso shuddered to a halt as its head continued moving, spinning upon the neck stump. The blue

fires winked out in its ghastly eyes as the severed head bounced to the flagged floor.

"Whitley?" asked Gretchen, her voice weak and fearful.

The Werewolf shook his shaggy head, unable to look at the Werefox. Taboo and Krieg ran up to them, the Behemoth and two of the Hawklords behind them. All were slick with rotten flesh and splintered bone from their battle with the undead. They faltered as they approached, spying the girl on the floor. Taboo raised her weapon, ready to strike the wounded Wyld Wolf.

"Stay your spear, Taboo!" cried Gretchen, raising a hand to halt the Weretiger. "That's Trent Ferran, Drew's brother."

Resheathing Moonbrand, Drew bent and picked Whitley up in his powerful arms. Her head lolled into his chest.

"I've a favor to ask of you all," said Drew as the moans of the dead and the snarls of the Wyld Wolves echoed in the hall. "Should anything happen to me, someone must get Whitley to her father. She cannot be left behind."

Krieg stepped forward, squeezing Drew's shoulder briefly before taking the slain Bearlady from him.

"She'll get home, my lord," said Count Carsten, his voice grave. "Fear not."

"And my brother," Drew went on, looking down at Trent pityingly. "He needs help. There must be hope for him, some way of reversing whatever foul magicks Darkheart cast upon him."

He turned away from the monster, his broken heart unable to deal with any more misery this day. His world was in ruins. There was only one way he could seek retribution for this awful night. Lucas had killed his love, and Hector had brought about the horrors that infested Icegarden. He glanced at the stairwell the Lion had taken. The grim laughter no longer sounded in the hall, nor did the snarls of the Wyld Wolves. Only the dead raised their voices in chorus, a symphony of hungry moans as myriad blue eyes spied the Werelords in the cloisters.

"Seek the higher levels, my friends," said Drew, suddenly spurred into life. "Find balconies, some way out. Do not linger within this hall."

"The staircase," said Taboo, gesturing to the portal in the wall. "Where does it lead?"

"To Lucas. He seeks Hector, and I'm going after both of them."

"Both of them?" gasped Gretchen. "What will you do if you find Hector?"

The lycanthrope's amber eyes glowed with vengeance. The Werefox stepped up to Drew, placing her russet clawed hands over the White Fist of Icegarden.

"Whitley wanted you to save Hector, remember? He's still our friend."

"Look at the madness that surrounds us, Gretchen. There's just one way to save our friend. His body's lost. There's only his soul that we can put to rest now."

"Drew, no," she said, gripping the gauntlet as he tugged it away.

Then he was off and running, leaving his allies behind him, bounding through the doorway and up the narrow, cold staircase on lupine legs, Moonbrand lighting the way ahead. He heard Gretchen scream for him to stop. He heard Krieg snorting, bellowing for him to wait for them. He heard Taboo hiss as she sprinted after him. His eyes remained fixed on the curving staircase, the foul stench of the Werelion choking his nose, throat, and heart.

6

THE LONG SLEEP CALLS

THE GREATSWORD CAME down, again and again, cutting, chopping, scything. The misty air glittered and shone, a fog of red, tasting of salt and metal and bittersweet revenge. Duke Manfred kept on climbing, cloven feet churning up the earth as he gave chase across the moorland, the Lionguard cloaks drawing his wrath like a red rag to a bull. Another of them fell beneath his wild strokes, hitting the peat, his hoof coming down to crush the fool into the earth. A noise made him turn, the sword striking the onrushing skirmisher, but not before the man's hammer had struck the Staglord's bloody head.

He fell to his haunches, breathing hard, the world turning. He lifted his head, the moon almost blinding him as if he was

staring upon it for the first time. *Where am I? How did I come to this place?* Tufts of yellow grass sprouted out of the boggy moorland all about him, steam rising into the cool summer night. His thighs, his hands, his chest were slick with blood. *Is it mine?* There were open wounds across his body no doubt, but there was too much of the red stuff for it all to be his. *How many have I killed?*

His head thundered. He reached up with his hands, fingers broken and twisted, finding his antlers snapped and severed, one tine hanging loose like a splintered branch. The rage that had powered him, on into the battle, through the enemy lines, up the valley to chase down the Redcloaks, had suddenly deserted him. He tried to pick his greatsword up from where he had dropped it on the ground, but his hands refused to obey. He lifted his head, about to call out, but thought better of it. He might be surrounded by the enemy for all he knew.

Confirming his worst fears, the Lionguard and skirmishers began to appear through the peat mists that shrouded the moor. The enraged, berserk roars of the Staglord had clearly ceased, and they had returned to investigate. Finding bravery in numbers, what they discovered in the mist was not a monstrous beast from the Barebones, the mighty Lord of Stormdale. A bloody, beaten old man awaited them, in sight of death's dark door, the long sleep awaiting.

Manfred sighed and looked up at the moon. *Did I do right by you, Milo? My beautiful boy, did I do right? I'll be seeing you soon enough.*

He closed his eyes as the Redcloaks closed in around him.

A horn blew, crisp and clear, calling the Catlord soldiers away from the beaten Werelord. They looked up across the moor, as the ground began to thunder beneath them. The sight of the Knights of Stormdale, cresting that ridge, pounding down the hill toward them on their mighty steeds, broke the Redcloaks' morale in an instant. The deserters ran, this time back down the hill toward the fighting, Staglords and cavalry from the Barebones felling them as they fled.

Manfred looked up as one horse circled him, the rider silhouetted by the moon above. He jumped down from his mount, armor clanking as he landed. The duke recognized the antlers straightaway as the Staglord knelt and embraced him.

"Father," said Lord Reinhardt, rocking as he held the old man in his arms.

Three daggers left, and two of those were in his hands. He was deep into enemy territory, and his bandolier was looking woefully low on knives. The odds weren't looking good for Bo Carver. Still, he had Reuben Fry with him, and that was something. The two had become firm friends since their worlds had been turned upside down in Highcliff, and there was no man Carver would rather have beside him in a tight spot. Fry had long ago discarded his bow, the fight now coming down to hand weapons. His breastplate was gone also, tossed after an ax

had almost cleaved him in two. Sword and knives in hand, the roaring of the waterfalls filling their ears, the two men waited for their moment as the Vermirian Guard ran past, reinforcing the enemy lines.

The men leapt down from the rocky outcropping that had served as their hiding place, each one clattering into, and taking out, a handful of the black-cloaked Ratguard. As they struggled to their feet, Carver and Fry worked fast, darting in and out with their blades, finding the weak spots in the armor where greave and plate met. Two of the Vermirians fell backward, off the bluff into the Robben Falls. The others fell gurgling, no doubt regretting their fine-looking—and cumbersome—midnight plate mail as they dropped back down to the dirt. A handful were still on their feet, turning back to run into the two foes who had found their way behind their lines.

Before the Vermirians could engage with their enemy, there was a roar as a mighty arm smashed into them. The enormous swinging limb of Lord Ulik, the Wereape of World's End, scattered the soldiers as he charged up the rocky valley toward them. The men wailed as they followed their comrades into the water. Half blind from his crushed eye, the Naked Ape had to pull back from attacking Fry and Carver, recognizing them at the last moment. A giant among Werelords, the Apelord was good to have on their side. The beast pointed across the fast-flowing falls to the hills southwest.

"Their lines are broken," gasped Ulik, deadly teeth catching as he spoke. "Your Staglords have arrived, and the men of the Longridings are close behind me. I sense victory!"

Fry smiled and clapped Carver's chest.

"My lord!"

The voice was small and came from on high. Carver didn't look straightaway—after all, who on earth would address *him* that way? Curiosity made him glance up. His heart sank. Pick, the girl from Highcliff who had shadowed his every step since they had fled their homeland, was perched atop the rock he and Fry had hid upon.

"Stay there, girl!" he shouted angrily, running quickly around the edge of the outcropping. By the time he had climbed up to the top to reach her, he heard the first scream below him. He looked over the rock.

An enormous Catlord had emerged from the darkness, its black fur camouflaging its approach. It wore a chain skirt, like a northman's kilt, with a shining sickle hanging from the hip. It now stood over Lord Ulik, driving a giant silver spear into the Wereape, pinning the goliath to the rocky ground. Fry lay a few feet away, struggling to get up, clearly having been clobbered by a blow from the Werepanther. Goldhelms appeared all around them, staying close to their master and commander. Farther down the gorge, the first of the Horselords were approaching, led by the blond Lord Conrad. He spied the Panther.

"Oba!" the Werestallion cried, pointing his greatsword

toward the giant of Bast. "I challenge you to battle!"

"All in good time, Pony!" hissed the Werepanther as his Goldhelms leveled bows upon the humans and therians from the Longridings. The beast turned back to the Ape.

"Well, well," said High Lord Oba. "Seems you *did* run away and play tattletale with our enemy, Ulik, eh?" He twisted the silver spear, provoking a terrible wail from the Wereape. "Well, join them you shall," said the Panther, ripping the weapon out and preparing to strike it into Ulik's chest. "In hell!"

Before he knew what he was doing, Carver had leapt onto the Catlord. He landed across Oba's shoulders, legs wrapped around the Panther's neck, knives in each hand stabbing down hard. Each dagger found the flesh of the monster's face, neck, and shoulders, plunging in and out in quick succession, a frantic series of blows that drew blood every time. The Werepanther roared, reaching back over its head to seize the human. Carver felt an enormous paw close over his right arm, gripping tightly. The daggers tumbled from his hands, and the bones broke like balsa wood as Oba hefted him into the air and tossed him onto the bluff's edge beside Fry. The Thieflord saw stars momentarily before Reuben Fry's pained face shifted into view.

"Fancy seeing you here." Carver grinned at the Sturm-lander through gritted teeth, his one good arm reaching for the bandolier, and pulling out the last knife. The silver spear rapped his knuckles, cracking Carver's hand and sending the

dagger skittering away off the edge. Oba came to stand over them, sneering at each in turn, the Pantherlord's furious face a mask of blood.

"Pathetic, useless humans," Oba spat. Bastians and Lyssians all watched, deadlocked at the head of the valley. "You dare to defy me, High Lord Oba, the better of all your betters? Worthless worms! Who do you think you are? This is your place, squirming in the dirt before me, groveling for undeserved mercy! You would challenge me, a Werelord? Then you may die as Werelords, both of you!"

Oba snapped the giant silver spear in two, shifting a fragment into each hand and brandishing them over the thief and the soldier. Preoccupied by the snapping of the weapon and the Pantherlord's roaring voice, neither the Catlord nor the Goldhelms noticed the girl who had stealthily crept up behind the Pantherlord. Pick's hands worked deftly, unhitching the silver sickle from Oba's belt. She tossed it to Carver as the Werepanther of Braga turned its hate-filled gaze back onto the humans.

Carver was fast, catching the blade in his off-hand and lashing out. The sickle tore a perfect line across Oba's vast, dark stomach, from left hip to right breast, before Bo changed angle, dropping his aim and ripping back up the other way. The broken pieces of the spear clattered from Oba's hands as the Werepanther staggered, trying to stuff its insides back into its body. Oba looked at the humans, eyes wide with horror and disbelief, as the end fast approached. The Goldhelms

were stunned, stumbling clear as their godlike leader shambled through them, finally toppling onto the rocks beside the falls.

The water of the Robben River ran red, all the way down to the lake far below.

The cheers started at the head of the valley, where the waterfalls raced and roared. They rolled downhill, gathering momentum, breaking the resolve of every Bastian in their path and stirring the souls of every Lyssian. By the time they reached the shores of Lake Robben, the cheers had become screams of delirium, outpourings of raw emotion as free men and women of the Seven Realms embraced one another in celebration.

Count Vega stood on the battlefield, the ground clogged with the bodies of the fallen. He was no longer the fearsome Shark of the fabled *Maelstrom*. He was the dashing buccaneer pirate prince once again. Until he met Drew Ferran, Vega had never dared to imagine a day when the Catlords no longer held Lyssia beneath booted paw. That hope would come in the form of the young Wolf had been totally unexpected. Drew had trusted Vega when all others wouldn't, had believed in the Sharklord when the others called him a liar, a ne'er-do-well. Vega grinned to himself. He would turn his back on all the wealth in the ocean to continue serving by the Wolf's side. Well, most of it, anyway.

He turned and began to wander down through the mists, back toward the beach. He passed Greencloaks and Longriders along the way, northmen and southerners. They all saluted the count, his actions during the battle already the stuff of legend. The enemy was routed, dropping sword, shield, and spear and running for the hills. Those who hadn't fled had surrendered, the Furies of Felos taking them prisoner under the dutiful eye of Tiaz. The Tiger had been a more than capable ally. Who knew if their paths would cross again when all this was over?

Vega would certainly be glad to see the back of Opal. The Pantherlady's looks hadn't become any warmer over the months. Vega shook his head. It would all be behind them soon enough. He had Shah to think about now, and Casper. That the terrible war could reunite a family was something the Sharklord could never have dreamed of. He just needed to fix up the *Maelstrom* and then their adventure could truly begin. There was a world of oceans out there, just waiting to be navigated and charted. Perhaps the old Tern Florimo could accompany them? A good pair of eyes was always of use.

Vega never saw the man approaching behind him. He turned at the last moment, surprised to find Djogo there. The Sharklord was about to speak, to congratulate his comrade on a war well won, when he felt the silver dagger in his belly. It went in again, and again, the warrior stepping away from the count, a wild look in his one good eye. A passing Green-

cloak shouted, having witnessed the attack, before he raced forward, giving chase to Djogo as the former slaver ran off.

Vega collapsed onto the riverbank, so close to the *Maelstrom,* he could see her silhouette through the fog. He could see another dark outline, too, on the opposite bank. The Beauty of Bast stood there, watching him as he keeled over. She nodded once, and then turned, swallowed forever by the mist.

7

LIGHT AGAINST NIGHT

HIS FRIENDS WERE far behind him, and only enemies lay ahead. Enemies and an endless procession of steps. His legs burned from the exertion, his entire body dizzy and disoriented from the constant spiraling climb. The cold wall seemed to be leaning in, looming on his left, drawing closer at every turn. The claustrophobia had hit him a hundred footfalls ago. There was no sight of the Lionlord, but his scent was thick in the air—plus something else, a rotten, sweet smell that reminded Drew of his days back on the farm on the Cold Coast. Dead sheep and cattle, found in ditches or meadows, taken by means both natural and foul: corpses had an unmistakable stench, especially those that had been left in the sun, decomposing as death worked its unavoidable magic upon the flesh. That

odor was in his lungs now, drawing him ever higher.

Another fresh smear of blood on the wall, the red drop-lets still trickling down, confirmed Drew's suspicions. Lucas was just ahead. Drew pushed on, forcing his body to continue even though every muscle and sinew cried out for mercy. The anger that had fueled his swift ascent remained, but his sorrow intensified, magnified in every passing moment. Whitley remained at the forefront of his mind, his bighearted friend who had inspired him to such great things. He couldn't imagine a world without her. Perhaps when he hit the summit of the tower he would simply keep on going? *Perhaps the heavens have a place for me, and Whitley's waiting?*

Drew saw the moon's dim glow reflected by the uneven steps ahead, bouncing off the crooked walls and calling him. The power of that strange light spurred him toward the inevitable confrontation with his half brother and his best friend. Or at least what had been his best friend. Brenn only knew what Hector had become since last he'd seen him.

Voices raised in anger bounced down the stairwell, a violent struggle clearly under way at the summit. The Werewolf bounded up the remaining stairs, the White Fist clawing at the bricks now. He burst onto the tower top, instantly buffeted by a gust of wind.

The Werelion was locked in a struggle with a black, wraithlike form. At first, Drew assumed it was Hector, until he realized the figure was too tall, too rangy. Spindly legs carried

the man, bedraggled boots rolled down around rotten ankles, arms swinging, skeletal fingers snatching. Blue fires roared in the dead man's sunken face, his splintered teeth already grinding meat from where he had taken a piece out of Lucas. Two longknives sat neglected in sheaths on the dead man's hips, his tattered brown cloak hanging loose from disheveled shoulders, fastened in place with a Boarshead brooch.

Behind the dueling monsters, a third figure stood, black cloak whipped by the wind, moon shrouded in clouds at his back. It was only now that Drew realized the frightening height he had reached. He was reminded of his ascent to the peak of Tor Raptor, ancient burial site of the Hawklords of the Barebones. But the vertigo he'd experienced there was nothing compared with this. The stone platform on which they stood was only ten paces across, with the fighting corpse and felinthrope taking up most of it. A firm push would send any of them over the low, tumbledown wall that circled its edge. The Werewolf's eyes narrowed as he glared beyond the roaring Werelion and the hungry Child of the Blue Flame. Hector stared back and smiled, his face ghastly and white.

"They fight for our entertainment, Wolflord," said the magister, holding his hands out wide as if crucified. His left hand was a gnarled, black branch, fingers withered twigs that twitched in the breeze. The skin was stretched tight; what muscle remained was drained of fluid, wrapped about brittle bone. Drew blanched, horrified by what had become of his friend.

"What happened, Hector?" Drew called over the snarls and moans of the combatants. "How did you come to this?"

"Hector's dead, Wolflord. You address Blackhand, Lord of Icegarden."

"Lord of death, more like," sneered Drew, his eyes returning to Lucas and the dead man as the Lion now forced the corpse to the stone deck. The king's claws descended at speed, ripping at the risen Boarguard and rending it apart. Enraged and covered in wounds, Lucas lifted the dismembered body, which was still shuddering spasmodically, and flung it from the tower. It disappeared into the night in a shower of torn, rotten flesh.

"Poor Ringlin," muttered Blackhand. "He served me well in life. And death, for that matter."

Lucas looked up, panting, the Lion's mane bristling as the king switched its gaze from magister to Werewolf.

"All together again, eh?" snarled the Werelion.

"I know what you're here for," Drew said, ignoring the Lion's sarcasm. "But let me deal with Hector. I know you seek vengeance for our mother's death—"

"She was never *your* mother," snarled the king. "Turning up at the end of her days to pretend at being her boy doesn't make you her son!"

Drew could see the magister shifting now, reaching behind his back to withdraw something from the recesses of his robes.

"All good things must come to an end," muttered the Werelion through bloody teeth, raising the Wolfshead blade.

"Bad things get their endings, too," replied Drew, lifting Moonbrand before him.

"I hope your little Bear enjoyed her end. She did die, didn't she? Apologies for not hanging around to see it, but she had the same pained look on her face as her brother when I killed—"

Moonbrand struck the Wolfshead blade with such ferocity that it sheared the steel weapon in two. The Sturmish sword continued on, scything down to land in the Werelion's shoulder blade. Lucas roared, striking back, the broken metal of Mack Ferran's old sword finding Drew's left breast. The Werewolf howled as the Lion drove the weapon home, the sundered metal twisting in Drew's chest. The brothers rolled across the exposed tower top, swords coming loose as they grappled with one another, each blade clattering across the stone summit.

Lucas had found his way on top of Drew. He was Drew's junior, but even in human shape he had outgrown Drew. In therian form, the difference in size was even more extreme. The Lion's shoulders were broader than the Wolf's, and the chest was a great barrel of knotted muscle, mane thick and shaggy about its throat. Teeth marks from the undead scarred the golden fur, but Lucas paid them no heed, lost in a vengeful furor. The White Fist of Icegarden was all that kept the king's jaws from Drew's throat, the Wolf's elbow locked as he kept Lucas at bay. The Lion's feet came up, clawing at Drew's belly,

tearing strips of gray skin from his guts as the monster tried to disembowel the Wolf.

Blackhand danced about them, laughing, as the two fought. Drew caught sight of the thing in the magister's hand now, a twisted length of ugly, burned metal that appeared to be a lightning rod. Its ends were pointed and the magister twirled it in his necrotic hand, awaiting his chance to turn it upon Wolf and Lion. The Boarlord darted toward the struggling brothers, thrusting the rod into the melee like a spear, catching the Werewolf's thigh with a glancing blow and bringing it back bloody. It was only a scratch, but cold, sickening pain radiated from where the rod had struck him. Drew tried to ignore the sadistic antics of the magister and the effects of the twisted spear, instead concentrating all his strength on the hold around Lucas's throat. The clouds parted and the moon bathed the Bone Tower in its silver light.

The White Fist burned bright like a beacon, squeezing all the tighter, all the harder, about the Lion's throat. Drew saw Lucas's eyes widen as the bladed fingers dug into the flesh, puncturing the skin. All of Drew's anger and sorrow poured into the arm, his hatred for all that had been done to him, all he had endured. The Lion's paws came up to its throat as it began to shift back to human form, pink hands gripping the Sturmish steel gauntlet. Drew shook him, snarling, tears streaming down the Werewolf's muzzle as Blackhand laughed behind him.

"Kill him, Wolflord! Snap his neck! Break him so I may put him back together again!"

Blackhand's terrible words were ringing in his ears, stirring him from his deadly deed, bringing the boy from the Cold Coast back to the world of the living. A blond, gangly youth hung from the clenched White Fist, eyes rolling in his head. Drew released his hold, letting Lucas drop to the floor with a wheezing gurgle. The Werewolf turned to the magister, whose face darkened.

"What kind of Werelord are you that you're incapable of killing this wretch? This is the Lion! The beast that took everything from you!"

Hector struck out again with the lightning rod, aiming for the Werewolf's belly. Drew twisted, catching it in the White Fist's grasp. Whatever dark powers were at his old Boarlord friend's disposal, Drew was instantly sure of one thing: the rod was the key. Wave after wave of terrible magick rolled over him, coming straight from the magister. The enchanted gauntlet flashed gray, its light quenched by a dark fire that poured out of Blackhand. Drew dropped to his knees, his own energy suddenly leeched from him through steel glove and lightning rod. The gray fur that coated his body receded, his muscles shrinking, all the power of the lycanthrope and the moon pouring out of him and into Blackhand. The magister snorted and squealed, tusks breaking from his pale, sweaty face as he

laughed, body shifting, popping, and bursting with muscles as the Boar came to the fore.

"What power!" cried the magister. "Hector, are you watching this? Can you feel it, brother?"

His old friend's choice of words wasn't lost on Drew. *Brother? So it's* Vincent *who is in control of Hector's flesh!* Drew tried to release his hold on the rod, but the White Fist was having none of it, as if soldered to the twisted bar. He was human once more, the Wolf lost to him, the gauntlet useless. Drew gasped, fighting the magicks Blackhand marshaled.

"Snarl away, little Wolf! Look at you—you're nothing!" proclaimed Blackhand. "Some good your White Fist did you, eh?"

"I have another," said Drew. His right fist caught the magister sweetly across the jaw, the blow causing Hector to fly across the platform, the rod yanked from the White Fist's grip. The Boarlord landed near the tower's edge, head bouncing off the rubble parapet with a crunch.

Drew clambered up from the stone floor, unsteady, wind almost propelling him into the night. A movement in the corner of his eye made the hairs on the back of his neck stand on end: the beast within him sensed the coming danger, but he was too slow. The broken steel of the Wolfshead blade struck home once more, plunged deep into his shoulder. He fell forward, the sundered sword sliding out of his flesh as he collapsed onto the stone deck of the tower. Drew looked back as

Lucas stood there; the blond boy's eyes were wild, a tortured smile almost carving his face in two, sweat-slicked locks clinging to his brow. He struck down with the broken blade, again and again, threatening to deliver the killing blow at any moment. Drew rolled, dodging each swing, but only delaying the inevitable as his stamina drained away.

"Lucas."

The girl's voice came from behind the king, sudden and surprising, and the Werelion spun about to face her. He shuddered to a halt, the rage that possessed him dissipating in an instant. The broken sword tumbled out of his hands, clattering onto the flags. He was face-to-face with Gretchen, the flame-haired girl he had once been betrothed to, her green eyes burning into his. He looked down. In her hands she held the broken tine from a young Staglord's antler, slick with Lucas's blood. The gaping hole in the Lion's left breast told its own tale, the life pouring out of his open heart. Lucas wobbled away from where Gretchen stood by the stairwell, shaking his head in disbelief as he tottered to the tower top's edge. His heels caught the parapet and he wheeled backward into the night.

Gretchen rushed forward, helping Drew rise, the young man wincing with every movement. He felt dead inside, heart and soul drained of life even as the Werefox hugged him. She was whispering to him, words of grief, of relief, of sadness and joy, but he heard nothing. Drew looked past her to the crumpled body of the Boarlord. Giving Gretchen a squeeze of the

forearms, he nodded to Blackhand as the magister stirred, raising his bloody brow from the rubble. The Boar was gone, the sickly human face returned.

"Drew?" whispered the magister, the venom that was there earlier gone now. "You came back for me, my old friend."

Hector was crying now, tears mingling with weeping wounds as pink rivulets raced down his pale cheeks. He reached up, both hands held out, wanting to embrace his friends. As his eyes landed upon the dark, twisted limb, he paused, then shuddered and heaved as it twitched, skin squeaking as he formed a leathery fist. Drew watched as the knuckles threatened to tear through the foul flesh. Hector's gaze came back to his old friend.

"It was Vincent," he whispered. "I haven't been myself since you went, Drew. It was one thing after another; I made all the wrong choices. Where were you, Drew? I needed you."

"Lyssia needed me, Hector," said Drew as he crouched before the other. "I thought you were safe back in Highcliff."

"The danger was within." Hector sighed where he lay. "It was the magicks, the magistry, the communing. Once I uncorked it, the djinn was out of the bottle. I didn't realize until you were gone just how much you meant to me."

"And you me, friend."

The two young men hugged one another on the tower top, Gretchen weeping at their backs.

"You were my moral compass, Drew."

"And you were perspective, Hector," said the Wolflord with a sad smile, rising again. "You taught me so much, about the world, about the Werelords, about what's expected of me. You tempered the chaos in me, mate. You made me a better man."

Drew stepped away, disappearing briefly behind Gretchen. When he returned, he had Moonbrand in his hand.

"What are you doing?" said the Fox of Hedgemoor.

"What needs doing," said Drew, stepping over the Boarlord where he lay.

"You can't do this," said Gretchen, voice full of dismay, horror, and anger.

"He can and he shall," said Hector. "Vincent will return. I can feel him stirring already. He has mastery of this body now: I haven't been in control for so long now. His vile owns this bag of bones."

"There has to be some other way," said the Werefox. "Don't do this, Drew. Whitley wanted you to save Hector, remember? She wanted you to cure him."

Drew looked at the girl through red-rimmed eyes. He weighed Moonbrand in his hand as the white flames raced up and down the glowing brand.

"This is how we save him, Gretchen. This is the only cure, can't you see?"

She turned away, unable to watch Drew as he stepped over his friend. Hector lay there, arms out wide, broken in the rubble.

"Do you remember?" Hector coughed. "So long ago, we spoke about this moment."

"We did?"

"The prophecies always pointed to this day. The Seven Realms broken, a battle between brothers, dead walking the earth, a Champion of Light versus the Night. I always thought, growing up, that I could be that champion—blame the bookish daydreamer in me—but look at you, with the White Fist of Icegarden! It suits you. Turns out I was the other," he said, looking across at the twitching black limb. "I was the Night."

Hector looked back at the Wolflord. "Who would've thought all those miserable prophecies would lead us here, eh?"

Drew tried to smile, but his brow was furrowed, the tears a flood.

"I'll see you at Brenn's table," whispered the Boarlord of Redmire, closing his eyes. "I love you, Drew Ferran: my king, my brother, my best friend."

Drew sniffed back a tear and raised the white sword high. "Brenn, forgive me."

And Moonbrand descended.

8

A FINAL FAREWELL

THE ROBBEN VALLEY was a scarcely populated shire situated between the foothills of Sturmland and the rolling hills of the Dalelands, and nothing remarkable had ever happened there before. The few people who dwelled there were farming stock, generations old. Living in a sleepy vale with an even sleepier lake, the good folk of Robben were used to a quiet, unremarkable life. All that had changed when war had come to the north, the Battle of the Seven Realms unfolding right on their doorstep. For the first and only time in Robben's peaceful history, the green and pleasant valley was the center of the attention. Specifically it was the scene of the greatest carnival Lyssia had ever witnessed.

Those who had played their part in the war were many

and various, and in years to come there would be hermits in the most far-flung corner of the realms who would claim to have been there that day. The Werelords of all the ancient noble households had each been represented, chief among them those from the Dyrewood, the Barebones, and the Longridings. The pale therians of Sturmland had answered the call, Bears and Wolves of the whitest fur fighting alongside one another just as in days of yore. Even the Lords of the Dalelands who yet lived had joined in, chief among them Baron Mervin. The Wildcat of Robben had reclaimed his reputation of old, seeking out the fiercest foes on the front line and surviving while others fell. This wasn't a war that was won by those great and glorious therian lords, colossal though their effort was. The true victor was humanity.

The Werelords were blessed by Brenn with something close to immortality. They were long-lived, way beyond the life span of humans. They could be harmed by few things, chief among them silver, magick, and their own tooth and claw, although a clean hit to the heart would most surely stop them dead. With such supernatural resilience, the fabled Lords of the Seven Realms were afforded a comfort in battle that humans would never experience.

Yet it was three humans who had climbed farther up the valley than any Werelord, deep behind enemy lines, finally coming face-to-face with High Lord Oba, the Werepanther of Braga.

There were many wondrous victories that night—Count Vega in the river, Duke Manfred on the moors, King Faisal on the lakeshore, and Baron Mervin in the vanguard to name but a few—but they all paled beside the fall of Oba. The Pantherlord was brought crashing to the rocks above the Robben Falls by an archer from Sturmland, a reformed rogue, and an orphan girl from the poor quarter of Highcliff. All three humans, and all three the most celebrated champions in the days, weeks, and months that followed.

Fry, Carver, and Pick were the ones who would be remembered long after all had departed for the long sleep. In those first days, with the war won and the prisoners in chains, people traveled from far and wide just to meet them. Young and old, the fearful and the frail, all wanted to be there, to celebrate with their brethren, to cheer the brave heroes of the Battle of the Seven Realms. And those who could not make the journey would tell the tale of being there, repeating it so often in the following years that they would finally convince themselves that they spoke the truth. Lie became myth became fact. The scribes originally wrote that there were fifty thousand who fought in that final battle. In years to come that number would swell tenfold.

Drew walked through the multitude of revelers, Bergan's words ringing in his ears. The duke had been his first port of call when he arrived back in camp on Bravado. The horse had been found in the snow-laden pastures beyond Icegarden's

walls, having evaded the dead that had swarmed the White Bear city. The remainder of Drew's party were still marching south, back to the Wolf's war camp. He hoped their encounters with the dead were done. The Children of the Blue Flame could keep Icegarden for now. Later, Drew's allies would be back in numbers to purge the city of all signs of Blackhand's awful residency. At some point, down the road, the Sturmlanders would have their home back. Whether they could vanquish the memory of the horrors that had befallen it was another matter entirely.

Count Carsten had flown on ahead, carrying Whitley back to her father. When Drew had returned to a chorus of cheers and salutations, he felt sick to the pit of his stomach. Every step Bravado took brought him nearer to confronting the Bearlord. The conversation that had followed hadn't been what he'd expected.

"She went of her own volition, Drew," the heartbroken duke had said, within the confines of his tent. Whitley had been laid out as befitted a Lady of Lyssia, Lady Greta and Miloqi having prepared her for her final journey back to Brackenholme. "I don't blame you, my boy. You would've dissuaded her—as would I—if you'd known her intentions. She did it for love, lad. And she didn't die in vain—she saved her friends, who helped save the kingdom."

The two had embraced, away from the prying eyes of the singing, celebrating masses beyond the tent.

"You're needed out there, lad," the Bearlord had said, words stifled by tears. "The people need to see you, need to know that you've lived while others have fallen. Raise your chin, Drew Ferran. Smile for them, wave to them, even if your heart is breaking. That is the way of kings."

So Drew had walked from the tent, shaking the hands of those who had fought in his name, accepting their adulation, their love. He smiled, he toasted, as he made his way through the camp, while inside he was broken.

They had triumphed, against all odds. Lyssia was free once more. Hopefully, the Seven Realms would never again be enslaved by the Catlords of Bast. If the walk he had taken to Bergan had been hard, the one he now undertook was doubly so. He no longer had Bravado to carry him. It was his own leaden feet that took him to the river's edge to the great dark ship that sat beached in the shallows, her belly torn open.

Drew walked up the gangplank that had been lowered to the bank, the *Maelstrom* quiet while all around the party raged. The vessel was pitched over like a drunk, her sails hanging limp and forlorn in the breeze, her crew nowhere to be seen. No doubt celebrating, along with every other soul in Robben, and who could blame them? The crew of the pirate ship had seen more of this war than most. It was only fair they could now raise a glass and voice in triumph.

Figgis waited for Drew at the top of the gangway, the old pirate nodding as the Wolflord approached. Here was one of

the toughest men Drew had ever met, his small frame belying the strength and rugged determination that had allowed him to live this long in such a dangerous profession. The man's leathery face was more downturned than usual, and the young Wolf noticed a tear upon his cheek. Drew paused as he passed to squeeze the old sailor's shoulder in sympathy. Then he was past him, through the hatch and down the tilting steps to the captain's cabin.

Vega wasn't alone. Duke Manfred stood by the threshold, Bo Carver at his side. The precocious pickpocket, Pick, stood beside the Thief Lord, her hand in his, her face a mask of sadness. Miloqi and Mikotaj waited in the shadows on the opposite side of the entrance, hidden behind the open door, the big White Wolf grunting an acknowledgment at the arrival of his distant cousin. Eric Ransome, captain of the Bastian warship the *Nemesis*, saluted Drew, but the act was tired and halfhearted, his eyes returning to the figure on the bed.

Baron Eben rose from the foot of the cot, snapping the latches shut on his medicine bag. The young magister had been busy, nowhere more so than aboard the *Maelstrom*. Lady Shah and Casper sat on either side of the bed, seemingly asleep. Eben spied Drew suddenly and cleared his throat.

"Come along," said the Ramlord of Haggard. "I think some of us could make ourselves scarce. The hour approaches."

He nodded at Drew as he trudged past him, the White

Wolves and Ransome following him out of the door. Carver turned to follow, only for Pick to release her hold on his hand to rush to the bed. She threw her arms around Casper, the boy surprised by the show of affection, raising trembling fingers to briefly brush hers before she dashed from the room. Carver looked back, his face hard.

"Farewell, old mate," said the Thief Lord, the serpent tattoo that flashed across the side of his face writhing as he grimaced. With that, he followed the child from the room. Only Manfred remained, standing at attention, his head wrapped in bandages, his face battered almost beyond recognition. Drew walked toward the captain's cot.

Vega wasn't dead, not yet anyway. There was still some fight in the Sharklord. Eben had spent the hours since those fateful blows nursing him, keeping him breathing and comfortable, long enough for Drew to see him. The Wolflord stood beside Shah, the Hawklady of Windfell looking up, gray eyes unblinking but dry. Perhaps she was all cried out?

"Do I smell a Wolf on my ship?" wheezed Vega, his eyes fluttering over, his skin a ghostly pallor. That infamous smile appeared, as he looked upon the young lycanthrope.

"What do you need?" asked Shah. "Tell me and I'll do it, Vega."

The Sharklord raised a hand and stroked her fine cheekbone.

"I would have my friend, Drew Ferran, sit with me a while, my love," he said. "Take Casper. Stretch your legs. Fear not, I'm not going anywhere. Not just yet."

She held his hand in place against her face, crushing his knuckles against her cheek before relinquishing her grip. Casper craned over and hugged his father, gentle but firm, slow to let go. Shah moved about the bed, tapping her son's back and slowly pulling him away.

"Come, Casper," she whispered. "You heard your father. We'll return momentarily."

The boy rose and went with the Hawklady, looking back all the while as he disappeared out the door and up top. Drew sat down on the bed, the mattress creaking beneath his weight.

"And what can I do for you, friend?" he said, managing a smile as Vega looked at him.

"It's been an adventure, hasn't it? Who could've imagined it would lead us here, eh?"

"I'm sorry I wasn't here."

"You're here now."

"But I could have done more," said Drew sadly. "Things went to hell so quickly."

"Went to hell? We won the war, Drew Ferran. The Seven Realms are free again. You're the toast of Lyssia, lad."

Drew shrugged. "Many played their part. None more so than Carver."

"Aye, a strong man there," said the Sharklord. "And to

think, there were some who expressed doubts when I suggested we call upon his assistance!" He glanced over at Manfred by the door. The Staglord snorted.

"If you recollect, Vega, the man was bound in chains and a prisoner of Westland at the time."

"A prisoner of Leopold's, Manfred," corrected the Sharklord. "Remember, one man's criminal is another man's freedom fighter."

"Always with the gray areas, eh, Shark?" Manfred smiled, unable to argue with his friend at this dark hour.

"I always look for the best in people, Stag. I saw it in you, didn't I?"

Manfred chuckled as Vega grinned, suddenly racked by coughs. Drew took a waterskin from beside the bed and raised it to the count's lips, the pirate prince drinking thirstily. He smacked his lips and rested back into his pillow.

"I'm going to abdicate," said Drew, his voice but a whisper.

"You're going to what?" gasped Manfred.

"I don't want Westland, I never did. I'm not a king, and I never shall be."

"You led your people into war, lad. If that doesn't make you a leader, what does?"

"I didn't say I couldn't lead, Manfred. I know the good fight when I see it. I led the Seven Realms against the Bastians with one purpose: to free a people oppressed, a people under the boot of those who thought themselves better."

Manfred shook his head, but it was Vega who spoke up.

"You mean to give it to them, don't you?" said the Shark.

"Them?" asked the Stag, confused.

Drew turned to Manfred, who now stood at the foot of the bed. "Humankind shall have Westland. They've earned it: true freedom, free from the rule of Werelords."

"This is unheard of—"

"Yet it shall happen," said Vega, cutting the Stag off. "Does this really come as a surprise to you, Manfred? We've known the lad's thinking all along. You've never hidden your feelings on this, have you, lad?"

Drew shook his head. "Blame being raised by humans, if you will. I know this is right."

"You do realize," said Manfred, "that some folk are happy to be ruled by the Werelords?"

"I do, and they may seek out such servitude in the other six realms, but they'll find no such mastery in Westland. And those who find themselves in a land where therians rule should be allowed to move freely to the west, to seek out a new life as they see fit. That has to go both ways, Manfred."

The Staglord nodded ruefully. "And who would rule this brave new land?"

"Carver, Fry, Ransome," said Vega. "There are many who could form a government there."

"That was my thinking," said Drew. "Brave men and women who've proved themselves in the eyes of Lyssia."

More nods from Manfred as he warmed to the idea. "That's three fellows there who've earned the right to rule."

"If they want it," said Drew. "Remember, not everyone's born to rule." Drew's destiny had thrust him into a position of power, a figurehead for the Seven Realms, but at heart he was still the dreamy shepherd boy from the Cold Coast.

"I'm sorry about Whitley, lad," said Vega. Manfred joined him, placing a fatherly hand on Drew's head. The Wolflord was rocked by the sympathy but tried not to show it. It was taking all his mettle simply to face Vega without crying; mention of the girl from Brackenholme could tip him over the edge.

"I'm sorry about Djogo," replied Drew.

"I know," said Vega, wincing. "Who'd have thought he had such an ax—or silver knife—to grind with me? I don't think I ever spoke to the chap."

"Why did he do it?" asked Drew.

Vega smiled. "I fear Opal put him up to it. She never did forgive me for the hand I played that got her to turn on her kin. It's no secret that the man was in love with Shah. And he'd been in with Opal since we sent her to Azra. I suspect her words were poison to his ears."

"I can't help but feel responsible," sniffed Drew.

"Nonsense," said Vega with a splutter, sweat beading his pained face. "I hold Djogo no ill will. The poor soul has been used, and it would've happened sooner or later. A man can't live a life such as mine without making enemies along the

way. I think the ledger's looking pretty full with folk who want me dead. Perhaps they'll be getting their wish, eh?"

"Did they capture Djogo?"

"No," said Manfred. "He's at large. As is Opal. There are others, too, who weren't accounted for in the enemy's ranks. Vanmorten for one."

Drew's growl rose in his throat. The Ratlord was the one Werelord who seemed to have dodged justice in all of this.

"You've still got that fire in your belly, lad," said Vega, clasping the White Fist of Icegarden with both hands. "Good, good. That'll see you through this. You're turning your back on kingship, but not life."

"I've still work to do," said Drew. "The war is won, but some battles still need to be fought."

"I'll be there by your side," said Manfred solemnly, hitting his breastplate with a fist.

"You've family, Your Grace," said the Wolf. "They await you in Stormdale, those who have survived. You need to be with them."

The Stag muttered an objection, but it was hollow. He wanted to be with his people more than anyone, especially having lost his youngest in the war.

"I'd like to be by your side," said Vega, "but I fear I cannot join you. That ship's sailed."

Drew brushed Vega's forehead, smoothing dark locks away from damp skin.

"Stop looking so sorry," said Vega. "If it weren't for you, I'd never have found Shah again. I'd never have been able to reunite my boy with his mother."

"But you deserve time together. Fate brought you back to each other for a reason."

"Fate's a fickle, funny bugger, eh?" laughed the Sharklord. "No, it's time for the Pirate Prince of the Cluster Isles to go on one final journey, Wolflord." He reached up and squeezed Drew's trembling shoulder. "It has been my honor to serve you, Drew Ferran. That you took a chance on a traitorous old fish like me showed me that it's never too late, that no soul is ever truly lost."

"Farewell, Count Vega," said Drew, his will broken, tears now flowing. "I'll see you at Brenn's table for that feast one day."

"Not for a long time, lad," said Vega, leaning back into the pillow and closing his eyes. "Not for a good long time."

PART VII

THE COST

I

The Girl in the Tree

THREE MONTHS HAD passed since the Battle of the Seven Realms, and summer had turned to autumn across Lyssia. The Longridings had been reclaimed by the Horselords, and the Barebones returned to the protection of the Staglords of Stormdale. The southern mountains were as safe as they had ever been, with the watchful eye of Count Carsten and his Hawklord brethren policing the peaks from their ancient home of Windfell. The Dalelands had enjoyed a bountiful harvest, seeing their goods swiftly down the Redwine to Highcliff and onward into the wider world. The Council of Humans saw to the fortunes of this fledgling realm, Westland reborn with High Governor Carver and General Fry leading the way,

Admiral Ransome marshaling the White Sea along the Cold Coast.

Peace remained elusive, old miscreants haunting the hopeful. He may not have been the sheriff of the Badlands anymore, but the villain Muller seized control of Highcliff's Thieves Guild. He wasn't alone, either. It was rumored that the reformed rogue Ibal had returned to a life of crime, joining Muller as a silent—but giggling—partner. The Cluster Isles remained a lawless world of untamed water, the pirates who called it home quick to return to business both fair and foul. Baron Bosa had assumed the role of Steward of Cutters Cove, the Werewhale guarding the throne until a worthy liege could be found. Few suspected he had any intention of expediting that search. Other realms still struggled, Sturmland feeling the bitter approach of winter, and the city of Icegarden as yet unreturned to White Bear control. The undead still reigned within those frozen walls. Perhaps spring would be the Sturmlanders' chance to take back what was once theirs.

The vast and sprawling Woodland Realm was the untamed wilderness it had always been, home to all manner of dim and dark peril. The Dymling and Dyre Roads were no longer the overgrown avenues of tangled briar and ivy, feared by human and therian alike, that they had been when King Leopold had reigned. The brave souls of the Woodland Watch and the traveling Romari had made them their own, settlements and halfway

houses breaking up the great highways and providing shelter from the Dyrewood's more dangerous denizens. Chief among those sanctuaries were Darke-in-the-Dyrewood and Bracken-holme, homes to the Bearlords of the old forest. Defenses had been rebuilt, and trade had returned. The brown, red, and gold leaves of autumn now littered those tired old roads.

While light had reclaimed the Dyrewood, evil yet lurked upon Brackenholme's doorstep.

Drew reached into the closet and unhitched his green cloak from its peg. He slipped it around his shoulders, fastening it beneath his chin by the Wolfshead brooch. He checked himself in the mirror.

"Not bad for a fellow of the Woodland Watch," he said to himself.

"They'll take anyone these days," said Bergan, causing the lad to start. He turned, finding the old Bear standing in the doorway to his room, grin glowing from within his bushy nest of ruddy whiskers.

"You don't knock in Brackenholme?"

"You're in my house now, lad. Don't believe in locking doors and whatnot."

Bergan smiled as Drew picked up his pack from the foot of his bed. Whitley's bed. He paused, looking around the chamber.

"Is it as she'd left it?"

"Pretty much," sighed Bergan. "It's not like she was ever one for the girly things in life. She had a closetfull of fancy

dresses that were never worn. Leave that to the Gretchens of this world, she always said. Her heart belonged to the Woodland Watch. And you, of course."

Drew stepped up to the old duke and hugged him. It had been a strange few months. Turning his back on the rest of Lyssia, he had returned to Brackenholme with the Bearlord, the forest the only place in the Seven Realms where he felt he belonged.

"This is where she and I would have come, Bergan. We wanted to make Brackenholme our home together."

"And it is your home, Drew, now and forever more. That blessing you and Whitley undertook in Robben only confirmed what I already knew. We're family, Drew, you and I. I love you as my own, never forget that."

The young man smiled and nodded, hitching the backpack across his shoulder.

"You're sure I cannot join you?" asked the Bear.

"You've been away from your people for far too long," said Drew assuredly. "Leave this work to the Woodland Watch. This is my score that needs settling."

The two left the room, marching through Brackenholme Hall as they made their way toward the bamboo cages that would carry them to the ground far below. The duke was not about to wave him off just yet: he would accompany him to the city gates before sending him on his way. The Bearguard escorted the pair into the lift and with a grinding of winches

they were away, floating down alongside the Great Oak's trunk, the city approaching below.

Where Brackenholme had once been reduced to smoking timbers and piles of ash, townhouses, inns, and shops had risen. The work was ongoing, and it would be some years before the city was truly returned to its former glory. Yet still, the sight of the people scurrying about, industrious and hopeful, was cause for great joy for the therians.

"I'll meet you at the Dyre Gate," said Drew when they climbed out of the lift's barred door as it hit the ground. "I've business to attend to first."

"You're off to see him, correct? Well, you might want to visit the Queen Beech first," said the Bearlord. "There's something you'll want to see."

Drew nodded and was away, unsure of what the duke meant. Bergan knew who the lad was visiting—the young Wolf a slave to routine—but clearly he wanted him to call by the dead tree first. He made his way along the street, smiling at townsfolk and Romari when they recognized him, returning their waves and greetings. Drew passed beneath the boughs of the White Tree, the giant pale oak the home to the House of Healing, walking on to the remains of the Queen Beech.

The enormous tree had perished during the Battle of Brackenholme, the fires devouring it root and branch, leaving an ugly black trunk and a giant pile of ash. With tender hands,

the Romari had set to work upon it, cutting away the burned bark, stripping back the charred timber and exposing the wood beneath. Their artisans and craftsmen had set to work with hammer and chisel, carving a memorial to those who had lost their lives, not just in Brackenholme but across the Seven Realms.

Drew stood in silence, staring at the scenes and faces that adorned the beautiful sculpture. His old friend Red Rufus was there, carved wings eternally outstretched, but it wasn't the Hawklord who caught his eye. He had seen the work of art a number of times, but there was a recent addition to the frieze. The likeness was remarkable. Drew gasped, stepping forward on unsteady feet.

"You're missed, Whitley, each moment of every day," he whispered, raising his hand and letting his fingertips brush a cheekbone of perfect, polished wood. "The world lives on around me, yet I'm in limbo, lost without you. How do I carry on? Tell me, please, my love."

Whitley's face remained motionless, of course, her expression frozen within the grain of the tree trunk forever, but at that moment something peculiar happened. Clouds passed by overhead, briefly plunging the city into darkness. As the light changed, so did the shadow across the Bearlady's face, her features shifting before Drew's eyes. For a moment, it looked like she was smiling at him, and the Wolf's heart caught in his chest.

"Tricksy, isn't she, when the light plays upon her face?" came a familiar voice from nearby. "Then again, she always was a bit of a minx."

A teary-eyed Drew turned and found the Romari Yuzhnik leaning against the sculpture. His shirt was missing, broad chest still soaked with sweat and covered in dust and shavings. A tool belt hung loose about his hips. Whitley's image was the giant's handiwork.

"She was," replied Drew, marveling at his craft. "She's incredible. I don't know what to say. Words can't express what this means to me."

"I don't seek your gratitude, Drew. Do this for me, though, and for Whitley's memory." He stepped up to the youth and gripped him by each shoulder. "Live, lad. Don't linger in misery, waiting to join her. She wouldn't have wanted that. Live a life worth living."

Drew clapped his hand and the White Fist of Icegarden onto Yuzhnik's thick knotted forearms and nodded, the sun now bright overhead. He took one more look at Whitley, kissing his fingertips and brushing her lips, before setting off on his way once more.

He had been in Brackenholme for nine weeks now, and not a day had gone by when he had failed to pay a visit to their guest in the Garrison Tree. He made good time across the city to the enormous, gnarled black tree, bare twisting branches reaching for the sky high above like skeletal fingers. The irony

of this being the residence they had settled upon was not lost on Drew. The City Watch saluted him as he entered in a manner deserving of a captain of the Woodland Watch. He had been reluctant to accept the title, but there was no hiding the esteem the soldiers held him in. *This was my home too, once,* he mused as he climbed the giant spiral staircase, passing the cell he had been thrown into long ago, upon his first visit to Brackenholme.

As he climbed the steps, he wondered how his friends were all faring. Taboo, Krieg, and the Behemoth had all sailed home to Bast in the company of Tiaz. War no doubt awaited them there as the Catlords quarreled for dominion over the jungle continent. The Tigers were in better shape than any, though, with the free peoples of Bast now aligned with them. He wished them well and prayed they would meet again one day. Of Opal, there was no sign, and who knew what had become of Djogo? Those Werelords of Bast who had been defeated, such as Count Costa and the Lionlords, Lex and Luc, had been sent home free men. Drew hoped that this amnesty might appease the Panthers and Lions, but he feared the worst.

Faisal was back in Omir, taming the Desert Realm, the Doglords and Hayfa a thorn in his paw still as they would forever be. The Jackal knew he had a friend in Drew, though, and if he ever needed him, the Wolf would come running. The phibians of the Bott Marshes had gone back to the water, their chieftain Shoma slain in the river fight, Kholka taking his place in

the tribe. The Frogmen were no longer strangers, never again to be hunted or demonized by the people and therians of Lyssia. And the old seadog Figgis had taken the *Maelstrom* for his own since Count Vega's demise, the clever Ternlord Florimo joining him as they repaired the pirate ship and returned it to the open oceans again.

They had put their guest in the highest room of the Garrison Tree, a former observatory that looked out over the north of the city, giving a fine view of the Dymling Road as it cut its path straight through the Dyrewood toward the Redwine and the Dales. A guard nodded, pulling a chain from his pocket and turning it in the lock of the black timber door. Drew rapped the knuckles of the White Fist on the wood, manners always in mind, as Tilly Ferran had always schooled him. The door swung open and he entered.

2

THE WOLF HUNT

ALTHOUGH IT HAD once been an observatory, it was now a library, the books from Redmire Hall having been salvaged from its ruins and sent south. Books on history, geography, the great races and nations of Lyssia. Tomes on language and legend, maps and scrolls as old as Brenn himself, but not a word of magick upon any one of them.

Hector looked up from where he sat on a bench beside the window, perched upon a cushion, the chill autumn wind blowing through the room. He snapped the book shut and placed it awkwardly on the seat as he rose, the young Boarlord still getting used to life with only one arm. The evil was gone from him, although the scars would haunt the magister until his final day.

Hector smiled as Drew entered, and Drew returned the grin.

"An early visit today," said the magister. "To what do I owe the pleasure?"

"I'm going away for a few days. There's been an incident in the Dyrewood."

"An incident?" said Hector. "That sounds serious."

"It could well be."

"Would you like me to come with you?"

Drew smiled awkwardly. "That's not going to happen, Hector."

The Boarlord nodded slowly. "That's right. You don't trust me."

Drew shrugged. "That may be, but I'll ask you this: do you trust yourself? Can you be sure that Vincent is gone, never to return?"

Hector raised his left arm, the limb severed just below the elbow. He didn't answer, simply staring at it, his face pale and his mind elsewhere. He was thinking back to the events atop the Bone Tower in Icegarden, Drew figured, and the grim events that had unfolded. The Werewolf had climbed that tower intent on stopping two tormented souls, Lucas and Blackhand. The Lion had been slain, and when the chance came to kill the magister, Drew had faltered. It was no necromancer lying before him: at that moment it was dear Hector's voice that had emerged from the magister's corrupted body. The Wolflord

had made a snap decision. The evil was in the withered, necrotic limb that twitched with a life of its own. Moonbrand had descended and the dark hand had spun from the tower top, disappearing into the night. The Hawks had carried them from the Bone Tower's summit, beyond the walls of Icegarden and away from the undead hordes.

"Vincent may be gone, but the scars will remain forever," said Hector, glaring at his shortened arm.

"We're all left counting the cost," said Drew. "None escaped Icegarden unscathed that night."

He had personally carried Whitley's body back to Robben, declining all offer of help from his friends. He had been unable to relinquish his hold on her, at least until he found Bergan. Upon reaching the Wolf war camp, Hector had been spirited away to the Daughters of Icegarden along with Trent. As the White Bear magisters cleaned and stitched Hector's wound, others had set to work on the cursed Wolf Knight. Drew's brother was still on the mend, even now. Drew wondered if Trent would ever be truly healed. He wondered if any of them would.

Hector looked back at Drew. "So how long do I stay here, Drew? A week? A month? A year?"

"Are you not happy here, Hector? Is the room not furnished to your liking? I had the books brought from your libraries. I wanted to make it feel like home."

The Boarlord's smile was forced. "It's a prison cell, Drew."

The young Wolf tried to return the smile, but he couldn't. When he spoke the words caught in his throat.

"I swore an oath atop the Bone Tower that I would take you into my care, Hector, and I'm not about to break that. It's not just that you mean the world to me; it's more than that. We know what happened in Icegarden, we saw the power that you could wield. I can never allow that to happen again. Not on my watch."

"So you're my jailer then, Drew?"

"Oh no," replied the lad from the Cold Coast. "I'm so much more than that."

Drew hugged Hector and felt the tension break instantly, the Boarlord sagging in his arms, falling into the embrace. He heard the magister sob as he whispered in Hector's ear.

"I'm your friend."

"What's keeping him?" said Mikotaj from where he sat astride the black stallion, the horse stepping nervously with the hulking Wolf of Shadowhaven upon its back. It whinnied, prompting a curse from the barbarian as he swatted its mane with his hand. "Oi! Quit it, or you and I will have a falling out."

"Not fond of horses?" asked Trent Ferran where he lounged in Storm's saddle, the chestnut-brown mare snorting at him contentedly, pleased to be reunited with her lost master.

"I wouldn't say that. Cook 'em right, they can be quite tasty,"

replied the White Wolf as the mount protested once more.

"How do you feel?" Bergan asked Trent. The Bearlord stood nearby, General Harker holding the reins of Drew's white charger, Bravado, awaiting the captain's arrival.

"I'm all right," Trent lied with a smile. Lady Greta and the Daughters of Icegarden had worked their craft upon him, purging his body of the poisonous Wyld Magick that had transformed him from man into beast. The physical features of the lycanthrope had disappeared, driven from his flesh, but his mind was still tormented by the dark desires that had seized him that night in Icegarden. Those images returned in the form of nightmares, keeping him awake at night when the moon was at its fullest in the sky, leaving him sick with fever and slick with sweat. The monster appeared to be gone, yet some of it remained: heightened senses, an instinctive understanding of how the Wyld Wolves thought. How they hunted.

"You'll be wanting to get back to Gretchen in Hedgemoor, eh?" said Mikotaj.

"When this work is done. Not until," Trent replied. "What about yourself? Surely Shadowhaven awaits?"

"It does indeed," sighed the pale-haired giant. "All in good time, though. The place is a ghost town still, more rubble than city. Nobody's in a hurry to bend their backs while Icegarden still needs taking from the dead. No, Shadowhaven can wait a little while longer. And besides, it's colder than a White Bear's whatnots up there!"

All four laughed before spying Drew Ferran, captain of the Woodland Watch, as he marched down the Dyre Road toward them. He had a spring in his stride, purpose to his step.

"Thanks, Harker," he said, smiling to the general as he took Bravado's reins.

"My pleasure, captain," said Harker, patting the mighty charger's flank as Drew climbed up into the saddle.

"What do we know, then?"

"One of them was spied by a family of woodsmen twenty leagues south of Darke," replied the general, his smile now gone from his face.

"Did it attack anyone?" asked Mikotaj.

"It went for a boy, but a few well-placed arrows saw the beast away and the boy to safety." Harker handed a map to Drew. "It's marked on there, as best we can tell according to Baron Redfearn's scouts."

"We can't let it bite anyone," said Trent. "It spreads through the blood, remember?"

"Don't fret," said Mikotaj. "You were bit and you survived, didn't you?"

"I was strong," replied Trent, more anger in his voice than he'd wished, prompting a raised eyebrow from the northman.

"Do we know if it's Darkheart?" asked Drew.

"I suspect not," replied Harker. "The Wyld Wolf in question had blue woad markings on a mangy pelt. Darkheart's still out there."

"And we'll find him," said Drew, never more sure of his words. Those Wyld Wolves that had survived the horrors of Icegarden had fled south to their former homes in the forest, tails between their legs. These were the chieftains of the various Wyldermen tribes that were hidden in the darkest, dankest corners of the Woodland Realm. Some might even return to their people. With the disease as virulent as it clearly was, that could spell disaster in the Dyrewood, the potential consequences horrific.

"We'll find them all," added Trent, passing a dark look to his brother. Drew knew the meaning. There was one, more hated than Darkheart, who had slipped the noose as the war rumbled to a close: Vanmorten. Where the Ratlord was, nobody seemed to know, but that would not put the brothers off his scent. They would have revenge for the monster's crimes, chief among them the murder of their mother, Tilly, so long ago. The Rat could run, the Rat could hide, but the Ferran boys would find him.

Trent coaxed Storm forward with a tap of the heels, and Mikotaj's horse followed, the northman gripping the reins tightly between great, white knuckles. Bergan placed a hand on Drew's knee before he went after them.

"You all right, son?"

Drew knew what Bergan meant. "She should've been with us today. She knew these forests better than anyone."

"She is with you, son," replied the duke, reaching up to tap

Drew on his studded leather breastplate. "In here. Always."

Drew smiled, reassured by his old friend's comforting words.

"And how was our guest this morning?"

"Well," said Drew, his smile slipping. "It will be some time before Hector is fully returned to himself—if ever. He needs watching. We must remain vigilant, Bergan."

"I'm just glad we got him back, almost in one piece," replied the duke, patting Drew's leg. "Don't worry, I'll watch over him like a Hawklord while you're gone."

"You do that," said Drew. "We could've done with Shah for a task like that. I often wonder where she ended up."

"Aye, odd her and the boy just up and going like that, wasn't it?"

"And taking Vega's body with them, too."

"Without so much as a good-bye," said the duke, shaking his head in dismay.

"Some folk like privacy when they bury their loved ones. Shah will have taken Vega to somewhere that meant something to him, a place dear to his heart. Our friend deserved a fine bed for the long sleep."

"He didn't look all that tired the last time I saw him," said Bergan, his whiskers twitching as he tried to hide a smile.

Drew stared hard at the bushy bearded therian. "What in Brenn's name are you grinning about, old man?"

The Bearlord of Brackenholme suddenly clapped Bravado's rump, causing the horse to rear up on its hind legs, kicking at the air.

"On your way, Drew Ferran," bellowed the duke, huge chest booming with laughter. "Brenn's speed my boy! You've wolves to hunt!"

And Bravado was off, kicking up dirt and sending showers of dead leaves into the air in his wake. Drew bent low in the saddle as the others followed, the Bearlord's laughter still ringing in his ears as they charged down the Dyre Road and into the woods.

PROLOGUE

xxx

THE WALDEN WOODS HORROR

The twigs snapped underfoot like skeletal fingers crushed before they could snatch and seize hold. The teenager's steps were hurried, kicking up wind-tossed leaves and weather-beaten branches as she swiftly climbed the slope. She glanced back occasionally, spying through the trees the neighborhood lights, twinkling into life at dusk. Her dorm backed up to the woodland's edge, her bedroom window overlooking the forest, this wild, wonderful world, right at her doorstep. His world.

Her eyes darted, searching the shadows on either side of the trail, checking to see that she was alone. He was a recluse for good reason; the folks who lived in this quiet corner of Lincoln, Massachusetts, were suspicious of strangers. Where better for him to hide away than up here, in the woods? She knew how he felt. She'd never fitted in, always the outsider, even in her own family. It wasn't easy

being a Goth when one's younger sisters were preppy, pony-loving princesses. She'd imagined life might get easier once she got to college, but she remained a square peg in a round hole. Yet those misfit days were behind her now. That the two of them had found one another was a miracle. It filled her heart with hope that there was somebody out there for everybody, even the loneliest soul.

Stepping through the forest, the young woman emerged at her destination. She stopped for a moment, taking one last cautious peek back the way she'd come; nobody on her trail, nobody in pursuit. She turned about, toward her lover's home. The old mill loomed out of the darkness, its windows boarded, the stream rushing through its broken waterwheel. It looked sinister at twilight, but that didn't bother her.

It gave her a thrill, truth be told. Spooky things got the pulse racing, the blood pumping; they made her feel alive. A nighttime rendezvous in an abandoned timber mill? This was their secret place. She reached for the long black scarf about her neck, fingers twining through the material to brush her flesh. She would be in his arms again soon enough. She'd waited too long for his kiss.

"Lovely evening for a stroll!"

She looked up, startled to see a figure standing in the tree line at the top of the slope.

"Who . . . who's there?" she asked, squinting through the dim, dusky light. "Come out where I can see you. I'm not scared, you know."

He stepped out of the shadows. He was just a kid, a middle-schooler. His face was hidden within the hoodie cowl that poked out of his bomber jacket's collar. The scuffed leather had seen better days, as had the drainpipe jeans and battered Chuck Taylors. In his right hand, a yo-yo spun lazily up and down; he made it rise and fall with the deft skill of a seasoned slacker. Over his shoulder he carried a khaki satchel, the bag resting against his hip. Finally, the boy tugged the hood back, his grin emerging in the gloom.

"You should be."

MAX HELSING HAD HOPED HIS SMILE MIGHT PROVE disarming to the young woman in black. Unfortunately, accompanied by those words, it just came across as creepy. She gave him a sideways look, reaching a hand into her pocket. Perhaps a can of pepper spray in there? Or something worse? Not that Max was too bothered. Nothing could be as bad as last summer's Colorado job and the Case of the Cold Canyon Killer. The petrifying spitting venom of a dust dragon had turned his baseball cap into a bonnet of stone. That was his favorite hat, he recalled with a pang.

"Sorry," said Max, pocketing his yo-yo and raising his hands peaceably while stepping closer. "I didn't mean to freak you out. I promise, I'm totally harmless."

"That's close enough," she said, backing away in the direction of the ruined mill. "What are you doing here?"

Max made an embarrassed face. "Well, I was kind of hoping I could dissuade you from going in there."

He pointed at the dark building. She stole a glance, as if it might have transformed since the last time she looked.

"Why's that?" Her hand emerged from her pocket, clenching something solid and rectangular. It looked ominously like a gun. Max cringed; okay, so that could possibly rival the dust dragon.

"Haven't you heard? Legend says the old mill's haunted. Well, at least the locals do. They say it's cursed. That terrible things happen to anyone who enters. Some big bad juju went on here in the past."

"So?"

That wasn't the reply Max had hoped for. Usually the "big bad juju" line would put even the most numbskulled norm off. The fact that it hadn't only confirmed what he feared.

"So you're not scared easily? Cool. Maybe we can go in together?"

The woman eyed him suspiciously. "You shouldn't be here."

Max strolled toward the building, its double doors slightly ajar. He peered through the gap, the dark void impenetrable. A host of smells assailed his nostrils, none of which was pleasant. He was getting the musty aroma of mold and damp, a hint of rotten timber, and the sweet scent of decaying flesh; a heady bouquet indeed. This was the place, all right.

"I said you shouldn't be here," repeated the young woman.

Max looked back at her. She was in her late teens, no doubt a student from the university in nearby Waltham. A Goth, too, judging by her dark attire. He might have known; they were so often Goths. He spied the scarf bound around her throat. Hiding something? Before he proceeded any further, he needed to discover just how deeply she'd been glamoured.

"There's no harm in taking a look inside, is there?" he said finally, fishing a flashlight from his bag. "It's abandoned, isn't it?"

"It's not abandoned. Somebody lives here."

"Don't be silly. Nobody would *choose* to live in a wreck like this."

"My boyfriend does."

Max arched an eyebrow as he seized a door and tested it. It groaned, resisting his pull. "Boyfriend? Is he a hermit?"

"He just doesn't get along with people," said the student, her words both cautionary and concerned as she stepped suddenly toward him. "You really should leave."

"It doesn't look like he's in," said Max, before ducking between the doors into the gloom beyond.

While she called after him, he flicked his flashlight switch. A bright beam lanced through the pitch black, the atmosphere alive with a swirling sea of dust particles. Max gagged now, the woodland aromas no longer providing adequate cover for the stench. This was the lair, undoubtedly.

Behind him, the Goth girl struggled through the entrance, cursing the intruding twelve-year-old. Max ignored her objections, instead searching the chamber for signs of life. Or worse . . .

Exposed rafters were vaguely visible in the darkness overhead, the rest of the ceiling shrouded in shadows. A rusted saw was suspended from a wall bracket up high, while log chains hung like iron curtains against the boards. The odd hand tool remained pegged in place, covered in cobwebs after decades of neglect. Long-forgotten offcuts littered the dirty floor, wedges of rotten timber that crawled with spiders and slugs.

"When you say he doesn't get along with people, what do you mean exactly?"

"He doesn't like crowds. Can't say I blame him." She seized Max by the shoulder and spun him around. "I said you shouldn't be here, and I meant it."

PUFFIN BOOKS
An imprint of Penguin Random House LLC
375 Hudson Street
New York, New York 10014

First published in 2013 by Puffin UK, a division of Penguin Books Ltd.
First published in the United States of America by Viking,
an imprint of Penguin Young Readers Group, 2013
Published by Puffin Books, an imprint of Penguin Random House LLC, 2016

THE LIBRARY OF CONGRESS HAS CATALOGED THE VIKING EDITION AS FOLLOWS:
Jobling, Curtis.
War of the Werelords / by Curtis Jobling
p. cm.
Summary: "While the war between the Catlords and the Wolf embroils the Seven Realms
in chaos, Drew must take his final stand against the man who has become Lyssia's deadliest
villain: his own best friend, the Boarlord Hector, whose powers of dark magick are raging
out of control"— Provided by publisher.
ISBN 978-0-670-78559-9 (hc)
[1. Werewolves—Fiction. 2. Adventure and adventurers—Fiction. 3. Fantasy.]
I. Title   PZ7.J5785 War 2013   [Fic]—dc23 2013024215

Puffin Books ISBN 978-0-14-242578-7

Printed in the United States of America
Designed by Jim Hoover

1 3 5 7 9 10 8 6 4 2

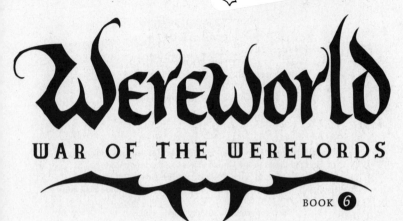

CURTIS JOBLING

PUFFIN BOOKS